EVERLASTING LOVE

EVERLASTING | BOOK ONE

DEBRA ST JAMES

INSPIRATION

This story was inspired by the lyrics ...

In Repair by John Mayer

DEDICATION

This book is dedicated to my husband.
The man who has saved me from the darkness on more than one
occasion.

I love you more than you realize.

To the men and women who fight for our freedoms.
Our world is a better place because you're in it.

Thank you for your sacrifice.

PLAYLIST

In Repair ... *John Mayer*
I Don't Trust Myself ... *John Mayer*
C'mon People ... *Richard Ashcroft*
Shy Guy ... *Diana King*
(Baby I've Got You) On My Mind ... *Powderfinger*
Standing Still ... *Jewel*
Don't Let Me Slide ... *Tedeschi Trucks Band*
Have a Little Faith in Me ... *Olivia Penalva*
Angels ... *Robbie Williams*
All I Want Is to Be With You ... *John Mayer*
Iris ... *Goo Goo Dolls*
Resolution ... *Matt Corby*
In Your Eyes ... *Peter Gabriel*
Hero ... *Enrique Iglesias*
Never Gonna Let You Down ... *Colbie Caillat*
Brighter Than The Sun ... *Colbie Caillat*
Scars ... *I AM THEY*

You can check it out here:

https://tinyurl.com/everlastinglove-spotify

PROLOGUE

SHANE

I NEVER WANTED TO BE LIKE MY FATHER.

I know, more often than not, kids strive to emulate one or both of their parents, but I never once wanted to be like mine.

He's military through and through—hell, his entire family is—and while he may have come back from fighting overseas, he never really *came back*. His body may be here, and he may work in a job he doesn't particularly enjoy to pay the bills, but his mind is still lost on the battlefield thousands of miles from home.

Throughout most of my life, he's been trapped in memories instead of making new ones with a wife and son who love him.

Sadly, I knew I would never escape following in my father's footsteps. The assumption that I would join the army weighed heavily on my shoulders. There was no way I could be the first to break the chain of the generations that came before me, and in all honesty, I didn't want to break away from tradition. I wanted to prove that I could go to battle and return unchanged.

I didn't want to be a shell of a man when I came home.

I thought I'd be different.

I thought my mind was stronger.

But I didn't understand what war does to a man.

PART ONE

TWO YEARS AGO ...

1

SHANE

I laughed today. It wasn't forced, and it wasn't for show to make my friends and family feel better. It burst from deep within and across my lips unbidden.

It was genuine and felt … *completely foreign*.

And I immediately drowned in guilt so deep I thought I'd *stop breathing*.

2

SHANE

With the warm sun at my back, I take the two steps up to the brown-painted double doors of the tan brick building. This place—or rather some of the people inside—has saved my life on more than one occasion, and now that I'm somewhat back on my feet, I like to visit regularly so I can give back where I can. The nondescript exterior of the building gives nothing away as to what's inside, but every single person who enters knows how important this place is and is grateful for its very existence.

A simple brass sign to the left of the large doors is engraved with two words: *The Bunker*.

The name is more than fitting. Just as a bunker is a safe place during turmoil, so is this place. However, the turmoil that leads men and women to these doors isn't from outside forces but from within. Battles that were once fought on a bloody battleground have now taken up residence in the minds and souls of the survivors, and it's not so easy to leave it all behind. What happened to each of us, and the experiences we were subjected to, have left us fundamentally changed. Scarred in ways we don't know how to assimilate, how to accept, or how to move forward from. But through it all, we know we can come here at any time of the day or night and find someone to talk with, or if we don't feel like talking, we can sit or spend time here knowing we're not alone.

As I breach the doorway, a sense of calm washes over me and my façade falls away. I don't have to pretend that everything's great here. I don't have to pretend that my skin doesn't feel too tight when I'm walking down the street, and I don't need to fake smiles to make the people around me think that I'm not fundamentally different from how I was *before*.

Before everything turned to shit.

To be fair, I think I've turned a corner. Life doesn't always feel so damn heavy, and it doesn't feel like a mammoth task to climb out of bed each day. I'm beginning to see color again, and some days I feel like maybe I can fit back in with society. *Some* days.

"Sutton," Nix calls as I step into the large café area immediately to the right when I enter. While everyone here has experienced some horrific shit, he's the *only* man here who knows *exactly* what I've been through because he was there the afternoon everything fell apart and my life changed forever. He's my former Sergeant and has been integral in my progress. I'll always be grateful for his support and compassion.

I weave around several tables in the open space to reach him. When I do, I place the box of spray paint on the table and hold out my hand so I can pull him into my body and slap him on the back. "Steele. Good to see you."

"You too. It's been a while." Our schedules haven't lined up for quite some time; he's been busy with his security business, and I've been busy working for my long-time friend and now famous musician, Toby Summer. He gestures toward the chair opposite. "Join me?"

"Sure, I'll grab a coffee." I place my order at the counter and carry my coffee back to Nix's table, then take a seat moving the box of paint to the floor. "How's business?"

"Busy." He fidgets with his spoon. "I'll need to bring on one or two more guys."

"That's great. I'm happy for you." I take a sip of the steamy goodness in my cup. "You deserve all the success, man." He's worked damn hard to get his business off the ground. Sometimes I wonder where he finds the time with a family at home.

"Thanks." He smirks. "How are things with the rock star?" He wanted me to work for him, but I couldn't refuse my childhood best friend when he asked me to be his bodyguard after a mentally unstable woman inserted herself into his life.

I huff out a laugh. "Living the high life. He's doing a Labor Day concert tonight with a seven-year-old who conned him into giving her guitar lessons."

Nix's eyes widen. "How the fuck did that happen?" He takes a sip of his coffee.

I shake my head as I snicker. "I have no clue, but she's a sweet kid and working with her has been great for him." I spin my spoon between my fingers. "He met her when he volunteered at *Music for my Heart*, the music and dance school for deaf and hard of hearing kids." He nods. Most people around here know of the new center run by the husband and wife team, Louis and Xanthe. "She's profoundly deaf but determined to learn how to play the guitar. He's been impressed by her commitment and dedication." If I'm honest, getting to know her has been pretty great for me, too. Poppy has a way about her that draws you into her orbit, and it's an awesome place to be. "The concert will be something to see."

"Sounds like it'll be a great night." He shifts in his seat and takes another sip of his coffee.

I nod. I'm surprised I'm actually looking forward to it. "Do you know if the bikes are ready for delivery?"

"No idea. I haven't been here long myself." He glances away, then returns his focus to me. "Have you seen Hope and Evan lately?"

My chest tightens at the mention of their names, and I have to consciously take a breath. I nod slowly. "Yeah. I see them regularly. I've been helping to coach Evan's soccer team every second week when their regular coach can't make it, and I do what I can to help Hope when she needs something done around the house." My stomach clenches when I think about everything they've lost. The moments they'll never have with Wyatt, our army buddy.

He studies my face closely. "I'd be happy to help, too."

I shrug. "I know. But you have your own family and a business to look after. I don't have anyone." I swallow the lump that always forms in my throat at the reminder.

Turning to lighter topics, we catch up while we drink our coffee, then make our way out to the workshop. When we walk inside, one of the guys is busy working on a bike. I unlock the caged shelving and add my paint to the rest of the cans. I always bring a few cans with me to bolster the collection of paint for the bikes we restore for underprivileged kids.

"Hey, Michaels," I call.

He tips his chin toward me and Nix. "Hey."

"How are things?" Nix asks.

Robert stops attaching the pedal of the bike he's working on. "Not bad. We're running a little behind schedule with the bikes for the *Mission Community Center*." He tips his chin toward a couple of tubs of parts that look as though they've already been painted.

I was worried that would be the case. "I have a couple of spare hours today. Tell me what needs to be done." I rub my hands together, ready to get them dirty.

Robert points back to the tubs behind him. "Those bikes are ready to be reassembled."

Nodding, I step closer to the tubs. "No problem. Steele, you wanna get started on that one, and I'll do this one."

We get to work assembling the bikes while we listen to classic rock, and before I know it, the two bikes are completed and added to the collection. Looking at our handiwork, I take note of the range of colors, sizes, and styles of bikes that families no longer wanted or needed. Each one has been rescued from the landfill and lovingly restored to its former glory—ready for a new owner who wouldn't normally have the opportunity to own a bike. These bikes may make a child happy or they may provide transportation for someone to get to and from work. We don't discriminate against whom we gift these restored bikes. If they need a bike, they get one. It's as simple as that.

"Thanks, guys. Akerman will load them onto the trailer when he gets here, and we'll take them to the community center tomorrow."

"No problem." We shake hands and say our goodbyes.

I walk out of the building with a pep in my step. I always leave here feeling better than I did when I entered. It's amazing how a couple of hours of doing manual work that will help someone else can clear the mind and cleanse the soul.

TOBY AND POPPY walk off stage together with matching grins, and I can tell from here that my best friend is floating among the clouds. I've watched him play in packed stadiums to tens of thousands of fans, and not once have I seen him so at peace and full of pride. Toby's parents, his twin sister Kate and her husband, Oliver, step out of the auditorium and walk toward us. Hugs are given freely to Toby and Poppy as their excitement bubbles over.

I do my best to stay on the periphery to watch over everyone, but Toby's mom wraps her arms around me and pulls me in tight. When she steps back, she cups my cheek and her eyes soften, making the muscle in my chest miss a beat. She always makes it a point to check in with me, especially since I came home. "How are you?"

"I'm good, Mrs. S." It's my standard response.

Creases form between her brows while her blue eyes, exactly like her son's, scan my face. I work to keep my features relaxed and neutral—I don't want to worry her. She doesn't need to know I'm on high alert and my adrenaline's swirling through my system like a tornado as more and more people crowd into the foyer. I'm itching to step back from the family so I can keep my view clear and observe from the sidelines. Toby would say that I can relax at an event like this but I can never be too careful with my best friend and his family's safety. Time away taught me to expect the unexpected. Eventually, she must see what she needs to see and nods as she releases me from her motherly hold.

Toby's parents have always welcomed me into their home and family as if I were one of their kids. I remember being astounded by their openness toward me—particularly Mr. Summer, because from the time my father returned from service, he was never what I would call a *loving father*. Their warmth and love were always given freely even though I wasn't theirs. The lines often became blurred for me, and there were times when I considered them parents; more so than my own. Their love for me has always been unconditional, which was something I didn't have at home—well, not from my father anyway. It was such a foreign concept for me, but the more time I spent with the Summer family, the more accustomed I grew to the way their family worked. I would find any excuse to spend time at their home to escape mine because I felt more comfortable with them. They accepted me. It was as simple and as complicated as that.

Poppy takes off across the foyer, and I snap my head around to keep her in my sight. It's easy enough to do when you're a full head taller than the majority of people in the room. That little girl has stolen my best friend's heart, and as a result of how important she is to him, I've now included her under my protection. I watch her fling herself at a woman, and confusion swamps me for a moment until my mind catches up to what I'm seeing. Cassia, my best friend's high school crush, stands with Poppy in her arms, her face full of happiness and pride.

Shit!

I quickly turn toward Toby and check if he's seeing what I'm seeing. His face says it all. And while I may be able to protect him from a physical threat, I can't protect his heart from shattering further with this discovery. I can't believe after the time they spent together recently, that she would keep such a huge secret from him. I watch my long-time friend gather his composure and make his way toward Poppy and her family. He won't outwardly show any emotion other than that of a professional musician even though I know him well enough to recognize the tightness around his jaw and eyes. The bunching of his shoulders and the rigid way he's holding his body is a dead giveaway. He's livid and I don't blame him. I would be too.

Poppy's grandmother, Rose, who we met recently at one of Poppy's lessons, rushes in first, hugging Toby and thanking him. Then she turns and introduces her family to us. My eyes stray to the gorgeous woman who's standing slightly behind Cassia and Rose. She has a toddler in her arms, who can only be hers because she's like a mini version of her, and she scans us with a level of distrust I haven't seen in a long while. Her smile seems forced, but she's putting on a good show for her family. *Interesting*.

"This is my older daughter, Violet, and her daughter, Jasmine." I reach forward to shake her hand, and I shit you not, as soon as my palm makes contact with hers, tingles erupt. I dart my eyes from her hand to her face to see if she felt anything out of the ordinary and catch her clear cerulean eyes widening slightly as her brows dip a little lower. She obviously felt something, too.

I swallow quickly and lift my chin as I extricate my hand from hers, immediately missing her warmth. "Hi, Violet. Hi, Jasmine. I'm Shane."

Wearing a shy smile, Jasmine burrows her face into the crook of her mother's neck while I do my best to be polite and not let my gaze linger on Violet's tanned complexion, but I'm knocked a little off-kilter by her stunning blue eyes. Her daughter has almost the same coloring as her, and I bet they turn heads wherever they go. Toby told me Cassia had an older sister, but I hadn't given it much thought until now. I look around their group to see if she has a husband or boyfriend, but it seems they are on their own tonight. Maybe he's working, or something.

She tilts her head back to maintain eye contact. "Hey, Shane." She turns her attention toward her daughter and adjusts her position on her hip. "Jasmine, say hello to Shane." Her voice is like warm honey, smooth and sweet.

Jasmine turns her head slightly, staying burrowed in her mom's neck, and her smile widens slightly. "Hewwo, Sane."

My heart skips a beat at her tiny voice, and the tension I always hold across my shoulders eases slightly. I step a little closer and smile at the tiny angel, stretching muscles I rarely use. "Did you enjoy the concert?"

She pulls further away from her mom, her confidence growing, and nods. Her smile grows and her eyes twinkle. "I sore did. Poppy was 'mazing."

I chuckle mildly, glancing at her mom, trying my best not to make my perusal obvious. "She sure was. She's been practicing really hard."

We're interrupted when Cassia announces it's time to go home. Poppy's not having it though. She's begging her mom for something. I guess I'd better start paying attention and learning more ASL because I have a feeling we're going to be spending more time with Poppy outside of her guitar lessons, and I want to know what's being said. I watch Poppy put her signature move on Toby, and I know we'll be heading out with Poppy and her mom before he nods his head.

Violet chuckles quietly beside me. "Poppy's so good at getting exactly what she wants."

I turn my head and drop my eyes to Violet's face, doing my best to avoid looking at her sensational cleavage. "She certainly is. I've never seen anyone as skilled as her."

Violet nods, her eyes twinkling in the overhead lights. "I know right? I should get her to teach me her ways." She readjusts Jasmine, and I want to take the child from her and ease her burden

—I don't know why, because I sense she doesn't *need* help but for some reason, I *want* to help her. "I guess we'll see you at *Brain Freeze.*"

"I guess so." I despise impromptu outings.

The tension that had released from my shoulders moments ago is back, and I blow out a long, frustrated breath. I can't perform the proper surveillance to ensure Toby's safety but it's not like I get to decide these things. We're going to the most popular ice cream shop in the city. It'll probably be mayhem. And if it's not, it will be as soon as word spreads that Toby Summer is in the house.

We all head out of the foyer and to our cars. Toby climbs in my SUV, drops his head back on the passenger seat, and blows out a long breath as I study him carefully.

"Well, that was fucking awkward." I rub my hand over my short hair. "Did you know Cass was Poppy's mom?" Of course he didn't know. How would he have known such a thing? We've never seen Cassia with Poppy, and I know she never spoke of her daughter—keeping her a secret.

Without lifting his head from the headrest, he turns toward me. "Nope."

Laughter bursts out of me. Something that's been happening occasionally since that first time. Each time it happens, the guilt becomes marginally less—*marginally*. I'm fairly certain it won't ever completely disappear. "Only you, man. This shit could only happen to you. What are the fucking chances that the only time you decide to teach a kid you don't even know from a bar of soap how to play the guitar, she's the daughter of your high school crush?"

He doesn't answer me. What can he say?

As his silence fills the cab of my vehicle, I pull myself together, start the engine, and drive us to *Brain Freeze* to meet everyone for ice cream. "You realize I haven't had a chance to vet this place or book it out so you're not bothered by fans?" I don't even know the fucking layout properly. I haven't studied the entry and exit points or what's close by.

"Yeah, I know. Sometimes it's good to be spontaneous. We'll manage." Being spontaneous sucks when your job is to plan things down to the tiniest detail.

We all arrive within moments of each other, moving into the shop together. The girls lead the way, with me, Toby, and Oliver following close behind. I survey the area outside of the shop, noting the alleyway to the right and the number of cars parked down the street. With only one door into the building and a wall of glass windows, I should be able to keep an eye on Toby easily enough. When we enter the premises, I take note of the booths along the walls and the tables positioned neatly throughout the space. The jukebox in the corner and the long counter displaying ice cream. There's one door through to what I assume is the kitchen and probably an office and another door with a sign for the bathrooms. I open the door and check to find two doors leading through to male and female facilities. There are nine people in the building as far as I can see, two serving and seven customers prior to our entry. I think we'll be okay.

3

VIOLET

My eyes keep straying to the giant of a man with dark hair and even darker eyes. As many times as I drag my gaze away from him, I find myself sneaking glances. I'm not sure if I'm being as covert as I hope, but I can't stop watching him. He moves with a gracefulness that doesn't match his size while his eyes constantly dart around the shop, and I'm genuinely surprised he hasn't cracked a tooth with the way he's clenching his jaw. I'm certain I'm not crazy, but I *felt* something ignite inside me when we touched in the foyer; it was weird and unexpected. I can't stop thinking about how small my hand was in his and how safe and protected I felt just being close to him. He has this presence about him that screams, *you're safe with me.*

"Mommy, taste my ice cweam." Jasmine raises her ice cream to me, so I bend down and dart my tongue out for a lick.

"Mmm. Your ice cream is delicious."

Cassia steps toward me, holding two ice creams. "Here ya go. Cookie dough for you."

I take it from her. "Thanks. I could have bought ours."

Cass swipes her tongue up the side of her icy treat. "I didn't pay for it." She chuckles. "You missed Toby and Oliver arguing over who was going to pay." She widens her eyes at me with a grin.

My mouth drops open, and I shoot my gaze across the shop to Toby and Oliver, who still look to be arguing. Being a billionaire, Oliver Stone could afford to buy the actual shop. To be fair, Toby probably could too. "I'm sorry I missed it. I always seem to miss out on the good stuff. Who won?"

Her lips widen further. "Toby."

I wiggle my eyebrows up and down. "Maybe you should go lick your ice cream in front of him and show him your skills."

Her face drops. "I don't think he'll ever speak to me again after the way I've treated him and the secret I kept."

"You didn't know he was Poppy's guitar teacher. I mean, what were the chances?"

"I know, right?" Cass blows out a breath. "Vi. If I'd known how accepting he would be of Poppy, I would have never shut him out. I'm devastated that I've hurt him the way I have."

I move closer and wrap my free arm around my sister. "So you apologize. Explain your reasons to him." I glance across at Toby. His face looks like thunder for some reason. "I'm sure he'll understand. He seems like a decent guy, and you already know he thinks the world of Poppy."

Out of the corner of my eye, I see Shane move closer to Toby and look at something on Toby's phone. His face turns hard, and the tic in his jaw seems to take on a life of its own. Toby walks over to us and gently touches Cass's elbow. "Can I talk to you quickly about something that's just come up?" he asks as he keeps his voice low.

Cass glances around, trying to make sense of Toby wanting to talk to her. I'm not surprised since she thought he'd never want to speak with her again. She pauses her gaze on me for a moment, and I try to convey that him wanting to speak with her is a good sign. I think she picks up on my silent message and moves away from everyone so they can talk. Fingers crossed he's the upstanding guy he seems to be. Though, I wouldn't be surprised if it isn't a front. Some guys seem to be pretty good at faking it until they suck you in. I shake my head, trying to dispel the negative thoughts. Not every man is like Allen or our dad or Cass's ex and Poppy's father, Jake, for that matter.

Allen. Just thinking his name sends disappointment sliding through my veins like tar and sours my mood.

Shane moves closer to the booth where Poppy and Jasmine are enjoying their ice creams as they both lick up the side of their cones to collect the melted sweetness. Luckily I brought my wipes; the girls are going to need them. I check that Poppy and Jasmine are okay and step closer to Shane, trying not to notice how good he smells or how his heat seems to radiate from him and wrap around me. I tilt my head back to make eye contact with him. "Is everything okay? Toby seems pissed about something."

He huffs out a breath, rubs his hand over his short hair, then glances over his shoulder at the girls. His features soften, and he turns his attention back to me. "Someone posted a video and photos of Poppy and Toby's performance on social media," he says softly, and my mouth drops open. "They specifically named Poppy, and Toby's worried about unsavory people having the information."

"That was quick."

He nods. "People don't waste time spreading the word about Toby, and when it hits social media it quickly grows out of control." That tic in his jaw is back.

I place my hand on his arm in reassurance, feeling the same tingles as before and trying to ignore how right his muscles feel beneath my touch. "Poppy will love the attention. Don't stress."

He snaps his focus back to me. "You don't get it. Poppy is a really cute kid. Some psycho could come after her. She could be at risk now, and so could your daughter by association. They're both such beautiful girls," he murmurs the last part. "Toby never wanted any publicity surrounding the concert because he wanted to protect Poppy. You have no idea the sick stuff people can do."

My heart goes all gooey inside. His concern for the girls' safety hits me right in the muscle behind my ribs. "Sorry. I didn't realize. Thank you for being concerned about the girls but I'm sure it'll all blow over quickly. It's not like Poppy will be spending much more time with Toby now the concert's over." Will she? I don't know if the lessons have an expiration date.

He glances at Toby and Cass, and I follow his gaze. Cass and Toby are wrapped in each other's embrace. "I wouldn't be so sure about that." Shane smirks at me.

His entire face changes with a simple tilt of his lips and my heart speeds up. The tingling I felt at a simple touch spreads through my body and makes a direct hit at my core.

For fuck's sake, Violet. Don't even think about it.

After the day I've had, my core shouldn't be tingling and my heart shouldn't be racing for anyone with a dick. They're all assholes. Allen being the biggest one of them all, closely followed by Jake and my father.

Just thinking about how all of my things were dumped on the guest bed so his whore could hang her clothes in *my* closet and store her crap in *my* drawers has anger filling my body from the tips of my toes to the ends of my hair. My heart pounds harder, sending blood rushing through my veins as I think back to this morning.

I rap my knuckles against the door. I need to be sure he's *not here. He promised he wouldn't be home so I could stop by to collect my and Jasmine's things.*

I blow out a long breath, relieved there's no answer. Today's the first day I've felt strong enough to come here, and I don't want to face him. As angry as I am, beneath all of that, I'm hurt beyond repair. I trusted him to keep my heart safe—I mean I trusted him enough to have a child with him, and he treats us like this. I still can't believe he kicked us out. He fucking kicked us out of our own home. I shake my head, still in disbelief.

What an asshole!

I slide my key into the lock and open the door slowly, listening for any noises. Nothing. The tension I was holding in my shoulders evaporates, and I quickly pick up the boxes I brought and close the door behind me. Making my way through what was once my home, I feel eerily detached from the mess that greets me. Our home never looked like this when I was here because I *would always clean up after* him. *I had pride in our home, unlike my husband. Ex-husband. Is he my ex yet? Or does he only become my ex once we're divorced? I guess we're no longer together, so that would make him my ex—right?*

I spin on my heel and turn my back on the mess. I just want to get clothes for me and Jas as well as her favorite toys and books. The rest can wait. I head straight to Jas's room. Everything is exactly as we left it, so I pull open her drawers and grab as many of her things as I can. As I fill each box with clothes, toys, and books, I carry them out to the car. Looking around her room, I'm satisfied I have enough of her things to get her through until we settle everything officially. It's mostly excess toys that she doesn't play with anymore that I've left behind. With a sigh, I close her bedroom door and make my way to my bedroom. Well, I guess it isn't mine anymore.

I fill my lungs with a deep breath and open the door. The first thing that hits me is the scent of perfume. Perfume that isn't mine. What the hell? I step fully inside and take a moment to look around. I notice a lacy bra that isn't mine hanging out of one of the drawers, and as I scan the room, other unfamiliar items grab my attention. I guess his whore's been spending time here now that we're not together.

I move woodenly toward the drawer to investigate further, disgusted at the fact that she's put her bra in my *drawer alongside* my *underwear. I'm going to have to wash everything. My stomach rolls uncomfortably at the thought of her stuff touching mine. With two fingers, I pull her bra out of the drawer and toss it onto the messy bed, then open my drawer fully, ready to scoop up my bras and panties. My eyes widen in disbelief as I take in a drawer full of underwear that's not mine. I quickly close it and open the next drawer to find the same. Repeating the process, I find all of my drawers filled with some other woman's clothes.*

I feel violated.

She would have gone through my drawers and touched all of my things. Or maybe Allen did it. I don't know which is worse. I quickly walk over to my closet, and when I open it, I'm confronted with the same thing. All of my things are missing, replaced with another woman's stuff. My hands shake as I take in the jeans and sweaters. Skirts and boots. Feminine dresses and blouses.

Maybe he lost interest in me because I wasn't feminine enough on top of giving most of my focus to our daughter. Not that it matters now. He's made it clear that I'm no longer what he wants. After everything I put up with. Disgust consumes me over staying for as long as I did. God, I was a fool. But I thought I was doing the right thing for Jas.

I spin around, scanning the room, looking for my things. It's like I never lived here, and honestly, in this moment, I wish I never had. I step out of the bedroom on shaky legs and make my way down the hallway to check the cupboard there. My things aren't there. He'd better not have given my stuff away. I'll fucking kill him. Anger fills every cell in my body, and I tear through my home like my hair's on fire; opening and closing doors until I stop dead in my tracks at what greets me when I open the door to the guest bedroom.

A gasp escapes and I cover my mouth. I don't know if it's because of the emotional build-up I've been feeling about coming here today but tears immediately burst free along with a violent sob. There, on the bed, all of my clothes lay discarded. Just like my marriage. Just like me. I'm unsure if I'm sad or angry; both emotions seem to be warring with each other for dominance.

How dare he treat me like I never existed. Like I wasn't once the most important person in his life. And the way he's dismissed

Jasmine. His daughter. His *fucking daughter. That thought takes my fury to a whole new level.*

I guess anger wins out.

A warm hand on my lower back breaks me from the memory and a shiver makes its way up my spine. It's only then I realize how stiffly I'm holding myself. "Are you okay?" Shane's warm breath feathers across the side of my face in a gentle caress, sending my senses into overdrive.

I glance up at him. His dark brows are slashed low over his eyes and his features are full of concern. Concern that's directed at me. A stranger. It's been a long time since I've had anyone of the opposite sex show concern for me. I draw in a long breath and try to clear my thoughts. "I'm not okay but I will be. One day," I add and force a smile. "Thanks for checking in."

"You're welcome." He tips his head in acknowledgment and then steps away. The space beside me feels cold and empty the instant he moves, leaving me feeling vulnerable and exposed. I sigh. *Stop it, Violet.*

He and Toby fall into a deep discussion, and Cass gains everyone's attention. "As wonderful as this evening has been, it's time we get this superstar-in-the-making home to bed."

I chuckle and turn to look at the little superstar whose mouth and chin are covered with sticky ice cream. I'm so freaking proud of her. I love how she goes after what she wants, and I pray she never loses that. I hope life doesn't steal her wishes and dreams. That her sparkle never diminishes. Jasmine watches her cousin with adoration, and I couldn't want for a better role model for my daughter.

WE ALL PILE into Cass's car, Mom taking her turn in the back seat with the girls. I twist my body so I'm facing my sister and drop my voice to keep our conversation between us. "Soooo ... don't think I didn't notice."

Cass glances at me and then quickly returns her attention to the road. "Notice what?"

"Don't play innocent, Cass. I saw you hugging Toby. Not bad considering you didn't think he'd ever speak to you again."

She exhales a long breath and her shoulders slump. "He's worried that some weirdo is going to come for Poppy after videos and photos of them performing together ended up online."

I nod. "Yeah, Shane said something similar. Surely it can't be *that* bad." I feel like they're overreacting a little.

"That's what I said, but Toby was adamant that something bad may happen to Poppy so he's going to have Shane watch over her."

I snap my head back around to my sister. "What? You don't think that's overkill?"

She huffs. "Of course I do but he was ... determined." She glances at me. "He really cares for her, Vi. He doesn't want anything to happen to her." Her tone softens, and the shame in her voice is noticeable.

My heart goes all squishy for the second time tonight. Poppy deserves to have someone who really cares for her outside of our girl squad, and so does Cassia. I reach over and squeeze Cass's arm. "Of course he does. Everyone falls in love with Poppy. You realize this means you'll probably see more of Toby."

She lifts and drops one shoulder. "Maybe. Or, he could avoid me. He won't be the one watching over Poppy, so I doubt I'll see him."

"You could go over and talk to him. Sort things out."

"Yeah, maybe. I'll definitely apologize, but as for anything more ... I don't like my chances." She glances at me. "Don't think I didn't notice you talking to Shane." She winks as she deftly changes the subject.

Shit. I knew I should have kept my distance. My sister knows me too well. I shrug as nonchalantly as I can. "He's easy on the eyes, and it looks like we may get to see him more often." I wiggle my eyebrows. "We deserve some eye candy on the regular. Don't you think?"

Cass chuckles. "We sure do."

When we arrive home, I gently unbuckle Jas from her car seat and lift her into my arms, careful not to wake her. I glance up at the house as I quietly close the car door. I can't believe I'm a twenty-nine-year-old woman with a three-year-old daughter, and I'm living at home with my mom, sister, and niece.

I exhale a long breath filled with defeat.

I never thought my life would turn out like this. It should never have turned out like this. When I met Allen, I knew he was a player and didn't want anything to do with him. I kept blowing him off, but he persisted and was determined to prove to me that he'd changed his ways and had become a one-woman man. Boy, he fooled me. Never again will I fall for some man's smooth charms. I've learned my lesson.

I climb the stairs and lay Jasmine on her bed, remove her shoes, and head into the bathroom for a washcloth to wipe away the stickiness of the ice cream. She's going to have to miss out on brushing her teeth tonight because I refuse to wake her and then spend the next two hours trying to get her back to sleep. As I wipe her chubby cheeks and her sticky fingers, warmth and gratitude that she's mine fill all the empty spaces inside of me. Allen may be an asshole of epic proportions but he gave me the best gift of my life. Equal parts of guilt and happiness war with each other that he doesn't want to be involved in her life, and I won't have to share her with him, and that she's going to grow up without a father figure just like I did. I carefully slide a pull-up on since she didn't go to the bathroom before she fell asleep, and then I change her into her pajamas. I run my finger gently along her soft cheek and kiss her forehead, then step out into the hallway to find Mom standing outside her door waiting for me.

"She's out like a light," I whisper.

Mom smiles softly. "Such a cherub." She glances at the door and then hooks her arm through mine. "Come and have a cup of chamomile tea with me."

We head downstairs and into the kitchen together where Mom already has the kettle boiling and two cups on the counter. "Isn't Cass having tea?"

Mom shakes her head. "No. She wanted some time to snuggle with Poppy." I grin because that's probably what I'll do when I finish tea with Mom. I love snuggling with my girl. Her first three years have gone by so fast, and I fear the time for snuggles will come to an end before I'm ready. She pours the hot water into the cups and carries them to the dining table. "I wanted to check on you. I know today had to be difficult."

I study the woodgrain pattern of the table and think back to earlier. I felt like I'd been sucker punched in the gut while simultaneously having the rug pulled from beneath my feet. "I don't understand how I was so blindsided. I knew he'd been cheating, but I guess I hadn't expected him to move her into our home." I trace my finger over the rim of my cup. "How did I not expect that?" I whisper, my throat clogged with pain and betrayal. "Why did I stay with him for so long and overlook his cheating?" Where the hell was my self-respect? I'm so disappointed in myself. I didn't stand up for myself *or* my daughter. How did I let him treat me as less than for as long as I did?

Mom reaches over and gently lays her hand over mine. "Because you always like to think the best of people, Violet."

"I wish I didn't. Then I wouldn't have been so surprised ... and hurt."

Mom's gaze softens and she smiles sadly. "But then you wouldn't be you." She squeezes my hand. "And I wouldn't want you to change because you're perfect exactly as you are."

My bottom lip quivers and the backs of my eyes sting. "Maybe I shouldn't have focused so much of my attention on Jas. He felt neglected and looked elsewhere for the attention I wasn't giving him. And judging by the clothes in the closet, he wanted someone more feminine."

Mom tsks. "I know that's what he said to you, honey, but that's simply an excuse coming from an immature man who wasn't getting his way." I open my mouth to interrupt but Mom holds up her hand, shaking her head. "I don't want to hear it, Violet. A mother's focus needs to be on her baby, and the husband's focus should be on caring for his family and supporting his wife. There's no excuse. And as for being feminine, you needn't worry about that. You're plenty feminine, Vi. Don't let that thought fester in your head."

My argument dies, and my shoulders drop from around my ears. I know she's right. I know there's no excuse but I still wonder.

4

VIOLET

It may be a holiday for everyone else, but being an employee of a state park means I don't get today off. The park will be busy, so it's all hands on deck, so to speak. Walking into the busy office, I find everyone prepping to head out to their designated areas. Checking the map, I find the area my partner and I have been assigned to today and breathe a sigh of relief when I see we've been designated a section that isn't quite as popular as other areas of the park. It's also my favorite spot because the views are endless, and in the springtime, gorgeous wildflowers cover the area.

There isn't a cloud in the sky today, so I slap on a layer of sunscreen, grab my radio, backpack, and medical kit and head back out to meet Tristan at our SUV. I love working with him. He and his wife had a baby boy two months ago, and I love watching his face light up whenever he talks about them. He is one proud husband and daddy, and he shows me there are *some* men in this world who dote on their partners and are selflessly dedicated to their families.

"Morning, Vi," Tristan calls from the driver's seat as I stow my stuff in the back. "Didn't think you were gonna make it in time."

I huff as I climb into the passenger seat. "It was tough getting out of bed today. Mom didn't realize I had to work and kept

Jasmine entertained quietly so I could sleep in. Which meant my little alarm clock didn't wake me." I put on my seatbelt and turn toward him. "I'm still waking up."

He chuckles as he starts the engine, and we make our way slowly toward our section of the park, winding along the main road which snakes through the preserve. "Noah slept six hours last night, so I'm feeling refreshed and rejuvenated. I can't remember the last time I had such a long stretch of uninterrupted sleep."

"Probably about two months ago." I wink at him. "I remember the first time Jasmine slept through the night like that. I woke in a panic thinking something was wrong with her."

Tristan nods. "Yeah. I have to admit my heart was racing when I woke and saw the time. It didn't go back to its normal rhythm until I knew he was okay."

"But everything was okay, right?"

He glances at me and grins. "I wouldn't be here if there was anything wrong."

My heart melts. Of course he wouldn't be here because his family comes first for him. Always. "So do you think this is the start of him sleeping through the night?"

"I don't know." He shrugs. "I'd like to think so but after watching my sister's kids, I know their sleep patterns can change quickly at this age. I'm not getting my hopes up."

I snicker. "Isn't that the truth? Just when you think you have them worked out, they do something completely different."

We fall into companionable silence as we travel toward our destination, and I take in the beauty of the park. Because today is a holiday and we expect the park to be busy, we won't be doing our usual monitoring tasks, instead, we'll keep our eyes peeled for visitors who need help, directions, or just want to know a little more about the environment and local flora and fauna. I don't enjoy days like these, even though I sometimes run school visits to educate kids about our indigenous flora and how introduced weeds affect our local plants and animals. I prefer to be observing, recording, and monitoring the native flora and the invasive species that have found their way into our beautiful park. Leading a project to remove weeds and plant more native species is one of my favorite parts of the job.

We pull up as close as we can to our spot for the day and climb out of the vehicle. Overhead, the familiar rasping scream of a red-tailed hawk pierces the air. Shielding my eyes, I look up to find it soaring elegantly above us. The mild fall breeze kisses my face, and I smile as I watch the hawk with wings outstretched.

So damn beautiful.

I look back down the hill and out across the expanse of the park enjoying the sun on my skin, and my grin widens. I can't believe this is where I work; *this* is my office. I've never been one to be cooped up inside, always feeling happier and more grounded when I'm outdoors. Even knowing I'll have to deal with the public today—more than usual—I still love my job. Every day is different, and although I know this park like the back of my hand, it's forever changing according to the season. I don't know how people can work inside all day where everything stays pretty much the same day in and day out. I would be bored out of my mind—I can't even contemplate the possibility. Here, the landscape changes daily, from spring wildflowers to snow on the tops of the mountain in winter, to a drier landscape in the summer. It doesn't matter the time of the year, the park always steals my breath.

Tristan whistles long and low. "Didn't take them long to get up here."

I glance at him and then follow the direction he's pointing down the hill. A group of mountain bike riders are making their way toward us. "Damn. They were fast."

The track they're using is rigorous and steep for bikers on a good day. On a bad day, it can be muddy and almost impassable, but that doesn't stop some hardcore cyclists; we've seen all sorts up here. The riders fly straight past us without slowing, and I'm concerned at their lack of consideration for others on the track. If they have no respect for us, they certainly won't think twice when they come across hikers using the same track.

Once they're out of sight, I turn to Tristan. "How did the night hike go on Saturday?"

He tucks his hands in his pockets and rocks back on his heels. "Really well. The kids were thrilled when they saw the scorpions glowing under the UV blacklight flashlights."

"Oh yeah, I—"

"Hey!" We both turn toward the voice shouting at us to find a man waving frantically from the crest of the hill the cyclists disappeared over mere moments ago.

I take off at a sprint and shout over my shoulder, "Bring our stuff!"

As I reach the cyclist, he takes off. "Over here," he calls, waving his arm for me to follow.

When I crest the hill, I see the carnage. It looks as though two cyclists are down but there are three people on the ground. With panting breaths, I come to a stop and quickly assess the situation. At first glance, everyone is conscious, which is a good sign. The two cyclists are being helped to their feet by their friends, leaving one hiker on the ground with a large man kneeling beside her. I drop to my knees next to the woman. "Hi, I'm Violet. I'm a park ranger here. Would it be okay if I check you out to see if I can help you today?"

The woman nods, her face scrunched in pain. "Of course. I'm Fiona and this is my husband, William."

I say hi to Fiona, then glance at her husband. "Hi, William."

"Hello." He tilts his chin to me, and I notice the shake in his hands, probably from shock. "I told Fiona it wouldn't be a good idea to hike today. She wouldn't listen to me," he snaps.

I give his snappy words a pass, he's probably grumpy because his wife is hurt, and he's worried about her. I nod so he knows I've heard him, but direct my question to Fiona. "Can you tell me what happened?" As she explains about the cyclists coming around the bend too quickly for her to get out of their way, I scan her body for any wounds. She has some abrasions on her hands where I suspect she reached out to catch herself as she fell. "Are you in any pain?"

Tristan drops our medical supplies beside me and rushes over to the two cyclists who are already up and about.

"I landed pretty hard on my hip, so that's quite sore," she says with a shake in her voice, indicating the level of pain she's experiencing. Judging by the silver in her dark, chin-length hair, she's probably about the same age as Mom, and I don't want to risk any further injury by moving her.

"I think it would be best if we call an ambulance to come and get you. Hips can be tricky things, so I think we should keep you as still as possible. Would it be okay with you if we call for help?"

She and her husband both nod. "Certainly. We're covered for an ambulance."

I nod and step away to call it in on my radio, then check with Tristan if the cyclists need any help, and they don't. Once I know help is on the way, I return to the couple as William berates his wife for getting injured. "Serves you right. This is what happens when you don't listen to me. I didn't want to come out today. If we'd stayed home like I wanted, you wouldn't be lying on the ground with a sore hip. And now we have to go to the damn hospital, and God only knows how long that's gonna take," he yells at his wife.

I drop to my knees, ignoring the husband, and set about cleaning the abrasions on the heels of Fiona's hands, biting my tongue to stop myself from telling William to give it a break. Fiona doesn't need his grumpiness right now; she needs his support. "An ambulance is on the way. It shouldn't be too long. Do either of you have any water with you today?"

Even though it's not a super-hot day, sitting in the sun for a long period means I need to keep the couple hydrated while we wait. While they share a drink of water, and he continues to quietly berate her—*dick*—I head back over to the cyclists. I'm so pissed at them. They flew past us without any consideration, and I'm sure they didn't find their manners as they crested the hill since the evidence of their lack of care is currently sitting on a dirt track. As I step closer, I hear Tristan lecturing the young men. They're lucky he beat me to it because I wouldn't be holding back and maintaining the level of professionalism he's showing them. In fact, they should be dropping dead any moment from my evil eye as I glare at them.

Tristan makes them feel guilty enough that they finally show some respect and apologize to Fiona and William, who only grunts in return, saving all of his mouthiness for his wife. I'm pretty sure I can't roll my eyes anymore today or I'll be too dizzy to work the rest of my shift. One would think an apology would have been the first thing out of the young men's mouths, instead, they had to be *told* it would be a good idea to apologize.

What is wrong with people?

Where are their manners? I shake my head—feeling like I'm channeling my mother right now.

Finally, Tristan guides the paramedics to us, and after I explain everything that happened and what I've done for Fiona, they carefully situate her onto a gurney and carry her to the roadside, where they parked, and load her into the back of their ambulance.

"Thank you so much for all of your help today," Fiona calls.

"You're welcome. I'm sorry your hike ended the way it did today." I only hope she's not too seriously injured and that her husband stops with the negativity. I wave to her and her husband as the paramedic closes the doors. The cyclists are long gone, leaving me and Tristan alone. I radio the main office to give them a description of William and Fiona's car so there's a record at the end of the day if it's still in the parking lot. That way we know we don't have to send out a search party for any unaccounted park visitors.

"Well, I don't know about you, but I think we've had enough excitement for one day," Tristan says as he pulls out his thermos and pours himself a coffee.

I grab my water bottle. "I hope she's okay." I take a drink. "I was so pissed at those boys and their lack of common sense."

"I could tell." Tristan snickers. "That's why I thought it would be best if I spoke with them."

I nod as we each prop ourselves in the back of our vehicle to enjoy our morning snack. I peel my orange while Tristan unwraps a giant piece of chocolate brownie. "Jesus, sure you couldn't pack a bigger piece of that?" I huff out a laugh and take a bite of an orange segment.

He looks affronted. "I could have brought the whole tray." He bites off a large chunk and chews, making a big deal about how delicious it is. I'm pretty sure just looking at the sweet treat has added another inch to my damn hips. "So, how was Saturday?" I widen my eyes at my long-time friend, startled that he's asking me about Shane. How does he know? Am I that transparent? When I don't respond, he adds, "You know, picking up your stuff from your place."

Oh, *that*. It's a testament to the effect Shane had on me that my mind skipped right over the shit show of the day, passed over Poppy's concert on Saturday night, and straight to meeting Shane Sutton: bodyguard extraordinaire and setter alight of women's panties. I blow out a long breath. "It was worse than I anticipated." Tristan takes another bite of his treat, which I could do with right about now, while I explain how my ex and his whore dumped all of my stuff on the guest bed so she could move in. "And when I say dumped, I mean dumped. Like they carried the drawers into the room and tipped them out. Then took all of my clothes from the hangers, rolled them up, and threw them on the bed."

His eyebrows shoot up in surprise. "What a fucking dick!"

I nod, finishing off another segment of orange. "I know. I can't believe I'm actually married to the guy. Can't wait 'til I divorce his slimy ass."

The rest of our day goes smoothly, free of medical emergencies —thank goodness. We share some native flora and fauna knowledge with a couple of hikers who are interested in learning more, and then we make our way back to our office to sign off for the day.

THE SECOND I open the front door, my little girl throws herself at me so I bend down and scoop her up. "Mommy, you're home!" She wraps her little arms around my neck and kisses each of my cheeks.

I burst into laughter at her happiness to see me and rub her nose with mine as I hold her tight to me. "How's my girl?"

"I be a good girl." I bet she has. She's such a sweet little thing; I don't know how I got so lucky.

Mom comes out of the kitchen with a grin. "Oh my gosh, you didn't even get completely inside the door."

"That's okay. I'm glad my girl is so happy to see me." I bounce Jasmine in my arms, making her giggle.

"Come see what we pwanted today." Jasmine releases my neck and wiggles down my body, taking my hand in hers.

"Hang on and let me close the door, then you can show me all the things."

She releases my hand, running toward the back of the house —probably to put her boots on—while I close and lock the front door. Mom takes my backpack from me and I kiss her cheek.

"How was your day?"

"Busy. I'll tell you all about it later. Thanks for looking after Jas today." Mom will never know how much I appreciate her looking after Jasmine for me on the days I work. She's been doing it for me ever since I returned to work part-time after my maternity leave ended. She manages to do her work from home when Jas naps or is occupied with an activity, and on the days I don't work, she does her work on site and meets with clients.

"I'll look forward to hearing all about it, but you'd better get your butt outside before Jasmine star—"

"Mommy! Where are you?"

Laughter bubbles out of me and Mom. "So impatient, that girl of mine."

"Sounds like someone else I know." Mom snickers, giving me a wink. I guess the apple doesn't fall far from the tree and all that.

I wave to Poppy, who is practicing guitar, on my way to meet Jasmine at the back door. When I look down I notice she has her boots on the wrong feet, but I leave her be. She'll work out that they feel odd when she starts to walk, or she won't, it's not like it matters. She slides her small hand in mine as excitement lights her little face. Her blue eyes twinkle with the anticipation of showing me what she did today.

We step out of the house and onto the back porch. Jasmine tugs me eagerly down the steps to the raised vegetable beds. "Oh my, you've been busy today."

"We did wots of pwanting today." She tugs me forward and we stop at the first garden bed. "We pwanted bwoccowi here and cabbage here." She points at the neat rows, then drags me to the next bed. "We pwanted cawwots and wettuce here."

Jasmine tries to drag me to the next garden bed, but I stop her. "How many lettuce plants did you plant today?" She shrugs. "How about we count them together and find out?"

"Otay." We count each tiny seedling together. "... eight, nine, ten!"

"That's going to be a lot of lettuce."

She turns to me with wide eyes. "It is. Wucky we wike wettuce."

"Sure is."

We spend the next thirty minutes in the garden as Jasmine points out all the seedlings she planted with Mom today, and we spend extra time counting each one. "Woah, we pwanted a wot of pwants today, Mommy."

"You sure did. I can't wait until they grow so we can eat them." I tickle her stomach, eliciting giggles—the best sound in the world.

"Me too."

We spend the next twenty minutes collecting ripened tomatoes, snap peas, and squash, which we take inside and wash, ready to use for dinner. Jasmine manages to *sneak* some peas while we work. I'm not about to complain that she's eager to eat vegetables. So many mothers from playgroup complain about how hard it is to get their little ones to eat their vegetables. We have no such problem with Jas because she's excited to eat the vegetables we grow. She loves being part of the entire process. Same with Poppy.

ONCE DINNER IS over and done with and we've cleaned up the kitchen, Jasmine and Poppy head into the playroom for a little while before I start getting Jas ready for bed. As we put Cass's dinner in the microwave for her to heat when she gets home, I tell Mom about the events of the day and how a poor woman was knocked over by the mountain bikers who were in too much of a hurry to be considerate of the hikers on the track.

Mom's eyebrows almost fly off her face. "Lucky you and Tristan were close by."

"I know. I dread to think how they would have managed if we weren't there to help."

Mom pats me on the arm. "I'm so proud of you, Vi." I feel warm all over with her words. She's always been supportive of me and Cass.

I turn and hug her close. "Thanks, Mom. I'm so lucky to have you as my mom."

When she pulls back her eyes are a little glassy, and she gives me a lopsided smile. "I'm the lucky one." She squeezes me tight, then heads off to shower, and I spend some time playing with the girls until Cass arrives home. Jasmine goes to bed before Poppy, so once

Cass has finished her dinner, I bathe Jasmine and get her ready for bed.

"*...When the first stars of evening appeared in the sky, Koala Lou crept home through the dark and up into the gum tree. Her mother was waiting for her. Before she could say a word her mother had flung her arms around her neck and said, "Koala Lou, I DO love you! I always have, and I always will." And she hugged her for a very long time.*" God, I love this story by Mem Fox. I sigh as I close the book, and Jasmine looks up at me with a sleepy smile.

"I wove Koawa Wou, Mommy," Jas tells me in her sweet sleepy voice.

I brush her silky hair away from her face. "I do, too."

"Mommy?"

"Yeah, baby girl."

"Where's Koawa Wou's daddy?"

Oh shit! Here we go. I didn't even think about that when I bought this book for Jas the other week. I scoot down so I'm able to rest my head on her pillow and face her directly. "He was probably at work."

"Is that where my daddy is? At work?"

I swallow past the lump in my throat and rub my baby's back with soothing strokes. "Well, yeah, your daddy goes to work every day."

"But what about on the weekend?" Her little brows scrunch down over her tired eyes as she thinks. "He was home on the weekend."

"You're right. He was always home on the weekend."

"Why doesn't he visit us?"

I'm stumped as to what to say to my daughter. I'm supposed to have all the answers, but right now, I have none and no idea how to come up with a suitable response.

"Did he forget about us?"

My mind skips back ...

"Wook at all the bubbwes, Mommy." Jas holds up her soapy hands with an excited giggle.

"So many bubbles. Make sure you get all the dirt off from the garden," I prompt.

"I wiw, Mommy." She scrubs and scrubs her hands.

"Thank you for all your help pulling out the weeds."

"It was fun!" she cheers loudly.

"Shh, remember, Daddy's still asleep."

Her eyes widen. "Sowwy, Mommy."

"That's okay. Come on, let's rinse the soa—"

"Can you two shut the fuck up? I'm trying to fucking sleep!" Allen shouts from our bedroom.

Jas's head snaps up to me, her eyes wide and shimmering. I have to bite my tongue so I don't tell him *to shut the fuck up. I don't know how many times I've told him not to speak like that in front of our daughter. We finish rinsing the soap off quietly, and then I dry our hands, then take Jas to the kitchen to make her lunch. I slice half an apple, a small carrot, cucumber, and cheese and place them in a Bento box with some crackers for her along with a glass of milk.*

I slide the items onto the table in front of her. "I just need to check on Daddy. Can you be a good girl and stay here for Mommy?"

Jas nods as she takes a slice of apple and a slice of cheese and pops them into her mouth. I stroke her soft hair and kiss the top of her head, then turn on my heel and head for my husband who's finally awake. Stepping inside our bedroom, I close the door behind me, and when I turn around, Allen's lying on his stomach, his head turned away from me. I take the four steps to the side of the bed and snap, "Don't speak like that to me or our daughter again. I've told you that language is unacceptable around her."

He rolls over and sits up, his face creased from the pillow but he looks pissed. "Maybe you should take your fucking precious daughter and get the fuck out. I'm sick and tired of being told what to do and what not to do. I'm a fucking man, not a child."

I fold my arms across my chest as my blood boils. "Maybe you should act like a fucking man *instead of a child. I'm not going anywhere. If you don't like it, you leave."*

"This is my home!" he shouts. "Last I checked, I pay the fucking mortgage around here. And I can't remember the last time you treated me like a man. Maybe if you sucked my dick occasionally, you'd remember who the boss is around here."

I shudder at the thought of having any part of his body anywhere near me. "Why in the hell would I suck your disgusting dick when you're sticking it God knows where at every opportunity?"

"Why do you think I go looking elsewhere? You spend all of your time with that fucking ugly brat out there," he thrusts his arm toward the door, "and ignore me. I wish we'd never had that damn kid."

He may as well have lunged a dagger straight into my heart. "You asshole," I whisper, holding back the sting of tears. He can say whatever he likes about me, but he went too far when he brought Jas into it. "If we leave, we're not ever coming back, so you think long and hard about what you're saying to me."

He looks up at the ceiling as if he's thinking, then smirks at me. "Get the fuck out and take the brat with you." When I don't immediately move because I'm in shock that things have exploded like this, he shouts, "Get the fuck out, now!"

I move toward the door. "You'll fucking regret this. I'm packing and then we're outta here."

"I won't fucking regret it. What I regret is agreeing to have a kid with you; an ugly one at that. This is the best fucking decision I've made in a long time. I want you gone in the next two minutes or I'm gonna throw that ugly kid out the front door."

"You were my biggest mistake," I grit out and leave him in the bedroom. Closing the door quietly behind me, I lean against the cool surface and catch my breath. Hold it together, Violet. Just get out of here and get to Mom and Cass. Then you can fall apart. *I draw*

in a deep breath and blow it out, then repeat the process until I'm certain I won't cry as soon as I see Jas.

Pasting on a smile, I head to the kitchen to collect my daughter. "I think we should go visit Gramma. What do you think?" I fake enthusiasm for my daughter's sake.

She throws her little arms up in the air. "Yay! Wiw Poppy be there?"

"I'm pretty sure she will." I grip her beneath her arms and swing her onto my hip. Grabbing my keys and purse, I head out the door and don't look back.

Shaking myself out of the memory, I kiss Jas's forehead and use my finger to smooth out the creases across her forehead. "How could he forget you? I think he's just been busy." She smiles at me, and it breaks my heart that I've just lied to my little girl but the alternative is unacceptable. I don't want to break her heart. I never want her to know that she was cast aside by her father, but I need to come up with something better to say because as she grows older, that answer isn't gonna fly. I kiss the tip of her nose. "Now, it's time for sleep. Remember that I love you more than all of the wildflowers on the earth."

She wraps her tiny arm around my neck and pulls me in close, rubbing her nose against mine. "I wove you, Mommy."

And that. That right there is the best thing that's happened to me today.

5

SHANE

"WHAT TIME ARE YOU COMING OVER TODAY?" I can practically hear the frown in Mom's voice and picture the deep lines stretching across her forehead.

"I'm not sure if I can make it today."

Mom's sigh fills the line. "It's your birthday. I would like to see my *only* child on his birthday." She's good at laying on the guilt—I guess she's seasoned at it since she's been doing it for years. She'll be the only one in the house who *wants* to see me on my birthday. Dad couldn't give two shits. "I don't ask for much." I roll my eyes. "You know just as well as I do that we don't know how many birthdays we have on this Earth." Fuck! She's pulled out the big guns now. Not that she realizes exactly what that comment means to me directly; it's more about her losing her sister at a young age.

"All right." I sigh. "I'll be over …" I look at the time. "In an hour. Will that suit you?"

"Perfect." Her voice brightens, and I can imagine the smile lighting up her face. "I'll see you then." I nod even though she can't see me and ready my finger to end the call. "Oh, and Shane."

"Yeah?"

"Thank you."

I end the call and drop my gaze to the ground at the gratitude dripping from her voice. I've been ignoring messages from Toby, Nix, Mrs. S, and Hope all morning, but when Mom's name lit up my phone I couldn't ignore her. It's not completely her fault I hate going there. Nothing's really changed since I was a kid. She still loves and cares for me as much as she's capable of even if *he* doesn't.

I finish washing my SUV and then head inside to shower. On the way to my parents' home, I ruminate over my conversation with Mom. Guilt and shame swallows me—she had to practically beg to see me on my birthday. What sort of a son plans to stay away from his parents on his birthday? She's always tried to make a fuss, even though it was often only the two of us acknowledging my special day. Out of guilt, I make a detour and stop at Cass's shop. I'll feel a little better if I show Mom that I appreciate her efforts by giving her some flowers.

Cass is busy and there are a couple of people waiting before me, so I choose a bouquet from one of the tubs as I get closer to the front of the line. When I finally make it to the counter, Cass's eyes are wide with surprise. "Hi, Shane." She looks around and I know who she's looking for.

"He's not here."

Her shoulders drop slightly, disappointment washing over her features before she realizes it. Her face smooths out, and she smiles at me, dropping her eyes to the flowers in my hand. Her eyebrows rise as she asks, "For someone special?"

I look down at the colorful arrangement. "Just for my mom."

Cass's smile widens. "Oh, she'll love them." She reaches for the bouquet. "Let me tie a ribbon around them for you. What's your mom's favorite color?"

I picture all of Mom's favorite things. "Teal."

"Oh, I have a gorgeous teal ribbon with gold flecks through it." She holds up a finger. "Back in a sec." She disappears from view through the side door I know leads to the back of her store, then hustles back out holding up the ribbon. "Will this be okay?"

I dunno. It's just ribbon but I can tell this means something to Cassia so I nod. "Looks great."

Her smile is wide as she wraps the stems with the ribbon. She clearly loves doing this stuff. "Uh, how's Toby's arm today?"

Damn, I probably should have checked on him today after he was hit with a baseball during our visit to the park with Cass and Poppy yesterday, but I've been too busy avoiding everybody. When I dropped him off at home last night, he was floating on cloud nine because he got to spend the afternoon and evening with Cass and Poppy. "I ... uh ... haven't spoken with him today. I'm sure he's fine, though."

"Oh. I figured you guys see each other every day."

I shake my head. "*Almost* every day. He's home writing, so I have today off." She snips the end of the ribbon and holds up the flowers for my approval. "They look great. Thank you." I grab my phone out of my pocket to pay.

As we're waiting for the transaction to be approved, Cass asks, "Any special occasion?"

"Nah, just visiting my folks and thought I'd surprise Mom."

"Oh, that's so sweet. Have a great visit."

"Yeah, thanks." I step through the glass door, and back onto the street. A scrawny kid is running toward me, holding a woman's purse in his hand and looking over his shoulder. I follow his line of sight to find a woman shouting after him. Stepping out from the doorway, I grab the back of his shirt as he reaches me and lift him clear off the sidewalk. He kicks out with his feet, connecting with my thigh before I shift him farther away from my body.

"What the fuck, man!" He swings his arm out to try and hit me, but his reach is too short. "Put me down. This is fucking assault."

Stupid kid.

The woman catches up to the boy, her chest rising and falling quickly. She scowls at the kid and then looks up at me. "Thank you so much."

"You're welcome. Is this your purse?"

The kid drops the purse on the ground, the contents spilling everywhere—little punk. "Put me the fuck down. I don't have nothin'."

"Yeah, it is. I'd just taken some money out of the bank to pay for my kids' school fees. Thank God you caught him."

I nod. "You wanna call the cops? I'll keep him until they get here."

"Thanks." She drops to her knees and collects everything from the sidewalk, including her phone. Pressing the screen she dials nine-one-one and talks to the person on the other end. While she explains what happened, two officers patrolling the street come to a stop in front of us.

"What's going on here?"

The kid flicks his arm out toward me. "This guy's assaulting me."

Both officers turn their attention toward me, their eyebrows high on their foreheads as they wait for my explanation. The woman who had her bag stolen ends her call and steps closer. "Officers. Thank goodness you're here." She points to the kid I'm still holding off the ground with one hand while I balance Mom's flowers in my other hand. "This boy stole my purse, and this kind gentleman stopped the little thief."

"I ain't got no purse, lady." He looks at the cops. "It's all bullshit."

"Watch your mouth, kid." The cop turns to me. "Is that what happened?"

I explain how I stepped out of Cassia's shop and what I saw. "I just reacted on instinct. I didn't *see* him steal the purse, but he was running with a lady's purse as she shouted after him. It only took a second to put two and two together."

A man steps out from the small crowd that's formed around us. "*I* saw the boy snatch her purse, officer."

"Fuck," the boy spits as he goes limp in my hold.

The officer nods and grabs his notepad as we each take turns recounting the events. All the while, I keep hold of the boy. "Okay. Thank you, I think we have everything we need. You can put the kid down and we'll take him to the station and call his parents."

"Fuck no! I'm not going back home. My dad'll kill me."

I place him on his feet, and once I'm sure the officer has a firm hold on the boy, I release him. "We'll talk about it on the way to the station."

As the cops take the boy away, the woman steps closer to me. "I don't know how I'll ever thank you. I've been saving that money for the past six months. If I'd lost it ..." Her bottom lip trembles. "I don't know what I would have done. Thank you so much."

I force a tense smile. I'm just glad I could help; I don't need any thanks for that. "It was nothing."

"It wasn't nothing. It meant a lot to me and my sons."

I sense she's not going to let it go unless I accept her thanks. "You're welcome. Glad I could help." I hold up the flowers for Mom. "I need to get going." Mom's going to be wondering where the hell I am.

"Oh, of course. Well, thank you again."

I tip my head and walk toward the parking lot.

I PULL into Mom and Dad's driveway, and dread fills my stomach like lead. I know exactly what I'll find when I step inside—I can see it clearly in my mind's eye. I walk along the paved walkway to the front door and knock.

After several minutes, the door opens, revealing Mom. A smile lights her tired face when she sees it's me. "Oh, I'm so happy you're here. I was worried you'd changed your mind." She steps back to allow me into their home. It's a different house from the one I grew up in. They decided to downsize when I went into the army. "Happy birthday!" She wraps her arms around me and holds me tight. The top of her head barely comes to the middle of my chest as I awkwardly return her hug while holding her flowers.

"Thanks, Mom. Sorry I'm late. I needed to make a stop on the way." I hold out the flowers for her.

Her eyes soften, and she brings her hands up to cover her mouth as she looks between me and the flowers with her dark eyes, exactly like mine. Such a simple gift, yet you'd think I bought her a diamond-studded necklace. "Oh my gosh, they're so beautiful. Thank you. You didn't need to bring me anything, I'm just happy to see you." There she goes again, making me feel guilty for my lack of presence. "Come in. Come in." She moves to the side so I can step inside fully, and I pull the door closed behind me, locking it.

To the left, I spot Dad sitting in his usual spot in his recliner. Several empty beer bottles litter the table next to his chair, and one of his favorite war movies plays loudly on the television. Judging by the scene currently playing, it's *Full Metal Jacket*. If he's not working at the post office, this is where he can be found, except when Mom manages to drag him out of the house every once in a while. He doesn't acknowledge me as I follow Mom—who's favoring her left side—into the lounge room, even though he had to have heard me at the front door.

"Look who's here," Mom says, trying to push excitement into her voice. "Shane's come to visit on his birthday." Without taking his eyes off the screen, he grunts at me and then takes a long pull from the beer he's holding. I don't even take his lack of response personally anymore. He's been like this for as long as I can remember. Lord only knows how or why Mom's stayed with him for this long. For a long time, I felt as though she'd picked him over me since she never called him out on his behavior toward me, not that he treated her any better. She sighs and her shoulders drop, some of her energy leeching out of her body. "He even brought me some beautiful flowers." She tries again but he's shut us out completely now.

I stride past her and into the kitchen, stopping short at the sight that greets me. Now I feel like an asshole. A *happy birthday* banner is strung across the window that looks out to the backyard, and a birthday cake, complete with candles, sits in the middle of the kitchen counter. She has balloons tied to the back of the chairs and some of my favorite snacks from when I was a teenager on the table. I find it hard to swallow around the lump in my throat at what she's done for me. What she's always done for me on my birthday. She may have chosen him over me but she's never stopped trying to show her love for me.

She limps past me, mumbling under her breath as she goes. She opens a cupboard up high and tries to reach the top shelf, which is laughable with her small stature. I step up behind her and grab the vase that she was trying to reach and take it to the sink to fill.

"Why are you limping?"

She waves me off. "I had a bit of a fall a few weeks back. It's nothing." *Nothing?* Did he fucking hurt her? Is he that far gone now?

"How did you fall?" I ask in a tone harsher than she deserves.

"It was a nice day, so I convinced your father to go for a walk. Some cyclists were going a bit fast around the bend and didn't see us in time and knocked me over. It was nothing."

"What the hell, Mom? Why didn't you call me?"

"You're so busy, and it really was nothing."

"It wasn't fucking nothing. We ended up in the back of an ambulance, woman!" Dad shouts from the living room.

"An ambulance? Jesus, Mom. It must have been pretty bad." I clench my jaw and look at her. "You should have called me."

"Why would she do that? It's not like you give a shit about her," Dad calls out from his chair. I guess I deserve that. It's not like I'm around all that much.

She waves me off, dismissing my concern, and busies herself with the flowers, placing them in the vase and then finishing off the display by tying the ribbon around the glass. "These are stunning, Shane. Thank you so much." She places them in the middle of the table, then pulls out a chair for me like she didn't just tilt my world on its axis. What if it had been worse? Would they have called me then? "Come. Sit. I'll make us a coffee and we can catch up."

"I can do it since you're hurt." It's the least I can do since I'm such a shitty son.

She grabs my arm and tugs me toward the chair. "I'm fine. Let me spoil you." I reluctantly sit, and while the coffee machine does its thing, she places the birthday cake on the table right in front of me.

My immediate thought is that I don't deserve her attention and care. Her kindness. Her love.

She places our coffee on the table and sits beside me, dropping her hand over the top of mine and squeezing. "I'm so happy you came." I swallow past my guilt. She doesn't deserve my absence but I can't stand to be in the same place as Dad. "Tell me how you've been." She tucks her chin-length hair behind her ear.

I look at Mom. For the first time since I arrived, I take a moment to study her face closely. She looks tired. Really tired. The lines etched across her forehead are deeper than the last time I saw her, and there's more gray in her dark hair. "How about you tell me how *you've* been?"

"Oh, you know, nothing much changes around here." Her eyes slide toward the lounge room as if she can see Dad in his recliner through the walls. "But the young couple next door had a baby"—she scrunches her eyebrows together as she thinks—"must be about six months ago now." A smile touches her lips. "Penny. Such an adorable little girl. So happy and calm. Reminds me a lot of you when you were that age." She clutches her shirt as she remembers, and her lips tip up slightly. "You were such a good baby."

We spend the next thirty minutes drinking our coffee while she tells me all about her neighbors and how she takes them a cooked dinner a couple of nights a week so they get a break. "I remember what it was like when you were a baby. Some days didn't go to plan, and I was so tired in the early days. A home-cooked meal prepared by someone else would have been a godsend. And Myles works some Saturday evenings, so I keep Rory company if she doesn't have plans."

"Fiona. Bring me a beer," Dad calls from the other room.

Mom rises immediately to do his bidding, a flush coating her cheeks. As she passes across the threshold into the lounge room with his beer, she asks, "Why don't you join us, William? We can sing to Shane and cut the cake."

"He's not a boy anymore, Fiona. He doesn't need a damn birthday cake, and he certainly doesn't need us singing to him like he's a damn child," he snaps at her.

When she steps back into the kitchen, her cheeks are even more flushed and she doesn't make eye contact with me as she collects the matches and a knife. She takes the seat beside me and lights the candles, then smiles at me. "Are you ready for my terrible, off-key singing?" she asks, as though Dad didn't just belittle her.

"You don't have to sing, Mom. Dad's right. I'm not a child anymore."

She covers my hand with hers. "I want to sing 'Happy Birthday' to my son. Today is as much about you as it is about me, you know. Don't deny me my celebration." I don't miss the *please* that she leaves unsaid as she looks at me pleadingly.

I nod and force a smile to my lips. "I'm ready."

Her smile is instant, and happiness bleeds through her face quickly, lighting her eyes. She draws in a long breath and then sings 'Happy Birthday' to me, her eyes never leaving my face. I chuckle at the enthusiasm she puts into the rendition, and when she's finished I lean forward to blow out the candles but she stops me with her hand on mine before I can let out a breath. "Remember to make a wish." Her eyes trace my face, and I nod slowly, then take my time to think of a wish.

What I really want to wish for isn't a possibility.

If I could have one wish.

One single wish.

It would be that Wyatt was never blown up and he was here to watch his son grow up and love his wife because I know damn well that if he'd returned, he'd appreciate his family not ignore them. My thoughts turn dark, and I get lost in my guilt that I'm sitting here *celebrating* my birthday when Wyatt no longer has birthdays to celebrate.

Mom squeezes my hand, bringing me back to the present. My second wish would be for her to finally leave my father. She deserves so much better than him. She deserves to be loved and honored by a man. Not ignored and treated like a maid.

But then I do the same to her, don't I? I don't treat her like a maid, but I ignore her.

I push her away.

I've put a wedge between us. I've been doing it for years.

I don't come to visit her, allowing *him* to keep me away, which only punishes her; not him. Anger and self-hate ooze into every cell in my body as I realize what I've been doing by staying away. It started when I was a teenager because I hated my father. I would spend as much time as possible with Toby at his house, just so I didn't have to deal with Dad, but it grew into something out of my control since I returned from service. It became less about hating Dad and more about not feeling worthy of Mom's love and affection. Or her pride. She was ... *is* so damn proud of me. Because she doesn't know. She doesn't know what happened to my friend, and she doesn't know what happened to me. I've never told her. I've never told anyone. Not even my best friend.

I turn to the woman who's only ever loved me. "I'm sorry, Mom."

She narrows her eyes at me, the lines across her forehead deepening. "What on earth for?"

"For being such a shitty son."

She bats at my arm. "Don't be ridiculous. You're the furthest thing from a terrible son." Then she pauses and studies my face closely. "Where's all this coming from, Shane?"

"I was just thinking about my wish, and it was for you to leave Dad. To find someone who doesn't ignore you or treat you poorly. But then I realized that I do the same."

Her shoulders sink, and her brown eyes develop a sheen to them that wasn't there a moment before. "Oh, Shane. You both have your reasons. I wish you would talk to me. That I could help you in some way." She squeezes my hand. "But hear me. I'll never leave your father because I love him and ... he still loves me in his own way. There are things you don't understand." There's steel in her voice. A determination that can't be missed.

"But I *do* understand, Mom. That's the thing. I've been there. I"—I tap my chest—"*know* what it's like." A tear escapes the corner of Mom's eye, and I reach up to wipe it away with my thumb. "I'll try to do better. Be better."

And now I know my wish.

I wish to be a better man.

To fight my demons and to come out the victor.

I blow the candles out, and Mom hands me the knife with a nod and a shaky smile. I cut the pound cake—my favorite— careful not to dislodge the strawberries decorating the top, not touching the bottom as per Mom's instructions, and she takes over to cut three slices. She takes a piece through to Dad and then returns. We eat the cake in silence and enjoy the treats she made especially for me. And this time when I leave, I promise to visit more frequently.

Mom reaches up and cups my cheek as we stand beside my SUV. "You visit as you feel comfortable. I know I can sometimes lay it on pretty thick, and I probably make you feel guilty, but I understand you're busy and life gets in the way." She *still* doesn't understand. "I know you came back a changed man, and I've gathered that you've experienced terrible things. My hope is that one day you'll feel ready to talk with me about it."

My heart splinters at her hopeful expression. "I'm not sure when that'll be."

"That's okay. I'm not going anywhere." She wraps her arms around my middle, and I have to suck in a sharp breath so I don't break down like a baby in her embrace. I don't deserve her acceptance or her understanding. Her limitless compassion blows me away and makes me feel unworthy. "I love you, Shane. I miss you, and I hope one day you find your way back to me."

I can only nod as I squeeze her tight and press a kiss on top of her head. Then I peel myself away from her and head home to spend the rest of my birthday alone—the way I intended to spend the day.

6

SHANE

 to my skin as I bake in what feels like an oven. The heat is oppressive, coming at me from all directions as I crouch behind the low limestone wall, using it to hide my presence while I scope out our surroundings. The intense heat feels like it's sucked all the oxygen out of the atmosphere. I struggle to take a full breath, and when I do, dust invades my lungs in this fucking shit hole. What I wouldn't give to be enjoying an icy cold beer at home with Toby and Wyatt— neither of them have met yet, but I think they'd get along great even though they're very different people.

The local kids play soccer in the open area next to their school, kicking up plumes of off-white dust as their bodies shift and turn. Mothers walk quickly with their heads down low, attending to errands they need to get done. Mangy dogs scamper among the heaps of garbage left along roadsides. Everything looks as it should for this time of the day. The voice of my team leader crackles in my ear, "Anything?"

"Looks clear."

"Move forward."

"Copy that." Staying low, I move along the wall until I come to the edge of the building. Using the side of the crumbling structure to *shield me from possible attack, my leg muscles thank me as I stand to my full height. Resting my back against the wall, I raise my head, checking the tops of the buildings around me. Out of the corner of my eye, a slight movement on the roof of the building to my right catches my attention. Twisting my body to get a better look, a sudden force sends me flying through the air.*

I jolt upward, waking in a pool of sweat. Fuck, I haven't had one of those dreams for a while now. My hands shake as I untangle the covers from around my legs and twist around to place my feet on the cool hardwood floor. I drop my elbows to my knees and hold my head in my hands as I work to get my breathing and thumping heart back under control. I'm not sure where the dreams come from because they're never the *actual* event that forever changed my life. It's always some vague twist on what happened.

There's a chill in the air, and my bedroom is still in complete darkness so I check the clock on the nightstand. Four a.m. Great. I got about two hours of sleep. My sleep patterns have been shit for years, and there seems no end in sight. Blowing out a long breath, I stand and push my legs into my sweats, pull my sweater on, run my fingers through my hair, and head to the bathroom to take a piss before making my way to the kitchen.

I flick the switch for the kitchen light as I cross the threshold and start the coffee machine. When I step over to the fridge to grab the milk my lips tip up as my eyes land on a drawing Jasmine made for me. She made me promise that I'd put it on display so it would make me smile whenever I looked at it. I'm not sure why I put it on my fridge; it's not like she's going to know whether or not I display it. My lips drop back into their normal position. What that sweet little girl doesn't realize is that I don't deserve to smile.

I grab the milk, and when I close the door, the drawing catches my eye again and my heart does something strange, the same as it does whenever I think of Jasmine and her mom. Every morning when I collect Poppy for school, Jas is waiting at the front door for me with the cutest smile and sparkling eyes. She kisses and hugs her cousin as she steps through the door, and then wraps her little arms around my legs, looking up at me with her innocent eyes and grin as she tells me to have a good day. I shake the thoughts out of my head, make myself a cup of coffee, and grab my Kindle.

Stepping into my dark living room, I place my coffee on the small coffee table, then grab the blanket from the back of the couch and settle in. Taking a sip of the steaming goodness, I close my eyes for a moment to absorb the warmth, then wake up my Kindle. I've been looking forward to starting this book by a new to me author, Janet Elizabeth Henderson. *Lingerie Wars* features former special forces officer, Lake Benson, and promises to have me laughing my ass off, but we'll see.

And yes, I read romcoms. Don't judge.

When I wake from a nightmare, I need something light to break me fully out of the memory, and I've found they help *most* of the time. Not always, because some nightmares are worse than others, holding me captive far longer than the tentacles of sleep should allow, but I'll take *most of the time* as a win. One of the psychs at *The Bunker* suggested I read a book to help me break out of the grip of my nightmares, and I promised to give it a try. I started reading more stereotypical types of books for a guy like me but they didn't work. It wasn't until I stumbled across a free romance book online that I found it actually helped. So I've stuck with it.

I drop my eyes to my Kindle and begin reading as I sip my coffee. *Jesus, how old is this guy? How is he already having a mid-life crisis? And what the hell is he thinking taking over his sister's lingerie store?* I lose myself in the story, huffing out a mild chuckle here and there. Objectively, the book is funny. Hilarious even. But my ability to truly enjoy anything seems to be on a permanent hiatus.

Soft light creeps around the edges of my blinds, and I glance at the time. Seven. Time to start getting ready for the damn parade. I should have gone to the sunrise service today, but I generally try to avoid watching the sunrise. I don't like to be reminded of a new day.

A day that Wyatt doesn't get to spend with his family.

Another day that I'm still here while he isn't.

I run my hand down my face and take a moment to think about today—Veteran's Day—and what it represents. To think about Wyatt and everything he left behind. Everything his wife and son lost that afternoon. The fact that he's not here to march alongside me as he should. Guilt floods my veins once again as it always does when I think back to that day. I drop my head into my hands, blow out a long stream of warm air, and blink quickly to hold back the sting of tears. I don't know how many times I've cried in private over what happened that day. Life is so damn unfair sometimes. He was a good guy and had a family who loved him. My hands ball into fists, and I shoot to my feet. *Fuck this.*

Tucking my Kindle away, I fold the blanket and place it neatly on the back of the couch, wash my coffee cup, and head into the shower to try and wash away the blood on my hands. No matter how many times I've scrubbed my body since that afternoon, the stain of his death won't wash away, and I'm stuck with this feeling of immense guilt that it should have been me.

When the water turns cool, I step out and dry myself. I slide my boxers up my legs and then my dog tags over my head. The cool metal against my skin feels foreign these days where it once was so familiar. I grip them in my hand and take a moment to think about what it means to wear the uniform I'm about to put on. Most would say it represents courage and honor but I wouldn't use either word to describe how *I* feel when I wear it.

To me, it represents death, failure, destruction, desolation, despair.

Loss and the deepest sadness.

Grayness.

Cold.

Loneliness and isolation.

Guilt and suffering.

It's a reminder of the worst time of my life and the end of a good friend's life.

I draw in a deep breath and blow it out again, then turn my attention back to my dresser and the second set of dog tags. Picking them up, I run my fingers over the indentations and read the words.

SULLIVAN
WYATT E.
626-16-4325
A NEG
CATHOLIC

I couldn't refuse Hope when she gave them to me at soccer and asked me to wear them today just as she has each year since my return. It's truly an honor to wear them but it's also my punishment.

My burden.

I slip them over my head, the weight of them like a heavy anchor, and I drop to my ass on the edge of my bed. I let the pain wash over me. I feel it, allow it to fill me up, and then take slow, deep breaths in and out to release it. That's what the psych told me to do when I feel overwhelmed, and it helps with the worst of it. It doesn't stop it completely, but it makes it manageable.

Climbing to my feet again, I methodically dress in my service uniform. If Wyatt's dog tags felt heavy, this fabric is heavier. It may as well be made of lead instead of cotton. With each article I put on, the weight across my shoulders increases and my skin grows tight and itchy. If it weren't for showing my respect for one of my dearest friends—marching because he's not here to do it—I wouldn't participate in today's parade. I wouldn't leave my apartment. Before I change my mind, I grab my stuff and head out the door.

The Bunker is busy this morning. Men and women dressed in their service uniforms congregate in groups according to the unit they were in when they deployed clearly identified by the fabric patch on their right shoulder. I spot Nix outside speaking to Troy, another former Ranger from a different battalion, and make my way toward them.

Tipping my chin, I greet them. "Steele. Gallagher."

"Sutton."

I tuck my hands into my pockets and rock back on my heels, clenching my jaw. The guys keep talking but all I can hear is the blood rushing through my body. I want today over and done with. I look out over the community garden and try to fill my head with more recent memories that don't leave me feeling desolate. Jasmine's sweet smile. Poppy's bright energy. Violet's vivid blue eyes. The lost look on her face when we went for ice cream, and the way my heart pounds faster every morning when I collect Poppy for school, hoping to get a glimpse of the woman.

A strong hand drops onto my shoulder and I tense. I was so lost in my head, I missed Troy stepping away and Nix moving closer. I must be losing it to be caught so unaware. "You okay?"

I study Nix's eyes, noting the tightness and concern. "Not really. Just need to get through today and I'll be better." I dig my fists deeper into my pockets. No point lying to the man, he already knows the worst of it.

He squeezes my shoulder. "I know you find days like this unbearable, and you feel undeserving to wear the uniform but it's simply not true." I shrug out of his hold and take a step away. He lowers his voice. "It wasn't our fault, and nothing that we could have done would have changed the outcome, Shane. But as many times as I've told you this, you insist on carrying the blame solely on your shoulders. You weren't the only one there when it happened. You're not the only one who carries the guilt of Wyatt's death, but you're the only one who seems to think the blame lies solely at your feet. It doesn't."

I drop my head to look at the floor because I can't deal with the sincerity shining in his eyes. He truly believes what he says. However, my guilt is acute. If I'd been more aware of my surroundings—listened to my gut—I could have warned Wyatt before it was too late.

THE ROUTE for the parade seems never-ending, and we've only been marching for about half a mile. Thousands of people line both sides of the street, proudly waving American flags, dressed in red, white, and blue. National pride and gratitude ooze from the spectators as their cheers pierce the air. I keep my head straight and eyes forward, not seeing anything other than the head of the man in front of me. I don't want to hear people calling out their *thanks* from the sidelines. I don't want to see the pride they wear on their faces for us.

After we round the final corner, the end comes in sight and relief that this is almost over fills me. Over the pandemonium of the crowd, a sweet voice breaks through. "Sane! Mommy. There's Sane! Sane!" My lips tip up automatically, and I glance without moving my head toward the voice. Sure enough, there's Jasmine in her mother's arms. Her tiny arm wrapped around Violet's neck and in her free hand, an American flag. She's waving it high in the air at me. "Sane!"

"Yeah, baby girl. It's Shane," Violet says, and I'm astounded that with all of the noise, their voices are as clear as a bell.

"Why isn't he waving at me?" I can hear the disappointment in her voice, and my heart cracks. I never want to disappoint her because I sense she's already had enough of that in her short life.

"He can't right now, JJ."

The most I can do is tip my head slightly and hope she notices because I don't want her to think I haven't seen her. I lose sight of them as I move past but for some reason, my steps don't seem quite so heavy and the uniform isn't quite as uncomfortable now. I stand taller and finish the march with a sense of pride I hadn't been feeling until I heard that sweet little voice.

7

VIOLET

"Mommy. Can we fowwow Sane? I wanna say hewwo." She places her tiny hand on my cheek and turns my face toward her, forcing me to tear my eyes away from Shane's retreating back. All wide shoulders tapering to a narrow waist and tight butt. Long, thick legs taking sure, confident strides. I swallow.

Shane looked fantastic dressed casually in jeans and a button-down shirt at the concert, so fantastic that each morning when he comes to collect Poppy for school, I make myself scarce because I need to keep my distance. So I watch him come and go from my bedroom window. Where I'm safe. And far enough away that I won't *accidentally* throw myself at his feet.

I focus on my daughter. "Uh ... I don't really think we can, JJ."

"Why not?" Her eyes turn sad and her bottom lip drops.

I tuck her soft hair behind her ear. "Because there are too many people."

She perks up a little. "But we could twy."

I don't want to disappoint her so I nod my head once. We're close to the end of the parade, it shouldn't be too hard. "Okay. We'll try, but I don't want you to get sad if we can't find him."

Her eyes and lips widen as she nods her head quickly. "I pwomise."

Keeping Jasmine tucked in my arms to make it easier to maneuver through the crowd, I head in the direction the servicemen and women are marching. People are packed tightly together so it's a challenge and very slow going. By the time we make it to the end of the route, he'll most likely be gone. Even if we find him, he'll probably be busy with his friends or doing whatever he normally does after the march, but at least Jas knows I'm trying to follow through for her.

Since leaving Allen, I feel it's important to keep my promises. She's had enough disappointment to last her a lifetime. Not that I think she misses Allen all that much because he never really paid attention to her when we were together but *I* know and understand what she's lost. The lack of a father figure in her life will be missing forever. Feeling responsible for her loss, I hold her tighter to me. If I'd chosen a better man ... I can't go there right now so I shake off the thought.

We get to the endpoint of the parade, and hundreds of men and women in their uniforms mill about the area as they connect with their partners and kids.

Now I feel stupid.

Jas and I don't belong here. We have no relationship with Shane, and I've been doing my best to stay away from him. After my initial attraction to him, I felt it was the safest thing to do. I'm not ready to open my heart and life to another man.

Jas bounces in my arms. "Mommy! I see Sane." She points toward him, and I follow with my eyes. Sure enough, she's managed to find him among the hordes of people.

I push up onto my toes to get a little more height and wave to try to get his attention since he's facing us. He looks as though he's talking to someone, but I can't see properly over the crowd. I weave my way through the people toward him, hoping Jasmine can say hello before he leaves.

Who am I kidding?

I also want to say hello and appreciate the hotness up close that is Shane in his uniform. I may have sworn off men but I can still appreciate a hot guy when I see one. *Well, that's what I'm telling myself.*

Jasmine waves her free arm in the air. "Sane! Sane!" she shouts. It's so sweet how excited she is to see him. Every morning she waits by the door with Poppy so she can say hello to him and wish him a good day. She even drew him a picture of herself in the garden—her favorite place to be. She was so excited when he agreed to put it on his fridge; I thought she was going to bounce right out of her skin.

His eyes catch on her, and his lips tip up, causing crinkles to form around the corners of his eyes. My heart pounds a heavy rhythm in response, and heat fills my cheeks. *Wow!* If I thought he was handsome before, he's just skyrocketed to another level with that smile. I wouldn't mind being on the receiving end of one of his smiles. But I'm pretty sure he doesn't do it all that often.

We make it to him in a few more steps, and that's when I see who he's with. His smile is still in place but mine's disappeared. "Jasmine." He looks at me. "Violet." I don't think I imagined the deeper rasp of his voice when he said my name, sending tingles through my body. *God, Violet. Cut it out.*

Jasmine wriggles in my hold, and I have to tighten my grip as she reaches out her arms toward Shane. "Sane!" She opens and closes her hands and pushes her body away from mine toward him. "I sawed you in the pawade."

He chuckles as he takes a step closer to reach for her, checking with me if it's okay if he takes her. I release my grip and she climbs across into his arms. I think my ovaries just exploded at the visual of my daughter in the capable hands of Shane Sutton in his uniform. *Holy hotness!* His attractiveness is flying out of the stratosphere now. "I saw you, too. Thanks for coming out to support us."

She presses her hands against each of his smooth cheeks. "Mommy aways bwings me." She says it like she's been coming to the parade for the past fifteen years, not four. And I'm certain she doesn't remember the first time I brought her because she was a baby and slept through the entire thing. "Why didn't you wave to me?" Her little brows furrow, causing a deep divot between them.

He starts to answer but is interrupted by the beautiful woman he's with. "Shane?"

Shane's face drops, and he quickly passes Jasmine back to me then turns around to include the woman, who's holding the hand of a boy, in our conversation. "Hope. Evan. This is ... uh ... Violet and Jasmine. They're ... uh ... friends of my boss?" His voice rises at the end as if he's asking a question.

"You're named after flowers," Evan blurts.

I smile at him. "We sure are. All the girls in my family are named after flowers or plants."

Hope smiles. "That's so cool."

I nod. "It sure is." She reaches out her hand to me and I take it. "Hi. Nice to meet you."

"You too." I take a step away, putting distance between us. Of course, he has someone. A gorgeous someone. I'm not sure why my brain automatically thought he was single. This is good. In fact, it's the perfect way to squash this attraction I've felt toward him from the second I laid eyes on him. It's like an icy cold shower which is exactly what I need right now.

"It was so much fun watching you in the parade," Evan says. His face is alight with happiness. "When I'm older I want to march just like my dad." He looks up at his Mom. "Dad marched, didn't he?"

She visibly swallows and strokes her hand over his hair. "Yeah, he marched in parades. Not this one, though." *So, he's not Shane's son.*

Evan's eyes light up. "I could be just like Dad." Shane nods, sadness draping his features, and Evan turns his attention to Hope. "Could I march next year, Mom?"

Her brows furrow and she glances up at Shane. "Uh, I don't think so."

Shane grips the boy's shoulder in a fatherly way. "You need to be in active service or a Veteran, big guy."

The boy deflates. "Will you teach me how to march so when I can I'll be as good as you?"

Shane's jaw clenches and that tic I noticed at *Brain Freeze* is back. "Sure. It's pretty easy."

Hope smiles down at her son, but there's a sadness behind her eyes that anyone would recognize. Her eyes dance from me and Jas to Shane and back again. "Okay, Ev. We should leave Shane to his afternoon. Say goodbye."

Evan's face fills with confusion. "Why? I want to hang out with Shane like we always do."

"He's busy." Her eyes flick back up to me. "We'll see him on Monday at soccer." She turns her attention to Shane. "Will you be at soccer practice this week?"

"Yeah, I don't see why not. But I need to stop by over the weekend to cut your grass." Evan folds his arms across his chest and I recognize the stubborn set of his chin. He's not prepared to budge. Shane turns his attention to Evan. "I could show you how to march after I finish the yard work."

"Really?" His eyes open wide.

"Sure. Why not." Shane smiles at the boy, ruffling his hair.

I feel like we're intruding so I step a little closer. "Uh, we have plans so we'll get out of your hair. We just stopped by because Jasmine wanted to say *hi*." I jiggle Jasmine on my hip as I semi-lie —we both wanted to say *hi*. "Jas, say goodbye to Shane. You'll see him tomorrow when he picks Poppy up for school."

She turns her megawatt smile on Shane. "Bye, Sane."

He leans in and hugs Jas while she's in my arms, partially wrapping me in his embrace. He smells freaking amazing, and I shamelessly draw a deep breath of his delicious scent into my lungs. Clearly, I've lost my morals somewhere along the way to be enjoying his closeness in front of his girlfriend. I'm no better than the whore who was screwing Allen while he was a married man. I work hard to keep my balance and not lean into the warmth of his body since that would be completely inappropriate. He pulls back and taps her nose with his finger. "I'll see you in the morning, Jasmine."

"Otay."

He sears me with his dark stare, and I feel it all the way to my core. He has a way about him that makes me feel like he only sees me and nobody else. It's like we're frozen in a moment of isolation where we are the only people around. "Will I see you tomorrow?"

Heat floods my body at the rasp in his voice. I'm pretty sure my face is beet-red at this point. "Uh ... uhm, not sure."

He nods. "All right then. Thanks for coming out today. Careful driving home." His voice has turned cold as he dismisses us, and I swallow past the hurt of his dismissal. It shouldn't matter to me.

"We will. Bye, Hope. Bye, Evan."

They both say goodbye and we leave, making our way through the thinning crowd back to my car. "Are you ready to visit with Aunty Quinn?" I ask as I situate Jas in her car seat.

She kicks her little legs and cheers. She loves my best friend from high school. But what she loves more than Quinn are her special guests. Jas and I sing along to her favorite playlist on the drive across town, and when we arrive, Quinn rushes out to meet us before I can turn off the engine of my car. She pulls Jas's door open before she even acknowledges me.

"Aunty Quinn!" Jasmine squeals.

"JJ." She unbuckles Jas's seatbelt and pulls her into her embrace, snuggling her close. "I've missed you."

I chuckle as I climb out of my car. "Don't worry about me."

She pokes her tongue out at me. "I see you more than I see this one."

"I guess so." Our paths sometimes cross when Quinn has to release a wayward snake in the state park where I work. I grab Jas's bag and we head inside.

Jas wriggles in Quinn's arms so she places her on her feet, giving her the freedom to take off toward Quinn's guests. "Barney's so big now!" Jas shouts from the front room. Barney is a Western fence lizard. Yep, that's right, a lizard. And he's Jas's favorite with his blue underbelly.

Barney only has two front legs, and Quinn didn't think he'd survive on his own after she witnessed him being pecked by birds so she brought him home. Her front room often acts as a type of halfway house for reptiles of all species, shapes, and sizes that may be injured or misplaced. Some can be released back into the wild, while others, like Barney, stay with Quinn forever.

Quinn chuckles. "He sure is. Did you notice he has new lady friends?" She points to a spot toward the back of the aquarium where two smaller lizards are basking in the sunlight streaming in through the window.

I do a double-take. "Are they albino Western fence lizards? They don't have any color."

Quinn nods. "Yep. A couple found them in their yard and called me. I'm not sure what to do with them. I don't think they'll make it on their own."

"Yeah, they'd be easy prey for predators." Thank goodness for Quinn and her kind heart.

Jas presses up on her toes and almost squishes her nose against the glass to get a better look. Her eyes widen when she spots the two females. "Oh, I'm gwad he's got some fwiends. I was wowwied he was wonewy." She watches them closely.

Knowing that Jas will be captivated for the next fifteen minutes or so, Quinn makes herself a coffee and me a tea. "How was the parade today?"

"Crowded."

"It always is. I'm impressed that you make the effort every year."

I shrug. "It's my small way to show my appreciation for everything the service men and women have given up for us." I feel it's the least I can do. If it weren't for those men and women, we wouldn't have the freedom we do.

She nods and smiles at me. "You have a good heart, Vi. I made wraps for lunch. Hope that's okay."

"Of course. I'm starving so I'll eat anything."

She places our food and drinks, a cup of milk for Jas, and Jas's favorite home-baked cookies on the dining table. We both take a seat, and she fills me in on her latest escapades capturing snakes from backyards and homes across the city. She loves her job but what she loves more is the surprise on her client's faces when a woman turns up to wrangle the local snakes. They generally expect a man to turn up and deal with the unwanted reptiles.

Her phone rings as she takes her seat. "*Quinn's Capture and Release.* How can I help you?" She listens for a bit. "Where did you say you are?" She listens again and then rolls her eyes at me. "It's probably a Northern Pacific rattlesnake. They *are* dangerous if they feel threatened, so give it a wide berth and you'll be fine." She listens some more. "No, I'm sorry, I can't collect the snake from a state park. That's where they live." The person says something else. "I'm sorry. No, I can't make an exception. I'd lose my license if I removed a snake from a state park for no good reason." She pauses. "As I said, just give it plenty of space. It doesn't want to hurt you." The person on the phone must say something else. "No problem. Have a great hike. Goodbye." She ends the call and chuckles. "I swear, Vi, some of the calls I get."

"So they wanted you to collect a rattlesnake from a hiking trail?" I'm not surprised. People like to get out in nature, so long as it's not *too natural*.

She nods. "Yup. I'm not sure what they expect when they're in a state park."

I roll my eyes. "Oh, trust me. We get all sorts of requests when people are hiking through our park. They even want us to keep the bushes trimmed away from the trails so they don't have to touch the foliage. It's ridiculous."

Jas races into the room and climbs onto the chair in front of her cup of milk. "You made my favowite cookies. Fank you, Aunty Quinn."

Quinn chuckles and bops her on the nose. "Of course. I know how much you love them. But you have to eat your wrap first, okay? How was the parade?"

Jas nods as she kicks her feet back and forth. "It was gweat. We sawed Sane, didn't we Mommy?"

She's so obsessed with the man, and I have to admit he hasn't been too far from my thoughts since we first met. Quinn raises a blonde brow at me. "Who's Sane?"

"His name is *Shane*, and he's Toby Summer's best friend and bodyguard."

Quinn's eyes widen and she holds up her hand. "Woah, back up, sister. Toby Summer?" Her eyes grow even wider, and I'm worried her eyeballs are going to pop right out of their sockets. "Explain." She makes the come here motion with her hand.

While Jas munches on her wrap, I fill in Quinn about Poppy's guitar lessons with none other than Toby Summer and how we had no idea he was her guitar teacher until we went to the Labor Day concert at *Music for my Heart*.

"No way!"

I nod. "Yes, way. Funny thing is that Cassia crushed on him in high school, and now he's famous and has been teaching her daughter how to play guitar. Mom even met him and didn't realize who he was."

She chuckles. "Oh, this gets better and better. So his bodyguard was in the military?" I sigh and I'm sure my cheeks are flushed pink at the thought of Shane in his uniform. Quinn's lips widen, and she points her wrap at me. "There's something going on there. I can see it all over your face."

I shake my head adamantly. "There's nothing going on. Jas sees him each morning when he comes to take Poppy to school. She's taken a liking to him."

Quinn shakes her head, her grin still in place. "I think someone else might have taken a liking to him too." She winks at me.

I dart my eyes to Jas. She's concentrating hard on picking the chocolate chips out of her cookie, and I don't think she's listening to our conversation. "He's really ..." I fan my face and mouth a single word, "hot."

Her brows rise halfway up her forehead. "Nice."

"Yeah." I sigh and Quinn wiggles her eyebrows. "Don't even think about it. I'm not ready, and he has a girlfriend ... maybe. She was there with her son after the parade."

Quinn's shoulders drop and so does her smile. "That's a shame. You could have had a little fun with him to help you get back on your feet."

"He doesn't come across as the *bit of fun* type. He's pretty quiet and intense, shy even."

She pouts. "That's disappointing."

I shrug and hope that's the end of the conversation. I need to put Shane out of my mind. I'll get myself too worked up over something that will never happen, and I need to stay far away from men.

"Can I hold Barney, pwease, Aunty Quinn?"

"Of course. Go and wash your hands. You know we have to be careful not to give him any germs."

Jas cheers and hops down from her chair, heading straight for the bathroom while I carry our dishes to the sink and wash them. When Jas returns, Quinn carefully collects the lizard and motions for Jas to take a seat. She places Barney on Jas's lap and my daughter's expression turns serene as she gently strokes along his back just the way Quinn showed her. I swear the lizard preens under my daughter's attention. The smile on Jas's face is bright so I snap a photo of the moment to show Mom and Cass when we get home. Jas spends time snuggling—if that's the right word to use—with the two new female Western fence lizards, and Quinn gives her the honor of naming them.

"I fink we sould caw this one Pechunia and this one Daffodiw." She looks up at us with the broadest smile and pride fills her face.

Quinn giggles. "They're great names. I love them. Now I have to work out how to tell the girls apart so I don't call them the wrong name."

Jas and Quinn study the two lizards closely. "This one has a wittwe bit of yewwow on her toes. Se sould be Daffodiw 'cause they're yewwow too."

"Good idea. Thanks for helping me name the girls."

"No pwobwem."

"It's time for us to go. Say goodbye to Aunty Quinn."

Jas and Quinn hug each other tightly, and Quinn carries her out to the car for me and we head home so Jas can have her afternoon nap and I can catch up on laundry. With five females in the house, the laundry piles up quickly.

8

SHANE

"Hɪ, Sʜᴀɴᴇ!" Eᴠᴀɴ ᴄᴀʟʟs ᴀs ʜᴇ sᴘʀɪɴᴛs ᴛᴏᴡᴀʀᴅ ᴍᴇ, his lips spread wide as his mom follows behind. She has a permanent black cloud hanging over her, one that matches mine. I'm pretty sure if it weren't for Evan she would have given up on this life. It's a double-edged sword for her. He looks so much like his daddy that he's a constant reminder of what she's lost, while also being the most important thing he left behind. He throws himself at my body, giving me no choice but to catch him as if he didn't just see me on Saturday. He's so full of life and fun, which is exactly how his father would want him to be.

"Hiya. You ready for practice?" I dip my chin in hello to Hope as she stops in front of us, watching our exchange.

"Sure am. I practiced my sprints yesterday. Mom timed me." He turns to his mom. "I've improved my time, haven't I?"

She musses his hair as she giggles at his excitement. "You sure have. I'm excited to see how you do with getting the ball down the pitch toward the goal."

"All right, let's go." Evan runs forward, full of energy, toward his friends near the pitch who are already warming up, leaving Hope and me to follow behind. "How are you doing?" I ask her since this is the first moment we've had alone. She seemed really down at the parade and again on Saturday when I did the yard work, and I'm worried about her.

She shrugs. "Okay, I guess." She looks away from me. "I, uh, I've decided to go back to group." Her voice is shaking as she gives me her update. "I think it's time, Shane. I can't keep living in this limbo where everything's gray."

I nod. "I get it." Wrapping my arm around her shoulders, I pull her in. "I'm proud of you for making the decision. Wyatt would want you to get the help you need. Let me know if you need me to watch Evan for you." A wrenching pang hits my chest at the mention of my buddy's name, though I'm more accustomed to calling him Sullivan. I pull his tags out of my pocket and hold them out for Hope.

She takes them and closes them in her fist, raising them to her chest and pressing them against her heart. The relief that they're back in her hands and out of mine feels like an elephant just climbed off my chest. "How about you? When are you going to get the help you need?" I release my hold on her and put space between us.

"Don't start. I'm doing just fine." And I am. I'm better than I was.

"No, you're not. You're still only going through the motions." She grips my forearm, pulling me to a stop. "It wasn't your fault, Shane."

I don't want to go through this shit again. I fucking know I didn't blow us up. But he died lying not far from my unconscious ass. If I'd listened to my gut. If I hadn't been knocked out, I may have been able to get help. He may have fucking survived. He had a fucking wife and son who loved and adored him, I had no one—*it should have been me!*

I pull my arm away like she's burned me and make my way toward the kids on the team, leaving her standing in place. I know she's trying to help, but it's not as if she has her shit together; she needs to concentrate on herself and her son and forget about me.

Clapping my hands loudly, I gain the kids' attention. "Coach Mathers can't make it today, so you're stuck with me. Let's get ready to do our drills." The kids cheer loudly, running toward the cones I've already set up. I guide them through some basic stretches before demonstrating what they need to do. "Okay, I want you to jog slowly to the cone at the other end and then back again. Make a line behind each cone. Let's get started."

The kids run in pairs up and back then repeat the process running backward. Evan smiles the entire time throughout the warm-up drills. We switch it up and do some practice passes before playing five-on-five on half the pitch. Evan's speed has improved considerably since last week's practice, and he's managing to keep the ball close to his feet, making it difficult for his opponent to take possession of the ball. "Good one, Evan. Keep it up!" I call out, glancing around to see if his mom's watching. She's holding her hands above her head, applauding her son's achievement.

When practice is finished, I walk Evan over to Hope. "You guys have done well with your training. Keep it up and you'll be the fastest member of your team to run the wing." I ruffle Evan's sweaty hair.

"Thanks, Shane. I did my best." He looks up at his mom. "I'm hungry. Can we get burgers, please?"

Hope bends down to collect Evan's sports bag. "Sure thing. I think you've earned it, big guy."

"Yay. Shane, you'll come. Won't you?" Evan turns his excited eyes to me, and I glance up to check if it will be okay if I tag along. If I go, it means I can pay for their meal and Hope can save her money. I know it's not much but I like to help wherever I can.

She nods slightly and I turn my attention to Evan. "Thanks for the invitation. I could eat a burger." I pat my flat stomach.

We climb into our cars, and I follow them to Pier 7 and *Declan's Diner*. The diner's been here since the pier was built, and it hasn't lost any of its original vibe. Sure, it's been updated over the years, but the owners have always been careful to stay true to its origins, maintaining its authenticity. The three of us step inside, and even though it's Monday night, it's still packed—just like it always is. The noise of the grills sizzling, people placing their orders, and numbers being called fills my ears. I scan the diner, noting the patrons, their positions, those lingering by the jukebox, and those waiting to order. Nothing seems amiss.

"I'll order if you guys find us a seat." I gesture toward the far back corner where I'll have a clear line of sight to the door, then line up to place our usual order. While I wait for our number to be called, I continue to scan the diner and pier outside the large glass windows. Everyone's caught up in their discussions without a care in the world, and nobody's watching what's going on around them. I wish I was still oblivious to the darker side of people and didn't feel the need to be on high alert all the time. It's fucking exhausting.

When my number's called, I grab our order and take it to Hope and Evan, placing the correct items in front of the pair, then I take a seat, adjusting it to make sure I can see the room clearly. Evan practically tears the paper off his burger and shoves it into his mouth.

"Oh my gosh, Ev. Slow down. You'll choke on your food," Hope scolds, wrinkles forming across her forehead.

"Sorry, Mom. I'm really hungry."

We eat quietly for a few moments, and Evan must have satisfied his initial hunger enough to take a breath. "I've been practicing my marching. Mom says I'm looking good."

I chuckle lightly. "That's good, big guy, but did you do your homework? Between soccer and marching practice, it doesn't sound like you have much time left."

"I did my homework, didn't I, Mom?" He turns to Hope.

She swallows the fry she's chewing. "You did." She turns her head in my direction. "He made himself a timetable so he could allocate enough time to the tasks he wants to achieve." Her eyes are full of pride as she shares her son's approach to time management, and the muscle in my chest clenches. Not only does he look like a miniature version of his father, but he also has his father's approach to organization. I catch Hope's eyes and note the glassiness in them.

"Mom, can I have a quarter for the jukebox?"

I dig into my pocket and give him a couple of quarters. "Here. Knock yourself out, big guy."

Hope and I watch him at the jukebox, making his selections. She turns her attention back to me. "So ... uh ... Jasmine's a cutie pie."

I keep my eyes on Evan to ensure he's safe. "Yeah, she's a cute kid."

"Her mom's attractive." My eyes snap to hers, noting the question there before dropping back to Evan. "Anything going on there?"

I swallow. "Nope." My heart thumps heavily behind my ribs, and blood rushes into my ears at the thought of something happening between me and the gorgeous bombshell.

"Why not?"

Without taking my eyes off Evan, I answer with gritted teeth. "You know why."

"Wyatt died. You didn't." I hear the heaviness in her voice, the utter pain buried inside those words, and I turn my head to study her closely. Her delicate features are drawn tight, and her shoulders are bunched up around her ears. Her thin arms are crossed over her body as if they can somehow shield her from the pain that oozes from inside.

"Exactly," I murmur. I'll never understand how she doesn't blame me for her husband's death, but never once has she laid the blame where it belongs. She doesn't even blame the kid who had the explosives strapped to his body. The kid I trusted on several occasions because ... well because ... he was just a kid, and we'd spent numerous hours playing with him and his friends. A kid who was probably about Evan's age if I had to guess.

Her small hand reaches across the table, aiming for the top of mine, but I snatch my hand away before she can make contact. I don't need her sympathy *or* her compassion. What I want is for her to blame me. Get mad at me. Hate me. But she doesn't get it.

"You're allowed to be happy, Shane. To build a life and have a family. Wyatt would hate that you deny yourself the way you do."

I shake my head. "Can you stop already?" I snap and stand abruptly. "I need to go." I spin on my heel to say goodbye to Evan and then feel like a complete and utter asshole all the way out the door. I couldn't sit there and have Hope lecture me for the umpteenth time about how I should live my life. I felt as though I was going to crawl out of my skin. I can't look into her perpetually sad eyes and watch her son without being swamped with guilt so strong I feel like I'm drowning. But I can't leave without ensuring their safety, either, so I position myself opposite the door of *Declan's Diner* so I can keep an eye on them. When they leave, I watch as Hope notices my car still parked in the lot and looks around for me before she climbs in and drives home.

I RING the doorbell at the usual time and wait. Not a single sound comes from inside. Normally, I can hear the girls, but I'm greeted with utter silence. I press the button again and try to peer through the stained glass inlay of the front door. Finally, movement catches my eye.

"Uh, hi, Shane," a muffled voice calls through the heavy door. "I'm sorry. I forgot to call you this morning."

That sounds like Cassia. "Is everything okay?" I call out.

"Uh, no. We all have the stomach flu—all five of us. We won't be leaving the house anytime soon. I'm sorry you came all the way here for nothing." Shit, that's not good.

"That's okay. I don't mind." I wonder how sick Violet and Jasmine are. "Can I get you ladies anything to help?"

"No, I don't think so. Thanks anyway."

Damn. "Okay then. Bye. I guess I'll see you guys whenever you need me over the Thanksgiving break?"

"Thanks for everything. We'll be in touch. Bye, Shane." I step away from the door, my phone in hand ready to text Toby. "Shane," Cassia calls out.

"Yeah?"

"Can you please let Toby know we're all sick and Poppy won't be at her lesson today?"

Already on it. "Sure, Cass. Take care. Bye."

"Bye, Shane. Thanks."

I climb into my SUV and shoot Toby a message.

ME

Cassia and all the girls are sick with the
stomach flu

I wait for a while to see if he wants me to do anything, but a response doesn't come—which is not uncommon for Toby. It's early so he may not even be awake yet, especially if he was up late working in his studio. I start the engine and make my way across town to his home. Traffic is heavy, and by the time I arrive at his place, I need to flex my fingers several times to release the tension from holding the steering wheel. People drive like goddamn idiots, even in rush-hour traffic. Parking my car in his garage, I make my way upstairs, checking the studio first. It's empty with sheets of music strewn across the table, so I head downstairs to his lap pool. Sure enough, he's swimming, something he tries to do whenever he has the chance. He says it helps him focus. I stand at the edge of the pool and wait for him to notice me.

Two more laps of the pool and he finally spots me—the guy's not great with being aware of his surroundings. He stops at the edge of the pool closest to me and rests his arms on the edge. "What's up?" He wipes the water from his face.

"I went to get Poppy for school but all the girls are sick with the stomach flu. I messaged you but you must have already been in the pool."

He pushes up and out of the water and I hand him the towel that he had lying close by. "I need to go check on them." He dries the excess water from his body as he strides inside.

I expected as much since he's been spending so much time with Cass and Poppy. "I'll take you when you're ready."

"Thanks, man." Toby gets ready in record time and we stop at the market and drug store on the way to pick up the essentials for the girls. When I pull into the driveway, Toby climbs out of the car before I can turn off the engine. "I'll call you if I need anything."

"Sure."

He slams the door, and I wait until he's inside before I leave. I envy my friend because he can go inside to look after his girls, something I don't have any right to do but wish I did. I hate the thought of the girls being sick but the thing I hate most is that I can't protect them from this. I can't make sure that Violet and Jasmine are okay. I can't care for them the way they deserve to be looked after. I have to trust that Toby will look after *all* of the girls, not just Cass and Poppy.

After all, this is the way I want it, right?

I *want* to be alone.

Don't I?

Yes, I do. It's what I deserve.

I pull onto the road and make my way over to *The Bunker*. I'll get lost in some bike restoration so I don't feel completely useless.

9

VIOLET

Thank God that's over. I still feel weak, but I'm a thousand times better than I was. I can't believe we were all taken down at the same time by a microscopic bug. I run the brush through Jasmine's hair as I think about the last few days and how I was barely able to crawl out of bed. I'm certain I was freaking delirious for some of those days.

Thank goodness for Toby.

I had my doubts about him, but he truly is a good guy. My lips tip up at the memory of his pink cheeks when he offered to help me shower and the way he stumbled to clarify that he couldn't help me the same way he helped my sister but he could sit outside the door. He was so adorable. And the way he confessed how much he loves Cass and Poppy made my heart expand to double its size. I'm thrilled for my sister, if not a little envious that she's found such a great man who is obviously devoted to her and her daughter. I don't know anyone who deserves it more than they do.

I tie the rainbow ribbon in Jas's hair and slide her long curls behind her shoulders. She smiles up at me in the mirror. "Fank you, Mommy."

I kiss the top of her head. "You're welcome. The ribbon you chose looks great with your rainbow sweater dress." I glance down at her unicorn rain boots which almost come up to her knees and smile at the way she insisted they were the perfect addition to her outfit.

She spins around on her toes. "I wove it!" She flings her little arms up in the air, and I giggle at her delight. Oh to be three and think everything is amazing. I only hope I can help her hold onto her joyfulness for as long as possible.

I tap her on the nose. "Can you go downstairs and wait with Gramma? I need to check on Aunty Cass."

She nods. "Otay, Mommy." My bundle-of-energy takes off downstairs and I wander into my sister's bedroom which is a mess. Cass stands in the middle of her room wearing her bra and panties, her hands in her hair.

"What's up, Sis? You're all over the place." I plop down on her bed, looking around at the pile of discarded clothes.

She throws her hands up in the air and huffs. "I dunno what to wear. I want to make a good impression. Plus, I want to erase the last images Toby has of me. I wanna look good, but I can't work out what to wear." Ahhh, this explains it. We all looked awful when Toby was here looking after us and I guess I'd feel the same if, say, someone like Shane were to have seen me at my worst. That reminds me, I wonder if he'll be at Thanksgiving dinner today. My heart flutters at the thought of getting to spend any time with the man. Then I remember he has a girl-friend ... and I mentally squash the thoughts. I don't understand why I'm having such a hard time remembering the guy is unavailable.

I stand and carefully study the clothes on Cass's bed as well as the ones still in her closet. I pick up a pair of jeans that always look amazing on my sister and a sweater I know shows her amazing curves and matches her coloring well. "What about these black, skinny jeans with this red sweater? You can wear your knee-high boots. They always look amazing on you."

She doesn't look convinced as she chews on her thumbnail.

"You think that'll be okay to wear to Thanksgiving with his whole family?"

"Of course. Why not?"

"I wanna look classy."

"You'll look classy and casual. Sexy, even." I wink at her. "C'mon, you're running out of time."

She smiles at me, and I know I've managed to put her mind at ease. "Thanks, Vi. I'll be down in a minute."

I blow my sister a kiss as I leave her room and head back to my bedroom to check my outfit one last time. I twist this way and that as I check out my reflection. I chose my green sweater dress because I thought it would be cute if Jas and I wore matching outfits, not that our dresses are the same color. I don't think I can get away with wearing a rainbow dress at my age. I smooth the knitted fabric over my wide hips and straighten my belt.

Objectively, I can see I look good in this dress, great even but there's that little voice of doubt that's been getting louder since splitting with Allen that says I'm nothing special. If I were special, he wouldn't have cheated the way he did, right?

I draw in a long breath and blow it out slowly, along with the negative thoughts. Thinking like that won't get me anywhere. I wouldn't want my daughter to think poorly of herself, so I need to make sure I squash those thoughts—lead by example and all that.

The doorbell rings, so I grab my coat and take the stairs to the foyer. It's mayhem. Toby catches Poppy just in time as she takes a flying leap at him, Gramma Iris is laughing her ass off at her great-granddaughter's antics, and Mom's bustling her way out of the kitchen carrying one of the three casseroles she baked this morning. I say hello and catch Jasmine so I can put her coat on before stepping into the kitchen to grab another casserole. I'm not sure why Mom thought we'd need to take not one but three dishes with us. We're going to the home of a billionaire for goodness sake. I'm pretty sure our Thanksgiving dinner will be fully catered.

I'm the last to follow everyone out of the house, so I lock the door behind me. Suddenly, everyone seems to stop dead in their tracks, and Cass almost knocks the casserole out of Mom's hands. Pretty sure my chin has dropped to the pavement at the sight of the fancy limousine parked in front of our humble home with a handsome bodyguard holding the back door open to boot. My eyes drop down his well-built body, taking in his faded jeans, heavy boots, and a button-down shirt complete with a waistcoat. His outfit looks effortless, yet he looks like he just stepped off of a runway for Tom Ford. My traitorous body reacts to Shane without permission, and I squeeze my thighs together to stem the instant throb at the apex of my legs.

Jas takes off at a sprint. "Sane!" She dives for the man, and he quickly steps away from the back door of the limo to catch my daughter. I'm not exactly sure why Jas is so attached to him—he barely speaks—but she's enamored just the same. He swings her up into his arms and rests her little butt on his forearm as he watches her closely. She looks tiny in his hold as she spreads her arms out wide as though she's showing him something huge then throws herself into his body and wraps her little arms around his neck.

His lip twitches like he wants to smile but can't quite remember how to do it, and his eyes find me still standing on the porch. Within an instant, his eyes have dropped and scanned me from head to toe and returned to mine with a degree of heat that I've not felt from a man in a long time. Heat zaps through my body at the same time self-consciousness overtakes me. I pull my coat across my body trying to hide my wide hips the best I can with the one free hand I have. His eyebrows dip over his eyes as I cover myself. *Why on earth did I think a sweater dress that hugs every single one of my curves was a good choice?* Shane returns his attention to my daughter, and I finally fill my lungs with a fresh breath.

Toby must notice our surprise at the car. "I figured everyone would fit in this. Hope you don't mind."

Mom responds quickly, always worried that she's offended

someone. "Not at all. I was surprised, that's all. It's very thoughtful of you to organize a ride. I figured we'd be following behind you and Cass."

"This makes it easier. C'mon, let's go." He says it like it's no big deal he organized transportation for all of us, when in fact it's a big freaking deal. It shows exactly how much he loves my sister and niece. I can't help the smile that crosses my lips for my sister. We all head for the car, me keeping my eyes locked on my daughter still resting in Shane's very capable hold.

He says hello to each member of my family while holding Jasmine like it's of no consequence. When it comes to my turn, I swallow the nervousness that seems to take hold whenever I'm in Shane's presence. His eyes grip onto mine like a fist and don't let go. "Violet." His rich voice rumbles through me like a freight train straight to my lady parts and I'm surprised I'm still standing from that single word.

"Uh, hi, Shane." I attempt to smile but I'm not convinced I actually make it happen.

"Pass me the casserole, Vi," Gramma says as she pokes her hands through the open limo door.

I pass it to her, then push my loose hair behind my shoulder so I can reach forward to collect my daughter from Shane's arms. I try to keep my eyes away from his face, focusing on Jas as much as possible without seeming rude. "C'mon, JJ. We need to get in the car."

"I want Sane to come too."

I grip her little waist, and Shane releases her, helping to transfer her to my arms. "Don't worry, Angel, I'm coming too. I'll be sitting there." He points toward the front of the car, and my heart skips a beat at his term of endearment for Jas and the easy way it rolled off his tongue.

The smile on my daughter's face is instant, and if I didn't think it would be weird for me to be ecstatic that he's coming, I'd smile too. I hold myself in check but my lips do tip up of their own accord at this news. Shane notices and his cheeks rise too. Jas gives Shane's neck one last squeeze and then releases him, dropping her body weight into my arms, and even though I was expecting it, she knocks me a little off-balance. Shane quickly reaches around my body and scoops me into his with Jas sandwiched between us.

"You okay?" he asks as his eyes trace every inch of my face. His grip on me is sure and strong, making me feel safe.

I swallow the riot of emotions that have taken flight through my body and nod, grateful that Jas is tucked between us and he can't feel the heavy thuds of my heart, making me almost dizzy in his presence. Once he's certain I have my balance, he releases me and I say my thanks before climbing into the limo. I choose a spot right up front near Gramma, who's sitting behind the driver—that way I can avoid looking at Shane. I'm aware of his every move as he closes the back door and makes his way to the front of the vehicle. When he climbs into the passenger side, I instantly realize my mistake. I may not have to look at him, but I'm surrounded by his spicy scent. It'll be impossible to hold my breath the entire way so I'm going to have to suck it up and be a big girl and try not to let his intoxicating smell affect me too much; my first intake of breath is potent, and the next one is the same.

I wonder if I'll ever get used to the way he smells and the effect it has on me. I imagine our paths are going to cross on a regular basis so it's something I'll *need* to get used to and train myself to ignore.

Jas bounces on my lap with excitement so I tighten my arms around her little body and kiss the top of her head, taking a moment to draw in her sweet apple-scented shampoo in an attempt to drown out the sexy smell of the man behind me.

I'm brought out of my head by Gramma's finger poking my thigh. "Are you listening to me, Vi?"

I turn to look at her. "Huh?"

"I thought so. Off in a world of your own." She raises her graying brow. "I said you two girls look adorable in your matching outfits." She strokes her hand down Jas's hair. "Did you plan it that way, or was it a coincidence?"

I chuckle. "Sorry, Gramma. Uh, I guess, I planned it that way. Sometimes Jas likes us to dress the same, though my dress isn't quite as colorful as hers." I squeeze Jas for good measure.

"Why don't you have wainbow cowors, Mommy?"

I *feel* Shane tune into our conversation. "I suppose I could have bright colors on my dress but my favorite color is green while you like *all* the colors."

"Why don't you wike aww the cowors?" Little divots form between her brows and I hear Shane chuckle behind me.

"I *do* like all the colors. Especially when I'm admiring the wild-flowers in the park. Wearing lots of colors doesn't suit me like it does you."

"But you're so pwetty, Mommy. You sould wear aww the cowors." She squeezes my cheeks in her tiny hands.

I chuckle and rub her nose with mine. "Thank you, JJ." This kid's good for my ego.

As the limo pulls up a long driveway, Toby's twin sister and brother-in-law's home comes into view and all I can do is gasp at how gorgeous it is. If Toby is truly serious about my sister, her life is really about to change. We pile out of the car, Shane helping each of us with our balance. I'm the last one out because of where I was sitting and when his hand wraps around mine, shivers race down my spine. He gently tugs me to my feet and with his mouth close to my ear, and his warm breath ghosting across my flesh, he whispers, "Jasmine's right. You're pretty enough to wear all the colors."

He pulls away and releases me before I have a chance to absorb his words. By the time I realize what he said, he's moved away, leaving me in a puddle of goo.

It appears that Toby's entire family has descended on us and I don't have time to think about Shane's compliment. I collect the casserole from Gramma so she can greet the two other elderly ladies who have come out to welcome us. I try to stay at the back of the crowd since I feel like a tag along but Kate, Toby's twin sister, makes her way to Jas and me.

She hugs us both. "Hello again. We're thrilled you guys could make it. I hope you're feeling better."

"Thank you so much for the invitation. We appreciated it since we were nowhere near prepared for the holiday. We are feeling better, mostly. I don't know about Mom and Cass, but I still have occasional bouts of feeling weak and dizzy."

Kate's brows dip low over her gorgeous cobalt eyes which are exactly like her brother's. "Let me know if it gets too much, and I'll find you a quiet place to rest. Okay?"

Oh my gosh. How sweet is she? "Sure, thanks, but I don't want to impose when you've already been so generous."

She squeezes my arm. "I assure you, you won't be imposing. Now, shall we go inside?"

A van pulls up as we make our way up the steps to the large front door, and I wobble a little as I spin around having turned too quickly. It's taken me longer to get my appetite back and I've still been feeling light-headed since the stomach flu took us all out. Shane grasps my elbow and helps me to balance, his eyebrows cutting low over his warm chocolate eyes. "Are you okay? That's the second time you've lost your balance today."

"I'm fine, still a little dizzy from the virus. Thanks for catching me." I try to pull out of his grip, but he holds me tighter and guides me inside. He walks through the quiet home with familiarity, guiding me to the back where it seems Kate and Oliver have everything set up for our Thanksgiving dinner. "Here, let me have your coat, and you can take a seat. Can I get you a glass of water? Anything?"

I look up into his concerned face and smile. The backs of my eyes sting and that tell-tale tingle is forming in my nose. *Do not cry.* Just because a man is showing you care and concern does not mean you can break down and sob like a baby. I drop my gaze from his.

"Thanks. I'm okay. I ... uh ... need to keep an eye on Jas. I'll be fine. Promise."

"No problem. I can keep an eye on Jasmine for you. It's not like I need to do anything for Toby in this setting so I basically have nothing to do." My heart expands to double its size with his offer. Allen never once offered to look after Jas if I was unwell but Shane didn't hesitate. Not even for a second. "Why are you looking at me like that?"

"Huh? Like what?" *Shit. How was I looking at him?*

"Like I was speaking a foreign language or something."

I chuckle awkwardly. "Sorry. I was just thinking." I need to change the subject before he asks what I was thinking about. He doesn't need to know what a loser I'm married to. "Are Hope and Evan coming today?" That's good Violet. You've finally remembered the man is happily taken. He looks at me completely puzzled. Maybe he's forgotten that I've met his partner and her son. "You know, I met them on Veteran's Day." I raise my eyebrows.

"I know who you're talking about but why would you ask if they're coming today?"

"I figured your girlfriend and her son would be here since it's a family day."

He stands to his full height and takes a step away from me. He holds his body rigid and that tic returns to his jaw in full force. "She's not my girlfriend. She's the wife of a friend." He spins on his heel and stalks away from me leaving my head spinning. I admire the play of muscles across his back through his waistcoat as he tucks his hands in his pockets while moving farther away from me. *Damn.*

"Mommy, wook what Kate gived me." Jas bolts toward me holding a book above her head. She holds it in front of my face, too close for me to be able to see what it is. I take it from her as Kate comes up to us, chuckling.

"I hope you don't mind. I love to give the kids from the shelter

I volunteer with gratitude journals for Thanksgiving. It's kinda become a tradition. I didn't want to leave Jasmine out of the fun but I know she's a little too young to write what she's grateful for. I hope she likes to color."

Can this family be any kinder or more inclusive? First, they invited us all to Thanksgiving dinner and now they've included Jasmine in their gift-giving traditions. I look up into her kind eyes with gratitude. "Thank you so much, Kate. She loves to color"—I look down at the book and smile—"and she loves flowers, so this is perfect."

"Toby gave me a couple of hints." She winks.

"Thank you." I slide my hand down Jasmine's hair, careful not to displace her ribbon. "Did you say thank you, baby girl?"

She nods enthusiastically. "I did, Mommy."

"She did. She has such beautiful manners. Her and Poppy." Kate taps Jasmine's nose.

"Can I go pway with the kids, Mommy?"

"Of course. Go make some new friends with Poppy." She races off to join the other kids.

"She's such a sweet girl." Kate smiles as we watch my daughter run to the opposite side of the room.

"Thanks. I think I'll keep her for a while." We both chuckle.

"Anyway, I must keep moving. Help yourself to the special punch." She raises her eyebrows when she says *special punch* and I decide to make it my mission to taste test the punch since I'm not feeling dizzy anymore.

I grab two glasses of special punch and take one to Cassia. I hand it to her and then clink my glass against hers. "Cheers, Sis."

"What are we toasting?" She takes a sip of her drink and her eyebrows shoot up. "Mmm, this is delicious."

I knock her shoulder with mine. "Celebrating your first Thanksgiving with your new in-laws, of course."

She chuckles. "You don't know that for sure. I think you're getting ahead of yourself."

"Oh, but I do." I hold my glass out and sweep around the room. "This is your future, Cass. How does it feel?"

She flushes pink. "If this truly is our future, it feels pretty darn great."

I give my sister a side hug. "I'm so damn happy for you, Cass. And for Poppy, too. They love her like they've known her since she was a baby."

"I know." She lifts her chin toward the kids. "They've taken Jas in, too."

My heart swells watching Kate's parents fussing over both of our girls. Our family is so small and insular, so this is a fantastic treat for them.

"Dinner's ready on the buffet, everyone. We'll serve the kids first. Then the adults can get their own," the man who turned up with all the kids calls out over the noise with his deep baritone. The woman, I'm assuming is his wife is busy gathering the kids from the shelter and guiding them toward the buffet.

"Thanks, Roman," Oliver calls.

Cass and I make our way toward our girls so we can serve their food but Toby cuts in before Cass can make it to Poppy, and just as I reach Jas, Shane steps in close and scoops up my girl with a tip of his chin in my direction.

"Hey, Angel. Let's get you some dinner."

He holds her one-armed and her tiny arm slides around his neck, her little hand holding his mostly smooth jaw like it's the most natural thing in the world. I watch in fascination as he relaxes the muscle he usually clenches beneath her hold. It's quite remarkable how different he looks when he's not so tense. He carries her to the table and grabs a plate, placing it on the table each time Jas points to something she'd like to eat so he can add her selections. He *could* put her down, it would certainly make the process easier.

Once she's satisfied, he carries her to the table where the kids are sitting and places her plate in front of an empty seat. He grabs a cushion to boost her seat and then places her carefully on the chair, pushing her closer to the table. Just when I think he's finished, he collects a knife and fork and cuts Jas's turkey and vegetables into bite-sized pieces.

Jas looks up at Shane with stars in her eyes. "Fank you, Sane."

He leans down and kisses the top of her head. "You're welcome, Angel."

I turn and leave the room before I burst into tears in front of everyone and spoil the party atmosphere. A man taking care of my daughter shouldn't send me into a fit of tears but it honestly does. I've had my moments since leaving Allen where I've regretted marrying him, but ultimately he gave me Jas, so I can't truly regret him. But in this moment, I truly regret that Jas doesn't have a better man for a father. A man who will dote on her and treat her like the little angel she is. A man to show her that she deserves to be treated well and to never accept anything less. A man who loves being with her and values her for the great person she is. The regret is so strong it feels like an enormous boulder sitting on my chest and I struggle to take in a full breath. A sob escapes when I'm far enough away from everyone, and I drop my face to my hands.

Today is a day for feeling thankful, but it's hard to be grateful for the way things have turned out. And when I watch Jas with Shane, well ... it makes me wish for things that are far out of the realm of possibility. While he seems to have a lot of time for Jas, he barely gives me the time of day which is fine. *Totally fine.* I don't need to mess up my life with another man anyway.

Though, something deep inside me says that Shane wouldn't actually mess up our life but pull it together.

10

SHANE

The instant I saw Nix's name on my screen while Toby was doing his interview, I knew something was terribly wrong. When he told me Cass and her employee, Sam, had been attacked in her shop, I dry heaved and then I pulled myself together to break the worst possible news to my best friend.

Probably the hardest thing I've had to do since facing Wyatt's widow and child was tell Toby that Cass and Sam had been attacked. Beaten to the point they needed to be hospitalized. I'm surprised I wasn't paralyzed with the amount of guilt swamping me. My broken pieces were already holding together tenuously and with the news, I feared I would break beyond repair. But I needed to keep it together so my friend could fall apart.

He wanted me to stay back and watch his girls instead of him during this press tour but *I* knew better.

I fucking knew better. Detest grows in the pit of my stomach and threatens to burn me alive from the inside out. What would I know?

It's laughable really that I thought I knew anything at all.

I drop my face into my hands and pull on the short strands at the top of my head but the pain isn't enough to drown out these feelings of inadequacy and failure.

Again.

How many times will I fail the people around me?

When will I learn that I can't be trusted to make important decisions regarding anyone's safety?

I watch and rewatch the footage of Cassia and Sam's attack over and over again as my penance for my poor decision-making. Cassia was fucking heroic in her actions to protect Sam and her unborn baby from the fucking maniac she used to date. She fought like the warrior she is against Jake, who looked as though he was on something that gave him almost super-human strength. When she jumped on his back and tore at his eyes, I wanted to leap to my feet and applaud her. But when she was lying helpless on the floor and he stomped on her lower leg, breaking it, I wretched. *Fucking wretched.*

I shoot to my feet. I can't sit around here feeling sorry for myself. I need action. I need to do whatever I can to make the situation better. I grab the thumb drive containing the video footage of the attack, lock up the shop, and climb into my SUV.

Nix is already at the police station with his man, Len, when I arrive. I want to pulverize Len for his carelessness. He was supposed to be watching the girls. I trusted him. *Fucking trusted him.* My fists clench as my anger vibrates through every muscle but I'm not sure who I'm more angry with—Len or myself?

From the doorway, I catalog his visible injuries and the way he's holding his ribs—he looks as though he's gone a couple of rounds with Tyson—as he speaks with the police officer.

Nix notices me first and walks toward me with his hand outstretched. "Sutton." His tone is reminiscent of our time together in the army when he had the right to talk to me like he was in charge.

I ignore his hand. Too furious for niceties. "How the fuck did this happen, Steele? Markham was supposed to be watching the store." Anger laces my harsh tone, and it's taking everything inside of me not to rip Markham limb from limb. I trusted him. I trusted him with the most important people in Toby's life, making them the most important people in mine.

Nix presses both palms against my chest, stopping me in my tracks. I didn't realize I was surging forward like a bull seeking to destroy the red cape. "Remember where you are, Sutton."

I draw in a deep breath, then blow it out and repeat the process several times. Rage still burns through every molecule of my body but I need to push it down. Now is not the time nor the place to make a scene or be aggressive. Once I calm my temper, I join Len and Nix at the counter with the police officer and hand over the thumb drive explaining what's on it. Because the system was installed by a professional security firm, *Steele Security*, the footage can be used as evidence.

Thank fuck.

At least I did something right.

After spending an hour and a half going through everything with the police officer, I climb back into my SUV. I lean my head against the headrest, blow out a long breath, then smack the shit out of my steering wheel. I'm so damn pissed, and I'm on the brink of exploding. I need to fucking punch something.

I shoot Toby a text.

ME

I watched the footage of the attack

You should be fucking proud of your girl. She
fought him like a champion to protect her friend

TOBY

Thanks, bro

ME

I've taken it to the police and filled in the
necessary paperwork

TOBY

I appreciate it, thanks

ME

No problem. Let me know if you need anything

TOBY

Will do

I drop my phone onto the console and start the engine, giving it extra gas for good measure. I head straight to *The Bunker*. It's the one place I can go and beat the shit out of something and someone will keep an eye on me from a distance to make sure I don't go completely feral.

There'll be no questions, no judgment—exactly what I need.

Pulling into the parking lot around the corner, I fly out of my car and climb the steps, drag open the large door, and storm inside straight to the gym room. I take a minute to remove my button-down shirt and boots, put on a pair of gloves, and then start with a couple of warm-up hits to the bag. One punch, then two, and I lose track of time. The pounding of leather against leather sets a frenetic soundtrack—sweat trickling down my back, my muscles tensing and aching, my flesh contracting and flexing—as I try to expel the rage and anger that's bubbling inside of me like a volcano ready to blow. I increase my intensity, adding side kicks as my lungs burn and my eyes sting as they fill with sweat. Furious grunts leave my lips with each expulsion of breath as the shadows across the room lengthen and darken while the chain holding up the bag creaks against the wooden beam. I punch and kick the bag like a madman until my muscles turn to Jell-O, and the adrenaline in my system is depleted. I drop my heavy arms and lean against the wall, sliding down the smooth surface until my ass hits the padded floor, wincing at the pain in my back. Raising my knees, I remove the gloves and rest my arms on them, then lean my head back against the wall as I work to catch my panting breath.

"Feel better?" Nix's calm voice breaks the silence, and when I drop my head, I find him leaning against the doorjamb with his arms folded across his chest. "I didn't think you were ever going to run out of power." He takes a step into the room and drops to his ass across from me, mirroring my pose against the opposite wall.

I grunt. I don't have the energy to put my thoughts into words right now. He gets comfortable but remains silent. And waits.

"It's my fault Cass and Sam are in the hospital. I fucking failed them," I whisper into the near darkness.

"Explain to me exactly how you failed those women, Sutton, because last I checked you weren't even in the state." Nix's voice is firm but laced with compassion.

"If I'd stayed behind like Toby wanted, I would have been the one watching over them. Cassia's ex wouldn't have gotten past me."

"Maybe. Maybe not." He shrugs like it doesn't matter. "There would have been a point where you would have needed to take a piss or grab something to eat and if he was determined to get to those women, he would have found a way. Whether you were the one watching over them or not." He studies his hands dangling between his knees. "Markham isn't a pushover. You know this. He was gone ten minutes, tops."

"He shouldn't have fucking been gone at all. His job was to stand outside that door and watch over the women."

"No one's beating themselves up more than he is right now. I promise you, he feels as though he's let everyone down." I grunt. "I don't know where this complex of yours is coming from, Shane. You are not responsible for every terrible thing that happens."

I interlock my fingers and clench my hands together. "I don't feel responsible for *every* terrible thing that happens. Just the awful shit that happens to the people I care about that I could have prevented." My throat grows tight and the air feels as though it's thinned in the room as I struggle to draw in a proper breath. "I *should* have prevented it," I murmur the last words.

"Okay, let's work through this."

"I don't want to fucking work through this," I explode. Jumping to my feet, I stalk toward Nix.

He rises but keeps his posture relaxed. "How could you have prevented the attack that killed Wyatt? How was that your fault? I was there too. I was the officer in charge, and I let you guys play with the kid while on patrol." He tilts his head to the side. "Explain how you're the only one to blame so I understand."

"I should have known that kid was hiding something when he sought us out to play with him just outside our camp. I should have warned Wyatt not to play soccer with the kid. It was off. The whole thing was fucking off. But I didn't listen to my gut."

Nix drops his voice low. "And Wyatt would have laughed you off, man. He loved playing soccer with the kids because it helped him feel closer to Evan. You know this." He reaches up and squeezes my shoulder. "It was his little piece of home, and he wouldn't have walked away from that kid begging him to play. You need to move past this."

Air rushes out of my lungs in a gush, and I bring my hands up to rest on my hips, dropping my head to study the padded floor beneath my feet. "I don't know how."

"For a start, you need to put the blame where it belongs. And that's at the feet of the assholes who packed that bomb and sent a kid to blow himself up to take out half a dozen soldiers." His voice rises. "They're the ones to blame. Not you. Not me. Not even that damn kid wearing the explosives. Put the fucking blame where it belongs, Shane." He squeezes my shoulder to the point of pain. "Wyatt wouldn't want you to carry this burden. It wasn't your fault." I risk looking at Nix's face. It's full of compassion and understanding. "There was no scenario that day where you are to blame for anyone's death or injuries. Let it go, soldier." He pauses. "Same goes for what happened to Cassia and Sam. None of it was your fault. Let that go too before it festers and eats you alive."

The backs of my eyes sting, and before I can stop them, tears escape and roll down my cheeks, dropping onto the mat beneath my feet. They flood from me, releasing years of built-up pain and blame in rivers that coat my flesh and burn a path from my very soul.

Nix doesn't move. Doesn't say a word. Doesn't release his grip on my shoulder. He stands with me as I break apart.

Exposing my pain.

Releasing my burden.

Shedding my guilt.

When the tears finally subside, I wipe my face with the heels of my hands and run my fingers beneath my nose.

"Thanks, man."

He silently nods and then walks away, leaving me alone. I suck in a deep breath and another and another until I feel more composed. Grabbing my boots, I slide my feet in, then collect my shirt and make my way outside to climb in my SUV to head home.

My phone buzzes with a text, interrupting my morning coffee.

TOBY

Hey, man

Would you mind bringing Violet to the hospital?

I don't think she should drive on her own

ME

Sure. I'll leave shortly

How's Cass?

TOBY

She's sore but I'm thankful she's alive

Thanks, man

ME

Do you need anything?

TOBY

A change of clothes would be great right
about now

I check the time. Visiting hours aren't for another couple of hours, but I've missed seeing Poppy and Jasmine—let's not forget, Violet—so it won't hurt to head over a little earlier. I shower and dress, then grab my stuff and drive to Toby's place to collect what he needs.

On my way past the mall, I pull in at the last moment and park. I don't know what I'm looking for exactly but I don't want to show up empty-handed for the girls. I want to do something nice for them during this awful time. I wander into the bookstore. Kate always says that books make the best gifts, and I trust her judgment since she's a teacher. I wander through the kids' section but nothing captures my attention. I notice a sign out of the corner of my eye that promises good things so I wander over to take a look. The section is full of music books so I browse the shelves until I find a music diary I think Poppy will love. Toby was saying that she could easily write some of her own tunes with the way she played around with the arrangements for the concert so this should work. I tuck it under my arm and go in search of a book for Jasmine. She loves being outside in the garden and spending time in nature, so I head to the kids' science section to look for a book I think she might like. None of the books look age-appropriate, so I move to another section. Browsing the books, I don't know what I'm looking for and can't make up my mind.

A woman approaches me from the side. "Hi. Can I help you find something particular today?"

"Uh, hi. Yeah. I'm looking for a book for a young girl who loves gardening and spending time in nature. Do you have anything she might like?"

The woman's face lights up. "I do." She takes three steps away and bends down to collect a book from a low shelf. She carries it to me and displays it with a flourish. "How about this one? It's really popular and it's a timeless classic."

I read the title. *The Lorax*. I look at the woman as I flick through the colorful pages. "What's it about?"

"It's about the Lorax, a little guy who becomes an advocate for the trees. A business owner is destroying the trees in the name of progress and the Lorax prevents further progress by stepping in and speaking on their behalf. It's a great story and perfect for a little nature lover."

I nod. "I'll take it. Thank you."

I purchase both books and step out of the store to head back to my car, only to be distracted by a tea shop. I know Violet enjoys her tea. Would it be weird if I bought her a gift? She's probably worried about her sister and it may put a smile on her face even if for a moment.

What could it hurt?

I step inside and make my way around the store looking at all of the fancy teacups and pots available. I want something practical, so I settle on a double-walled plastic tumbler with a green screw lid and tea infuser. It should be durable enough for her to take to work. It doesn't have any fancy designs like the teapots and cups, but it's useful for her day-to-day activities. I buy it and climb into my car.

Stopping at Toby's place, I throw a few things into an overnight bag for him and make sure his place is secure before heading across town to pick up Violet.

That woman.

She's so far out of my league and off limits, it's not funny. Yet, she's the first woman in a long time that's woken something long dead inside me and garnered my interest. It's obvious she doesn't trust easily. Whatever happened with her ex has definitely hurt her and left her scarred.

It's interesting to think that we both carry scars.

Our scars may be different but they've still left a lasting legacy that impacts us both in the way we respond to situations and people. I saw the way she held back her pain at Thanksgiving, escaping the room to cry in private. I followed her but let her have her moment in peace. She looked fucking broken, and I wanted so badly to scoop her up and promise to keep her heart and soul safe.

Ha! *Yeah, because you've done a stand-up job of keeping the people around you safe so far.*

I shake my head and try to dislodge the image of her crying from my mind. Instead, focusing on how her dress hugged her curves and showed the athletic line of her legs. Her slim waist and wide hips looked fucking sensational leading to shapely thighs and strong calves. What I wouldn't give to have the privilege of tracing the length of her body with my tongue.

Great. I huff with frustration. Now I've got a boner.

I turn up the radio and focus on the mindless chatter of the announcers—I swear they talk more than they play music. It's not long before I pull into Rose's driveway and climb out of my car. I collect the gifts from the passenger seat and close the door.

When I spin around to face the house, I suck in a sharp breath. Bundled up on the front step sits Violet. She looks small and fragile, even though I know she's strong and capable. When she raises her head, the sight of her swollen eyes and red nose stops me in my tracks. Even though it's a sunny day, the temperature is downright chilly but I don't think it's the reason for her red nose. The closer I get, the more details I notice. Like the glistening tracks of tears and the slight shake of her shoulders. The shadows beneath her eyes and the shakiness of her hands. I lengthen my steps and close the distance, then drop to my ass beside her on the top step. After I put the gifts down, I turn to her.

She's so damn beautiful.

"You okay?" I could fucking punch myself in the face. What a pathetic question. As if she's okay, dickhead.

She wipes her finger beneath her nose and looks away from me, shrugging her shoulder. "I-I've been holding it together for the girls since I found o-out about C-Cass." She breaks into a loud sob and she buries her face in her hands.

Wrapping my arm around her shuddering shoulders, I tug her firmly into my body, noting how well she fits against me. *Perfect.* I drop my lips to the top of her hair and plant a reassuring kiss there as I hold her to me trying to comfort her the best I can but I'm out of my depth here. Crying women aren't something I've been taught to handle. But I do my best. I hold her, stroking her silky hair and laying gentle kisses on the top of her head. I let her cry just as Nix allowed me the space to fall apart last night. She needs to get it all out as I did. I fill my lungs with her delicate scent—wildflowers—which is beautifully understated and so uniquely her.

The longer we sit and the more she cries, the thicker the blanket of guilt wraps around me. She's devastated because of a decision *I* made. One that left Cassia and Sam vulnerable to Jake. It's another burden I'll carry for the rest of my damn days. It reminds me of the choices I made and the choices I continue to make that fail the people around me.

She pulls back, putting space between us, and digs into her purse to pull out a tissue. "I'm so sorry. I don't know what came over me." Her eyes skate all around us, never quite landing on me and I wonder if she blames me for what happened.

"No need to apologize. I'm so fucking sorry Cass and Sam were so badly hurt that they ended up in the hospital. And I'm sorry you've all had to deal with the worry you have. If I could somehow change what happened and make a different decision, I would. You have to believe if I could, I would undo everything that's happened."

Her eyes narrow as she draws her brows low and a crease forms between them. I want to wipe her pain away with my thumb and remove her worry and anguish. If only it was that easy. "What do you mean?"

I swallow past the lump in my throat and man up. I need to own up to my mistake to the people that matter. And Violet matters. She matters a lot. I rub my hand over the top of my head. "I decided to leave Len behind to look after the girls so I could stay with Toby. I felt he was the one at greater risk from *fans*. I never factored in Jake, and that was my biggest mistake and my true regret." I do my best to keep my eyes locked on Violet's to show her how sincere I am in the hopes that she understands the regret I'm drowning in.

She places her cold hand on mine as she shakes her head back and forth repeatedly. "No," she whispers. "How could you have known Jake was so unhinged? You made the best decision you could with the information you had." I shake my head in denial and she squeezes my hand. "You need to listen to me. None of us hold you responsible in any way. You shouldn't either."

"We'll have to agree to disagree on that, Blue. I can't forgive myself and I won't." She presses her lips together in a tight, straight line and I can tell she's unhappy with my response. "Are you ready to go?" She nods, so I climb to my feet to help her up. I pull her into me and trap her arms at her side as I hold her tight. "I'm so fucking sorry, Violet."

She drops her forehead to my chest and tries to reciprocate my embrace but I tighten my hold to keep her hands in place and away from me. I don't deserve her care and tenderness. After a while, I step back, ensuring she has her balance, then bend down to collect the gifts I brought.

"What are those?" She points to the bag.

I raise the bag balanced on the end of my finger. "I missed the girls, so I brought them something small. I was hoping to see them and give these to them before we go."

A smile touches her lips ... and it's *everything*.

11

VIOLET

He bought the girls gifts because he missed them. Within the span of a few minutes, he managed to break my heart *and* surprise me. I can't even think about the pain in his voice when he took responsibility for Cass and Sam's attack without my eyes stinging and my throat closing up. He couldn't be more wrong about where the blame lies. Jake is the only one to blame. He was the one who lost control and beat two women so badly they ended up hospitalized. I don't understand how Shane, a good man with a good heart, can possibly blame himself for such a heinous act.

"I'm sorry. The girls aren't home. Mom took them to the movies to distract them from Cass being in the hospital. Jas is too young to understand, but Poppy's upset that she can't visit with her mom. They left not long before you arrived."

His shoulders slump and disappointment takes over his features. "Fair enough. Maybe you can give them to the girls when you get home." He drops his eyes to his feet, then looks back up at me. "There's ... uh ... there's something in there for you, too." His cheeks pinken slightly and it's adorable to watch such a big man grow embarrassed.

I step closer and poke my finger into the top of the bag to open it enough to peek inside. "Really? I love gifts."

He thrusts the bag toward me. "Here. You can take it now." Once I have the bag, he tucks his hands into his pockets and rocks back on his heels. The tic in his jaw comes to life, and I drop my eyes back to the bag.

I dig my hand into the bag to pull out the gifts. Two books and a travel tea mug. Warmth fills my body on this cold day at his thoughtfulness. I drop the books back into the bag and open the box of the travel mug. It has a green lid—my favorite color. I flick my eyes up to his face. That sexy tic in his jaw has taken on a life of its own as he studies me carefully. Is he worried I won't like it? I smile at him and lean forward to embrace him. His entire six-foot-three frame tenses; it screams *don't touch me*, so I freeze in place and drop my arms. "Thank you. I love it. It'll be great for work."

He nods once and rubs the top of his short hair, messing up the strands. "I thought it looked robust enough to handle your line of work." He makes it sound like I'm throwing myself off cliff faces, but I can't fault his thoughtfulness.

I tilt it this way and that. "I think it'll be great. Some days I have to hike a bit to get to remote locations for my weed surveys and a hot cup of tea would be fantastic when I take a break. Especially as the temperature drops." He nods again. He's always been a man of few words, but his inability to accept a *thank you* takes it to a whole new level. "I'll put these inside and we can get going. I need to hug my sister."

He waits for me, then places his hand on my lower back to guide me to his SUV. Opening the door, he helps me inside and draws the seatbelt across my body, fastening it. His spicy cologne fills my senses without warning making my blood heat; he always smells so damn good. I'm not sure I'm going to survive being trapped in his car with him and his intoxicating scent because I can't hold my breath for that long. Even after he closes the door, his scent lingers. He climbs in and starts the car, then glances over at me. "You can select the music if you like."

I scroll through the options on the screen—noting our similar tastes in music—and find one of my favorite playlists on Spotify: *Rock Classics.* "Hope you don't mind. I love this playlist."

Shane glances at the screen and shrugs. "That's a pretty safe choice." He returns his eyes to the road, leaving me to my thoughts which immediately return to Cassia.

Mom said I needed to be prepared because Cass is a mess. That's why she decided to keep Poppy away from the hospital for now. It would be too upsetting for her to see the result of the attack. My stomach rolls at the thought of seeing my sister lying in a hospital bed as a result of Jake's violence. I can't imagine the terror she must have felt. My nose tingles and my eyes fill with tears. I blink them away as much as I can, but when the first tear breaches my eyelid, the rest follow quickly.

Shane can't see me cry again. He already bears the guilt of the attack, and I don't want to add to his misery so I turn my head toward the window to hide my pain and worry.

God, I hope she's okay.

Twisting my body slightly, I do my best to hide my face as we drive toward the hospital. Dread grows heavier in my stomach, and I fear I'm going to be sick so I wrap my arms around my stomach to hold myself together. After what feels like forever, Shane pulls into the parking lot of the hospital and climbs out of the car. He walks around to my side to open the door, and I keep my head down, hoping my loose hair will hide the fact that I've been crying again, but he's too observant for that.

Right there, in the parking lot, he wordlessly pulls me in tight to his firm body, and I bury my face in his chest. For the second time today, he holds me as I cry. He doesn't rush me or make me feel like I shouldn't be upset. He quietly holds my broken pieces and allows me to have my moment. I'm certain he has no idea how important his quiet support is to me as he rubs soothing strokes up and down my back. After a while, my sobs slowly turn to sniffles and I pull away.

"Thank you. I'm so sorry I keep losing it."

"No problem, Blue." I keep my face tilted downward, but he gently tips my chin up with the crook of his finger. "Take your time. I'll be here for as long as you need," he murmurs. My eyes drop to his mouth, tracing his plush lips, wondering how soft they really are. Does he have any idea how much his words mean? How much his kindness affects me? I don't think he does because Shane looks after people. That's what he does. It's all I've seen him do every time we've had any interaction.

But who looks after him?

"Thanks. I think I should be okay now." I suck in a long breath, then blow it out slowly and wipe beneath my eyes. Shane carefully pushes my hands away, cups either side of my face, and uses his thumbs to wipe away the evidence of my breakdown, following the action with eyes full of concern. His tenderness makes my emotions well again and I suck in a breath to hold any more tears at bay. I'm already embarrassed that he's witnessed me fall apart twice. I pull myself together and straighten my spine. After studying me closely, he must see the determination I have to hold it together and we both turn toward the hospital entrance.

Shane takes a moment to check on Sam, so he can pass on any information to Cass and Toby. I'm such a horrible person, I didn't even think about Cass's friend in my need to get to my sister.

The closer I get to Cass's room, the more my body shakes and my bones rattle with anxiety. It's been less than twenty-four hours since the attack, but it feels like it's been a week since I've laid eyes on my sister. I take deep breaths to strengthen my resolve to be strong for Cass as we make our way down the corridor to her room. Not long now and I'll be able to see that she's okay for myself.

Toby steps out of a room, and I freeze in place. "Hey." He leans in to hug me. "I was about to see if I can find any information about Sam and her baby. You mind sitting with Cassia?" He studies my face closely, his eyes full of worry but he must recognize my determination to be here for my sister.

"Hey." Shane pats Toby on the back. "Sam's up in maternity. She had the baby last night."

"Oh, okay. Maybe I don't need to leave Cass to find out." I love how reluctant he is to leave my sister. "Come in and say hello." Finally, we step into the sterile room.

Cass's eyes widen as her lips spread in happiness when she sees us. Shane moves forward first because I can't move from my spot just inside the doorway. My heart breaks for her and her bruised and broken body as I take in what I can see of my sister from head to toe. Not to mention the parts I can't see—her mind. I can't believe she's smiling. He kisses her forehead. "Hey, Cass. How are you feeling?"

"A bit sore and sorry for myself, to be honest," she says, her lips turned downward. I'm certain she's downplaying how she's feeling. "But thankful it's not worse than what it is."

"I watched the footage from the shop." I can't believe he watched the attack. I know I won't ever watch it. I don't want to see what happened. The aftereffects are bad enough. "You're a badass. I'm honored to call you my friend. What you did for Sam ..."—he shakes his head—"the way you fought with everything you had. You were ... *are* amazing. Don't forget that."

Cass blinks quickly at Shane's high praise. He steps away from the bed, making room for me but I can't move as I take in every visible inch of my broken sister. She's almost unrecognizable. Mom said she was a mess, but I didn't comprehend what she really meant. No wonder she didn't want Poppy to see her like this.

Cass holds out her good hand to me, and I step forward quickly. The sob I was holding back breaks free as I gently take Cass's hand, careful not to hurt her. We cry together, both of us shaking. I gently run my hands along the sides of her face, barely touching her as I study every inch and catalog her bruises and cuts.

"Oh, Cass. That fucking asshole. I want to hunt him down and do some serious damage. I want to—"

"Shh, shh. Don't do that. He's not worth any more of our time or thoughts." She shakes her head at me when I open my mouth. "No. I don't want to hear any more about it. I just want to forget it happened and wait for the justice he deserves to be served."

"It better be served, Cass. I'm so fucking angry he did this to you." I huff. "How dare he put his hands on you like this. Who does he think he is to hurt you so badly? I knew he was an asshole, but this is a whole other level of assholery."

"How's Poppy?" Cass changes the subject, and I work to tuck my anger away. It's better than the torrent of tears I've been crying but obviously, Cass doesn't want it.

"She's missing you. She knows that you've been hurt but she doesn't understand why she can't come and see you. Mom took the girls to a movie to distract them for a while which allowed me to sneak out of the house so I could visit you." I take Cass's hand in mine. "Do you need anything? Can I bring you anything from home? Any snacks?" I raise my eyebrows waiting for her to respond.

"I'd love my shampoo and stuff and maybe some fresh clothes. I'm not sure how long I'll be stuck in here." I can't believe I didn't think to bring anything with me but I was so focused on seeing her, my mind wasn't working properly. Even Mom didn't think to send anything with me because she was busy distracting the girls.

"I'm sorry I didn't think to bring anything with me. My only excuse is that I've been in shock that this happened to you."

Cass reaches up and tucks my loose hair behind my ear. "It's okay, Vi. Don't worry about it. It's not like I can use any of it just yet. I'm not even sure when they'll let me take a shower." She blows out a long breath. "I don't know how long I'll be here, and I'm already missing Poppy so much."

My heart breaks for my sister. I don't think I could be away from Jas for very long, I'm not sure Cass will be able to get through this without seeing her little girl. "Do you think you're going to be okay? I mean, I know physically, you'll heal, but ... mentally ... do you think you'll be okay?"

She presses her lips together in a straight line, her eyes move from side to side and her eyebrows dip and rise as she thinks. "I really don't know, Vi," she whispers. "I *know* I have a great support system around me, and hopefully Jake will be locked up so I feel safe, but I'm not sure."

I nod slowly and squeeze her hand gently. "I'm always here to listen for whatever you need. I love you so much. I've been so scared so I can only imagine the feelings swirling around inside of you."

A tear rolls down her cheek, and I move in carefully to embrace her as gently as I can as we both cry.

PART TWO

21 MONTHS LATER ...

12

SHANE

I position the polished plank of wood on the brackets, ensuring it's securely in place. "There. Now you have room for more books."

Hope smiles up at me. "Thanks, Shane. I appreciate you stopping by."

I pack my tools into my toolbox. "No problem. You know I'm happy to help whenever. Anything else you need done while I have my tools?" The front door slams and Evan storms through the house, his anger radiating from him like a wave. Hope and I look at each other with raised brows. "What the hell was that?"

She shrugs a delicate shoulder and looks away from me. "He's been angry lately. He won't talk to me."

"Did something happen at school?"

"I don't know. I spoke with his teacher, and they're not aware of anything, but he's been more aggressive at school lately." She heads into the kitchen and pulls a glass down from the cupboard. "I just give him some space to cool down, and he's usually okay after a while."

"I'm gonna go see if he'll talk to me."

"You can try. I don't like your chances."

I head off to find Evan. I can't believe the turnaround from the happy, placid kid to this one. And it seems it's a common occurrence. When I get close to his door, I can hear his game. "C'mon, asshole!" he shouts, and I push his door open fully and step inside.

"Hey, watch your mouth."

He glances at me over his shoulder. "You're not my dad. You can't tell me what to do." His careless words are like a roundhouse kick to the solar plexus. *Fuck!*

"Maybe not, but I know your dad wouldn't want you speaking like that."

He ignores me, his full attention back on the game he's playing, so I step in front of the screen to block his view and gain his attention. "Let's go downstairs and kick the ball around."

"I don't wanna kick the ball. I wanna play my game in peace. Leave me alone."

I snatch up the remote and turn the TV off.

"Why'd you do that? I was in the middle of my game!" He climbs to his feet and tries to grab for the remote but I hold it out of his reach. "Fuck you!" *Jesus. Where's the Evan I know and love? Who the hell is this kid?* He storms out of the room and downstairs, so I follow him. He bangs through the back door, leaving Hope gaping at him from the kitchen.

"What did you say to him?"

"Told him to watch his mouth, then invited him to kick the ball around." I raise my eyebrows and widen my eyes. "How long's he been like this?"

"A couple of months. He's getting worse."

"I haven't noticed this behavior."

"No, because he usually holds it together when he's at soccer practice, and you haven't been over to the house for a while."

"Only because you told me you wanted me to step back so you could learn to do stuff for yourself." I shove my hands on my hips in agitation. I was only doing what she asked.

A crease forms between her brows. "I wasn't laying any fault with you. I know I asked you to step back, and I'm glad you have.

You need to get on and live your own life, not spend your time here looking after us."

"But I want to help you guys."

"Shane, you feel obligated to help us because of what happened."

"I don—"

"Yes, you do. And I love you for it. Truly." She steps closer and rests her hand on my arm. "Wyatt would be so grateful that you've looked after us so well. But Shane, we all need to move on. I need to learn to be independent; I was relying on you too much. It's not healthy for any of us."

I wave my arm out toward the backyard where Evan is bouncing the ball on the top of his foot. "Yeah, and look at what I've missed. I had no idea he'd changed so much. That he was so angry."

"We'll work it out. It's just pre-teen stuff."

"I'm gonna spend some time with him. See if he'll talk to me."

"Good luck." She turns back to the counter to rinse her glass, and I suck in a deep breath and head outside.

I walk across the backyard toward Evan with slow steps, waiting for him to notice me but he keeps doing his thing and ignores me. "You wanna practice some tackles?"

He shrugs his shoulder and I can see some of his earlier hostility has subsided for now. "Sure."

"How about you try to get the ball off me to start?"

"That'll be easy, old man." Jesus. This kid's on fire with the insults today.

"We'll see."

We spend the next thirty minutes running, passing, and stealing the ball from each other. Evan's tackles gradually become more aggressive the longer we train. His foot connects with my shin at full force, and the kid isn't even trying to play the ball. "Hey, cut it out!"

"Are you growing soft, old man?"

I narrow my eyes. "Enough of the disrespect, Evan." His chest heaves as he works to catch his breath, and I lay my hand on his shoulder. He tries to bat it away, but I hold steadfast. "Talk to me. What's going on with you?"

"Nothin's going on with me," he snaps, trying to step out of my hold.

"This"—I circle my finger around him—"whatever *this* is ... isn't you."

"How would you know? You're never here anymore." Ouch! I crouch down so I'm at eye level with him, but he turns his head to the side.

"I'm sorry I haven't been around as much but all you have to do is message me and I'll be here. Whatever and whenever you need." He shrugs, keeping his face averted from mine. "If you want me to come around more, I'll make the time and effort for you."

"It doesn't matter, anyway."

"It matters to me. *You* matter to me." He turns his head so he's facing me, and I have to school my expression at the glassiness in his eyes. I wrap my arm around him and tug him into me, and the floodgates open. He sobs into my shoulder, and I drop to my knees so I can hold him properly. I sense this has been building inside him for a while now.

His body shudders and he takes in a deep breath. "I'm scared I'm gonna forget him," he murmurs into my shoulder. My stomach drops to the grass beneath us and my heart stutters. "Some things are getting harder to remember. And when I see my friends with their dads ... I ... I get jealous. I know I shouldn't but I can't help it." He draws away from me, swiping his hand beneath his nose. His eyes, which are exactly like his father's, are red and puffy. "What if I forget him?"

"Then you ask me and your mom to tell you about him." I rest my hand on his shoulder and squeeze.

"I try not to talk to Mom about Dad because it makes her too sad." I nod. I thought Hope was doing better, but maybe she's just become better at hiding it.

"Well, you can talk to me. Any time. We won't let you forget. I promise you that."

He drops his gaze to the ground. "I didn't think you cared anymore."

I sigh. "I always care, Ev. And I'll always be here for you. I may not come around as often because I wanted to give you guys some space to get on with life and maybe that was a mistake." I squeeze his shoulder again. "But it doesn't mean that I don't care because I do. I always will, no matter what happens or how big you get. I'll always be around."

He gives me a tremulous smile. "Thanks, Shane."

"No problem. When things get on top of you, talk to me or your mom. She's worried about you."

He nods. "Sorry."

I tip my chin up and ruffle his hair. "How about we go inside and see if we can score a slice of cake?"

His eyes light up and his lips spread wide. "Sounds good."

We make our way inside and while Evan heads to the bathroom to wash up, I find Hope in the kitchen. When she turns to me, I can see that she's been crying but she gives me a shaky smile. "Thanks, Shane."

In three short strides, I have her in my arms and she melts against me. "You don't have to do it all alone, Hope."

Her hands grip the sides of my shirt as she nods against my chest. "Yes, we do. We can't keep depending on other people. This is our reality and it's time we get used to it."

"I know you think you need to do it all. That you think you're being too reliant on others, but you didn't ask for any of this. You never planned to be a single mom, raising Evan on your own. You thought you'd grow old with your high school sweetheart and that was stolen from you. You're allowed to struggle and grieve and ask for fucking help, Hope."

Tears quietly stream down her pretty face and her lip quivers. "I-I just feel like it's been so long since he's been gone, and I should be in a better place by now."

Fuck, I feel those words with every ounce of my being. "There's no timeline for grief, Hope."

"I know," she murmurs.

Evan barrels into the kitchen. "Can I have some cake?"

Hope wipes her eyes, averting her face from her son. "Sure. I think you earned it after all that training. You were looking pretty good out there."

"Yeah, Shane made me work pretty hard." And we're back to the Evan we all know and love.

Hope makes a smoothie for Evan while I make us both a cup of coffee. She slices the chocolate cake and places three decent-sized pieces on the table for us to enjoy. "I'll be back in a moment."

"Is Mom okay?" Evan asks the second Hope clears the kitchen door.

"She will be. Just like you will be. But you guys need to stick together." I pull out a chair for him and then sit next to him. "You guys are a team. Just as you support your strikers on the team, you need to support your mom. Okay?"

"Okay. I will."

13

SHANE

Kate, Cassia, and Violet walk ahead of us into one of Toby's favorite restaurants, *Cristo's Taverna*, and I can't stop my eyes from dropping to Violet's ass with appreciation as she steps inside. I can see why some men have written sonnets about curves like hers—damn spectacular.

I tear my eyes away when Toby's shoulder bumps into mine, and I glance at him, noting his wide grin. Shaking my head to shift my thoughts away from Vi, I draw myself back to why we're out to dinner tonight, and I can't believe that in three short days, my long-time friend is marrying the girl he crushed on in high school. Nudging him with my elbow, I tip my chin toward the girls. "How's sixteen-year-old Toby feeling?"

When he turns to me, I swear his eyes are sparkling as his smile grows wider. "Sixteen-year-old me is fucking pinching himself, man." He points at Cass. "I can't believe she's mine. That we have a baby girl together. That Poppy and Daisy are my daughters. I must have done something right somewhere along the way."

Oliver huffs out a laugh. "You're a patient man. It drove me crazy that I didn't know how to find Kate after we first met. The length of time in between meeting her the first and second time only made me all the more determined to make her mine when I finally found her."

Toby and I snicker. "You wouldn't have smashed through Kate's walls if you weren't determined. It seems we both had the traits we needed to get the perfect woman for us," Toby proudly states.

Something happens inside my chest at the reminder they've both secured the women who stole their hearts and are now in solid, happy relationships that will last well into the future while I'm still single ... *by choice*. A certain someone has made her interest clear and if it weren't for the fact that I don't deserve her and her daughter, I'm sure we would have crossed the line from the friendship we've built over the last two years to something more. I'm finding it harder and harder to keep the lines drawn between us. But at times like these, where it's the six of us and it's painfully clear that Vi and I are not together in the same way as the other couples, I wish we were more than friends and that I was deserving of a place in her and Jasmine's lives.

We step inside to find Cristo exuberantly hugging each of the girls. With his arms outstretched, he steps toward Toby. "Congratulations! I'm so happy you've found the love of your life." He embraces him tightly, then releases him. "Come. Come. I have a celebratory feast planned for you all tonight."

He guides us to a table in the back which is blocked off with privacy screens from the rest of the restaurant, offering a modicum of privacy, and pulls out a chair. "My best table. Just for you."

"Thank you. You always make us feel special whenever we come here." Cass smiles at him.

Toby gestures for Cass to take the proffered seat, then sits next to her. Violet takes the chair next to her sister, while Kate sits next to Toby with Oliver next to her. That leaves me to sit between Violet and Oliver. I figured this would happen; I only hope I can keep my hands to myself. It's grown harder and harder to do since the woman tempts me like no other. I didn't think it was possible.

I thought I'd shut down that side of me when I watched Hope fall apart at the loss of her soul mate. I never want to experience that level of heartache. But the way Vi obviously loves her daughter, how independent and capable she is, and her determination to be the best version of herself, not to mention how damn beautiful she is has woken something inside me. Everything about Vi adds up to her being irresistible and too good for someone like me.

Since Cass moved in with Toby, I don't see Violet and Jasmine all that often, unless we're celebrating someone's birthday or a holiday.

It's torture.

Worse than that, I miss them.

I miss Jasmine's sweet nature which hasn't changed since she's grown older and started school. And I miss the bombshell sitting next to me. To be honest, it's probably a good thing that we see each other as infrequently as we do or the temptation would be too great.

As I pull out my chair, Violet smiles up at me. She's not as guarded with Toby and me as she was when we were first on the scene. Her smile is open and welcoming, and it's the worst possible thing for my control. I don't know how I'm going to make it through the evening without touching her in some way. Kissing her. Breathing her in like oxygen.

She tucks her loose hair behind her ear. "Hey."

I take a seat and turn to her. This close, even in the dim light, I'm able to take in her clear complexion and almost luminescent eyes. I clear my throat. "Hey, Blue." Her lips twitch, and I can't even remember when I started calling her Blue. It slipped out one day and continues to do so. She's never commented on the nickname but I think she likes it judging by the way her eyes brighten or lips twitch when I use it. "How are things with you and Jas?"

Cristo bustles to the table, interrupting her response, balancing a large platter in each hand. Behind him, one of his staff balances two more dishes and behind her, yet another waiter carries two more large dishes. He's always been incredibly welcoming and generous whenever Toby's eaten here, but this seems excessive. "A few of my favorite dishes. Enjoy!" He waves his arm out across the table and then leaves us to enjoy our meal before anyone has the chance to thank him, disappearing behind the screen that separates us from the rest of the restaurant. Toby isn't the only local celebrity at the table; Oliver has quite the name for himself around town, being a billionaire and all, so the screen separating us from the rest of the restaurant is appreciated and allows me the opportunity to enjoy the meal with my friends.

"Ah, man, Cristo knows how to put on a good spread," Toby says, and everyone around the table readily agrees.

Cristo returns holding two bottles of wine over his head. "I almost forgot the most important thing. We all need krasí to complement the meal!" He pours a little in each of our glasses and we all thank him quickly before he can disappear again.

Before everyone digs in, I raise my glass toward Toby and Cassia. "I'd like to propose a toast to Toby and Cassia." Everyone raises their glass. "Toby." I look at my long-time friend. "I've known you a long time. You're like a brother to me. When we were sixteen, I witnessed you falling for the woman beside you. I've watched you from near and far as you chased your dreams and I'm so damn proud of you. But I've never seen you happier than you are sitting beside Cassia, knowing that you're about to commit your future to each other. Cassia, thank you for making my best friend's dreams a reality. Toby, Cassia … may your marriage be long, happy, and full of all the love the two of you deserve." I lift my glass toward my best friend and everyone nods in agreement, mirroring my action. "And Toby. I'm glad you never gave up on your dreams, man."

"Hear, hear!" everyone responds together, and we all take a sip of our wine.

"Thanks, Shane." I nod with a full heart—glad I'm still here to share this experience with him. I pause for a moment, realizing that somehow my thoughts have shifted. I *am* glad I'm still here to share this moment with him. He's come a long way since he first crushed on the woman beside him, and I'm proud to have been on this journey with him and call him my friend. I wait for the guilt to swamp me and while it's there, it's not as overwhelming as it once was. I'm not sure when things shifted for me. It hasn't been obvious, but as I think back over the last two years, it's been a gradual change in the way I think about things and accept the things I can't change. I expect I'll still have my moments, but today I'm feeling positive so I'll take it.

We spend the next few moments passing dishes around the table and spooning portions onto our plates. As Kate, Cass, Toby, and Oliver discuss final plans for Saturday since the wedding is at Kate and Oliver's home, I return my attention to Violet. "So, how are things with you and Jas?"

Her smile is instant and the other conversations fall away. "She started kindergarten, and I've already been called in to speak with her teacher."

I bristle. "Why the fuck is the teacher calling you in for a meeting? She's a good girl."

Violet places her hand on my forearm, setting my skin ablaze through my shirt. I swear I feel every cell beneath her touch come alive. *Remember, she's too good for you.* "It was nothing bad. She wanted to talk with me about speaking with the kids about our native plants, and how important they are. Jasmine has been telling her classmates about my job and how important it is to look after our environment." She chuckles. "Apparently, she was telling the kids that she wants to be the Lorax and speak for the trees."

My eyebrows rise in surprise. I can't believe the book I bought for her when Cass was in the hospital has had such an impact. "Well, if anyone can convince people to look after their environment, it would be Jas. She can be very convincing." It must be a genetic thing because both she and Poppy seem to be able to persuade anyone to do their bidding. Even Toby and Cassia's daughter, Daisy, has everyone wrapped around her finger and she's only just over a year old.

Vi nods. "I know, right? Anyway, I'll be spending some of my day off next week speaking with a bunch of five-year-olds about caring for our environment and why it's so important."

"That's great. Do you do that sort of thing very often?"

She swallows a bite of food and I watch her throat bob up and down. My dick starts to thicken in my pants and I snap my eyes away from her to my plate, scooping up a fork of pasta. "Not in classrooms, but I often speak with school groups when they visit the park. I don't mind doing it because education is important if our native flora and fauna are to thrive but it's not my favorite part of the job."

"What is your favorite part of the job?"

Her eyes sparkle and her energy shifts. "My favorite part is just being able to spend my days outdoors in nature and get paid for it." She chuckles. "Some days, I have to pinch myself when I stop and look at the beauty around me. But the parts that I adore are monitoring and maintaining the habitat and knowing that I'm protecting our native flora and fauna. So many people don't even know which species are native and which are invasive or the negative impact invasive species have on our environment." She swipes her hair back over her shoulder. "Sorry, I'm sure you're not interested in hearing all that."

I sip my wine. "On the contrary. I love that you're passionate about what you do. The way you light up when you talk about your work or Jasmine is beautiful. Too many people work in jobs they're not happy with." Like my father.

A flush stains her cheeks, and she drops her eyes away from me. "Thanks."

We eat for a while, our elbows touching occasionally. My leg seems to have a mind of its own, moving closer to Violet until my thigh is touching her knee, and I'd love to drop my hand beneath the table and squeeze the toned muscle of her leg. I guess all the hiking she does keeps her pretty fit.

Kate and Cassia talk about last-minute preparations for Saturday, while Oliver talks to Toby about their honeymoon in Disneyland with the girls.

We finish eating and I shift in my seat to get more comfortable with a stomach full of rich food. I notice Violet sliding her hand back and forth across her stomach. "You okay?"

"Yeah. Just too full. The food was so delicious and I was a little greedy. Sometimes I have no self-control." She titters.

"Same. I couldn't resist having a little of everything."

She nudges my arm with her shoulder. "It's okay for you though. You probably have a great metabolism and burn off the extra calories quickly. All of that pasta and rich sauce will attach itself to my ass and thighs and probably never leave."

"I don't see a problem with that."

"Of course you wouldn't. It's not your ass or thighs," she shoots back. "Guys are lucky. They're not judged as harshly as women if they put on a little weight. In fact, the dad bod has become quite popular. Not that you would ever have to worry about that." My light mood falls away. I know I'm not dad material and never will be, I don't need the reminder. I sip my wine and shift in my seat, breaking contact with Vi. She drops her hand to my forearm and I want to pull away. "Are you okay?"

I take another, longer drink, of my wine and respond without looking at her. "Yeah."

Her hand squeezes my arm. "Are you sure? You seem upset."

I make the mistake of looking at her. The creases between her arched eyebrows and the way she's studying me like an insect under the microscope make my skin itch. I put that look on her face and it makes me feel like shit. I soften my posture and smile at her in reassurance. "I'm sure. Promise."

Her features relax and she returns my smile. That simple action makes my sour mood disappear, and I force the negative thoughts from my mind. Cristo brings out two platters full of delicious Greek desserts along with coffee for everyone. When I notice that Vi isn't drinking hers, I remember that she prefers to drink tea.

I stand, excusing myself from the table, "I'll be back in a minute." Heading toward the bar, Cristo notices me and heads straight over.

"Is everything okay? Do you need something?" he asks.

"Uh, yeah. Violet doesn't drink coffee, only tea. Can I please order a pot for her?"

Cristo smiles. "Sure. Sure. I'll arrange a pot of tea and bring it straight to the table."

"Thanks. Dinner's been great, and I can't wait to start dessert." I dig into my pocket. "Can I pay now?" I figure it can be my wedding gift to them.

He laughs. "No. This is my gift to Cassia and Toby." He winks. "You'd better get back before Toby and Oliver eat all of the desserts." Damn. Now I'll need to think of something else to get them as a gift.

I pat him on the shoulder and return to the table. Someone's put a plate at my place with a variety of treats. "I didn't want you to miss out. Toby's already on his second plate," Violet tells me.

I glance at Toby who's reaching across for another ball sprinkled with crushed nuts. "You wanna leave some for the rest of us, man?"

He pops it in his mouth and chews, gesturing toward the plate. "You snooze, you lose."

Well, if he's gonna be like that. I reach across and grab two balls, adding one to my plate and one to Violet's.

"Here's your tea, ómorfi kyría," Cristo says as he places a small tray with a teapot and cup on the table in front of Vi. He turns to me with a wink and says, "Courtesy of your companion."

"Thank you. You didn't need to go to so much trouble for me."

"It was no trouble at all. Enjoy."

Everyone around the table takes the opportunity to thank Cristo for the delicious meal and desserts and Violet pours her tea into the cup, her lips tipped up at the edges. "Thank you for this. I didn't want to make a fuss."

"You're welcome, but I don't think asking for tea could be considered making a fuss, Blue."

She takes a sip, closing her eyes in appreciation, and I have the sudden urge to lean forward and press a gentle kiss to her lips. I glance around the table, noticing Oliver and Kate leaning close together, whispering to each other while Cassia and Toby do the same.

"Hey," Violet whispers, breaking me from my observation. When I turn my head, her face is mere inches from mine. It would be so easy to lean forward and steal that kiss I was thinking about a moment ago. When I raise my eyes to hers, there's a hint of a smile like she caught me staring at her mouth, and she knows I'm tempted to kiss her. "I was wondering if you'd be able to help me with something."

"Sure."

She grins. "You don't even know what it is," she says playfully.

"Whatever you need, you know I'm happy to help."

She drops her eyes for a moment and fidgets with the ends of her hair. I've noticed she does that whenever she feels nervous or uncomfortable. "I know," she murmurs, her playfulness gone, and I'm not sure why.

I need to change her mood, so I bite into a zesty lemon slice and moan as the sweet and sour flavors burst across my tongue. I point to the same dessert on Vi's plate. "Eat that."

She looks at me and then, without question, scoops a piece up with her fork, places it on her tongue, then slides the utensil out of her mouth between her lips. Her eyes widen as she chews and then close in delight as she moans around the delicious treat. "Oh my gosh, that's so freaking good." I try to block out the huskiness of her moans of enjoyment and do my best not to think about how she would sound if I were to slide my dick into her pussy. Concentrating like I'm sitting for an exam, I work hard to focus on something else. *Anything* else.

Leaning across the table, I collect another slice to place on her plate and one on mine before Toby eats everything in sight. Violet chuckles as I make a big production of securing each of us another piece.

"Oi! What do you think you're doing?" Toby calls out across the table.

I lick my fingers slowly, then answer, "Making sure we don't miss out."

Everyone around the table laughs at our playfulness and now that Vi appears to have moved past whatever upset her moments ago, I nudge her with my arm. "So, what did you need help with?"

Her head snaps around the group and once she sees whatever she is looking for, she leans in close. "Mom and I have an idea for a wedding present."

I lean closer still to ensure our conversation stays between us. "Oh, yeah. Tell me more."

"Last summer, we noticed the area around Toby's pool—"

"I'll have to stop you there. It's Toby *and* Cassia's pool area now."

She smiles at me and nods. "Well, yeah. Mom and I noticed it's a bit bland. Everything else about their place is stunning but the pool area could do with some plants." I raise my brows and my lips tip up. "Anyway, we thought we could jazz up the area while they're away on their honeymoon."

I'm nodding before she can finish asking. "What do you need?"

"I don't suppose you could get me a key to their back gate? If I ask, it'll seem suspicious but I figure you already have access to all of that."

"Of course. I think it's a great idea. I'll give you my key after the wedding, and you can give it back to me after the honeymoon."

"Thanks, Shane."

"Can I contribute financially, so the gift is from all of us? I have no idea what to get them."

Vi smiles at me and it does something strange to me every single time. "Sure. We can work it out later. Mom can get the plants at wholesale prices through her business so that will keep the price down."

"Sounds good. Let me know what I owe, and I'll transfer it across to you."

"Perfect."

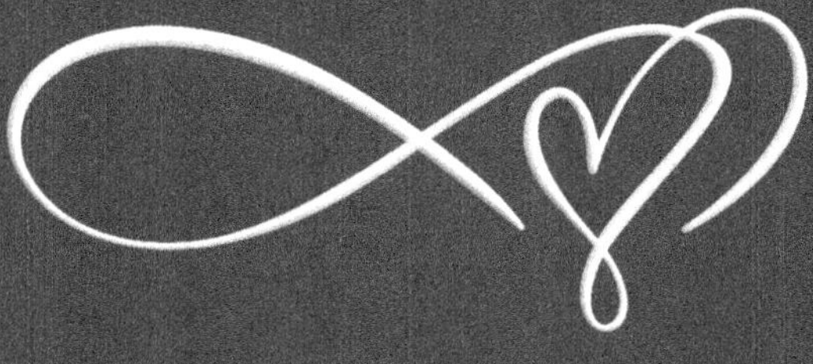

14

VIOLET

I knock on Cass's front door and wait. When the door opens revealing my sister, I can't help but peer around her to see if Toby—*oh who am I kidding, I'm really looking for Shane*—is around but neither man is in sight. "Hey,"—I lean in to hug Cass and she hugs me back—"are you ready?" We grew closer after I left Allen and moved back home, and I'm so happy that we've managed to remain close since she moved in with Toby, even though we don't see each other every day. I was an asshole to her when we were teenagers, pretending I didn't have a younger sister. I still can't believe I did stuff like that and that she forgave me so easily.

Cass blows out a breath and releases me to collect her overnight bag—she and the girls are staying with us tonight as a nod to tradition. She passes me the bag and then collects her purse from the entry table. "As ready as I'll ever be." She looks stiff and worried, not at all what I was expecting a bride-to-be to look like.

"Where are Toby and Daisy?"

"Toby's taken Daisy to her swimming lesson this morning, and Shane will bring Daisy to Mom's when he picks up Poppy and Jasmine from school this afternoon." Well, that explains why he isn't around. My skin flushes at the thought of seeing Shane this afternoon. Jas was so excited this morning when I told her Shane and Toby were picking her up from school today so Cass and I could spend the day together.

"Oh my gosh, I wish I was a fly on the wall to see the look on the other mom's faces when he turns up to class." I chuckle but Cass doesn't join in like she usually would—something must be wrong.

Neither of us would be considered high-maintenance girls but when Toby offered to send us for spa treatments, I thought it'd be fun—Mom couldn't make it because she's in the middle of a huge design for a rooftop garden in the city center and Kate couldn't take the day off work, so it's just me and Cass—but anyone looking at my sister would think I'm taking her to the gallows with the way she's acting. "You could be a little more excited," I prompt as she locks the front door.

She snaps her head to me. "I *am* excited ... nervous about tomorrow ... and thinking about everything I need to do but I'm definitely excited to spend time being pampered. I can't remember the last time I took some time out for myself. The shop's been so busy and with the girls and Toby's career ... it's a lot to juggle." She sighs.

As we walk toward my car, I nod. "Same." Well, not really the same, I don't have a rock star for a partner. I can't imagine what that's like. "Life is just so busy and this sort of stuff normally isn't on my priority list. But I can almost feel my skin cheering for this treat and my muscles relaxing at the thought of a massage."

We climb into my car. "Me too." She lays her head back against the headrest. "I can't believe I'm marrying the perfect guy tomorrow, Vi." Her voice is soft as she rolls her head toward me. "How is this my life?"

I take her hand in mine and grin. "You're meant to have this life, Cass. Don't question it because this is everything you deserve and more. I'm so happy you reconnected with Toby. I remember back in high school when you used to talk about him all the time even though you were dating Jake. I always wondered why you didn't date him instead."

She chuckles mildly. "Uh, that would be because I thought he hated me." She looks wistfully out of the windscreen. "How wrong I was. So much time wasted."

"Not really. If you'd dated in high school, you wouldn't have Poppy. Everything happens for a reason. You need to remember that."

I keep telling myself the same thing, hoping one day the message will sink into my brain. Reminding myself that I'm exactly where I need to be instead of dwelling on the stuff that's gone wrong in my life helps me to move forward and find happiness. Even in the simple things like spending time with Jas, taking photos—which I only recently discovered I have a talent for—and spending time with my family. It hasn't been easy the last two years since separating from and divorcing Allen, but I'm in a better place now. A happier place.

"You're right." Cass breaks into my thoughts and it takes me a moment to remember what we were talking about. "But what about you? When are you going to stop playing coy with Shane and go after the future you deserve?"

I start the engine. "He's not interested in me, Cass. I've made it clear that I'd be open to something with him but he misses ... or maybe ignores ... all of my cues. We're friends and I'm sad to say that I think that's all we'll ever be."

Cass huffs out a laugh. "You're both as clueless as each other. I was watching you guys the other night at dinner. The way you sat close to each other and served each other food. You also seemed to be having your own private conversations throughout the evening." She raises her eyebrows at me. "Oh, and let's not forget to mention how he organized a pot of tea for you. You guys definitely gave off couple vibes to anyone watching."

My cheeks flush at the memory of the way he looked after me

and readily offered to help me even though he didn't know what he was agreeing to. "Naturally we would pair off in that situation, but it's nothing more than the friendship that's grown between us. I wouldn't read anything more than that into it." I flick on my indicator to turn onto the main road away from the city.

Cass's lips tip up. "We'll see."

We spend the rest of the trip discussing the plan for tomorrow morning, steering the topic of conversation away from me and Shane. I pull into the parking lot for *Pure Harmony Day Spa* and turn off the engine. Cass and I both lean forward to stare at the building through the windscreen. Shit! This place is fancy. "Toby organized this, right?"

"Yep. Apparently, some rich Australian client of Oliver's recommended this place to Kate a while ago. Oliver sent Kate and her mom here for the day and they raved about it, so Toby thought this would be the perfect place for us. But I feel like maybe it's a little too fancy. How much do you think this place costs?"

I release my seatbelt and climb out of my car. Leaning back inside, I capture Cass's worried gaze. "Toby can afford it and he wants to spoil you. Let him. You can thank him tomorrow night." I wink and she finally giggles. "Come on. Let's go."

We make our way inside, and I can't stop my eyes from taking everything in. It's like walking through a bamboo forest as we enter the foyer which features a tranquil waterfall. I already feel Zen-like, and I haven't even made it to the reception desk. An older woman wearing pale sage smiles at us. "You must be Cassia and Violet. Welcome to *Pure Harmony*. My name is Jennifer."

Cassia steps up to the counter. "Thanks, Jennifer. I'm Cassia and this is my sister, Violet." She points to me over her shoulder with her thumb.

"Ah, the bride-to-be, congratulations on your upcoming nuptials."

"Thank you." Cass's eyes sparkle as she grins.

"Your partner has asked that we take the best care of you both today. Please follow me." She waves her arm out toward a door and makes her way forward.

Cass and I glance at each other, then follow her. The place is painted in muted greens and finished with light bamboo flooring and light gray stone feature walls and while it should feel cold, it's warm and inviting and the calming effect is instant. The sounds of nature play softly over hidden speakers, adding to the ambiance. I can feel the stress melting away from my body with each step I take. As I glance across at Cass, I notice she doesn't look half as nervous and bogged down in her to-do list as she was when I picked her up.

"This is our changing area. Lockers are provided to store your valuables and clothes. Robes are provided for your use. Please remove all clothing and use the disposable underwear provided. Your first treatment for the day is the float tank, so you won't want to get your underwear wet. Please enjoy the fresh fruit and vegetable platter and natural mineral water in the lounge off to the side. Lauren will be by to collect you both in a short while."

She leaves us in the changing area, and I'm pretty sure that neither of us really knows what to do right now. I mean we know we need to change, but this whole place seems unreal and oh-so serene. I'm used to serenity when I head out hiking and taking my photos of the natural world, but this is otherworldly. "I feel like a celebrity," I whisper, doing my best not to disturb the tranquility.

"Me too," Cass murmurs with a chuckle. "I guess we should get changed. Who knows how long a *short while* will be and we don't want to be late."

Once we're changed we meet in the lounge and grab a small plate of food each. We chat about our girls and how excited they are to dress up tomorrow. After about twenty minutes, Lauren collects us and guides us to separate rooms containing a float tank that looks more like a spaceship. I climb in, close myself inside, and amazingly float in the warm shallow water without any effort. Calming music plays and the lights dim low. Closing my eyes, I empty my mind and allow myself the opportunity to relax. Tomorrow will probably be crazy busy, and even though I love Jasmine beyond words, it's nice to lay in peace. Between her and work and life in general, especially with everything that needed to be done for the divorce to be finalized as well as terminating Allen's parental rights, I'm exhausted—mentally, emotionally, and physically.

I shut my thoughts down one by one but my mind snags on something Cass said—*you guys definitely gave off couple vibes to anyone watching.* As much as I swore off men when everything went to shit with Allen, I wouldn't be opposed to something happening with Shane. Getting to know him over the past two years, I've learned he's definitely not selfish (which I would like to think also translates to the bedroom), he's thoughtful, considerate, kind, and reliable. If he says he'll do something, he gets it done. And his hands. God, they're so big and strong. So capable, yet gentle. My core tightens at the thought of his hands on me in an intimate moment. I push my head beneath the water to wash away the thoughts. *Stop, Violet.*

Would I like to move our relationship out of the friend zone? Absolutely.

Is it ever likely to happen? I don't think so.

He's exceptionally skilled at keeping his boundaries in place. But what if I could sneak under his defenses? I lift my head out of the water and wipe the moisture from my face.

I must have dozed for a while because the next thing I know, the lights are slowly becoming brighter and the music grows a little louder. I follow the instructions and open the pod, then spend the rest of the day being pampered beyond anything I've ever experienced before. My skin is as smooth as silk and glowing with a freshness I haven't had since before puberty struck.

THE SIX OF us arrive on Kate and Oliver's doorstep right on time. When the front door eventually opens, Kate steps forward, squeals, and opens her arms wide. "Oh my gawd, you're almost my sister for real!" She draws Cass into an excited hug and they rock from side to side, laughing, and Mom and I grin at each other.

Kate embraces Poppy and then welcomes us all into her gorgeous home. I don't think I'll ever get used to being in the home of billionaire Oliver Stone and being made to feel so welcome. Considering how wealthy they are, they never make us feel as though they're better than us. On top of that, their home isn't showy; it's welcoming and warm, just like they are. They guide us to two rooms at the front of their home and I'm blown away by the setup. They've thought of everything for us and the girls; well above anything I would have expected. After Oliver gives his wife a not suitable for public viewing kiss, he leaves us to get ready. The excitement and happy energy in the room fills every inch of the space.

"Hey, Vi. I'm so excited that I'm almost related to you guys. I've always wanted a sister, and now I have two," Kate gushes.

I've always felt like the tag-along—which is unnecessary because Kate's always made me feel welcome—but the fact that she considers me part of her family as another sister brings my barely-held emotions to the surface. I reach forward and pull her into me, words escaping me for the moment. I've been worried I'd have to share Cass, but in reality, I've gained another sister. "Thank you. I'm so glad our families are joining together," I whisper as I squeeze her, my throat clogged with emotion.

From that point, the morning is a whirlwind of activity. Hair. Makeup. Photographs. Video. Flowers.

As Cass fiddles with the daisy and jasmine sprigs for our hair, I wrap my arm around her. "I'm thrilled for you, Cass. Toby has been so good for you and Poppy. He's an incredible man and I know, I just know that you guys were meant for each other and will have a long and happy life together." I smile shakily at my sister, past the emotions that have built up over the morning.

She swallows and wipes away a stray tear from her cheek, then holds me tight. "You know there's someone for you and Jas?" she whispers, giving me one of her looks. "You just need to be brave."

I nod. "I know." I plan to. "While I was floating in the pod yesterday, I decided to go after what I want. And I want him," I tell Cass and she grins at me, nodding with approval. Now I need to work out a way to get him to notice me and think of me as more than a friend.

Poppy and Jas walk back into the room, each holding one of Daisy's hands between them, and Mom follows behind smiling proudly. She loves being a grandma. Once Cass has gushed over the girls in their light-purple tutus the color of faded wisteria, we shuffle them back to the other room so Mom, Kate, and I can dress. Kate and I are wearing different styles of dresses in the same dark purple while Mom wears her dark gray mother-of-the-bride dress.

"You look gorgeous, Mom." Damn emotions clogging up my throat. *What is freaking wrong with me today?*

She studies my face. "Are you okay?"

I smile, or at least I try to. "I swear I'm happy for my sister. *So* happy for her. I don't know what's going on with me. I'm feeling overly emotional today, especially since we arrived here to get ready."

Mom's worry is replaced by a compassionate smile. "I know you are. But I can't help but wonder if today isn't a little difficult for you to process after the way things ended with Allen."

I shake my head slightly. "I don't think so. I think it's more about seeing how happy Cass and Toby are together. How *right* they are together. How much he loves her and the girls." I nod toward Kate. "We've never really been surrounded by happy and strong relationships before. It all feels foreign."

Mom's smile drops. "I'm sorry, Vi. As I've said to you before, I don't think I did you girls any favors by staying single all these years. I didn't show you that happiness in a relationship is possible. But it is. I believe that even after all these years and I want you to believe it, too. Don't do what I did and shut that part of you away. Open yourself to the possibility of a happily ever after. Do it because you deserve it, and show your daughter that there are good men out there and it's possible to have happiness." Her eyes have grown glassy during her speech, and I have to blink back the sting of tears. We hug, careful not to crush our dresses, and then Mom heads next door to spend a quiet moment with Cass.

"Mommy, I need to go to the bathroom, but I'm worried I'm going to mess up my dress."

I glance across at Kate. "I think the girls should hit the bathroom before the ceremony. It'll be a while before they get another chance."

Kate nods. "Good idea. Let's go." She collects Daisy and I take Poppy and Jas's hands in each of mine, and we lead them through to the bathroom, carefully holding their pretty dresses out of the way in turn so they can do their thing.

Poppy's almost vibrating with excitement once she's finished washing her hands. "I can't wait to show Daddy my pretty dress," she signs quickly.

"He's going to think you look beautiful," I sign back as I speak.

Poppy and Jas twirl their way down the hallway, while Daisy tries to keep up with her chubby little legs, giggling all the way while her short curls bounce around her face. Kate wraps her hand around my wrist and pulls me to a stop before we make it back to the bedroom. "I promise I wasn't eavesdropping, but I overheard your conversation with your mom."

I flush as embarrassment creeps its way through me. "Sorry about that."

She shakes her head, a furrow forming between her brows.

"Don't be sorry. I just wanted to say that my parents have always had a strong and loving relationship, yet before Oliver came along, I didn't believe I'd ever have what they have. I know how hard it can be to meet someone decent. Trust me, I had my fair share of douchebags." She chuckles. "Boy, did I give Oliver a hard time in the beginning. But ... he persevered"—a smile tilts her lips upward—"and I'm so grateful he did. Real love. A strong and happy love really can be found. It may even be right under your nose." She winks at me. "Now, let's go get our siblings married so we can see our guys."

I laugh along with her as we reach the closed door of the room in which Cassia is dressing. The girls are patiently waiting for us to open it, which Kate does with a flourish. As the door swings back revealing my sister, I freeze in place.

She looks like a goddess.

"Oh my gosh, you two look so gorgeous." Cass gasps as she scans Kate and me from head to toe.

Daisy runs forward, straight for her mom—"Mommy!"—and even though Cass is wearing her wedding dress, she scoops her up and fusses over her.

Poppy joins in and signs, "You look like a princess, Mommy."

Cass signs with one hand as she speaks. "Thank you, Baby Girl. You look like a beautiful princess yourself."

"I'm not a baby anymore!" She frowns as she quickly signs to her mom, which I guess is a fair statement since she is nine.

"You'll always be my baby girl," Cass says as she signs while I chuckle because that's exactly what Mom used to say to us when we didn't like being called her babies.

Kate holds out a gift to Cass. "Cassia, my brother's gonna pass out when he lays eyes on you." She chuckles, then hands her the small box. "Toby asked me to give this to you today while we're getting ready."

Cass opens the box, and her lips tip up as she runs her finger over a delicate piece of jewelry. Kate and I peer over her shoulder to spot a platinum necklace that has the word *Mrs* in script joined between two delicate chains and we giggle. "As if the rings on your finger won't tell people you're married, he has to add this piece to the mix," I say through my chuckles.

She holds the necklace out to me with a wide grin. "Would you mind putting it on for me?" I take it from her, drape it around her neck, and close the clasp securely. After it's in place, she studies herself in the mirror, smoothing down her dress. "I'm ready. I'm so ready to become Mrs. Toby Summer."

"All right. Let's get you to my brother." I'm not sure who's more excited about this wedding—my sister or Kate.

Cass asks if we should tidy up but Kate waves her off, telling us that Oliver has it covered—they've literally thought of everything. I can't believe Cassia's even thinking about it; I certainly wouldn't be. Tidying up would be the last thing on my mind if I were getting married. I'd be in too much of a rush to get to my man.

Beth—Toby and Cassia's wedding planner—meets us at the back of the house, ready to guide us through this last part and we get our first look at the backyard. It's beyond stunning and judging by Cass's gasp, she's happy with how it all turned out. The pots of lavender lining the path are beautiful and the scent is going to be divine as we walk toward the dock.

"Oh my gosh, you ladies all look stunning. The shades of purple are beautiful." Beth raises her eyebrows. "Are you ready to see your guys? They all look so ..." She fans her face and we all giggle. Well, Shane's not my guy yet, but that'll change soon if I have anything to do with it.

"I'm so ready! Thank you for everything you've done to make it look so incredible and ensuring the day runs smoothly," Cass tells Beth.

"You're most welcome. It's been my absolute pleasure."

At the first notes of Ellie Goulding's "How Long Will I Love You," Poppy and Jas step through the door together and follow the path toward Toby, Oliver, and Shane. Kate collects Daisy in her arms and follows the girls, leaving Mom, Cass, and me. I watch Jas leap toward Shane who bends to catch her easily as Poppy does the same to Toby. The three of us chuckle at the girls. Once Kate is halfway down the path, I quickly hug Mom and Cass and step through the doorway with a smile on my face.

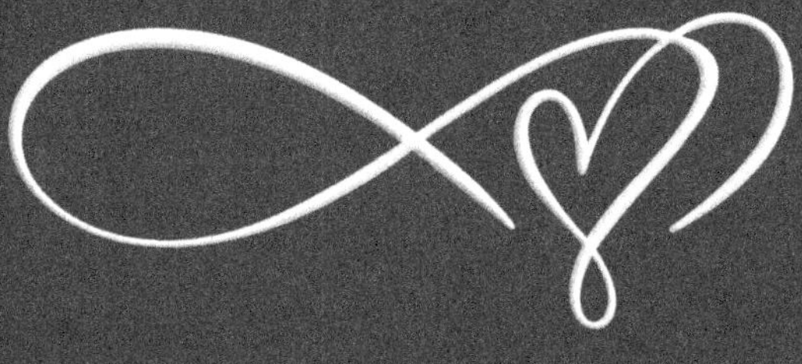

15

SHANE

Pulling my shirt collar away from my neck as sweat trickles down my back, I shift my feet for what seems like the thousandth time. Looking across at my long-time friend and employer, I note he's also shifting on his feet as a trail of sweat trickles down the side of his face. It's hot as Hades today. I fucking hate the heat. It reminds me of a time I've been working hard to forget. I don't know why they didn't choose to have their wedding in an air-conditioned room instead of Kate and Oliver's backyard. I get that it's a beautiful location and that it's private and has a great view, but it's unseasonably hot today.

"You worried she's realized she can do better than you and won't show?" I snicker. I know she won't find a better man than Toby. She knows he's the best and that he would lay the world at her and their daughters' feet if that's what she asked of him.

His eyes snap from the back of the house to mine. "Fuck off." He adjusts his jacket. "I'll hunt her down and drag her ass here myself if she doesn't show. I'll even let you use those skills of yours to help me." He chuckles. My body locks tight and my heart beats increase marginally at his words. It's not often he brings up my past, he knows not to. "Sorry, Shane. I didn't mean it like that." He brushes his hand through his hair, messing up his man bun. "I guess I'm nervous."

Giving him a sharp nod, I concentrate on releasing the breath in my body, relaxing my muscles one by one, and returning to the lighter mood of before. I remind myself that I'm as far away from that shit hole as I can possibly be. That my life is easier now.

Finally, the music begins to play. I lift my eyes to the back deck of the house, and I can't stop my lips from tilting upwards at the sight of Poppy and Jasmine making their way along the lavender-lined pathway toward us. Both girls look as cute as can be in their matching pale purple tutu dresses, complete with little white flowers in their hair. If you'd asked me two years ago if I knew what a tutu was, I would have thought you were crazy—but here we are. It's easy to tell they're cousins with their matching smiles. They run the last few yards, Poppy, leaping for Toby as Jas does the same toward me. This little girl is full of so much energy and joy, and from the very first instant she met me, she gave me the ultimate gift —her trust. She easily sucked me into her vortex with her sparkling eyes and mischievous smile, much the same as her mother did. She calms me and eases my mind; the effect someone so small has on me is mind-boggling.

"Hello, Shane." She smacks her lips against my stubble.

I laugh quietly at her excited hello. "Hey. Who's this pretty girl?"

"It's me, Jasmine! You remember me." She squeezes my cheeks in her little hands, and I chuckle, then place a kiss on her forehead. She drops her face, giving me a shy smile, which is unlike the little girl I've come to know since Toby and Cassia reconnected.

Glancing up along the pathway, I suck in a sharp breath when my eyes land on Violet. The woman is temptation incarnate on her worst day; I'm unsure how I'll make it through today without mauling her when she looks as beautiful as she does right now. Her stunning China-blue eyes connect with mine as I hold her daughter in my arms, and one side of her lips tilts up as she winks at me. She's sexy as fuck in a dress that highlights her athletic frame. The long slit up the front of her right leg affords me a glance of her toned thigh. Her tanned flesh begging for my hand to glide up along the smooth skin, followed by my tongue until I reach its apex.

Shaking my head, I remind myself I can't go down that road with her—I need to keep us in the friend zone, even if it's a struggle to remember to do so. She shouldn't be tainted by the darkness that's festered inside of me as a result of my time away. She's already been treated like shit and deserves to find a man who's whole and can be everything to her and Jasmine. Someone *better than* me.

I clench my jaw at the thought of someone else having the privilege to touch her. To kiss her. To love her. I look at Jasmine in my arms, and my gut sinks to think of her giving someone else her unconditional trust. What if they're undeserving of Violet and Jasmine? What then?

In a way, I've come to think of them as mine.

Violet makes it to the altar and this close, she looks even more beautiful if that's possible. I suck in a sharp breath, and I work to strengthen my defenses. I've managed to keep myself in check for this long, I can maintain it for today. *I hope.*

"Hi," she murmurs, her eyes dancing between me and her daughter.

"Hey. You look beautiful, Blue." *Probably not a good idea to use her nickname.*

Her cheeks flush a pretty shade of pink and her eyes drop away from mine for a moment. "Thanks. You look ... amazing." And that part of me that I've tried to lock away puffs out his chest that she likes what she sees when she looks at me. I doubt she would feel the same if she saw the real me.

She reaches across to fetch her daughter, but Jas clings tightly to my neck. I'm already sweating bullets in this suit and having her cling to me adds a couple of degrees of heat, but there's no way I'm going to make her let go. I'll hold her through the entire ceremony if that's what she wants. "She's okay with me."

"You're sure?"

I nod. "Yeah."

Violet kisses Jas's cheek, and I get a whiff of her soft scent. She winks at me when she pulls away, then takes up her position on the opposite side of the altar. Cass joins us, and then the civil celebrant begins speaking and Toby and Cass exchange their vows, but I'm not listening to a word. For some reason, my mind won't let go of the idea of me and Vi doing the same thing.

Creating a family together. Building a life. A beautiful life where I'm a better father than mine ever was. And I allow myself a moment to dream a little—imagining Vi round with my baby and spending weekends going hiking while she studies the plants and Jas splashes in the streams.

The civil celebrant asks for the rings, bringing my mind back to the present, and I shake the dreams and wishes away as I hand each ring to the bride and groom.

I GRAB another beer at the bar and that's when I sense her. She's been everywhere I am today, and my control is wearing worryingly thin. I'm certain she purposely brushes against me as she leans against the otherwise empty bar to order a drink, testing my resolve. "They're so happy," she whispers.

I glance across in the direction she's looking. "Yep. They deserve it. Toby's been so far gone for Cassia for a long time. He has to be the happiest man on Earth today, knowing he finally has her."

I drop my gaze to her; the woman who's taken up permanent residence in my mind she may as well have a key. A wistful expression blankets her face as she leans her back against the bar. "I want that. I thought I had it, but looking at Toby and Cassia, I realize I didn't even have a smidgeon of it."

My heart stops. "What do you mean? Surely you were happy at some point."

"Yeah, I guess. But not on such a deep level." She tilts her chin toward her sister and new brother-in-law. "Not like that. It was never like that." She swipes at her cheek, and I notice a few tears have escaped.

I place my beer on the counter, take her hand in mine, and lead her away from the bar and prying eyes. Nobody needs to see Cassia's sister crying at her wedding. I drag her outside the tent and down to the dock, so she can have her tears in private. As soon as her feet make contact with the wooden planks, she breaks down with her arms wrapped around her middle like some type of shield. She stands with the city lights shimmering across the water in front of her, her body trembling. Her loneliness and pain call to mine, and I can't leave her to cry alone so I pull her into me, trapping her arms between us as I wrap mine around her. I drop my lips to the top of her head, soaking up the softness of her hair and the wild-flower scent she always seems to have.

She tilts her head back to look up at me, the tears in her eyes shimmering in the moonlight. I don't know what possesses me, but I drop my head closer to hers. Our gazes lock for a long moment. I desperately want to close the distance and take that first kiss but I need to hold onto my last shred of restraint. She presses up and our lips meet for the first time in a soft swipe, sending sparks pulsing through my body like an electrical current. Her lips are softer than I ever imagined, and when her tongue darts out and slides against my closed mouth, I groan at the sensuality of it. Taking advantage, she slides her tongue inside my mouth and I work to hold myself still—she's more courageous than me. Her tongue slides against mine, allowing me to experience her taste and it's exquisite—better than anything I could have imagined.

But I can't reciprocate. If I do, I'll take her here against the damn boat shed and she deserves more than that. A hell of a lot more.

Violet pulls away, her eyes narrowed as she looks at me. "Kiss me back, Shane."

"No," I grunt like a damn Neanderthal. It's like her kiss has stolen my ability to communicate like a man. I draw my hips away from her body so she can't feel what her bravery's done to me.

She presses in, touching her lips to mine more firmly. The minx is determined to get me to give in, but I won't. I push her shoulders back slightly.

I fucking can't.

She draws back again. "But I want you to," she whispers harshly, annoyance in her tone. "I *need* you to. Kiss me."

"No." I shake my head to make my point.

"Don't make me beg, Shane. I've been emotional all day, and I'm vulnerable and horny right now and I want you. I need you to want me too." She exhales a harsh breath.

I can't admit to her that I *do* want her. It will be the invitation she's looking for to take things further between us. I've already let it go too far and I'm too messed up for her. I like a good fuck as much as the next guy, but she's not the woman you fuck and walk away from.

She's the woman you beg to marry you.

She's the woman you know you won't be able to live without once you sample her.

She's the woman who deserves a man who's whole.

That's not me.

She runs her finger down the lapel of my too-tight jacket, sending my pulse racing. I'm not sure how much more I can take. I don't want to hurt her, but I can't have her either.

I am only a man.

And she's so goddamn sexy without even trying on a normal day. Today, she's the most beautiful woman I've ever seen. "C'mon, Shane. Give me what I want ... *You*," she breathes against the base of my throat before pressing her lips against my burning flesh. She runs her hands down my pecs and over my abs, toward the waistband of my pants making my muscles twitch and my dick punch against my zipper. "Let me see the masterpiece beneath these clothes. I want to touch you."

Her words are like a bucket of icy water, and I snatch her hands in one of mine and growl. "No. I'm no masterpiece, more like a monster," I growl. Women think they want me. I look whole on a superficial level, but my scarred and damaged skin hidden beneath this suit represents the damage I hide on the inside. She doesn't need to see that.

Nobody needs to see that.

She draws back, her eyes catching mine. "Yes, I do. You're no monster." Pushing up on her toes, she presses her lips to mine in a rush and I groan with need, my cock growing ever harder and fighting against the fabric of my pants for freedom.

My control slips.

In a moment of weakness and a lack of self-preservation, I return her kiss as I walk her backward and press her roughly against the timber siding of the boat shed. Her back thuds against the unforgiving surface and a gasp escapes her pretty mouth. "You want me to kiss you? To fuck you?" I murmur hotly, my lips brushing her heated skin with each word.

She pants, her breaths licking the exposed skin at the base of my neck. "Yes. That's exactly what I want."

I press my heavy cock against her soft stomach, barely holding back my groan. "If I give you what you want, it can't be anything more than a dirty fuck in the dark," I whisper roughly in her ear as I weave my fingers through her silky hair.

She sucks in a breath, nodding her head slowly. When I draw back to scan her features in the limited light, all I see is pure unadulterated need.

Need and lust.

I can give her a release and then walk away.

I reinforce my shields, then deliberately slide my hand beneath the long slit at the side of her dress—the one that's been taunting me since she walked down the aisle toward me—and glide my rough fingers along the smooth flesh of her firm thigh. Touching her like this is better than I anticipated. *So much better.* A rumble escapes my lips at the feel of her beneath my fingers.

Her body trembles beneath my touch and the softest of moans escapes her puffy lips. How will I go back to never being able to touch her like this again? *Perhaps I should stop.* I've already let it go too far.

Fuck! I can't stop. Not yet. I don't want to.

She spreads her legs slightly, inviting me higher in anticipation of me reaching the apex of her sexy thighs. I take my time, enjoying the firm silkiness beneath my palms; she has sensational legs, and I want to trace every single inch of them with my tongue—memorize every part of her while I have this chance. My fingers reach the lace at the edge of her panties, my breaths stall in my lungs, and I glide the back of my hand over the front of her mound. Her heat scorches my flesh as her arousal wets my knuckles. Her pussy's going to be so fucking hot and wet. My dick thickens further, doing its best to break through the steel barrier of my zipper. Hooking my fingers in the elastic at her hips, I murmur, "I need these out of the way." I slide the panties slowly down her legs and then tap each foot to remove them from her. I don't need them tangling around her ankles and putting her off balance.

"Shane. Hurry up. Give me what I need," she whispers, desperation thick in her voice as her fingers slide into my hair.

I draw back quickly, almost losing my damn balance—I can't have her touching any part of me. Standing, I collect each of her hands in mine, then twist her panties around her wrists, binding them together, and then loop the fabric over a hook, designed to hold an oar, directly above her head.

"Wh-what are you doing?" Vi pants, her chest rising and

falling heavily. Her gorgeous tits heave with each breath, almost pushing her peaked nipples through the purple fabric.

"Making sure you keep your hands where I want them. No touching, Blue, or I stop," I say firmly.

She nods and I drop to my knees. I wish it wasn't so damn dark so I can see her clearly since this is the one and only time we'll ever be together. The muscle in my chest squeezes at the thought of some other man touching her like this, seeing her like this. Making her fall apart. I need to make the most of this moment and I'll have to work out a way to deal with it when she finds the man that's perfect for her and Jasmine.

Wedging my shoulders between her thighs, I slide one finger through her sweet lips from back to front and groan at the slickness already there. "You're so fucking wet and ready for me and I've barely touched you."

Violet moans, wordlessly pushing her hips forward as much as she can. I run my nose along her slit, savoring the heat and soaking up the scent of her arousal—storing it in my memory. My tongue slips out without any direction from me to taste her for the first time.

Heaven. Fucking heaven. I knew it would be.

Once. This is happening one time. I need to keep the reminder at the forefront of my mind. So I need to be in the moment and soak up every incredible second while it's happening.

"Mmm. Fucking delicious," I tell her as she rubs against my mouth, trying to hurry me along but I want to take my time. "Keep still or I'll stop." I push her hips back against the timber siding and insert one digit, then a second into her tight hole. She's so damn hot and wet that my fingers make a squelching sound, making my cock so hard it's almost painful. "Fucking juicy," I groan. Keeping my eyes locked on her, I watch closely, reading her body's cues so I can make this good for her. I want her to remember this moment. Her breasts rise and fall rapidly as she writhes beneath my touch like she can't get enough—*so damn stunning*.

"Shaaane, more!" She moans as I push in deep. "Harder, please." Her tight, hot walls contract around my fingers, welcoming me and inviting me deeper. I hear the hook rattle as I push my fingers in and out of her snug hole with a steady rhythm, ensuring I pummel her pussy lips each time. I'm not being gentle and her sounds of pleasure fill the stillness of the night as I lead her toward her orgasm, ensuring I pay special attention to the front wall with each thrust. The scent of her arousal fills my lungs with each panting breath I take and if it weren't so dark, I'm sure I'd be able to see the flush rising up her body as she heats. I bet she looks magnificent when she comes. What I wouldn't give to be able to see her clearly, but this is a one-time deal. A rock settles in my gut at the thought because if things were different … if I wasn't so fucked up … this is where I'd live. On my knees, spending my days and nights worshiping this goddess.

"Mmmm," I hum as I swirl my tongue around the bud peeking out at the top of her slit. Using tight, firm circles, I tease her, making her body shudder and her leg tremble on my shoulder as the heel of her shoe digs into my back, right over one of my surgical scars, and I wince. I relish the pain and use it to keep me grounded as Violet quivers beneath my tongue. I try to absorb everything about this experience so I can look back on this moment and remember the time I was privileged enough to touch her. To taste her.

"Oh, my God. Shaaaane!"

She whimpers as her walls tighten, and her clit pulses beneath my tongue. My cock begs for release—to feel her tighten and pulse around it. To feel her snug heat. I slow my strokes as she rides out her release on a sigh, her head dropping back against the timber siding. I bet she'd look fucking beautiful spread out on a blanket beneath the stars, breathing heavily, her tits quivering from her release.

Her body sags and I reluctantly remove her leg from my shoulder, carefully place her foot back on the deck, and take a few moments to smooth out her dress, prolonging my touch as long as possible while I work to get my body back under control which is going to take a mammoth effort. Climbing back to my feet, I take in Violet as best I can beneath the moonlight; sated from her orgasm, with heavy eyes and a half smile touching her lips. I'm certain if the moon was full, I'd be able to see the flush of her cheeks and a sheen of sweat glistening on her beautiful sun-kissed skin.

I dig my hands deep into my pockets to stop myself from reaching for her—from threading my fingers into her silky hair once again and pulling her still-swollen lips back to mine. To stop myself from kissing my way to her breasts and tracing every single inch of the beautiful pillows with my goddamn tongue. God knows I want to touch her every-fucking-where, but I can't. I shouldn't have let this go as far as it did but my control only stretches so far and she's so damn tempting. Stepping back, I give myself the space I need to breathe without her addictive scent overwhelming my senses but it's all over my face. I lick my lips, relishing the taste of the one woman I can't have. That I don't deserve.

Violet's head snaps down, her eyes narrowed. "Where are you going?"

"Back to the party. I gave you what you needed." I spin on my heel.

"Hey, how about releasing me?" she snaps.

Shit! She has me so discombobulated that I completely forgot I secured her hands to the hook above her head. I take the three steps back to her to release her, holding my breath to guard against her addictive scent, I untangle her panties and place the silky fabric in the palm of her small hand. Then drag the key to Toby and Cassia's back gate out of my pocket and dangle it in front of her.

"Here's the key you need." If I give it to her now, I can avoid her for the rest of the evening.

She takes it from me with shaky fingers and confusion all over her face and if I'm not mistaken … hurt. "Thanks," she mumbles.

When I turn to leave, her hand snaps out and grips my arm. "What about you?" She points down at the tent in my trousers with her chin.

"What about me?" I shrug.

I can't go there with her. Not with her. Anyone but her.

I shake off her hold and take long strides toward the side of Oliver and Kate's massive home feeling like an asshole and a coward for leaving Violet standing in the dark. Once I'm out of sight, I watch her gather herself as she holds herself up against the side of the shed to pull her panties on and I can almost feel her pissed-off vibes from here. Watching her stalk her way back to the tent, I breathe easier when she makes it inside. I need to calm my cock down before I can return to my best friend's wedding.

I can't believe I just crossed the line.

Not just crossed it, I *obliterated* it.

I'm fucked!

Completely and utterly fucked because I know I'm going to want to do that again and I can't.

16

SHANE

We arrive at John Wayne International Airport, and true to Peta's usual form as Toby's manager, we're whisked through the back corridors so we can get through the airport with a minimum of fuss. Toby's carrying Daisy while Cass holds Poppy's hand, and I'm following behind pushing the cart with our luggage. I'm reasonably certain Cass has packed for a month-long vacation rather than for the week we'll be spending in Disneyland for their honeymoon.

They quickly climb into the waiting car while I transfer our bags into the trunk, and then we're on our way to the resort. Toby is never one to stay in fancy places when he tours but he's gone all out for his girls for this honeymoon vacation. Toby said I didn't need to come with them, that Peta could organize a local security company, but after my poor decision-making where Cass was concerned, I wasn't prepared to let them out of my sight. You could say I have trust issues. My goal is to stay out of their way as much as possible so they can enjoy their family honeymoon. Working in the background is what I prefer anyway, ensuring the spotlight remains where it should be ... on Toby.

I open the door to the three-bedroom suite and Poppy runs inside with wide eyes and an even wider smile. She's signing too fast for me to keep up with her but Cass and Toby are having no problem following Poppy's excited conversation. I roll the luggage trolley inside and situate each suitcase in the correct room. Toby insisted that I stay in the suite with them, which made sense when he was single and on tour, but now it feels intrusive. As happy as I am for my best friend, watching him with his family is painful—a reminder of what I'll never have.

When I step into the living area, Cass is making coffee. "Would you like one?"

"Sure. Thanks."

She sets out an extra cup for me and drops a pod into the machine. "The girls want to head straight down to the park." She chuckles. "They don't want to waste a single second."

"No point being at Disneyland and hanging out in the hotel."

"Exactly." She hands over my coffee. "I have to admit, I'm just as excited. I always wanted to come here when I was a kid. Violet and I used to wish for a trip to Disneyland every birthday."

My heart thumps heavily at the mention of Violet's name and like Pavlov's dog, my mouth waters at the memory of her coming on my tongue last night.

Of her sighs and moans.

Of the look on her face when I walked away.

And if I breathe in deeply enough, I swear I can still smell the scent of her sweet arousal.

I fucked up so badly.

I've probably destroyed the friendship we've slowly built over the last two years, and if I have, I'll be left adrift without Violet and Jasmine to anchor me. I hate to admit that even though I don't see them all that often, I've come to depend on having them in my life. I know I don't deserve them, but that knowledge hasn't stopped me from dreaming about more.

The outer door slides closed, and I'm ripped from my thoughts. Toby saunters in with Poppy and takes his coffee from

Cass with a kiss. "Poppy wants to get down there. She already has a plan of what she wants to see today."

Cass signs to Poppy as she speaks, "You need to have a snack first. Sit with Daisy and have your juice and fruit, please. Then we'll start our adventure."

Poppy nods excitedly, signing, "Okay." Then, she heads straight for the small table and her sister.

I ROLL ONTO MY BACK, exhale a long breath, then throw the covers off. Climbing to my feet, I slip through the sliding door to the balcony. The park is quiet with limited lights illuminating the grounds for security purposes. Most people were respectful of Toby today with only one couple stopping to ask for a selfie. Fans tend to give him his space when he's with his family which is always unexpectedly considerate. Some days I still have trouble wrapping my head around how much Toby has changed from the boy I knew in high school. I'm so damn proud of the success he's achieved. He has no trouble going after what he wants and working toward his goals.

He's living his best life. Especially now he has Cass and the girls.

While I'm just going through the motions.

I've done a lot of work on my mental health since the explosion and losing Wyatt, but some days I feel as though I'm standing still. I may not feel as undeserving of my survival as I once did but my progress has definitely stalled, and sometimes I feel as though I'm going backward. But mostly, it feels like I'm wasting the chance I've been given.

I just don't know how to take those final steps to feel worthy when I've made so many damn mistakes and let so many people down. The task feels impossible. It feels too heavy.

Could it be possible to break through the final barrier that's holding me back? To go after what I truly want.

My mind automatically flies to the woman who is never far from my thoughts. Can I be the man who deserves Violet and Jasmine?

Standing in the darkness, I wonder ... am I ready? Will I ever be ready?

Sometimes I think I am, but then I go and do a dick thing like I did last night. It would have been the perfect opportunity to demonstrate to Violet that I care for her more than what I showed. But would she want me if she knew about my past and how I'm not the man she thinks I am?

Pushing away from the railing, I step inside and make my way to the mini bar. I study the selections Toby organized to have on hand and settle on a bottle of my favorite bourbon that he always stocks for me, then grab a glass to take back to my room. Padding back across the thick carpet, I quietly close my bedroom door and take a seat in the club chair near the window. Pouring a couple of fingers, I tip the glass to my lips, and take a drink, enjoying the warmth as it slides down my throat.

When I think about when things began to improve for me, it was when I met Vi and Jas. I know it seems cheesy but they brought color back into my world. Jasmine's sweet and trusting nature melted me from the very first moment she turned her smile on me, and the connection I felt to Violet the minute I laid eyes on her knocked me flat on my ass. I've done my best to keep some boundaries in place but the girls have been slowly wearing me down at every turn in the same way the waves shape the coastline. It's been a gradual process and hardly noticeable as it's happening but when I look back, the change is obvious and I wonder how I missed it.

But can I trust myself to keep Violet and Jasmine safe?

Or will I end up hurting them? Or putting them in a vulnerable situation?

I wouldn't survive if anything happened to either of them. I *know* I wouldn't. The devastation would be too great. I barely survived losing Wyatt. My entire body shudders and my stomach twists at the notion of a world without the girls who have grown to mean so much more to me than I ever intended. I swallow the rest of the bourbon and refill my glass as I contemplate a million *what-if* questions.

I grab my phone, pull up Violet's number, and hover my thumb over the green button ready to confess my feelings to her.

To tell her that I need her.

How much I want her.

Tipping my head back to look at the ceiling, I close my eyes with a frustrated growl and toss my phone to the bed. She deserves better than a long-distance confession in the middle of the night fueled by alcohol-induced bravado.

Doesn't mean I don't still want her.

Spreading my legs out in front of me, I run my tongue over my bottom lip, imagining her taste is still there. My cock wakes as I close my eyes and relive the events of last night. The way Violet took the first step and pressed her soft lips to mine.

She's always so damn brave.

So much braver than me.

I rub my hand—imagining it's hers—along the length of my quickly hardening dick. Something I could never allow to happen in reality. Fuck, what would it feel like to press the head of my cock against her mouth ... to slip it past her lips and slide across her tongue until I reach the back of her throat. My dick swells until it's hard as steel. Slipping my hand beneath the waistband of my sweats, I wrap it around the thickened length and squeeze. My pulse quickens and my breaths grow shallow at the thought.

Dropping my head back on the couch, I tug on my balls, then stroke up my length, swiping the palm of my hand over the crown, imagining watching it disappear into Vi's sexy mouth. I stroke and tug, swipe and squeeze, pushing my hips up as I close my eyes and visualize Vi falling apart above me. The way her body shuddered, the way she pushed her hips forward, the way she took what she wanted.

So damn hot.

Increasing the speed and pressure, I tighten my grip as I stroke my cock from base to tip. Every atom in my body lights up and feels as though it's rushing toward the base of my spine. Electricity shoots through my veins and thick ribbons of cum erupt, landing on my stomach, making a damn mess. *Fuck, that was fast!* If she were here, I'd be fucking embarrassed.

And now I feel like a piece of shit. I resisted doing this very thing last night because I'd promised myself I wouldn't disrespect her more than what I already had. What I did at the wedding was bad enough, but now this. I don't know how I'll ever look at her and not want her now that I've had a taste and relived the events with my heavy cock in my hand.

"THE GIRLS WANT to spend the day down at the pool. Daisy needs a little downtime today, so it works for everyone. Are you okay with that?"

I shrug. "It's your vacation. Whatever you guys want to do, I'm there. You know that."

Toby claps me on the shoulder and studies my face. "I still like to check in with you. It should be a quieter day, and I have an inkling the girls will want to nap this afternoon. I thought maybe you and I could head down to the bar for a quiet drink. I feel like we haven't caught up in a while."

"Sure. Sounds good." I wonder if he's picking up on the guilt I'm feeling for what I've done with his sister-in-law *and* with her in mind. Am I that easy to read?

We head down to the pool area and make our way to the quiet spot away from other families the hotel organized for us once I told them of our plans today. Poppy wastes no time jumping into the water, splashing loudly as she surfaces causing Daisy to squeal with delight. Cass carries her down the sweeping steps into the pool as Toby dives in from the opposite side, swimming a fair distance under the water before surfacing next to his family. I watch closely from the edge of the pool ensuring Toby and his family can have their fun in peace.

"Hey, why don't you come in?" Toby calls.

"Nah, I need to keep an eye on things." Plus I'm not ready to expose my scars and have to answer all the questions that are bound to stem from that. Maybe one day, but not today.

He splashes water at me but I step back with a smirk just in time to avoid getting wet. "Come on. Loosen up and have some fun."

I tip up my chin at him. "I am having fun watching your daughters climb all over you."

"I wouldn't have it any other way," he calls and I know he wouldn't. He's living his dream right now.

After a while, Poppy climbs out of the pool and signs, "I'm hungry."

I speak as I sign back, "Sit down, I'll get you a snack."

Cass ordered snacks to be delivered poolside, I just need to let them know we're ready for them so I call the number I was given for the kitchen and organize the delivery. Cass climbs out of the pool using the steps and wringing her hair on the way, while Toby lifts Daisy out at the side and climbs out by pushing himself up on the edge. The food arrives and we all enjoy the fresh fruit and cheeses under the shade of a cabana.

After a short break, they head back into the pool but Daisy starts to get grumpy and even Poppy's looking tired so Toby calls an end to the fun and we all head back up to the room so they can shower. As Toby predicted, the girls and Cass opt to take a nap, leaving Toby and me to head down to the bar for a drink.

The waitress stops at our table to take our order and even

though she does a double take when her eyes land on Toby, she maintains her professionalism which I know he appreciates.

"I can't believe we go home in a few days. This week is flying by so fast."

"Is your honeymoon all that you wanted it to be?"

He thinks on that for a minute, then begins to nod as his lips slowly stretch wider. "It's been better than I thought it would be. Mom, Dad, and Rose were insistent on leaving the kids behind and just having this time for Cass and me, but I'm glad we didn't listen. It's been amazing to share this experience as a family."

I nod. "You guys are certainly having a great time together, and you're giving the girls some amazing memories." I swallow past the lump in my throat. "You're a really great dad."

Toby swallows and nods his thanks as the waitress returns with our drinks, wedges, and chili wings. We thank her and both take a drink then grab a wing each—we're quiet for a while as we enjoy our snack.

"Do I need to order you another bottle of bourbon?" Toby asks out of the blue with raised eyebrows.

I swallow the food in my mouth. So he noticed but hasn't said anything. I wonder what's been going through his mind since I've technically been on the job and shouldn't have polished off almost the entire bottle on the first night. "Nah, I'm good," I answer as nonchalantly as I can manage, doing my best not to squirm beneath my best friend's gaze.

He studies me a moment longer, his blue eyes cataloging my features. "Everything okay with you?"

Do I feel guilty that I've never opened up to my best friend? You bet your ass I do but at this point, I have no idea where to start. I've never shared about my time overseas. He has no idea about the explosion that claimed my best friend and left scars so deep I doubted I'd ever recover. He knows not to broach the subject about that time in my life but I sense his hurt that I haven't willingly opened up to him. However, I don't think his question is about that and is directed at my more recent mood and whether it has anything to do with his brand-new sister-in-law and niece. I lift my shoulder and drop it, taking a drink of my bourbon to buy myself some time as I study his expectant expression. "Yep."

His face drops and disappointment washes over his features momentarily but he hides it quickly. "Good. I'm glad. I worry about you." I open my mouth to interrupt but he holds up his hand, and I close it again. "I know you don't want anyone to worry about you because that's your job to worry about us, but you're my best friend. You can't ask me not to care about your well-being."

I swallow past the guilt and drop my eyes to our food. I'm not sure what I've done to deserve such a true friend but in this moment I don't feel worthy. "I have trouble sleeping since I returned home. The army trains you to become a light sleeper, ready to leap into action." His eyes widen with surprise that I've shared something with him and I feel like an asshole. "Add in the stuff that happened over there, I also ... uh ... have night terrors." I rub my hand over the top of my head and clench my jaw. "Both things aren't conducive to a decent night's sleep."

His eyes trace my face and concern colors his features as he nods slowly. "Have you talked to anyone about it?"

"Yeah, I've been seeing a psych. I'm making steady progress and the night terrors don't happen as often as they used to."

He nods. "If there's anything I can do ..."

"Thanks. I know."

Sensing that he's pushed me enough for one day, he changes the subject. "I'm gonna call Finn when I get home and set up a time to play my new stuff at *Brady's Pub*."

"Let me know what you need." I know Finn's a good bar manager and he'll organize extra security, so there won't be much I'll need to do beforehand.

"Sure."

And just like that, my best friend reads the situation and my mood, guiding the conversation away from me as we chat about the logistics of his impromptu gig.

We head back up to our room and Toby excuses himself to join Cassia in their bedroom, and I shut myself away in my space.

I drop into the club chair by the window and drag my phone out of my pocket. What happened with Violet has been playing on repeat in my mind, and I'm concerned that things will be irreparable when I get back. Pulling up her number, I shoot her a text.

ME

Are we okay?

17
VIOLET

My phone buzzes as Tristan drives us back down the hill to the office so we can go home. Since Saturday, every day has felt like it's dragged. My mind keeps replaying my *private* time with Shane on the dock against the boat shed over and over, making the ache in my lady parts annoyingly persistent. I dig it out of my pocket, unlock the screen, and groan when I see *his* name. My heart stutters.

SHANE

Are we okay?

Tristan glances at me. "You okay?"

I take a sip of my tea from the cup Shane bought me, trying to buy some time. "Yeah."

Dropping my head back against the headrest, I blow out a breath and roll my eyes up to the roof of the cab. I don't know how I'm going to face him when he returns from Disneyland after what happened at the wedding. I threw myself at the man, and while he didn't immediately push me away, him walking away so easily after what he did to me stung like a bitch. It had taken me two years to recover my pride after Allen, and even though it took a hit on Saturday night, I refuse to let Shane's rejection drag me back to the depths that my ex-husband sent me.

I'm better than that.

Stronger.

Even though, I still feel weird about seeing him again. Will he acknowledge what happened between us or will he act like it didn't happen at all? Should I act like nothing happened? I have no idea what to do.

Tristan pulls into the parking lot and shuts off the engine, then turns toward me in his seat. "You've been off all week. If you need to talk about anything, I'm here. I know I'm not a chick, but I'd like to think we *are* friends after all these years."

Tristan is one of the few men in my life who shows me that not all men are assholes, and I love him dearly for that. He studies me carefully, waiting for me to spill my secrets but I don't feel comfortable talking to him about what happened with Shane. And I don't think he would really want to hear about it either. I may talk to Quinn about it because I feel like I need to work through the emotions surrounding what happened. I think I'll stop in on my way home and talk to her about it before I respond to Shane's text.

SHANE

Are you ignoring me, Blue?

I've never been given a nickname before, apart from my family shortening my name to Vi, and to be honest, I've wondered why that was. I thought maybe I wasn't a nickname kinda girl, but then Shane calls me Blue and I love it so much. I love the implied intimacy of it and the way he says it in that deep rumbly voice of his. Even when he uses it in a text message, it sends my girlie parts into overdrive.

SHANE

I can see you read my message

I groan and Tristan sighs. "C'mon, I wanna get home at some point. Spill."

"It's just Shane."

His eyebrows shoot up. "Oh yeah. He was the best man at the wedding, right?"

"Uh, yeah." I can't believe he remembered, though I shouldn't be surprised.

He studies me closely, and I can practically see his mind working to put the pieces together. Finally, his lips spread slowly until he's beaming at me. "Don't tell me the maid of honor hooked up with the best man." He pushes at my shoulder gently, and heat races up my neck and into my cheeks. "You did. You dirty girl," he says playfully while smirking at me. "About time you got back on the horse"—he wiggles his eyebrows—"or maybe I should say the D!" He bursts out laughing, and I whack his arm playfully.

"Cut it out." But I can't stop my giggles, and they bubble up at his hysterical laughter. "Such a damn comedian." I roll my eyes at him. He struggles to get himself under control but finally manages it, wiping the tears from his eyes. *Asshole.* "I'm not talking to you about this," I snip.

"Aww, why not? I'm hurt." He pouts like the child he's being right now.

"I don't know how Nicole puts up with you," I snark.

"C'mon, don't be like that." His humor fades away. "You can talk to me about this. God knows you had to listen to me enough times after Nic had Noah. It really helped us. I promise I can be a good listener."

That's true and he didn't hold anything back and it didn't make things awkward between us. I liked that I could help him and Nic find their way through those early weeks and months. How much to share, though?

He rests his arm on the steering wheel leisurely, waiting for me to speak. Twisting in my seat, I face him. "I'm not telling you everything that happened, but ..." The relief is almost instant, knowing I'm about to share at least some of what happened. I've felt as though I'm about to burst by keeping the events inside. "Saturday was an emotional day for me. I'm not sure why, but on and off, throughout the day I was close to tears. After all the formal stuff was over and we were dancing and hanging out at the reception, I got teary again and Shane pulled me outside away from the other guests. I guess so I could have my moment in private." Tristan's face softens, and he nods for me to continue. I look down at my lap because I don't think I can look at him when I tell him the next part. "He pulled me in and hugged me and it was exactly what I needed. Before I knew what I was doing, I kissed him. Well, one thing led to another and before I could return the favor, he was gone. And I don't know what to make of that. And now ... now I feel weird."

"Hang on." His tone makes me look back up at his face. "Did he kiss you back?"

I think back to Saturday night. "Uh, yeah. Reluctantly at first, then I felt him give in and things went from there."

"And then he walked away from you when it was over?"

Embarrassment floods me and I swallow past the rejection I felt when he left. "Yeah," I murmur, turning my attention toward the windshield. "I was pissed, but mostly embarrassed."

"Was he turned on or do you feel like what he did was out of some type of obligation to make you feel better?"

"Well, if the tent in his pants was any indication, I'd say he was turned on. He seemed to like what he was doing if his enthusiasm was anything to go by." I slap my palm to my forehead. That was way too much information.

Tristan's silent for so long that I glance at him. His expression is thoughtful as he rhythmically taps his fingers on the dash. "I think he's fighting his attraction to you."

My jaw drops. "Do you think so?" I'd hate to get my hopes up. Even though I've decided to pursue him, it'll certainly make things easier if this attraction goes both ways.

"I do."

"What makes you think that?"

"Uh, everything you just told me and the stuff you've told me about Shane in the past. From what you've said, he's *hands-on* with you if you haven't noticed." I look at him in confusion. "He *comforts* you when you're having a hard time." He wiggles his eyebrows again. "And you've said yourself how great he is with Jas."

Hmm, all true. "Why do you think he's trying to fight his attraction? We're both adults *and* single."

Tristan lifts and drops one shoulder. "Dunno. That's what you'll need to work out." He climbs out of the car, then rests his arm on the door, and leans back in. "Maybe he thinks he's not good enough for you." He closes the door and I climb out of the car.

"Or maybe he doesn't think I'm relationship material. I couldn't keep my husband happy."

Tristan stomps around to my side of the car before I can blink. Tension bunches his shoulders and he looks murderous. "Don't ever let me hear you talk about yourself like that again. That was all on Allen." I open my mouth to argue and he shakes his head. "I don't wanna hear it, Vi. Whatever you're about to say is bullshit, so don't say it. Don't even think it." I deflate, my argument dying on my tongue with his no-nonsense tone. He wraps a strong arm around my shoulder and tugs me into him. "You were too good for him." He kisses the top of my head and releases me but it's nothing like the way Shane does it when he's comforting me. "You okay? I need to get going."

I nod and give him a shaky smile. "Yeah. Thanks for the chat."

"Any time."

"Give Noah a hug from me and say hi to Nic."

"I will. Make sure you show JJ the photos you took today." He winks at me, and I burst out laughing. He means the photos of him doing a one-handed handstand on top of Crows Rock. He was so proud of himself and I have to admit his strength is impressive. However, it all fell apart when an *Alameda whipsnake* popped its head out of a crevice in the rock face surprising him and he lost his balance in spectacular fashion. Of course, I captured it all on my phone. Jas will get a kick out of seeing the photos.

"I'll send them to Nic. I'd hate for her to miss out." I chuckle as he climbs into his car, and I throw my backpack into mine, then place my insulated cup in the console. He tosses me the bird out of his window, then reverses and drives away leaving me shaking my head. I don't know how he did it but he just completely turned my mood around one-eighty degrees.

I grab my phone and read Shane's messages. We've messaged occasionally to arrange things over the years or to check on each other, which is exactly what these texts are. So why am I reluctant to respond this time? Who cares if he made me come harder than I ever had before against the boat shed? We're both adults. People have orgasms all the time. It was nothing special.

Yeah, right. I roll my eyes at myself at my own bullshit.

I hit respond.

ME

Yeah, we're good

SHANE

Good

I'll see you when we get back

Can't wait to see the transformation of the pool area

Sorry I'm not there to help

I'm glad he's not here to help. It would have been too soon and too weird to see him tomorrow.

ME

Mom and I have it covered

SHANE

Still sorry

I blow out a long breath, then toss my phone onto the passenger seat and head for home. I'm going to need my A-game to make sure I keep my cool when he returns. No more throwing myself at the sexy bodyguard. I need to take things slowly so I don't scare the man away. Maybe if I say it enough times between now and his return, I'll be able to stick to it.

18

VIOLET

was exhausted when I got home, but when Cass called at the last minute to invite me to watch Toby play tonight, I found my second wind. It's not often I go out on a weeknight, hell, it's not often I go out but I couldn't resist Cass's invite to *Brady's Pub* to watch Toby play. And while I enjoy Toby's music and am looking forward to seeing my sister, there's someone else I'm looking forward to seeing even more. I only hope I can control myself and not be awkward since this is the first time I've seen him since the wedding.

I bounce down the steps, toss my purse across my body, and find Mom curled up on the couch with her latest book which she places in her lap when she notices me. "Jas is asleep and I'm heading out. I'm not sure how late I'll be home, so don't wait up." I lean down to kiss her forehead. "I'll see you in the morning."

She smiles softly. "It's so nice to see you going out. Have a great time and give the others a hug from me. Do you want me to take Jas to school in the morning so you can sleep in?"

I shake my head. "No. I like to take her on the days I can. Thanks, Mom."

She smiles softly at me. "Okay. Enjoy yourself and I'll see you in the morning."

"I will," I call as I head out the door, grabbing a jacket on the way.

Climbing into my car, I head for Quinn's place. I invited—well *told*—her she was coming with me tonight. I need her to finally meet Shane so she can share her thoughts about him and whether she thinks there's a chance he's interested. I trust her judgment completely; years ago she told me to stay clear of Allen but I didn't listen, and I paid the price. He had me completely convinced he'd changed his ways—how wrong I was.

As soon as I pull into Quinn's driveway, she steps out of her front door, looking amazing in skinny jeans and a red sweater that makes her long blonde hair look like spun silk. Her dad wouldn't let her cut her hair shorter when she was young and now that she can cut it, she doesn't. She says she likes it long. People would be shocked to know what she does for a living when she's dressed in regular clothes.

She drops into the passenger seat. "I thought I was going to be late. I had to rescue a rattlesnake from an elderly lady's shed and by the time I drove far enough out of the suburbs to release it, I got caught in traffic coming home." She finally takes a look at me and smiles. "Oh my God! We look like we're going to a Christmas party with my red sweater and your green blouse!" We break into giggles as I reverse out of her driveway.

"Take a breath, Quinny." She takes an exaggerated breath and blows it out. "Thanks for rushing home to come with me tonight." I can't keep the tinge of nervousness out of my voice.

She shifts in her seat to face me fully. "Tell me you're not nervous. Because that's the vibe you're giving off right now." I open my mouth but before I can answer, she adds, "Don't lie to me either."

Damn it. That's what happens when you have a friend who

knows you so well. "I was going to say, *of course not*, but I am. Really nervous."

She pats my thigh. "You have nothing to be nervous about."

I try to push down my jitters. "It matters to me what you think of Shane. I'm worried I've made him into something he's not and you'll see through his façade and I'll kick myself because I missed the red flags yet again."

"I'm pretty sure you know what to look for now and to trust his actions rather than his words."

I hum. "Yeah, well, his actions spoke pretty loudly when he walked away from me after the wedding." I ended up calling Quinn and talking through the whole thing with her; I gave her all the details I left out when I talked to Tristan.

Quinn sighs. "I already told you. I agree with Tristan. I think he's holding back, maybe trying not to cross the line since you're his boss's sister-in-law. I'm looking forward to watching the dynamic." She raises an eyebrow, then smiles wide. "I can't wait to see Cass. It feels like forever since I've seen her. I can't believe she's married to Toby Summer." She fans her face. "I've seen pics of Toby with his *bodyguard* in the background and I have to say, your taste has certainly improved. So there's that." She winks at me as she snickers.

I pull into the parking lot down the street from *Brady's Pub* and we climb out of my car. Quinn hooks her arm through mine and we make our way to the front door. Thank God there isn't a line yet, the temperature's dropped rapidly over the last few days and it's too chilly to have to wait outside. Obviously, news hasn't got out yet that Toby's playing or it would be a completely different story. When we open the heavy door, I'm surprised by how crowded it already is. "I guess we didn't beat the crowd after all!" I shout to Quinn over the noise.

"At least we beat the line."

I nod. "Yeah. I don't like the idea of having blue toes."

We chuckle as we make our way through the crowded bar area

and take the stairs down to where the bands usually play. I've been to watch Toby play here a few times but this is the first time I've dragged Quinn along because she doesn't enjoy being in crowded spaces like this. If I thought the upstairs was crowded, then the downstairs is nuts. Toby hasn't even started playing yet and we can barely make our way through the crowd.

"Cass said she'd hold a table at the front right-hand side of the stage!" I shout, then grasp Quinn's hand and try to weave my way to the stage. Pushing my way through the throng of people is hard work and feels futile. I don't think I've moved more than a couple of feet.

Suddenly, the crowd parts like the Red Sea, and I almost lose my balance without people pushing at me from all directions. When I look up to work out why we suddenly have space to move, I spot Shane stepping toward us, giving everyone the evil eye as his jaw flexes. I sigh with relief and Quinn squeezes my hand; when I glance back at her, her grin is obnoxiously huge.

Shane steps closer, bending down close to my ear. His warm breath ghosts across my flesh before the deep rumble of his voice. "Hey, Blue." There he goes again with my nickname in that sexy voice of his.

"Hey. Thanks for the rescue."

"Anytime."

"How did you know I was even here?"

"I was keeping an eye out for you coming down the stairs. I didn't want you to have to struggle through all the people." He takes my hand and guides me through the parted crowd. I squeeze Quinn's hand tight to make sure I don't lose her as we make our way toward my sister, who's exactly where she said she'd be.

When we arrive at the table, Shane releases me and I instantly miss the security and safety of his hold. Cass leaps up from her chair and wraps me in a tight hug. "I'm so glad you could come," she says as we sway side to side as if we haven't seen each other for months not less than two weeks. "Thank you so much for our new plants. The area looks stunning."

I chuckle. "You already thanked us."

"Yeah, but I only thanked you over the phone so I couldn't hug you." She spots Quinn over my shoulder. "Quinny! You came."

She releases me and pulls Quinn in for a hug. Toby stands and repeats the process with me, then I introduce Quinn to Toby and Shane. Toby greets her warmly with a hug but Shane tips his chin with a quiet hello. Four of us settle around the table and Toby slides two glasses of Moscato across the table, while Shane stands behind me, keeping an eye on the crowd and I wonder if he's planning to stand sentry all night. I guess he has to work in a situation like this and can't join in.

While Quinn and I sip our wine, Toby and Cassia tell us about their honeymoon, well, the parts they can share, and before we know it, it's time for Toby to hit the stage. He grabs the mic and the crowd grows louder; the excited buzz in the air becomes overwhelming. I don't know how he does it but I guess he would have grown used to it by now; this is nothing compared to the size of the audiences he usually performs for.

"Thank you for coming out tonight. Your support means more than you'll ever know. I recently returned from my honeymoon—" The crowd goes wild. Wolf whistles and applause fill the room to an almost deafening volume and Toby chuckles, giving Cassia a wink. "With my wife and daughters. Man, I'll never get tired of calling this woman"—he holds his hand out to Cass—"my wife. I have to be the luckiest man on the planet." The crowd cheers loudly and when I look at my best friend, she reminds me of the heart eyes emoji with the way she's leaning forward resting her chin on her hands. "Anyway, I wanted to see what you thought of some of my new material." He strums a few chords on his guitar, and a hush moves through the room.

Toby plays song after song after song, keeping us all mesmerized with his deep raspy voice and meaningful lyrics. More wine is placed in front of me and Quinn, while Cass's water is refilled and the water jug is placed in the middle of our table. Our empty glasses are removed, and when I try to catch the waiter, he moves too fast to hear my request for an empty water glass. I push away to stand, ready to go after him, but Shane's strong hand lands on my shoulder, keeping me in place. "What do you need?"

"I'm driving, so I don't want another wine. I was going to ask for a water glass like Cass."

He listens intently, then nods. "I'll get it for you. You stay here."

He disappears into the crowd before I can thank him and Quinn leans in close. "I approve."

My lips tip up but I'm not sure how she's made her judgment so quickly. He's barely said two words which isn't unusual for Shane; it's not like he talks a lot. "Why?" I'm genuinely curious.

"Well"—she holds up her fingers and points to the first one—"first up, he was keeping an eye out for your arrival and instead of letting you battle the crowd, he did it for you and I get the sense he'll step into any battle for you." She points to the second digit. "Number two. He could stand anywhere close by and have a clear view of the room for his *bodyguard* duties, but he's standing right behind you. Like he's protecting you personally." I scoff at that and she shakes her head with a grin. "I'm serious. He's like a brick wall between you and everyone else." She taps her third finger. "Thirdly, you just had to make a move like you were going to stand and he was so in tune with you that he noticed immediately and then went to sort out your drink. Seriously, the man is ticking all the boxes."

When I glance at my sister, she's nodding in agreement with Quinn. I'm not sure how she could even hear what was said over the music. "I agree. Shane usually stands at the side of the stage to keep an eye on the crowd, never at the table. He only does that when you're with us."

"What? Really?"

Cass nods her head. "Really," she says, leaning in closer. "And he never leaves Toby's side when we're in situations like this. Tonight, he left it twice and both times were for you." My sister winks at me, and Quinn nudges my arm with hers.

"See," she says as she widens her eyes.

Well, maybe I *do* have a chance. I breathe a sigh of relief because if Quinn could see all of that in a short amount of time, then I haven't been making shit up in my mind which makes me feel better. And well ... Cass has been not-so-subtly encouraging me to make a move for a while now.

Shane returns to the table with a second jug of iced water and a couple of glasses. "Here ya go, Blue. Mind pouring me a glass?"

"Of course." I pour us both a glass of water and hold the jug up to Quinn who shakes her head in the negative. Cass's glass is still full so I don't offer her anymore. She must be driving tonight since I haven't seen her drink a single glass of wine.

After several more songs, Toby finally finishes his set for the night and stands to loud applause and wolf whistles. "Thank you for coming out tonight. I hope you enjoyed my new material, which I'm hoping to take on tour soon." I glance across to Cass but she's too focused on her hunky husband to notice. I've never seen my sister so happy, she almost seems to be glowing. Toby drops into the empty seat next to Cass and leans across to land a scorching kiss on my sister's lips. I turn away from them to look at Quinn, my heart aching for what they have. Quinn fans her face and winks at me, mouthing *hot* before bursting into giggles. God, I love her.

When Toby and Cass finally separate, Quinn and I congratulate Toby on his new songs, sharing which ones were our favorites.

"Thanks, ladies. Do you guys want to get outta here and grab a quiet nightcap? Cass and I found a great little coffee shop not far from here which is open late."

I look at Quinn to check if she's up for it because I already dragged her along with me. She might be ready to head home. "Sounds great. Let's get away from the noisy crowd."

While Toby packs his guitar into its case and chats to one of the managers, we stand and wait for him to return. I mentally prepare myself to fight my way back through the crowd but Shane guides us to the back area of the stage where there is another staircase leading upstairs to a door that opens outside. Thank goodness too, because I wasn't looking forward to the crush of people after Toby's performance.

When we breach the door, I inhale a deep breath of cool night air and shiver. I left my coat in the car in my excitement to see Shane ... *I mean* my sister.

Quinn doubles over in laughter. "Shit, I'm not even a rock star, and I felt like one the way we snuck out the back like that," she gasps out in between her chuckles.

Toby huffs out a laugh and points over his shoulder with his thumb. "That was nothing, right, Shane?"

"Definitely one of the tamer evenings," he agrees as he drapes his jacket over my shoulders without a word. His warmth surrounds me and his spicy scent fills my nose and it's almost as good as being wrapped up in his arms. When I look up at him questioningly, he shrugs. "You shivered." Like that explains everything and to him, it's as simple as that. Someone needed something, and he provided the best way he could.

I catch Quinn watching out of the corner of my eye and she shoots me a wink. "Okay, I'm ready to get my hot chocolate on. Where's this coffee shop?"

"Follow us. It's walking distance from here," Cass says as she loops her arm through Toby's.

They lead us out of the alley and past a cute French patisserie with white and yellow striped awnings over the large windows. I look up at the sign: *Harry's House of Crêpes and Croissants*. It must be new, I don't remember seeing this place here before. I admit it's been a while since I've been to *Brady's*. Mom loves crêpes, so I'll have to bring her and Jas here for breakfast one weekend. We cross the street and sure enough, the lights of a coffee shop come into view a couple of blocks away. Shane moves away from me to talk to Toby about something and Quinn takes the opportunity to lean in close. "As I said, I approve."

Before I can respond, she quickly scoots behind Toby and Cassia through the door Shane is holding open, leaving me to bring up the rear. Once I'm inside, I start to slide the jacket off my shoulders, but Shane's there, sliding it back into place. "You keep it. I can grab it off you next time I see you." He places his hand on my lower back and guides me toward the back of the coffee shop to the booth where the others are waiting for us. I slide into the booth next to Quinn and Shane pulls up a chair to sit on the end, angling himself so he can see the doorway. His eyes catalog the room and the few people occupying tables. It's something he does whenever we're out together.

Toby collects all of the menus before anyone can take a look. "This place has the best apple pie and homemade ice cream. It's almost as good as my mom's. Would you agree, Shane?"

"Definitely, this apple pie is probably the best I've tasted other than your mom's." He turns to me and Quinn. "I second the apple pie and ice cream."

"Well, that suits me because I freaking love apple pie," Quinn chirps.

"Hot chocolate all 'round?" Toby waits for us to respond and when we all agree, he taps the table and stands. Shane follows suit and they make their way to the counter to place our order.

Cass follows them with her eyes and I sigh internally as I watch Shane's ass flex in his jeans.

"What was that sigh for?" Quinn's question breaks me from my ogling.

"Huh, what?"

"You just sighed as you watched the guys walk away," my best friend points out.

I guess I didn't sigh internally after all. "Just admiring the work of art that is Shane's ass."

Quinn turns to study him and the longer she observes, the more she nods. "Yep. I approve of that man from the top of his head to the bottom of his feet and everything in between. He seems very well-proportioned." She wriggles her eyebrows up and down and we all break out into giggles like a bunch of high school girls at an all-girls school sleepover.

"I wouldn't mind finding out one of these days," I mutter.

Cass's eyes widen. "Does this mean you're actually gonna do something? It's not just talk?"

I draw in a deep breath and push my shoulders back. "Yep. I just need to work out how to go about it."

Cass and Quinn gesture for me to come in close and we huddle together. The two of them come up with a plan that I think may just work if I can dig deep enough to find my confidence. I mean I asked for what I wanted at the wedding, surely I can do it again.

"What are you ladies gossiping about?" Toby's voice breaks through our planning and we pull apart like kids who have been caught eating the last cookie and putting the empty package in the pantry.

"Just making some sister plans," Cass says breezily.

19

SHANE

I GRAB MY KEYS AND HEAD OUT THE DOOR. ON THE WAY to *The Bunker*, I run through how incredible Violet looked last night and how difficult it was to keep from touching her. It seems since tasting her, my resolve to keep things platonic is shaky at best and I don't know how to deal with it. I only have to look at her and my mouth waters like a trained response since sampling her at the wedding—almost like I can still taste her on my tongue. Even thinking about her now has me salivating and my cock thickening.

Pulling into the parking lot, I climb out of my car and instead of going in through the front doors, I head through the side gate so I can avoid talking to anyone. I'm not in the mood today. I want to get lost in some manual work without any interruptions and hopefully, being a Thursday will mean I have the place to myself. The workshop door is closed which is promising for a little solitude. Dragging open the heavy steel door, I breathe a sigh of relief when it's dark. I pull the door closed behind me and switch on the lights, pushing up my sleeves as I make my way to the workbench.

Sifting through the collection of discarded bikes, I choose one and begin dismantling it, ensuring I put all of the parts into the tub so nothing gets lost. Turning on my favorite Spotify playlist, I get lost in removing the decals and sanding the frame but it doesn't take long for my thoughts to return to Jasmine and Violet.

As I work with light, smooth strokes to remove the paint, I think about how sweet Jas is and what an asshole her father must be to have kicked his wife and daughter out. If Jas were my daughter, I'd do everything in my power to show her how much I loved and wanted her. I wouldn't kick her and her mother out of our home; I'd hold them as close as possible. My blood boils and my hand begins to move in rough, heavy strokes over the steel frame as I think about the asshole who hasn't reached out at all to his ex-wife and daughter.

What sort of man discards his family like that? A low-life piece of shit, obviously. My father may have mentally checked out on us, but he didn't leave, so I guess I should be thankful for small mercies. I have to wonder, though, is it better for the family if a disinterested father walks away or is it better if he stays? Both will have a negative impact. My mind whirls through various scenarios of *what-ifs* in my situation. How would life have been different for me and Mom if Dad had left or kicked us out? Would I be a different man than the one I am today?

Having him ignore me and Mom left deep fissures in my heart and on my soul. His behavior was the catalyst for years of self-doubt and created the belief that I'm not a good enough son. Would I still have that self-doubt if I'd grown up without him? Or would my wounds be different but just as painful? Would I still be questioning my ability to be a decent father and husband?

As I've grown older and watched Toby create a family, my thoughts have turned more toward the probability that I would be a shit father because that's the role model I've had. But then, when I'm with the girls and Evan, I always want to give them the best version of me. I want to forget all the shit in my past and be present and engaged with them in the moment. The problem is that there are also many times when I get caught up in the past and check out for a while, which isn't conducive to being a stable parent, further supporting my beliefs.

On the other hand, I look at Violet and Cassia whose father walked away and never looked back. Both women are strong, but there is a sense of loss and longing for something they never had. I watched Cass struggle with the fact that her father wouldn't be there to walk her down the aisle like so many other women get to experience. And even though Cass and Vi's bond with their mother is loving and strong, I've seen the way they watch Kate and Mr. S interact with longing looks. Their penchant for initially choosing assholes and being wary of Toby, who's a decent guy also suggests some deep internal scars.

So, which is better?

I run my fingers over the smooth steel frame of the bike as I try to make sense of my thoughts. Grabbing a dry cloth, I wipe away the dust and smooth out a spot of rust at the base of the frame.

I don't think either situation is ideal. A man needs to step up and be there for their family. End of story. And if he can't be everything his family needs him to be, then he shouldn't contemplate being a father in the first place. Simple.

The door bangs against the workshop as I wipe away the dust I just created and when I look up, Nix is striding inside. He tips his chin. "Hey."

I return the gesture. "Hey. You're not usually here this early in the day."

"Yeah, well, I needed to think, and working on the bikes is good for that." He selects a bike from the collection and starts to dismantle it, dumping the parts noisily into an empty tub, frowning the entire time.

Interesting. It seems I'm not the only one who uses the technique. "I'm here if you need someone to listen," I offer. Not that I'd be much help, but sometimes it helps to verbalize things and God knows he's had to listen to me enough over the years.

His head snaps up toward me and his eyes bore into me before softening. "Yeah, well, my wife served me with divorce papers this morning."

His words hit me like a freight train. Fuck! "Shit. I'm sorry."

He shrugs; his posture that of a defeated man. "I guess I deserve it."

"Do you want a divorce?"

"Fuck, no!" he almost shouts. "I love her and my family with everything I am," he says softly.

"Then fight for her. For your marriage. For your family." *Listen to me giving relationship advice.*

"I want to, but I've done sweet fuck all to deserve her since I got back, and I have no idea where to even start."

"I haven't been in your position, but I would think you need to show her you're the man she needs and wants. Step up and be the man she deserves. The father your kids deserve." *Maybe I should take my own advice.*

He grunts and we both fall silent, each lost in our task. I don't know what else I can say, and he came here to work through his thoughts, so I leave him be.

CLIMBING the stairs to my apartment—because the elevator's broken again—groceries hanging from my fingers on one hand, I look up as my foot lands on the final step to my floor and I freeze. My breath catches in my lungs when I spot the woman whom I can't stop thinking about leaning against my door, and my eyes automatically drop to her bare legs and hungrily trace every smooth inch until I reach the bottom of the jacket she's wearing.

My jacket.

For all intents and purposes, she appears to *only* be wearing my jacket, but that's probably wishful thinking on my part. However, if it's true, if she's only wearing my jacket and nothing else, then I'm totally and utterly fucked. I won't be able to resist her. It would be impossible.

She's so engrossed with something on her phone and unaware of her surroundings that she hasn't noticed me—which pisses me off. I could be anyone. Granted, I'm the only tenant on this floor at the moment, but she doesn't know that. "What are you doing here, Blue?" My voice comes out gruff as I make my way toward her.

She straightens where she stands, sliding her phone into her purse. "Returning your jacket." She gives me a coy smile, which isn't coy at all. She has to know the tilt of her lips is sexy as fuck and their silent invitation is impossible to ignore or refuse.

"Is that so?" I surge in, trapping her against the door with my much larger body, using my hips to keep her in place. Finding my control at the last second, I slow my approach and run my nose up the side of her neck. She tilts her head to the side with a sigh, giving me better access and I place a tender kiss against her pulse point, which is hammering a fast rhythm, mirroring mine. Her fingers glide through my hair, and her sudden touch is enough to bring me back to my senses and I pull away abruptly. I lock my eyes with hers, noting the blue I adore is being swallowed by her pupils. "No touching, Blue. That's the rule, or I stop."

Her eyes flick between mine for several seconds, then she nods once and drops her hands by her side. "Okay," she murmurs as she leans forward, searching for my lips. I trace my eyes over her features as I dip down and our lips make light contact—a slow swipe of soft flesh against flesh and I barely suppress a groan at the feel of her silky lips against mine once again. This wasn't supposed to happen but it truly was inevitable. Her tongue tentatively slides along the seam of my mouth, and I open, granting her access. She doesn't waste a single moment, flicking her tongue into my mouth. At the first sweep of her tongue against mine, I stop holding back. I slip my free hand behind her head, collect her hair in my fist, guide her mouth where I want her, and deepen the kiss without warning. She moans into my mouth, and even though she's not touching me with her hands, the touch of her supple body pressed against mine feels better than any previous lover's caress. Something I haven't had for a long ass time.

Her heart pounds against my chest triple time as our tongues sweep against each other. I tighten my fist and tilt her head to suit my needs, savoring her delicate flavor. She complies beautifully beneath my touch, and as our breaths combine, I get lost in her. In her taste and the feel of her lips against mine. This is everything I shouldn't be doing but damn if I can stop. This is a battle I'm tired of fighting, and I lay down my resolve at her feet.

Her ringtone sounds from her purse, and I unwillingly drag my mouth away. She slowly opens her eyes beneath a frown, her lips puffy from our kisses. "Why'd you stop?"

I dip my head toward her purse. "Your phone."

Pink stains her cheeks and awareness lights her eyes. "Oh, right." She digs in her purse but it stops ringing before she can fish it out.

While she sorts out her phone, I unlock the door to my apartment and drop my groceries onto the kitchen counter, putting the cold items in the fridge and freezer and willing my dick to calm the fuck down.

Vi rushes in, quickly shucking my jacket from her shoulders

and tossing it on the back of my couch—exposing her matching deep green lace bra and panties. Fuck, I was right! My dick wakes all the way back up at the sight of her sweet curves presented in green lace like a damn gift. She's so focused on the voice on the other end of the phone that she's completely oblivious that she's stripping in front of me. She's all business now; there isn't a hint of teasing in her actions, and her worried expression has alarm bells ringing loudly. "I'll be there as soon as I can. Thanks for calling." She disconnects the call and drops the phone on the counter. "I have to go."

I watch her carefully. She's not panicking, but her movements are efficient and I can see worry tightening her features. "What's going on?"

"Jasmine's been crying, and no matter what her teacher does, she's inconsolable. I need to collect her," she tells me without looking up as she drags out a pair of leggings and a sweater from her purse. If I weren't shocked by her words, I'd be impressed at how much she can fit in that bag of hers. She quickly drags the leggings up her legs, then slides her sweater on and pulls it down to cover her body. I step behind her and release her silky hair from being trapped beneath the soft fabric, then grab my car keys.

"I'll drive."

Her eyes rise to my face. "I can drive. I'll need to take her home, and it'll be easier in my car." She slides her feet into her flip-flops and then tosses her purse over her shoulder.

"Yeah, but you can't comfort her if you're driving. I'll come with you so I can drive, then catch an Uber home."

"Okay, but I can drop you back here." She nods once, then heads for the door with me hot on her heels. And even though she's in full mama bear mode, I would say she's even sexier now than she was when she was smiling coyly at my door less than ten minutes ago.

We climb in her car and within seconds, Violet's pulling out of the parking lot and onto the road, and I briefly wonder how I missed her car at the far end of the parking lot. "What do you think's upset her so much? She doesn't come across as a kid who cries for no reason." I don't think I've ever seen her cry. Oh, there was that one time when she fell and skinned her knee when we were all at the park, but I'd expect her to cry when she fell over.

Violet shrugs. "I have no idea but it must be something serious to make her cry like that."

If someone hurt my angel, I'll make their life a living hell. I don't care that they're possibly five years old. We pull into the parking lot, quickly climb out of the car, and make our way to the office to sign Jasmine out of class. When we finally reach Jas's classroom, Mrs. Diamond steps out to speak with Violet.

"I'm so sorry I had to call you. No matter what we do, we can't get her to settle, and she's too distressed to tell us what happened. She doesn't appear to be injured because we've checked her carefully."

"That's okay. Today's my day off, and I wasn't doing anything important." My eyebrows shoot up. Fucking around with me isn't important. *Good to know.* I stop myself from taking her words personally. Nothing would be more important to Violet than getting to her daughter, and that's one of the reasons I find her so damn appealing. So I swallow down my hurt ego and tune back into what's going on right now. "So what was happening when she started to cry?"

I don't know how Vi's being so calm. I just want to get to my girl and make sure she's okay. To see for myself that she's not injured and to find out what's gone wrong.

"It was lunchtime. The kids were playing." The teacher looks at a loss.

"Can I see her, please?"

Mrs. Diamond nods and steps back to open the door. Violet steps inside, and I'm unsure if I should wait outside or go in with her. She's so focused on getting to her little girl and doesn't give me any guidance.

"Are you coming in?"

My attention snaps to Jas's teacher. "Is it okay if I do?"

"Of course. If your name is Shane, she talks about you all the time. I gather you're very important to her." My heart swells from her words, and I tip my head and move inside. Violet's crouched down holding Jas close, but as soon as Jas spots me over her mother's shoulder, she escapes her hold and makes a beeline straight for me.

"Shane!" she sobs. I bend down and scoop her into my arms. I hold her close and study her puffy red eyes and runny nose while I gently stroke her sweaty hair away from her face.

"Who hurt you, Angel?" I ask as I make my way out of the classroom. Vi says something to the teacher, and then we make our way to her car. Jas's little body shudders in my arms and my protectiveness over her roars to life.

Vi opens the rear door and I dip down to situate Jas in her car seat, but her hold on my neck tightens so I stand back from the car. "I was hurt," she stutters.

"Where?" I run my hands over her arms and legs but can't find any injuries.

She holds her hand over her heart. "Here." My body locks into place and I look squarely at Violet who sucks in a sharp breath and places her hand gently on her daughter's back.

I tighten my hold on her. "Is your heart still hurting." Shit, should we go to the hospital?

She pulls back from me and looks me square in the eyes. Her puffy eyes break my heart. "It feels better now."

I turn to Vi, who's paler than I've ever seen her. "Should we take her to the hospital?"

"What made it hurt?" Vi asks her gently.

"When I was hanging upside down on the monkey bars, Jason pulled my hair and told me that I don't have a daddy because I'm ugly." She sniffles and swipes her hands across her rosy cheeks.

Every muscle in my body locks tight, and I want to spin on

my heel and go back to Jas's class and have a word with Jason. I don't fucking care that the kid's five. I catch Vi's eyes and she subtly shakes her head at me so I draw in a deep breath and blow out the anger that's pounding through my system ready to explode. I guess I should be thankful that her heart's fine, it's her feelings that are hurt. "You're not ugly," I say through gritted teeth. "Not on the outside and not on the inside. You have a beautiful heart which makes you beautiful all over. If anyone's ugly, it's Jason."

"Shane!" Vi glares at me.

"You think I'm beautiful?" Jas says at the same time.

I smile at Jas. "Yeah, I do." Then I frown at her mom. "What?"

She tilts her head to Jas and widens her eyes slightly. "We don't speak ill of peers."

I blink at her, then realize she was trying to speak to me in a way that Jas wouldn't understand but I would. I tip my head to acknowledge her. I guess it doesn't really set a good example if I say negative things about other people to her. *See, shitty parenting right there.*

"How about we grab a milkshake?"

The little girl in my arms wipes her hand beneath her nose and smiles at me and it's like the sun's come out of hiding. "Can I get a chocolate milkshake?"

"Of course." I smile at her, then turn to Violet, hoping I haven't crossed another line. "What flavor will you have, Blue?"

Her relieved gaze lifts to mine. "Uh ... maybe caramel if they have it."

"Sounds good. Let's go get milkshakes."

Jasmine wriggles in my hold and I loosen my grip so she can climb down my body and get in the car. I ensure her seatbelt is secure, then close the door quietly. When I turn toward Violet, she's smirking at me. "You wanted to pummel a five-year-old. I could see it all over your face."

"Well, yeah. He hurt Jas." I take her hand in mine and slip the car keys from her grip. Does she not realize I'd do anything to protect her and her daughter? Even from five-year-old bullies.

She shakes her head as her lips tip up. "Pretty sure that would be frowned upon."

I shrug as I help her into the car, slide the seatbelt into place, and make my way to the driver's seat. We make our way through light traffic to Pier 7 and *Declan's Diner*, arriving there in record time. Being a weekday afternoon, the parking lot is mostly empty. Vi climbs out of her car and retrieves Jasmine from the back seat just as she's probably done a thousand times before. I trail behind them for a few steps, but I don't like the distance so I bend down to scoop Jasmine up and place her on my shoulders enjoying her happy giggles and squeals of delight. Other people passing by grin at us, probably assuming we're a family so I grip Violet's hand in mine. She glances down at our joined hands, then up at me—her silent question clear.

I have no answer for her—the struggle to keep my hands to myself is exhausting—so I keep walking toward the diner without another word. We get to the diner and I duck so Jasmine doesn't bang her head on the door frame, then lead the girls to an empty table in the far corner where I can watch people entering and leaving. Old habits die hard.

"Okay, what's everyone having?"

Jasmine's eyes light up, and if I hadn't seen her tears for myself, I would never have believed she was so upset only thirty minutes ago. "Can I please have a chocolate milkshake and some fries?" She looks up at her mother for her approval, and Violet smiles.

"Of course. Shane, what do you want?" *Is that a trick question? I want a lot of things, none of which I can have but it doesn't stop me from wishing.* Violet climbs to her feet, but I beat her to it.

"You sit, I'm getting this. What would you like?" I command.

Her eyes widen and she swallows thickly. "Uh, I'll have a caramel milkshake and some fries too, please?"

I nod and then head toward the counter where I place our

order and pay for it, ensuring I keep my eyes on the girls at all times, then return to the table.

"Mommy, I need to go to the bathroom."

Vi stands—"Sure."—and Jas slides out of the booth. "Won't be long."

"No worries."

My phone rings, so I dig it out of my pocket. My landlord's name lights the screen, I press the green button and answer, "Shane Sutton."

"Hi, Shane. Roger here." The tone of his voice as he says the simple greeting puts me on immediate alert. I straighten my spine and reply with a grunt. "I'm calling regarding the letter I sent you two months ago about the building renovations. Work will begin on Monday, and it's been decided to start from the top floor and work down. That means I need you out for a month."

"What the fuck. It's Thursday. I need more notice to find somewhere to stay and move my stuff out."

"Yeah, sorry about that. The contractors only let me know last week."

"Last week!"

"Yeah."

I rub my hand over the top of my head and clench my jaw. "So, you could have told me last week and given me more time to sort everything out."

He sighs. "I guess. I've been busy."

"Busy?" I feel like a damn parrot, repeating everything he says.

Jas and Vi slide back into the booth, giggling about something, but I just want to smash Roger's head right now.

"Yeah. Make sure everything's out. I'm not taking responsibility for any damages to your property during the renovation." He pauses. "And when your lease renews, rent will increase twenty-five percent."

"You can't—" The call disconnects, and my words are left on the tip of my tongue.

Vi's hand lands on top of mine, and when I raise my eyes from my phone, her concerned expression eases my anger. "Are you okay?"

"Yeah." I clench my teeth.

A waitress brings our order to the table and Vi slides her hand from mine, leaving me untethered. "I have a chocolate milksha—"

"That's mine!" Jasmine almost shouts, eliciting a grin from the young woman.

"Chocolate is my favorite, too." The waitress winks at Jas.

She distributes the rest of the drinks and food, then leaves the three of us alone to enjoy our snacks. Not that I can enjoy mine because I'm so pissed at my damn landlord, each fry that lands on my tongue tastes like cardboard. While Jas is busy dipping her fries into her milkshake, Violet turns to me. "Who were you talking to on the phone?"

"My landlord. He's renovating the building and they've decided to start from the top floor and work down. I need to be out before Monday."

Vi's sculpted eyebrows dip low over her eyes. "Can he do that?"

"Apparently he can. He sent letters two months ago, telling us about the plan to renovate but he never gave us a timeline of when it was gonna happen."

"What are you gonna do? Where will you stay?"

"He can stay with us, Mommy!" Jas shouts with glee and both our heads snap toward the little girl who innocently invited me into her home.

"Uh ..." Vi turns to me. "I guess you could stay in Cass's old room if you get stuck."

"Yay! Will you read me my bedtime story and help me harvest the vegetables for dinner?"

"I don't think he'll be moving in today, Jas."

"Thanks for the offer. I can stay in a hotel or something."

"Definitely not. If that's your only option, then you should stay with us. Mom's going away for a sustainability seminar next week, so she won't even be there."

My eyebrows shoot up. "I'll need somewhere to stay for a month which feels like I'll be taking advantage."

"Please, Shane." Jas peers up at me, her eyes filled with hope. *How will I keep my hands to myself if I'm living under the same roof as the bombshell sitting opposite me?* "Please."

I pause, my eyes skipping from mother to daughter as I weigh my options. I could help out with Jas while Rose is away. I swallow past the lump in my throat and try to slow the rapid tattoo of my heart but it's no use. "Sure. What's our first story gonna be?"

She rolls her eyes to the ceiling as she thinks, and I know I've royally fucked myself over by taking Jas and Vi up on their offer when I look at Vi and the way her lips are tipped up in a sexy smirk. "*The Lorax* because you bought me that book, so you should read it to me."

"Sounds good."

SHANE

I close the lid on the last box I have and look around my bedroom. I'm going to need more boxes. Who knew I'd collected so much shit over the years?

A knock on my door echoes through my almost completely packed apartment, breaking the silence. I grab my long-sleeve T-shirt and throw it on, then head for the door. When I pull it open, my eyes land on Violet bent over collecting several flat boxes. Each time she tucks one beneath her arm another slips from her hold and falls to the floor. She's so focused on her task that she hasn't heard me open the door. I raise my arm to hold onto the door-frame and watch her struggle.

"Oh for fuck's sake!" she snaps at the boxes.

A chuckle escapes my lips before I can stop it and she bolts upright, spinning around to me at the same time, bringing us face to face. "Hey, Blue."

"Uh, hey." I watch her throat bob when she swallows and her eyes unapologetically trace my body. "I thought I'd bring these boxes over." She tips her chin down to the stack of boxes scattered in front of my door. "I've had them sitting in the garage from when I moved into Mom's and don't need them anymore so I thought you might be able to use them."

"Thanks." I bend down and scoop up the flattened boxes.

"I have more in the car," she offers as I take the boxes inside. "I'll grab them quickly."

"I'll help." I grab my keys and lock my door, then we head downstairs together.

"So, is the landlord gonna fix the stupid elevator while he's renovating the building?"

"I hope so. He's planning to increase the rent by a significant amount, so the elevator better be fixed." It's not like I have control over that. Maybe I should use this time to find somewhere else to live. Somewhere that charges more reasonable rent.

We make it to Vi's car and I collect the rest of the boxes as she makes her way to the front passenger door. When she steps back, she holds up a paper bag. "I thought I'd bring you lunch."

Not only did she think to bring me boxes to help with my move, but she also brought me lunch. "Thanks. You didn't need to go to so much trouble. I'm sure you have plenty of other things to do."

"Nope." She closes her car door with a swing of her hips and steps closer to me. "I had planned to take photos this afternoon but I can stay and help you pack."

My eyebrows shoot up. "Photos? Of what?"

As we climb the stairs back up to my apartment, she explains her photography to me. "I photograph different aspects of the park I work at and other parks around us. I started doing it after my marriage fell apart as a way to live in the moment instead of my thoughts spiraling out of control with a bunch of *what-ifs*." This is something I admire about Violet. She goes through difficult experiences but doesn't let them drag her down. She picks herself up and pushes forward.

"I'd like to see your photos sometime." We enter my apartment and I dump the boxes, then we both wash our hands. "You should go take photos. I can manage here." We unwrap our subs and I take my first bite. "This is great. Thank you."

"No problem." She shakes her head. "I can stay and help until it's time to pick up Jas from school. I like to pick her up on my days off. I always feel as though I neglect her on the days I work, so I like to make up for it on the days I don't." There's a smidgeon of self-loathing in her voice that doesn't belong there.

"You're a good mom."

She scoffs. "I wish I was. I've failed my daughter in the biggest way possible."

I'm not sure how she can possibly think she's failed Jas. "How so?"

"Last night she said something while we were coloring at the table. We've never spoken about what happened with Allen because I figured she was so young at the time and didn't realize what was happening. But last night"—she swallows and rubs her palm over her heart—"I found out that she understood a lot more than I realized. She remembered that he called her *ugly*." Her eyes grow glassy and she steals her gaze from mine. "I need to work out a way to help her deal with it all so it doesn't fester."

Who the fuck calls their kid ugly? Fury bubbles up inside of me like lava but I do my best to extinguish it for now so I can comfort Vi. Instead of tracking down her deadbeat husband and teaching him a lesson, I wrap my arm around her shoulder and tug her into my side. How can I keep my distance when I can plainly see she's in pain? I want to comfort her and take all of the bad shit from her shoulders. I want to protect her so nothing bad ever weighs her down again. "Do you think what happened at school yesterday triggered the memory?"

She shrugs. "Probably and I hate that she even has that memory. I was hoping she hadn't heard my argument with Allen and that she'd been spared his hateful words." She sighs like the weight of the world is resting on her shoulders. "I'm thankful she seemed okay when I took her to school this morning and she was fine when I left after my presentation to her class."

"She seemed okay when I left you guys yesterday but I still

wanted to pummel the kid who made her cry. And now, learning that her father called her that, I'm not gonna lie, I wanna smash something. Preferably his face." Even thinking about how upset she was yesterday makes me see red all over again. "Why the fuck is he calling her ugly?"

"She has a port wine birthmark across her stomach. Allen always made comments about it but on that last day ..."—she turns her face away from mine—"he actually referred to her as ugly." Vi looks back at me, her sorrowful eyes appear to be barely holding back her tears. "I'm guessing yesterday when she was playing on the monkey bars, Jason probably saw it." She tucks her hair behind her ear. "Most kids don't understand what it is and even some adults can be assholes about it." The derision that enters her voice when she talks about the adults—Allen—sends my hackles rising. I want to punch the asshole in the throat. The bastard.

I squeeze her shoulder. "Yeah well, she's a beautiful girl all the way to her beautiful heart, and I know you'll work things out. I'm happy to help in any way I can." She looks up at me and sucks in a sharp breath. I'm not even trying to hide the affection I have for Jasmine. "I love your little girl," I say softly. I've probably said more than is appropriate but anyone who meets Jas would fall in love with her. "I'd do anything for her because she only deserves happiness." I leave off that *she* only deserves happiness too but it's true.

She smiles tremulously. "Thank you. She loves you too just in case you hadn't noticed." We both chuckle and she pauses, studying my face closely.

I furrow my brow and narrow my eyes. "What?"

She points to my face. "You smile and laugh more than you used to when we first met. I like it."

My good mood threatens to vanish, but I grip onto it with both hands as I remind myself it's okay to find joy and be happy. "Thanks. I'm trying."

"Well, if I can help keep that smile on your face, just let me know." I nod and we return to eating our subs.

"So how did your presentation to her class go this morning?"

She giggles. "They all want to be park rangers so they can save the trees and flowers and all the animals now. So I'm guessing it went okay." My body fills with pride and I'm sure it's shining in my eyes, the feeling is that powerful. "What?"

"I'm proud of you."

It's her turn to be confused as the crease appears between her brows. "Why?"

"You're inspiring a whole new generation of kids who are gonna care about what happens to the environment. That's a big deal, Vi."

A rosy flush stains her cheeks and she drops her eyes from mine. "Thanks." She screws up the paper from her finished sub. "Allen always thought my job was a waste of time," she whispers as she glances up at me, then rises to her feet. The more I learn about her ex, the more I want to smash his face into a concrete pillar. "I need to get going if I'm going to be back in time for school pick-up." I narrow my eyes at her sudden change. "Are you sure you can manage here?" she asks on her way to the front door, keeping her back to me.

I quickly follow her and gently trap her between the door and my body before she has a chance to open it. I drop my head close to her ear and whisper, "Are you okay?"

She keeps her head forward and I hate that I can't see the emotion in her eyes. She's always been so easy to read when I can see the cobalt of her irises. "Yeah. I just need to get moving or I won't make it to the park and back in time."

"You sure that's the only reason you're running?" Her body stiffens, and I draw in a breath of her wildflower scent.

"I'm not running."

"If you say so." I step away from her body and grip the door-knob. She stands straight, stepping away from the door so I can open it. "You go take your photos." *Before I stop being a gentleman.*

"If you change your mind, just shoot me a text. Jas and I can come back after school and help you pack," she says, still not making eye contact, as she heads out the door.

"I'll be fine. Thanks for the boxes, and I'll see you over the weekend."

TOBY LIFTS one end of the couch while I grab the other. "You know I could have hired movers for you, and we could be down at the pub grabbing a beer instead."

I chuckle. "Yeah, I know, but this way I get to make you sweat."

"I sweat plenty when I'm doing *things* with Cass," he answers without missing a beat and my eyebrows shoot up in surprise. He doesn't normally share any private information about himself and Cass.

I roll my eyes. "Yeah, well we can't all work up a sweat that way."

"You could, bro, if you pulled your head out of your ass." I take the stairs backward, making sure I take each step carefully—I don't need to break my damn neck—and keep my lips sealed. "This is the perfect opportunity for you to get up close and personal with my sister-in-law." He wriggles his eyebrows up and down like a comedian.

If he knew I've already been up close and personal with his sister-in-law, he wouldn't be on my case right now but I don't kiss and tell. She doesn't deserve to be gossiped about behind her back —even if Toby is my best friend. "Shouldn't you want the best guy possible for your sister-in-law instead of encouraging me to go after her?"

I honestly don't know how I'm going to keep the lines drawn

between Vi and me while I'm living with her. I'll have to stay out of the way as much as possible. I can see a lot of hours spent at *The Bunker* in my future. Toby's in between tours at the moment, so he doesn't even need me because he dedicates his time to his family by being a stay-at-home dad for Daisy and Poppy while Cass runs her florist shop. Maybe Nix has some work to keep me busy.

He stops suddenly and I almost drop my end of the couch. "Are you fucking serious right now?" he snaps, pulling me from my thoughts. "You *are* the best possible guy for Violet and Jasmine."

"Yeah, I'm fucking serious right now. Are *you* for real?" I snap back.

"Of course I am. Look, I know your dad wasn't great and things at home weren't what they should have been when you were growing up and even now. I also *don't* know everything that happened while you were away and I can only imagine the shit you saw and the horrible things you had to do. I *know* your time away changed you. I'd have to be fucking blind not to notice and even then the changes in you would be impossible to miss." Hurt and disappointment flash across his face and guilt swirls in my gut that I still haven't fully opened up to my best friend about my time overseas. I'm not ready to tell him everything. "But Shane, and hear this my friend, you are the best man I know. Violet and Jasmine would be lucky to have you in their lives, and you deserve to have them in yours. I mean it."

My stomach drops, and my heart thuds in response as I swallow around the lump that's taken up residence in my throat. All I can do is nod and begin moving again. What can I say? I don't deserve his belief in me after what happened to Cass.

We load the couch onto the back of the truck and Toby rubs his hands on his jeans. "Well, that's the last of it. Do you need to do anything else here?"

"I'll quickly do a last check to make sure I have everything and lock up. I'll meet you at Rose's." Where the girls are spending time together. Rose insisted that I store my belongings in the garage to save money rather than pay for a storage unit. Like opening her home to me wasn't generous enough. She's even refusing to take any rent money but I figure I can do chores and maintenance around the house and buy the groceries to help out.

Toby heads toward his car and I call out to him, "Thanks, man." He nods at me. "For everything."

He pauses at the door of his black Impala. "Promise me you'll think about what I said."

I draw in a deep breath and blow it out. "I'll think about it." Considering that's all I've done since I met Violet and Jasmine, it's not a lie.

I PULL the rental truck up in front of the Phillips' house and climb out. Poppy and Jasmine race down the front steps wearing enormous smiles, and toward me like they haven't seen me for months. "Shane!" Jas calls out as she runs. These girls certainly know how to make a man feel special and welcome. I chuckle as they throw themselves at me in greeting and pick each of them up to carry back inside.

Rose is waiting inside the front door wearing a smile and holding a beer. "Welcome home, Shane. Come in and take a break, then we'll all help unload the truck." My heart skips a beat. She's always made me feel welcome in her home when she certainly had reason not to. I still can't believe she never held me responsible for Cassia's attack.

"Thanks, Mrs. Phillips."

She frowns at me. "Rose, please." I nod and place the girls on their feet inside the door, then take the beer from Rose's outstretched hand. "I made some snacks. Come and eat. You must be hungry."

I follow her through to the rear of her home where Cass and Vi are laughing about something and Toby's bouncing Daisy on his knee. The room is noisy and boisterous and while I enjoy my quiet solitude, the light mood of the room pushes the edges of my lips up into a grin.

Vi catches my eye from across the room and winks at me, then follows my path across the room with her eyes. I tip my chin at her and pull up a chair at the opposite end of the table as far away from her as possible. Rose places a cheese ball in the center of the table and Cassia and Violet climb to their feet to help her add various plates of cheese, fruit, dips, and crackers to the spread.

"Help yourselves, everyone." Rose glances around the table, then brings additional drinks for everyone. Once she's satisfied, she takes a seat at the table. "We've cleared out as much as we could from the garage for you. I hope there's enough space for your things. If not, we can stack some stuff in the corner of Poppy's room. She won't mind." She signs as she speaks so Poppy knows what's going on.

Poppy smiles and nods, then signs. "That's okay."

"I'm sure if I stack my things carefully, everything should fit." I clear my throat. "I appreciate you allowing me to stay with you and the additional space you're providing for my things."

"You're very welcome."

Conversation strikes up around the table as we eat the afternoon snacks Rose prepared, then everyone—including the girls—helps to unload the rental truck and stack everything neatly in the double garage. As I predicted, everything fits in the space so I don't have to take over Poppy's bedroom, which she still uses from time to time.

Once everything's unloaded, Toby takes Cassia and his girls home, and I return the rental truck. When I get back, it's early evening and close to dinnertime.

21

VIOLET

I rub a spot on the window like I'm trying to wear a hole through the glass itself as I watch my daughter lead Shane around our raised vegetable gardens. She animatedly points to the different vegetables, and I can tell by how fast her lips are moving that she's sharing all the knowledge she has about the different plants.

"I'm pretty sure that spot's clean, honey." My shoulders bunch and I turn to face Mom. "What has you so worked up?"

I point over my shoulder with my thumb. "The six-foot-three Goliath being led around our garden by my daughter."

Mom chuckles. "He's so sweet and patient with her."

I don't even try to cover my sigh because watching him with Jasmine is the weirdest form of foreplay. And I know I offered for him to move in while his place is being renovated but I don't know how I'm going to do this. "I don't know how I feel about having him in our space twenty-four-seven," I blurt.

She joins me at the window and watches the pair with a gentle smile. "She certainly took him under her wing from the get-go. I think she's been good for him and she blossoms under his attention." She turns to me. "Having Toby and Shane join our family has been great for the girls. They need to have those positive male role models in their lives."

"Yeah, but what happens when he meets someone and he's not around for us anymore? What happens to my daughter's heart then?" *And mine.* I turn my gaze to Mom. Surely she can understand the implications for Jas if he disappears from her life. The implications for me and my broken heart.

She turns to me, her expression thoughtful. "Do you really think Shane would abandon us completely? Abandon Jas like that?"

I turn back toward the window and watch him crouch down to Jas's level as they pinch some snap peas off the vine. He may not abandon us completely but things would definitely change. His focus would be on his own family, not ours. I wrap my arms across my body and shrug. "Probably not completely."

Mom wraps her arm around my shoulders and tugs me in tight. "Maybe you could use this time to convince him to stay."

I swivel my head to Mom. "Are you suggesting ..."

She raises her eyebrows with a satisfied grin and a shrug. "Show him what it would be like to be part of *this* family instead of hovering around the edges of it." She squeezes me and steps away as the back door opens and my whirlwind of a daughter steps inside with Shane close behind carrying a handful of peas.

"Gramma, I picked some peas to have with our dinner!" She pulls out a colander and climbs onto her step to place it in the sink. "Shane, can you put them in here. We need to wash them."

He raises a single eyebrow at me standing at the window as he wipes his boots on the mat, then follows my daughter's instructions. It was some kind of torture watching him lift and carry his boxes and furniture today; admiring his strength and the play of his muscles as they bunched and stretched. And now, it's another kind of torture, seeing his gentleness and patience with my daughter.

"How about some manners, JJ?" I remind her.

"Sorry, Mommy." She turns to Shane with a look of apology. "Sorry, Shane. Could you *please* put them in here." She points to the colander and he does as she asks with a smile that he always seems to have ready for her.

"Is there anything else I can help with?" he asks as he dusts his hands.

"Not right now. Why don't you go settle in? I've put fresh sheets on Cassia's old bed." Mom turns to me. "Vi, can you show Shane where to go?" She turns back to her task of peeling potatoes without giving me the opportunity to decline.

"I appreciate it. Thank you." He turns to me and I tilt my head for him to follow me. He collects the bag he left at the front door and as I climb the stairs I can feel his eyes burning into my back, or more accurately, my ass so I add a little more sway to my movements. He chuckles behind me and when I look over my shoulder, he's shaking his head and rubbing the top of his short hair. I know he's physically attracted to me, he just doesn't seem to want to do anything about it.

Maybe I can use this time to change that.

When we get to Cass's bedroom, I swing open the door and wave my arm out before stepping inside. Shane follows suit and places his bag on the end of Cass's bed, then turns around on the spot, taking in the space which isn't overly feminine but is definitely softer than his bedroom was. I move around the room, which suddenly feels tiny, opening and closing the drawers and cupboards to check if they're empty, which they are. "Since you're gonna be here a while, feel free to unpack and put your stuff here. The shared bathroom is at the end of the hallway." I move past him toward the door. "I'll show you where we keep the linen."

Without a word, he follows me down the hallway as I point out the linen cupboard, bathroom, and Jas's bedroom, skipping past mine.

Shane doesn't miss it though. "What's behind this door?" He points with his chin toward my closed bedroom door.

"Uh, that's my bedroom." He glances between his door and mine and his brows furrow slightly.

"So ... we're neighbors," he says slowly as if he's only now realizing that we're going to be in close proximity to each other.

"Yeah, I guess so." I tuck my hands in my pockets to stop myself from reaching forward to smooth out that crease between his dark brows. "Anyway, I'll leave you to unpack. Meet you downstairs for dinner."

"Thanks. I'll be down in a minute. I only have the basics to unpack tonight." I smile warmly at him and then make my way to the stairs. "Oh, and Vi."

I freeze at the rumble of his voice. The one I've imagined whispering dirty words in my ear. "Yeah?" My voice is breathy and the single word comes out on a rasp.

"Thanks for offering me a place to stay."

I glance at him over my shoulder and give him a simple nod. "You're welcome." I quickly leave before I plaster myself against his body and beg him to stay permanently.

When I enter the kitchen, I catch Jas peeking over her shoulder as she takes a bite of one of the peas she picked from the garden. I chuckle to myself as I walk over and ruffle her hair. "I saw that," I whisper lightheartedly close to her ear and she responds with a giggle.

"Sorry, Mommy."

"You don't need to be sorry. You can eat as many peas as you like, we can always pick more." I kiss the top of her head and grab the silverware from the drawer to set the table for four.

Four.

Shane Sutton will be sitting at our dining table, enjoying a meal with us. I mean I've shared meals with Shane before, but they were for social gatherings, they weren't ... *intimate* like this. I feel like he's going to see and experience aspects of my family life that are personal. And yeah, I know I want him but he's given no indication that he's remotely interested in anything personal with me. This is about us providing a place for him to stay.

Mom turns to Jas. "Jas, can you please tell Shane dinner is almost ready?"

"Okay," my daughter sings and skips out of the kitchen.

"Don't forget, I leave for the sustainability conference in the morning and will be out of town for a week."

I wave her off. "I remember."

Jas skips back into the kitchen, her tiny hand wrapped around Shane's fingers as she leads him into the kitchen, and if that image doesn't sum up her relationship with the stoic man, I don't know what else does.

Mom places the casserole on the table and then points to her usual seat at the head. "Shane. You can sit here."

He smiles at her, then pulls out each of the chairs at the table for us before taking his own. "Thanks, Mrs. Phillips. This smells delicious."

"Rose," Mom says in her firm Mom voice, and Shane looks chastised.

"I helped make the salad," Jas proudly announces.

He looks at her with wide eyes. "You never told me you were a chef."

Jas giggles. "I'm too little to be a chef, silly."

Mom points to the dish in the middle of the table. "Help yourself."

"Thank you." He dishes up for each of us before serving himself, and we all dig in.

We're all quiet for a few moments as we take the first bites of creamy chicken breast, baked potatoes, and fresh salad. "Thank you again for opening your home to me."

"You're welcome. It actually works out perfectly because I'll be away for a week and Vi was going to have to shorten her days to accommodate taking Jas to and from school. With you here, it will make things easier."

Shane is already nodding his head in agreement as I'm shaking mine in the negative. "It's okay. I've already made the arrangements for next week. I can take my daughter to and from school."

Shane wipes his mouth with a napkin, and as I watch him drag it across his lips, I find I'm jealous of a piece of tissue paper. "I was planning on taking Jasmine to and from school as part of this arrangement, so there's no need for you to change your schedule, Blue."

I understand he wants to contribute while he's here because Mom won't accept any payment, but he doesn't need to do my job. I also don't trust the other moms not to pounce on him the second they get the opportunity. There's no way he would have considered the hungry moms at school, and I don't want to subject him to all of that estrogen. I've heard some of the single moms talking about the things they get up to on the weekends with random hookups when their kids are with their fathers. Red tinges the edge of my vision when I think about one of them touching Shane or turning up at his apartment only wearing his jacket.

Before I realize what's happening, Shane's collecting the dirty dishes from the table and taking them to the sink. I was so caught up in my mind that I completely zoned out. Climbing to my feet, I collect the glasses and join him in the kitchen. "I know you feel like you owe us something for letting you stay here, but you don't need to clean up. I'll do this; it's my job." I try to nudge him away from the sink with a hip check but the brick wall that he is means he doesn't even move an eighth of an inch.

"I can wash a dish. It's no problem. I'm enjoying the food, I can do my share."

"Okay, I'll dry." I turn to Mom. "Would you mind bathing Jas for me?"

"No problem. Jas, let's go and get you bathed. Which pajamas are you wearing tonight?" Mom's voice fades as she leads my daughter out of the room.

As I watch Mom lead my daughter away and Shane wash the

first dish, the whole situation feels so very domestic, and I can't stop myself from picturing more evenings like this. Weeks turning into months and months turning into years of domestic bliss. A little brother or sister for Jas with Shane's dark hair and eyes.

"Hey, where did you just go?" He taps my arm with his elbow, and I tilt my head back to look at him.

Shaking my head to rid myself of the thoughts, I tilt my lips slightly. "Nowhere. Let's get these dishes done."

"Okay." Shane turns back to the sink and scrubs the plates. "I wanted to ask if there were any repairs or maintenance I could do while I'm here since your mom won't accept any rent."

I shrug. "We manage to do most things ourselves. I can't think of anything right now."

"Let me know if you do. I want to help."

He wants to help. Because that's what he always does. I swallow past the lump in my throat. "Okay," I murmur. "I'll let you know if I think of anything."

"Thank you." He picks up the casserole dish and scrubs it clean then rinses it. We spend the rest of the task in silence, occasionally brushing against each other. It feels so familiar and yet we've never done this before.

"Mommy, I'm all clean. Can we do some coloring now?"

"Of course. You set us up at the table and I'll finish putting these dishes away."

She scurries around the table, collecting everything we'll need, and then climbs onto the chair, opening the coloring book to the next page. Shane turns and rests his ass against the sink, folding his thick arms across his chest as he smiles at my daughter, making my chest constrict. Most of his genuine smiles are for the girls, and as sweet as it is, I wish I could steal more of them for myself because when he smiles for me it feels like I've won the lottery.

I take my seat next to Jas and open to the next blank page. Nice, I've been looking forward to coloring this one. I glance across at Jasmine's page. "Oh, that sunflower is going to look fantastic once you've finished."

"I love sunflowers. They always look so happy."

I nod and grin at my daughter. "Maybe I should have named you Sunflower."

She giggles but doesn't lift her eyes from the task. "That would be a funny name."

Mom wanders into the kitchen. "How about I make us all a cup of hot chocolate"—she says to the room, then turns to Shane —"and then you and I can retire to the living room."

Jas hums as she colors. This kid is in her happy place, and hot chocolate on top of that is the icing on the cake. Shane and Mom work side by side to make the drinks while Jas and I get lost in our coloring.

"Mommy, you did a great job of the twisty bark on the tree trunk."

My cheeks rise. "Thanks, Jas." I glance over to see how she's doing with her sunflower. "I love the colors you chose for the butterfly." She colors mostly inside the lines now. I've kept her early attempts at coloring, and occasionally I show her how much she's improved. She gets a real kick out of seeing her first pictures.

"Yeah, it looks so pretty."

Mom places our drinks on the table, and then she and Shane disappear into the living room. I can only imagine what she might say to him, and while I normally love spending this time with my daughter, coloring and talking about our day, I would love to be a fly on the living room wall.

I clear my throat. It's time to have a difficult conversation with my girl. I've been waiting to be alone with her and now's my opportunity. "Hey, I wanted to talk to you about what Jason said to you the other day. You know it's not true, right? You're not ugly." She stays quiet, but I notice a furrow form between her brows.

"I know," she whispers.

"Are you sure? Because you seemed very upset about it."

"He hurt my feelings." She looks up at me with wide eyes so much like mine. "And he made me remember that Daddy said I was ugly, too."

"I'm sorry your daddy said such hurtful words. He was angry at Mommy and thought he could upset me by saying mean things about you. Nothing he said was true. I want you to know that." I press my hand against her chest. "You have such a beautiful heart, there's no way you could be ugly. Not even if you tried."

She smiles up at me. "Shane said I'm beautiful inside and out. He doesn't say things that aren't true."

At five years old, she already has her bullshit meter fine-tuned. I wish I could say the same about myself. "Exactly. I would believe what he says, not what Jason or your daddy said." And how sad is that? I've just told my daughter not to trust her father.

She smiles at me. "Do you think he'll stay with us forever?"

I suck in a sharp breath as my heart drops to my gut at the hope in her eyes. "I don't know, JJ."

"I'll make sure I'm a good girl so he doesn't send us away like Daddy did." She nods once and returns to her coloring, and I try to blink away the sting at the back of my eyes. She remembers so much more than I want her to. I thought she'd forgotten. I'd *hoped* she'd forgotten. It's bad enough that I remember. It's horrific that a child her age remembers that her father didn't want her anymore.

I swallow around the thickness in my throat. "I'm just going to the bathroom. Back in a sec." I kiss the top of her head and leave the kitchen quickly to close myself inside the downstairs powder room. My tears break free, and I drop my head into my hands. My poor baby girl. No wonder she latched onto Shane. He's done nothing but show her kindness and care. He's been patient in ways her father never was.

Is that why I'm so attracted to him? Because he's good to my daughter? I know that's definitely part of it, but there's something about Shane that calls to me. I know he's hiding something dark from his time in the army. That he's keeping secrets from all of us. Whatever they are, I'm compelled to learn everything about him, to help free him from whatever traps him on the periphery of life.

Splashing my face with cool water, I check myself in the mirror. I'm not going to be able to hide that I've been crying so I take a few extra moments to gather myself before I head back out to my little girl.

I stop short when I step into the kitchen to find Shane leaning over my book, coloring with Jas like it's something he always does.

22

SHANE

I don't know the last time I colored a picture, probably in kindergarten. Where Violet's coloring is perfectly even within the lines, mine's not so great, but when I came in to wash the empty cups, I couldn't leave Jas sitting at the table on her own. I hear the door down the hallway open and close and prepare myself both mentally and physically to be in Vi's presence once again. I didn't think this idea through very well, and it's going to be tougher than I ever imagined to keep my walls intact while I'm living in close quarters with Vi and Jas.

I waffle back and forth between crossing the lines from friendship to more and keeping my distance. Sometimes I feel like I'm ready, and then other times I feel undeserving. But I *do* know that in the moments when my resolve fails me, I feel free from my self-imposed burdens and I'm so close to throwing all caution out of the window and taking what I want.

Vi pauses in the doorway and it takes every ounce of my strength not to look up at her and stay focused on my task. I hear her breath hitch and my eyes travel upward without permission. The sight that greets me makes my heart pound like thunder and I grind my teeth. She's been crying ... again. Probably over that piece of shit ex. She raises her chin and pushes her shoulders back, and I can almost see her restoring her inner power. She's a damn goddess.

"JJ, it's time to pack away now. Let's go brush your teeth and get ready for bed," she says brightly, but I can hear the undertone of sadness coating her words.

"Okay, Mommy." She packs her pencils into their case and closes her book. "Shane, are you still going to read *The Lorax* to me?"

I stack the coloring books together and zip the case closed. "Of course. Let me know when you're ready for me."

Her smile is instantaneous as she cheers, and I want to make it my mission to only put a grin on her lips ... never tears on her cheeks. She skips to Violet and slides her tiny hand into her mom's and waves at me over her shoulder as she leaves the kitchen.

"That little girl just loves having your attention," Rose says as she wanders into the kitchen.

"Well, that's good because she deserves all the attention she gets." I carry the girls' cups to the sink and set about washing the dishes as Rose dries and puts them away. "I hope you don't mind but I'm just going to check that all of the windows and doors are secure downstairs before I'm needed upstairs. It's a force of habit."

She steps past me and pats me on the shoulder. "You do what you gotta do to feel comfortable. I trust you." Rose leaves the kitchen and heads upstairs not having a single clue what her words mean to me. How they build a scaffold around a deep crevasse inside of me. Tension evaporates from my shoulders knowing she trusts me, which is unbelievable considering what happened to her daughter because of my shitty decisions. I methodically wander from room to room checking the windows and doors, ensuring the screen doors are also locked. I'm not sure what Rose and Vi normally do once Jas is in bed but it's too early to go to sleep. I hear the water turn on upstairs and assume Rose is showering so I head upstairs to check the windows. While I was in the backyard with Jas earlier, I checked for any easy entry points but everything looked secure.

As I step closer to Jas's bedroom, the girls' soft voices break through the quiet. I don't want to interrupt their time together but I'm drawn closer to the doorway so I can watch them. I've always admired how close Cass and Vi are with their girls, and it's no wonder they're great moms with a role model like Rose.

When I think back to my relationship with Mom, I remember how close we were. Dad always used to say I was a Mommy's boy when I was younger. I took it as an insult and began to pull away, putting space between us, but I missed her. Things only grew worse when I enlisted and then returned home injured. Keeping my secret meant having to keep my distance so I didn't inadvertently overshare. But there have been times when I could have used her comfort ... times when I craved that connection again.

"Do you think Shane still wants to read me a bedtime story?"

I step from around the doorway. I never want this little girl to doubt that I'll fulfill my promises. "Are you ready for your story, Angel?"

Her smile breaks free immediately as she nods. Violet brushes Jas's hair away from her face with a soft smile, then leans down to kiss her forehead. Pressing their foreheads together, Vi whispers, "Remember that I love you more than all of the wildflowers on the earth."

"Love you, too, Mommy." Vi kisses the tip of her nose, then pushes up from the bed but Jas reaches out to grab her hand. "Stay and listen, too."

"Okay." Vi hands me the book and lays beside her daughter. The two of them lying snuggled together on Jas's small bed make me ache for something I'll never have but wish I could.

I take it from her and sit at the end of the bed. I flick through the pages, realizing the story is longer than I originally thought it would be. Reading the book, I do my best to put on the different voices for each of the characters in the story. I have to say, I'm not a fan of The Once-ler—seems like a bit of a dick. "...*Give it clean water. And feed it fresh air. Grow a forest. Protect it from axes that hack. Then the Lorax and all of his friends may come back.*" I close the book as I finish and when I look up, my breath stalls in my lungs. Jas is asleep with her little lips tipped up slightly and Vi is watching her as she strokes her hair softly, a look of serenity on her face.

I clear my throat quietly, stand, and place the book on the side table. "I'll leave you to it. Good night," I whisper into the quiet of the room.

Vi reaches out and grips my hand, much like Jas did to her. "Hold on." She kisses Jas one last time, climbs from the bed, and tucks the blankets around her daughter, then leads me out of the room and into the hallway. "Thanks for following through with her bedtime story. I'm sure it's the last thing you wanted to do," she says softly, her eyes firmly planted on my chest.

I tip her chin up. "Don't ever doubt my promises. I always follow through." I watch her throat move as she swallows and I want to dip down and glide my tongue over the pulse point which is fluttering a fast rhythm at the base. Resisting her is becoming more and more difficult and I've been here less than six hours. She swipes her tongue across her bottom lip and her breaths come in short bursts. I rake my eyes over her, taking in her aroused state— like I'm not already struggling to hold myself in check, she has to be so damn tempting.

Fuck it!

I sweep forward and take her lips, using my hands on her hips to bring her body flush with mine. The blood in my veins hums to life, heating my body and surging to my dick. Her hands encircle my neck, so I quickly tug them free and step her backward so she's pressed against the wall. Gripping each hand securely, I raise them above her head and press them firmly against the wall without breaking our kiss. Her tongue tangles passionately with mine and it's so easy to get lost in her. To get lost in the feel of her against my body, her heart beating against mine. To get lost in her taste and heat. I press my hips tightly against her and the creak of a door opening down the hallway snaps me out of the spell Vi always seems to cast on me.

"Sorry to interrupt. I'm just grabbing a glass of water. Either of you need anything from downstairs?" Rose says with a smirk as she points downstairs.

I drop Vi's hands and take a giant step away from her, my back colliding with the opposite wall. I watch intently while a flush stains the cheeks of the woman I was just kissing as the realization dawns that we were caught making out like a couple of horny teenagers by her mom. "No thanks, Mom. I'm just gonna have a shower." She jerks her thumb toward the bathroom.

"You might want to make it a cold one," Rose shoots back with a snicker.

"Mom!" Vi admonishes.

"Just sayin'," Rose sings over her shoulder as she heads downstairs.

Vi chuckles and turns to me. "Well, that was embarrassing."

I rub my hand over my short hair filled with disbelief that I just mauled her in front of her mom. "Sorry about that. I'm just gonna head downstairs and watch some TV if that's okay."

"Sure. Make yourself at home. You don't need to check in with us."

I TOSS my pillow to the other side of the bed and climb to my feet. Sleep is a fickle bitch. Pulling on my sweatpants, I dig in my overnight bag for my Kindle but come up empty-handed. Damn. I must have packed the damn thing with the rest of my gear. I pause for a moment and try to remember seeing it over the last few days. It was on my bedside drawers, so it's probably packed in the box with that stuff. I head toward the door ready to find it. Thinking better of it, I grab a T-shirt and throw it on, then make my way downstairs to search among the boxes in the garage.

Turning on the light, I scan the stacks of boxes in the double garage. We were all stacking boxes in here this afternoon. I'm just going to have to move each one until I find the one I need. I move each box, methodically stacking them on the opposite side of the space.

"Who's there?" Vi's shaky voice echoes through to the garage from the kitchen, and I turn in time to see her silhouette in the doorway. She's carrying a damn baseball bat and I see red.

"What the hell are you thinking coming down here with a fucking baseball bat?" I take long strides to get in her space and snatch the bat out of her hands. "Now I have a weapon I can easily use against you," I snap.

Her hands fly to her hips, making her tits jiggle beneath the flimsy camisole she's wearing. "I was defending myself. I only let the bat go because it was you."

I grunt. "Sure." When I realize how close we are I take a step away from her. "What are you doing down here in the middle of the night, anyway?"

"I heard a noise and came to investigate." She huffs and takes a couple of steps around the garage. It's then I notice she's only wearing panties with that damn camisole and I pause to take her all in. Her hair's all mussed and I can imagine what it would look like after I've had my hands tangled in it. *Fuck.* "What are you doing?"

I follow her, keeping a safe distance so I don't maul her like I did in the hallway upstairs. My blood boils at the thought of her fighting off an intruder and my hand itches to slap her ass to teach her a lesson. "Considering I'm staying with you, you didn't think to wake me so *I* could investigate?"

One shoulder rises and falls carelessly. "I'm used to doing things like that for myself. Even when I was with Allen, he was barely home, so I'd have to do most things." He's an even bigger sack of shit than I thought. "Anyway, what are you doing down here? Shouldn't you be sleeping?"

"I never sleep well and tonight was no different. I was looking for something." I place the bat on top of a stack of boxes and move another box, turning my back to her. "You should go back to bed." I need to get her away from me.

She steps closer and shakes her head, causing her natural scent to fill the space. "What are you looking for? Maybe I can help."

I glance down at the box I'm carrying. "Found it. Do you have a box cutter?"

"Yeah. Hang on, I'll grab it." She spins and walks quickly inside, giving me a spectacular view of her ass covered in simple cotton panties. Shit.

I place the box on the workbench, adjust my cock, and wait. Violet returns a few minutes later with what I need. "Thanks." I take the cutter from her and slice through the tape. Meanwhile, she hoists herself up onto the bench beside me, stealing my concentration. Damn woman. She has no idea what she does to me. "You should go back to bed," I grunt.

"I'm okay. I want to see what you're looking for." She grips the edge of the workbench and crosses her ankles, swinging her feet back and forth. Her tits jiggle with each movement and my cock grows thicker; my breaths become choppy at the sight of her breasts free from the constraints of her bra. The cooler night air is making her nipples bead, and the position she's in presses them together beautifully. I'd do anything to be able to bury my face in the crease between them. I snap my head back to the box I'm opening. "What was so important that you had to come down here looking for it in the middle of the night?"

Without looking up at her, I grunt, "My Kindle." This woman turns me into a damn caveman with all the grunting I do because I have to concentrate on keeping my dick in my damn pants.

Her eyes light up. "Yeah? What types of books do you read?" She swings her feet again, and I suppress a groan.

I'm not ashamed of what I read, the books help me immensely but I don't think it's common for men to read what I read. "Romance books," I mumble.

"Pardon?" She leans closer and while I should send her back to bed and tell her to mind her own business, I like having her here with me and I find I want to share something with her nobody else knows. When I don't answer, she blows out a breath and begins to wiggle to the edge of the bench. "I should leave you to it. I'm clearly intruding." In a panic, I snap my hand out to hold her in place scorching my palm. I don't want her to go. I *should* let her go. It would be the right thing to do. I have nothing to offer her. "Shane?" I can hear the question in her soft voice.

My resolve is crumbling at my feet like the shattered glass of a windowpane. "Spread your legs, Blue."

"Shane?"

"Don't make me tell you again," I rasp. "Spread your gorgeous legs for me." I want to add *only for me*, but I daren't. Glancing down at the space that's now open to my gaze, the darker patch in the center of the fabric catches my eye—so damn responsive. Without taking my eyes from the damp area, I brush it with the back of my fingers and she responds by pushing her hips into my touch.

I move so my body is between her toned thighs and glide my palms along the silky smoothness until I reach the waistband of her panties. Each breath I take is filled with her sweet arousal and I almost feel dizzy. "Lift." She places her hands behind her and raises her ass off the workbench allowing me to slide the cotton down her trembling legs. "I read romance books, Blue." Placing the underwear on the bench, I drop my hands back on her thighs and slide them along the side of her body, tracing the beautiful flare of her hips to the dip of her waist, following the action with my eyes. "They help me settle after a nightmare." I don't look up at her face, I don't want to see her reaction.

Taking the fabric of her camisole with me, I glide my hands

higher, and my dick grows harder with every inch of flesh she allows me to expose. I'm a quivering mess inside that I'm about to see the woman of my dreams completely bare and she's allowing me to do so. She sucks in a sharp breath when my thumbs catch the underside of her breasts and then slide farther up until I reach her peaked nipples. "So damn perfect," I groan, and she sighs into the room as she pushes her tits into my hands. I squeeze the flesh roughly, making her squeak, then continue to slide the fabric of her top higher. "Lift." She raises her arms without question, and I relieve her of the fabric.

"How often do you have nightmares?" she asks breathily. I take a slight step back so I can admire what I've only ever imagined. Her body trembles beneath my gaze and uncertainty fills her China-blue orbs. "Shane?" she murmurs uncertainly as her brows furrow. I can't believe I have Violet Jamison naked in front of me. She's even more perfect than I could have ever imagined her to be.

"Less than I used to, but a lot of nights. I tried reading thrillers and mysteries, but they didn't do shit. Romance calms me every time and takes my mind off the torture in my dreams." She gasps, making her tits rise and fall, and I gently run the back of my finger over each peaked nipple. "Keep your hands on the surface behind you. You touch me and I stop. Am I clear?" My voice is a deep rumble, giving away my aroused state.

I glance up at her beautiful face and watch her swallow. "Crystal."

"Good girl. Now push those beautiful tits out for me," I demand. She complies beautifully, and I drop my head to suck one perfect nipple inside my mouth. I've been through hell, and I've never really given much thought to heaven but this has to be it. I circle her areola with my tongue, feeling the tiny bumps before biting the stiff bud. She moans softly as she pushes her tit farther into my mouth and grinds her hips upward, looking for friction. Fuck, I'd be happy to do this to her all night. I replace my mouth with my hand and move to her other breast while I slide my free hand toward her hot core. She opens her legs wider in invitation, and her fingers slide into my short hair. I immediately stop what I'm doing and stand to my full height, making her hand drop to her side. "What did I say?"

She looks confused at first, then I see the moment realization takes over. "Sorry. I ... I got carried away. I want to touch you. I didn't mean to break the rules. Please ... *please* don't stop," she whispers the last words as she drops her gaze from mine.

The head of my cock pushes past the elastic waistband of my pants, and I readjust myself. Her eyes drop to the action and she licks her lips, her pupils dilated to the point there's only a thin ring of blue left visible. I swipe my thumb across the opening, collect the precum, and lift it to her mouth, then paint it on her plush bottom lip. Watching her lip glisten with my arousal ratchets up my need to watch her fall apart. "Lick your lip, Blue."

Her eyes widen and her pink tongue darts out to taste my essence. God, she's so damn beautiful with her flushed cheeks and quivering breasts. I lean forward in a rush and press my lips to hers and I take. I push my way inside and pillage her mouth with vulgar strokes that steal her breath and empty my mind of everything but her.

I need more.

More of her.

More of her taste.

More of her moans and sighs.

I need her breath filling my lungs and her pussy squeezing my cock.

Weaving my fingers through her soft hair, I grab a handful and tighten my grip, then guide her head to allow me to kiss her deeper. I slide my other hand along the inside of her thigh, feeling goosebumps rise across her silky skin. When the tips of my fingers reach the crease between her thigh and her body, a long sigh escapes her lips and she readjusts her hips, seeking my fingers. I lightly scratch my short fingernails down through the small patch of curls above her slit until I make contact with her clit. Moving lower still, I find her opening and slide a finger inside her hot, tight opening and begin mimicking the action of my tongue in her mouth.

My breath falters.

My heart stalls.

My body quakes with need.

And her hips move in time, meeting my fingers as I slide them in and out, dragging along her silken walls. Her muscles tighten around the digits, and my cock weeps in my pants, punching against the soft fabric looking for an escape. I swallow her moans and whimpers with my kiss, greedily taking them and keeping them for myself.

Tearing my lips away from Violet's, I slowly, methodically trail my mouth down her neck as I tug her head back to give me better access. I nip the rapidly beating pulse point and then soothe the sting with a swipe of my tongue.

"Please don't stop," she cries.

"I won't." Leisurely, I kiss and lick my way across her collarbone and then move down to her breast, all the while pumping my fingers with even strokes in and out of her slick opening. "You're so goddamn wet for me," I murmur against her flesh. I can't wait to get my mouth down there and taste her again—it's all I've thought about since the wedding. Drawing her nipple deep into my mouth, I suck hard then swirl my tongue around the peak, drawing a long moan from deep within Vi. Pulling my fingers out, I push three fingers deeper into her pussy and am rewarded when her muscles tighten around me, gripping me within their silky walls, and Violet mumbles my name into the room like a prayer. A light sheen of perspiration glistens between her breasts beneath the garage light and I trail my tongue between them, licking the saltiness from her skin.

"Shane, please," she murmurs between panting breaths.

Using my free hand, I massage her breasts, pinching her nipples as I work my tongue down her body, around her navel, and lower still until I reach her clit. Crouching down, I get comfortable. Pressing my fingers against the front wall of her pussy with each rough thrust inside, I pulse my tongue against her clit, then bite it gently between my teeth. I can't tear my eyes away from the gorgeous woman who's close to falling apart beneath my touch—I don't want to miss a single nuance. I want to soak in every detail so I can store this experience away to revisit in the moments when life becomes dark.

Vi's legs tighten around my head, her back arches, and her head drops back on her shoulders as she pulses around my fingers, squeezing them like a vice and coming undone in spectacular fashion. Indecipherable mumbles fall from her lips, filling the quiet garage and my soul.

"You're so fucking sexy." Every single part of her was made just for me and the way she falls apart beneath my touch is designed to set me on fire.

The pink blush covering her body makes her glow beneath the light and I soak in every detail as I slow my movements and clean up her orgasm with my tongue. I swipe and swirl my tongue around her pussy lips and into her opening until I have it all because I'm a greedy bastard. Peering up her body, her tits heave with each breath as she draws oxygen deep into her lungs making her stomach quiver.

"Shit, I think I left my body." She drops her head forward and catches my eye as I lick my fingers clean, not wanting to waste a single drop. "Please tell me I can touch you now," she murmurs as a shiver moves through her body. I shake my head while I stand. Taking her hands in mine, I bring them between us and loop my arms around her, pulling her tight to my body. She sighs and drops her forehead to my shoulder, burying her nose in my neck. "You always smell so good."

I chuckle at her words. "Same."

She pushes back a little, and her blue gaze pleads with mine. "Please let me do something to make you feel good. I need to. I don't feel comfortable with the imbalance of you giving and me taking all the time."

I stroke her hair away from her face reverently, my gaze skipping between her eyes and her swollen lips. "You allowing me to touch you is all I need. I promise you don't need to do anything for me because that experience was a true gift." I press my lips to the tip of her nose and against her forehead.

Her eyes drop closed with a soft sigh, and then I startle at the feel of her hand wrapping around my cock. I push my hips back but she doesn't release her grip. My cock swells even more, and that's saying something considering it's already hard enough to hammer nine-inch nails.

"Blue. I'm serious. You don't owe me anything. I didn't make you come for any other reason than to make you feel good. My pleasure and enjoyment came from watching you fall apart beneath my touch. Knowing I could do that for you is the only reward I need."

She leans forward and kisses my Adam's apple. "What if I want to? What if I want to watch you fall apart beneath *my* touch? I *need* to know if I can do that for you. Please let me."

I study her guileless eyes closely. She's genuine. She really wants to do something for me. "Wait here." Once she nods her agreement, I quickly grab a cushion from my couch on the opposite side of the garage. Dropping it on the floor, I point to it. "On your knees." Her body shivers as she gracefully drops from the bench to the floor and then to her knees in front of me. Her beautiful tits rise and fall with her heavy breaths, and desire swirls in her gorgeous eyes as she looks up at me from her lowered position. "I've never seen anything more spectacular than you on your knees ready to let me fuck your pretty mouth."

She nods and her lips slowly spread into a sultry smile. "Use me, Shane. I want that so bad."

"Keep your hands behind your back. You can only use your mouth. If your hands touch me, we stop." My voice comes out gruff as I try to impart the importance of following this one simple rule. I watch her swallow as she nods her head once, the furrow between her eyebrows deepening. "I need your words, Vi. I need to know you understand how this works."

"I understand. No touching. Only my mouth." She moves her hands behind her back—pushing her perfect tits out—complying with my rule even though she's clearly disappointed. I can't risk her hands roaming and discovering the things I keep hidden. I don't want her to stop looking at me the way she does. And she would if she discovered what's hidden beneath the clothes I wear.

"That's my girl." She tilts her head back, her eyes locking with mine. I push the waistband of my sweats down slightly, and Violet licks her lips as I pull out my heavy cock. Stepping forward slightly, I tap the head on her lips and then trace them with the tip, moistening them with my precum. "You can pull your mouth away at any time. I'm not going to hold your head. If you want to stop, just lean back. Okay?"

She nods eagerly. "Okay, but I won't want to stop. I want this so badly."

"Open up." She does as I tell her. So fucking compliant and eager.

23

VIOLET

I can't believe I finally have Shane's cock in my mouth. I don't know how many times I've imagined what he looks like naked, and I still don't know—which is disappointing—but this is progress, and any small step forward with this man is worth taking.

He has a beautiful cock with that magic upward curve that women can only ever hope for. It's as perfectly proportioned as the rest of his body which means it's gonna be a struggle to fit it all in my mouth, but I'll give it my best shot. I want to give him the best blow job of his life so he begs me for more.

I can't say I've ever been the type of woman to get excited about sucking a man's dick, but for once, I am ... because it's Shane, and it means I'm working my way behind those steel barriers he keeps locked in place. I'm still astounded he shared something personal with me that I don't think he's shared with anyone else. His opening up to me gives me hope. It's a possibility for more someday. Maybe not soon, but sometime in the future, and if I'm patient, I can hopefully make him mine.

Because I want to keep him.

He's such a good man. A caring and strong man. A man with

morals and a good heart. He spends so much time and energy looking out for the people around him, it's time someone looked out for him. And I plan on making him feel good. Hopefully good enough to make him forget about everything else except me for a few moments.

Licking around the sensitive head, I slide my tongue through his slit delicately then down the thick length of his shaft and back up again. His cock jumps, and I have to quickly adjust my position to maintain contact—it would be so much easier if I could wrap my hand around the base. I repeat the process, ensuring I keep my strokes light and teasing and when he pushes his hips forward, I smile at his eagerness. He's finally beginning to let go, and that's exactly what I want.

I open wide, inviting him to push inside my mouth, and the smooth head of his cock slides against my tongue. Pushing upward, I take as much of him into my mouth as I can, then suck in my cheeks to increase the pressure around his length. A deep, sexy moan reverberates through the garage and he pushes his hips into my face; the musky scent of him fills my nose and heightens my arousal beyond anything I've felt before.

Who am I kidding? I only need to be in Shane's proximity, and I'm aroused. The man is my catnip. Disbelief fills my mind as my heart hammers, sending my heated blood racing through my veins. I feel dizzy that this is even happening. That he's letting me touch him. Even if it is only with my mouth.

When he slides his dick out, it's coated in saliva and satisfaction fills me that it's *my* saliva. I make an O with my mouth and swirl my tongue around the swollen head, then I plunge down the length of his shaft, taking it as deep as I can and breathe through my nose so I don't pass out—thank God I don't have a gag reflex. I bob up and down, using only my mouth, feeling his thick length sliding down my throat and back up again. I don't feel like I can do my best work without the use of my hands, but I'm determined, and if the rumbles and moans are anything to go by, I'm doing something right.

"Your mouth feels so good." His rumbly voice sends shockwaves straight to my core, and I moan in response as I suck him deep, then swallow. "Ah, fuck!"

His body almost vibrates with the pleasure that's building and his pecs tense beneath his T-shirt as he holds his body rigid. The veins in his neck bulge when tilts his face toward the ceiling and he looks as though he's in agony. *Beautiful* agony.

God, I want him to grab hold of my hair and tug on it. I want him to lose control. I want him to use me for his pleasure. To take what he wants.

Increasing my pressure, I bob up and down his cock, pressing my tongue to the underside as best I can and tracing the thick vein up the length of him. He swells in my mouth, and I know he's getting close. Saliva dribbles down my chin, and I struggle to take a breath, but I keep my eyes on him, moaning around his shaft as I do.

A groan rumbles from deep within him, and I match it with another moan of my own, ensuring he's deep down my throat as I do to give him as much pleasure as possible.

He begins to pull away, and instinctually, I reach up and grip his hips to hold him in place. Jerking, he takes a sudden step back, almost stumbling with the action, and at the same time, he explodes. His cum bursts out of him, painting my face and breasts, and my mouth drops open in surprise. His broad chest rises and falls rapidly as he squeezes his eyes closed and fists his hands. His orgasm drips down my face, and I bring my hand up to wipe it from my eyes.

"I'm so sorry, Shane. I didn't mean to touch you. I wasn't thinking in the moment, all I knew was I didn't want you to pull away," I apologize quickly, hoping my explanation is enough.

His eyes snap open, the warm brown of his irises tracing every inch of my face before dropping to my breasts and widening. "Fuck, Violet. I'm sorry. I never should have let it go this far. This was completely my fault."

I push up to stand, but he places his strong hand on my shoulder. "Stay. I'll clean you up."

The deep timbre of his voice sends a shiver racing through my body, and goosebumps fan out across my flesh. I drop my butt on my heels and wait as he leaves the room. Now that the adrenaline has worn off, I suddenly feel exposed kneeling on a cushion in the middle of Mom's garage.

Really, Violet. What were you thinking?

Shane returns and crouches down. "Close your eyes, Blue," he murmurs gently. I do as he says and then feel warm, soft cotton gently brushing across my eyelids, cheeks, nose, lips, and chin. "You're so damn beautiful." He softly wipes down my throat and across the top of my breasts and I feel bereft that he's removed his essence from me. "There," he whispers as he kisses the space behind my ear so softly I wonder if I imagined the touch of his lips.

I open my eyes and his brutally handsome face etched with concern fills my entire vision. My lips tip up in a shaky smile. "Thank you." Time seems to freeze as we pause for a moment, each of us watching the other. Me completely naked, him still fully clothed. And I can't help but notice the parallels in our relationship. I've been somewhat bare and vulnerable more times than I care to admit, while Shane maintains his composure and rarely lets his guard down. Tonight was the first time I've seen him slightly off-balance, and it was only for a moment.

He holds out his hand, and I place mine in his. "Let me help you." He tugs me to my feet, then collects my panties and camisole. Crouching down at my feet, he taps each shaky leg so I can put my feet through the legs of my panties, and then slides them up into place, ensuring the elastic is smooth at my hips. He leans forward and softly presses his lips against the front panel and I feel it through every cell of my body all the way to my toes and back again. Standing slowly, I tip my head back so I don't lose his gaze on me. "You're so damn perfect," he rasps. He taps my arms. "Lift."

I do as he says, and he slides my camisole over my arms and head, slipping the silky fabric down my body. Once it's in place, he dips his head and kisses each of my breasts over the fabric. My breathing becomes shallow, and I'm pretty sure I'm ready to rip the fabric from my body and beg him to take me here and now, to hell with the consequences. Without a word, he presses his lips to mine in a chaste kiss. "Thank you for tonight, Blue." Turning my body so I'm facing the door into the house, he smacks my ass. "Now back to bed, gorgeous."

I jump at the sudden strike, and when I look back at Shane over my shoulder, one side of his mouth is tipped up in a half smile, but I'll take it. He winks at me, and I feel as though some of the heaviness from a few moments ago has been lifted and that we'll be okay come morning. I *hope* we'll be okay.

I make it upstairs, close the door to my bedroom, and lean back against it, a genuine grin on my face. Holding in my squeal, I flop onto my bed, bouncing once before snuggling down beneath the covers and falling asleep almost instantly.

When I step into the kitchen, Shane's already leaning against the kitchen counter with a cup of coffee. He silently pushes a steaming hot cup of tea across to me, and I have to press my lips together so I don't outwardly smile. "Thank you."

"You're welcome." His eyes scan me from head to toe. "I offered to take your mom to the airport."

I sip my tea, my eyes dropping closed as I enjoy the warmth. "Thank you. I bet she loves you. She hates getting an Uber." I spin toward the fridge and gather what I need for Jas's lunch.

"I like to feel useful." He parks his butt against the counter and watches me prepare lunch and snacks for my daughter. Once it's ready, I grab the oats and set about making enough for all of us for breakfast. Shane slices some bananas and places the cut fruit and honey on the table. "Anything else I can help with?"

I shake my head. "No, I think we're good. Thank you."

"You don't need to thank me. I'm happy to help."

Jas skips into the kitchen with Mom hot on her heels. "I'm hungry, Mommy."

I lean down and kiss her soft cheek. "Well ... breakfast is almost ready. Can you please put the spoons on the table?"

"Okay." She grabs four spoons from the drawer and places one at each setting, moving her table setting closer to where Shane was sitting last night.

"Morning, love." Mom kisses my cheek and grabs a cup from the hook to pour herself a cup of coffee. "I have so much to do. I need to finalize the plans for the apartment project over on Twelfth Street before my flight later this morning. I won't have time to prepare dinner for you guys, will you be all right?"

"Of course, Mom. I *do* know how to cook dinner." I roll my eyes internally. Mom seems to forget that I had to run a household when I was married to Allen.

"I can cook dinner tonight, Rose," Shane says over the top of me.

Mom smiles at him with affection. "Thank you. You're an angel." She turns to me. "Did Shane tell you he's driving me to the airport?"

I nod as Shane says, "No problem."

We eat breakfast and clean up, then after saying goodbye to Mom, I wrangle Jas out the door. "Shane, are you coming to school with me? I can show you my favorite puzzle."

He glances up at me, then back to my daughter as we walk toward my car. "You want me there?" He sounds surprised, and I'm not sure why. Jas would glue herself to him if she could. She nods. "That sounds awesome. Do you think I'll be allowed?" My heart flutters and my belly flips as he smiles down at my daughter who's beaming up at him. I'll never get used to how open he is about his affection for the girls. I bet he doesn't even realize how incredible that is.

"Other daddies come into class," she tells him as she bounces on her toes and my heart thumps against my ribs. Shane doesn't miss a beat though.

"Then I'll be there."

"Yay!" she shouts as Shane buckles her into her booster seat.

"I'll follow you to school," he tells me as he closes Jasmine's door.

"You don't have to come to school. She'll expect you to come every day."

"Then I'll be there every day that I can. I have to coach Evan's soccer team after school today, but I'll be home in time to cook dinner."

Can an organ melt? Seriously, this man melts my heart with the time and attention he gives the kids in his life. I know he would do anything for them, but it's something else to witness a man *speak* through his actions as well as his words and all I can do is nod.

As soon as I climb into the driver's seat, Jas's voice fills the space. "Today's the best day."

We spend the drive to school singing along to Jas's favorite playlist while I try to control the butterflies taking over my stomach. When I pull into the parking lot at school, Cass and Poppy are waiting. The instant I turn off the engine, Poppy has Jas's door open and she helps release her cousin from her booster seat. The next thing I know, Cass opens my door. "Hey, Vi."

"Hey?" Confusion colors my greeting. "What are you doing here?"

"Can't a girl come say hi to her sister?" Uh, yeah, but this is highly unusual.

"Of course, but what about the shop?"

"Sam was happy to open for me today. I'm going straight there."

Jas wraps her arms around my sister's legs. "Hi, Aunty Cass."

Cass giggles and bends down to pick up Jas. "Hey, Jolly Jas." They both chuckle, and I take the opportunity to say hello to Poppy. Shane climbs out of his car and Jas wriggles in my sister's arms, so she places her on her feet. Cass raises her brows at me, then calls out to Shane, "Hey, Shane. Fancy seeing you here."

"Hey, Cass." He waits until Poppy looks at him, then signs hello to her.

"How's Daisy?" I ask.

Cass's smile grows wide. "She's great. Trying to talk up a storm." She wraps her arm around me, looks over her shoulder, and tugs me in close. "But that's not why I stopped by. I heard that a certain sexy bodyguard was caught kissing my sister in the upstairs hallway last night." She wriggles her eyebrows up and down, and my cheeks immediately flush, remembering what happened in the garage last night *after that* kiss. "Oh my God! I knew you two just needed to spend some time together and the fire would catch." Geez, if she knew what happened later, she'd be beside herself.

"Shh, keep your voice down." I pointedly glance around. "I'm not talking with you about this."

She sticks out her bottom lip. "Well, that's not fair."

"It's not like you shared the details when you and Toby got together."

She pulls away slightly. "I didn't share because you'd just left Allen and I didn't want to shove my newfound happiness in your face. I was being thoughtful. It wasn't that I didn't *want* to share. I would have loved to but I didn't think it was fair." Her gray eyes swirl with emotion and I feel like a bitch.

I wrap my arms around her and squeeze her hard. "I'm sorry I was in a shitty place and you couldn't talk to me. I feel like a selfish bitch now."

"You weren't." She shrugs. "Life isn't always good to us."

Poppy wraps her arms around her mom and Cass leans down to kiss the top of her head, then they sign goodbye to each other. I hug her and sign, "Have a great day."

Poppy places her fingers near her lips and then moves her hand toward me and down. "Thank you."

"Mommy, we need to get to class," Jas prompts.

"I know." I turn to Cass. "Gotta go but let's catch up. Maybe I can have lunch with you at the shop next week."

"Sounds perfect. But, Vi. Promise me you'll take this opportunity and make something happen."

I nod. "I will." *Don't worry, Sis, I'm already on it.* Literally. I barely hold back a snicker as we part ways with Shane hot on our heels.

Once Cass leaves, Shane holds out his hand for Jas and she slides hers into it with glee. "Lead the way." My eyes catch and lock at the sight of my daughter's tiny hand in Shane's much larger one, and my mind immediately sprints ahead to a future I would do almost anything to have.

Jas skips alongside Shane, making his arm bounce each time she hops, and if I weren't trying to hold my thoughts in check, I would be laughing at the comical sight. Jas's teacher is waiting outside the door to greet us when we arrive and my daughter drags Shane straight for her.

"Good morning, Jasmine. Violet."

Jas responds before I have the chance to open my mouth. "Good morning, Mrs. Diamond. This is my friend, Shane." She tugs him forward, and he holds out his hand for Mrs. Diamond.

Her lips tip up, then she glances at me as she takes his hand. "Nice to see you again, Shane."

He tips his head. "You too."

"I'm gonna show Shane my favorite puzzle."

Her teacher smiles and nods. "Well, you'd better get in there quick before all the other kids arrive."

We spend the next ten minutes with Jas as she drags Shane around her classroom showing him everything *except* her favorite puzzle. His attention is one hundred percent focused on her the entire time, so much so that he misses the blatant way the moms are checking him out. On a normal day, only one or two of the moms say hello to me but today, several of them act like we're the best of friends and introduce themselves to Shane, going so far as to put their hands on him as they speak. All I can do is grit my teeth and remind myself that he's not mine, and he's free to speak with whomever he chooses but seeing their hands on him grates me to my core. I'm somewhat mollified when he dismisses them in favor of lavishing Jas with his attention.

When it's time to leave, Jas wraps her arms around Shane's legs. "I didn't get to show you my favorite puzzle."

He scoops her up and I can almost feel everyone's ovaries exploding. "I'll come back again, Angel." He presses his forehead to hers, and her little hands come up to cup his smooth cheeks.

"Okay," she says brightly, then scrambles down his body to sit on the mat with the other kids.

As we make our escape, Shane shivers and I glance at him. "You okay?"

"Yeah. I just wanted to spend time with Jas." He looks behind us. "I almost feel dirty." So he *did* notice.

A laugh escapes me before I can stop it and I glance over my shoulder, spotting a group of moms watching us. "I'm pretty sure they're all licking their lips." I bump my shoulder into his side as I chuckle, and he wraps his arm around me to keep me in place. I hadn't considered that he's *hands-on* with me until Tristan mentioned it the other day but now that I think about it, he definitely is.

When we arrive at our cars, he drops his arm, leaving me feeling adrift. "I ... I ... uh ... guess I'll see you tonight." He rubs his hand over the top of his hair as his eyes trace over my face. "Have a good day at work." Turning away from me, he heads to his car before I can respond and my shoulders slump in disappointment. Not even a goodbye kiss. Damn.

I'VE BEEN RUMINATING over the fact that Shane didn't kiss me goodbye this morning, and after last night's ... *activities*, my pride is a little wounded. I'm not sure if I'm hoping for something that isn't a possibility, but I'm prepared to give the man grace since I know we have chemistry, and that he's definitely attracted to me. He opened up a little and shared something personal with me that I bet not too many people know. With each piece of himself he reveals to me, each little piece that gives me a peek into the man inside, the harder I fall for him. And I'm not even trying to stop myself. Focusing has been almost impossible today knowing that it'll just be Jas, Shane, and me home for the next week. *Almost like a family*.

I pull into the empty driveway and park. "Mommy, where's Shane?"

Releasing her seatbelt, I answer, "Remember, he had to coach Evan's soccer game this afternoon. He said he'll be home after that." *Home*. I like the sound of that.

"Oh, okay. Can we go watch?" Jas asks as we take the steps to the front door.

I unlock the door. "I don't know where they play. Maybe if you ask Shane, we can go watch another time."

"Okay."

We step inside and the faint smell of cooked steak hangs in the air. "Go wash your hands, and I'll make us an afternoon snack."

Jas takes her backpack to the kitchen and places her lunchbox on the counter, then hangs her bag on the hook in the hallway. When I open the fridge to grab some cheese and an apple, I see an enormous platter loaded with salad greens, grilled corn, tomatoes, red onion, and sliced grilled steak. When Shane told me he had soccer practice this afternoon, I figured I'd be cooking dinner even though he said he would. I never expected to come home to this but I shouldn't be surprised because he's shown me time and time again that he's a man of his word.

24

SHANE

They run off the field, and I notice Evan dragging his feet. One of his teammates nudges him gently and Evan pushes him back so hard, the kid falls on his ass. I jog toward the boys to help the kid to his feet. "Are you okay, Ronald?"

He brushes off his butt, "Yeah, thanks." He throws a dirty look at Evan and then heads toward his mom.

I catch up to Evan. "What was that all about?"

"He pushed me," he snaps, and my eyebrows shoot up. I thought we'd sorted out his bad attitude.

I grip his shoulder and pull him to a stop. "Watch who you're talking to. Now, what's going on?"

His eyes drop to the ground between us. "Nothin'."

Hope joins us at the edge of the field. "What happened?"

"Evan pushed Ronald so hard he fell to his butt. I'm trying to find out what's going on."

Hope frowns at her son. "Do I need to take the privilege of playing soccer away from you as well as your computer games?"

What? Hope never has to take things away from Evan. What the hell is going on? I look at her questioningly and she shakes her head at me.

"No, Mom," he says softly as he kicks the grass with the tip of his cleat.

"Say bye to Shane and get in the car. We'll talk when we get home."

Uh oh. He's in trouble. We watch Evan walk to the car with slumped shoulders and I turn to Hope. "What's going on?"

She releases a long sigh. "I had a police officer turn up at my door with Evan last Friday afternoon."

"What the hell?"

"Yep. My thoughts exactly."

"What? Why?" The Evan I know is so far removed from this boy.

She folds her arms and watches Evan climb into her car, then turns back to me. "He and his new friends thought it would be funny to steal stuff from the gas station. His friends took off when they were caught, leaving Evan to face the consequences on his own and he's not prepared to tell the officer who he was with." She runs her hand through her hair and the frustration is apparent in the creases across her forehead. "I don't know what to do with him." She huffs and looks back at her car. "I don't know how to deal with a pre-teen boy who has an attitude the size of Texas."

"Did the owner of the gas station press charges?"

She shakes her head. "Officer Taylor said the owner wanted to press charges but he suggested that since it was a first offense, a stern talking to and a ride in the police car should be enough of a deterrent from further misdemeanors."

"Well, that's something. Sounds like the officer is a decent guy."

She swallows and looks up at me, then away quickly but I catch something in her eyes that looks a lot like guilt. "Yeah, he was really nice and he sat and talked to Evan for a while about what he'd done and where a life of crime, no matter how small, could lead him."

I nod. "I can talk to him if you want."

"I'm not sure what you could add at this point. I've grounded him except for school and soccer. I've also taken away his computer time unless he needs to research something for school. He's not happy with me." She sighs heavily. "I never signed up to be a single parent, you know. It's harder than I thought it was gonna be."

I wrap my arm around her shoulder and begin walking toward the parking lot. "I'm here for support whenever you need it. I've stayed away because that's what you asked me to do, but if you need me, I'll be there. I promised Wyatt that if anything happened to him, I'd keep my eye on you guys."

She takes in a deep breath and blows it out. "I need you to stay away, Shane. I need to be able to handle everything on my own. I've relied on you too much, and that doesn't help me or Evan. It doesn't help you either."

We make it to her car. "But I promised."

She rests her hand on my arm. "I know you did. Wyatt promised me forever and look how that worked out," she says flippantly, then opens the back door of her car and pulls out a casserole dish. "I made you dinner." She offers it to me.

"I'm all right. I've already made dinner. I ... uh ... I'm staying with Toby's sister-in-law for a month while my building is being renovated. I prepared dinner before I came out, so I'm not freeloading on them." I'm not sure why I referred to Violet as Toby's sister-in-law. She's so much more than that.

Her eyes widen and her lips tip up. "You mean that gorgeous woman and her cute little girl?"

I nod and then push the casserole back into her hands. "I'd better get going. Let me know if you want me to talk to Evan."

"I will." I lean in to hug her goodbye. "And Shane."

"Yeah?"

"It's time you did something about Violet and Jasmine." She raises her eyebrows at me, and her eyes sparkle with mischief. It's a look I haven't seen on her for a long time and it gives me hope that maybe one day she'll think about moving forward.

"We'll see." I open Evan's door and squat down to his height. "You have my number, right?"

"Yeah."

"Use it. When you need something or to talk or whatever, give me a call."

"Like you care," he mumbles.

I gently grasp the back of his neck and tug his head up so I can see his face properly. Wyatt's eyes stare at me, full of hurt and anger. "I *do* care, Evan. Trust me, I do. Remember what I said ... I'm trying to give you guys some space to work things out for yourselves, but if you want to talk or hang out or whatever, I'm your man." I tug him forward and press my forehead to his. "And do me a favor. Stay out of trouble and look after your mom."

He attempts to nod. "Okay. I'm sorry I let you down."

I pull away a short distance and shake my head. "You let yourself down more than anyone else. This isn't who you are."

He swallows and his eyes glisten under the interior light of the car. "I know."

I kiss his forehead and stand. "Take care and I'll catch you in two weeks unless you need me before."

"Thanks, Shane."

I FINISH WIPING down the table while Violet makes each of us an ice cream cone for dessert. Silence falls over the room as we enjoy our sweet treat, and I tell them about soccer practice, leaving out the part about Evan knocking over one of his teammates. Jas has a million questions including if she can play soccer too, and I look at Violet for guidance.

"Maybe when you're a little bigger we can look at playing soccer. Okay?"

She nods. "Okay."

Jasmine takes a long lick of her cone to catch the drips, then turns to her mom. "Amber asked if Shane's my daddy." She looks up at me. "Are you my daddy now because you came into my classroom today?"

Vi sputters, so I reach over to calmly pat her on the back even though I'm anything but calm inside. "I'm not your daddy but I'd be happy to do daddy things with you whenever you need. Just get your mom to shoot me a message when I move back to my apartment. Okay?" My gut clenches at the idea of being separated from them.

She takes another lick of her cone as if she didn't just rock my world. "Okay."

How good would it be to be her daddy? The only problem is that I have no idea how to be someone's daddy. Mine was a shitty role model, so I'd probably fuck it up. There's no way I'd want to be responsible for disappointing the angel beside me.

I glance at Violet to find her eyes locked on me, a glassy sheen to them that has me turning my body toward her. "What's wrong, Blue," I murmur.

She shakes her head and looks down at her lap. "Nothing."

There's no way a woman looks close to crying and it's for nothing. But I can't imagine it's easy when your daughter asks another man, other than her father, if he's her daddy now. I'm intuitive enough to know that has to be difficult for a mom. Violet's so damn strong to be able to walk away from the loser she was married to and take on the role of the sole parent. I have so much damn respect for her.

I DROP my Kindle onto the bed and rest my head against the headboard. I think I've read the last page at least five times, and I still have no clue what I've been reading. A smile spreads at the memory of Jas greeting me at the front door and asking if she could come to soccer with me next time. Then my smile drops when I remember the look on Vi's face as she thanked me for making dinner. Like she didn't expect me to follow through with my promise to cook dinner. And then how she looked when Jas asked if I was her daddy now.

After we cleaned up from dessert and Jasmine was bathed and in bed, I came in here to hide out like the coward I am. I didn't want to risk being in close proximity with Violet without the buffer of Jasmine between us. I took things too far last night and she deserves more than a broken man.

I hear movement next door and close my eyes, picturing her in her panties and a camisole like the ones she was wearing last night. I rub my swiftly growing cock through the fabric of my sweats. Fuck. The way she fell apart beneath my touch. I hadn't even been here for a single day, and I already crossed the line I swore I wouldn't cross again. I just can't seem to keep myself in check whenever she's around.

A soft knock sounds at my door. Shit! She'll easily see my semi in these pants. "Just a minute," I call out and grab a long-sleeved T-shirt and do my best to rearrange my dick so it's not so obvious. When I pull the door open, I'm not sure if I'm relieved or disappointed to find Vi still fully dressed in her yoga pants that hug her hips and ass like a second skin and a sweater that falls from one shoulder, exposing a pale green bra strap.

She holds up a bottle of wine and two glasses. "Feel like a nightcap?" Jesus. I could use a nightcap, but not wine. I can think of something else I'd prefer to taste. I flick my eyes from the wine to her face and trace her soft features. Her bright eyes study me, waiting for an answer. Her throat bobs and I want to trace it with my tongue. "Come on, Shane. One drink. It won't hurt, I promise." She winks, then spins on her heel toward the stairs and my eyes instantly drop to the curve of her ass. She shoots me a saucy smile and wink over her shoulder and I know I'm in fucking trouble but it doesn't stop me from grabbing a black foil packet from the drawer next to my bed before I follow her downstairs. What can I say, I like to be prepared—old habits die hard.

When I step into the living room, the lights are low, soft music plays on the stereo, and she has a couple of candles burning. The room exudes seduction and so does the woman sitting on the couch. I should fucking turn around, go upstairs, and lock myself inside my bedroom like I planned. Instead, I walk toward the vixen and take the glass from her outstretched hand, then sit on the cushion beside hers. I feel like I'm having an out-of-body experience and I'm watching this all unfold from across the room because her willingly inviting me to join her is more than I fucking deserve.

She leans back against the couch, tucking one leg under the other, her knee touching my thigh. If I didn't know better, I'd say she's doing her best to look sexy, but I *do* know better and I know that Vi doesn't think that way. This is just her. "You seemed a little tense when you got home from soccer."

I blow out a breath and drop my head back on the couch. My hand automatically seeks out Vi's thigh and I lock my eyes on the ceiling. "Evan's been moody lately. He's not the boy he was six months ago."

"He's almost a teenager, right?" She takes a sip of her wine.

"Yeah, but this is more than that. He was caught stealing." She gasps. "An officer took him home to avoid the gas station owner pressing charges."

"Shit," Vi whispers.

"Yeah. And this afternoon, at the end of the game, he pushed a kid over for no good reason."

"What do you think is going on with him?"

I shake my head and roll my head toward her. "Apart from hormones, I think he's missing me. Hope asked me to give them some space but Evan seems to think I don't care about them anymore. Which couldn't be further from the truth."

Her hand covers mine and my usual need to pull away from

anyone's touch isn't there. I flip my hand over and link my fingers through hers. "It's not my business, but where's his dad?" My muscles tighten, and she has to feel the tension radiating from me. "Sorry. It's not my business. Forget I asked," she says quickly.

I rub my thumb over her knuckles. "It's a fair question." Am I ready to share? Vi's always shared everything with me. She's so fucking brave to be vulnerable and raw. Can I do the same? She squeezes my hand in quiet support. "His dad died in Syria."

Her expression softens. "Oh, Shane. I'm so sorry."

I take a moment to absorb her sympathy, something I don't normally accept. "He was my best friend over there, and I promised him that if anything ever happened to him, I would take care of his wife and son. It's what I've always tried to do since returning home but Hope asked me to step back because she felt she was relying on me too much. She wants to stand on her own feet. Which is fine, but I made a promise." I release Vi's hand and scrub my hand through my hair, gripping the short strands in frustration.

"I can't imagine how you feel about stepping back. You're a fixer." I scoff. "You *are*," she insists.

"Yeah, well, some things can't ever be fixed."

"I know," she whispers as she rests her head on my shoulder. I wrap my arm around her, holding her close, and we sit in silence— our breathing barely audible over the soft music playing.

SOMETHING PRESSES on my balls and my eyes snap open. I look up at the ceiling and then scan the surrounding area. It takes a moment to realize I'm still on the couch, and if the faint rays of sunlight streaming through the gaps around the curtains are anything to go by, it's morning.

Huh, how about that.

A warm body presses at my side while a smaller one wriggles

on my chest, and I look down. My lips stretch of their own accord at the sight. Vi is curled into my side, her face resting on top of her hand on my shoulder and her leg is thrown over both of mine. But she's not the only one using my body as her personal pillow. Jasmine is curled up in a ball on my chest wrapped in her blanket.

I desperately need to take a leak but I don't want to disturb the girls from their slumber and more importantly, I don't want to break this moment—it feels too significant. I soak it all in. Their trust in me, the feeling of being surrounded by two people who suddenly feel more important to me than anything else, and the sensation of hope blossoming in my chest that maybe I could have this on a permanent basis.

Stretching out my free arm, I check the time. Shit! It's seven. I'm pretty sure they need to get up. Yesterday, they were already up and getting ready for work and school by this time. I shift my arm beneath Vi and skate my fingers along her hairline, gently pushing her hair away from her face. She's so damn beautiful. Her eyelids flutter open slowly revealing sleepy oceanic irises. Her lips tip up slightly and she presses deeper into me like she isn't quite aware of what she's doing.

"Morning, Blue," I murmur. "We fell asleep."

She chuckles lightly, then her eyes drop from mine and land on her daughter. She instantly reaches for her little girl and strokes her back gently. "She must have come looking for me during the night. Sometimes she still crawls into bed with me."

Vi shuffles her leg higher, collecting my morning wood. "Hmpf." My body locks tight. It's not like I can control it but I don't want Jas to feel what's going on.

"Sorry," she apologizes and slides her leg off of me. "What time is it?"

"Just after seven."

Her eyes widen and her body tenses against mine. "Shit! We need to get up."

With her trapped between my body and the back of the couch,

I need to get up first. I wrap my arms around Jas and use my core muscles to get into a sitting position, then climb to my feet. She stirs against my chest, her tangled hair hiding her face, so I brush it away. Her eyes flutter open, much the way her mother's did, revealing her pretty blue eyes.

These girls are doing a number on me. I've been here less than three days and already we're having sleepovers and waking up together. I have no hope of staying here for one month and coming out of this situation unscathed.

Jas snuggles into me so I tighten my hold on her as Vi climbs to her feet and stretches her arms up to reveal a smooth swathe of toned skin. And in that moment, I know down to my soul that I don't want to come out of this unscathed.

"I'm just gonna run upstairs and have a quick shower."

I nod and follow her upstairs to get Jasmine dressed for school. By the time my foot touches the top step, Jasmine's fully awake and is smiling up at me. She wraps her little arms around my neck and lays a kiss on my bristly cheek. "You were sleeping on the couch with Mommy."

"Yeah, we fell asleep." We enter Jas's bedroom, and I place her on her feet.

"Why?"

I grab her brush and start to carefully brush the tangles from her hair thinking about everything we talked about last night. Vi gave me the space to share some happy memories about Wyatt; something I haven't done before. "We were talking and I guess we got tired."

"What were you talking about?" I grab an elastic and smooth her hair into a ponytail like I've seen her wear before.

"My friend, Wyatt, and how his son Evan seems sad, and I don't know how to make him feel better."

"Why does Evan feel sad?" She spins around to face me, studying me closely.

"I think he misses his daddy." Guilt snaps through my body

like a current, making my heart stutter and tightening my stomach. This guilt is different from before. I no longer wish it had been me who died because if it'd been me, I wouldn't be looking toward a possible future with this little girl and her mother.

She goes quiet for a long time and I realize my mistake. She probably misses her father. "Where's his daddy?" she asks softly.

"He's in heaven."

She thinks for a long moment and tips her head toward her shoulder with a small smile. "I always feel better when Mommy hugs me." She strips off her pajamas and grabs the school clothes she and Violet laid out last night. I spin around so she has privacy but not before I see the birthmark Violet told me about across her stomach.

I swallow past the thickness in my throat. "Hugs are definitely good."

"Yeah, I love hugs. I can give Evan a hug and see if that makes him feel better." My heart thumps against my ribs at her innate kindness.

"That's really kind of you. Maybe when you come with me to soccer you can give him a hug."

"Yay! I'd like that." She steps in front of me fully dressed for school. "I'm hungry."

"All right, let's go make breakfast." She slides her little hand in mine, and the trust she has in me makes me feel like the luckiest man on earth.

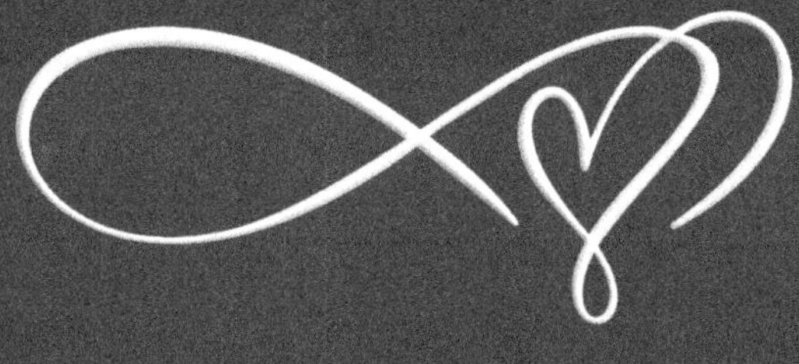

25

VIOLET

WELL, IT'S BEEN INTERESTING. HAVING SHANE HERE HAS changed the dynamic in the house. Every morning we've worked as a team to get Jas to school and me to work. At first, I tried to stop him because I'm more than capable of looking after myself and Jas but after day three, I gave up. It seemed to make him happy, and I know Shane well enough to understand that he likes to help others.

In other, more disappointing news, there have been no more sleepovers or impromptu orgasms in the garage. And even though I wouldn't say no to either of those things happening again, the night he opened up to me about his army friend was more intimate than any time we've spent together before that. It felt like an enormous step toward closing the final distance between us. I felt the shift in him. In us. And I don't think it was my imagination or wishful thinking. He's been different. Lighter. Freer. Especially with Jas.

My phone buzzes, and when I grab it out of my pocket, Mom's face is smiling at me. "Hi, Mom. How was the conference?"

"Amazing. I've learned so many new things and made loads of

new connections," she says, excitement filling her voice. "You'll never guess what happened."

"I'll never guess. Tell me everything." I lean forward, waiting with bated breath.

"Well, the second day at lunch, I was sitting next to a man and we were chatting about the industry. There was something familiar about him but I couldn't put my finger on it. Well, the next day we found each other again, and he commented that I seemed familiar. It took us the entirety of lunch to work out we moved in the same circle at high school. He moved away and lost touch with our group and well … life moves on, I guess."

"Oh, that's great, Mom. And how coincidental that you work in the same industry."

"I know, right? Anyway, he lives here and invited me to stay for another week. He's going to take me around and show me how he runs his business, then he might come out to visit me in a couple of months so I can return the favor."

"That's awesome."

"You don't mind, do you?"

I frown. "Of course not. You deserve to have a break. Stay as long as you like."

"Well, I figured you have Shane there to help you, so this is the perfect opportunity for me."

"Even if Shane weren't here, you could take time for yourself, Mom. I can manage. It's not like I didn't do everything for me and Jas when we lived with Allen." Shit that sounds like I don't appreciate her help. "I appreciate everything you do for us, but you're entitled to have some time for yourself. Have fun, see the sights, relax."

"Thanks, love." There's a long pause on the other end of the phone. "So, how are things going with Shane?" I get up to pace.

"Uh, good. Great actually." As Mom always does, she knows there's more and waits me out. "It's been really nice having him here and it feels like he *wants* to be here with us. Not that it's just a convenient place to stay while his apartment is renovated."

"Uh-huh."

"And ... uh, I feel like we're starting to build something." I fold my arm across my stomach.

I hear her sigh. "I'm so pleased to hear that, Violet. He's a good man, much like Toby."

"I know." I pace to the window and look across our backyard. "Anyway, I'll let you go and we'll see you in a week."

"Give Jas a big squeeze from me. Bye, love."

"I will. Bye, Mom."

I end the call and blow out a long breath. I can't stop the hopeful feeling that grows at the thought of spending another week with only the three of us. I grab my laundry and head downstairs. I'm not sure what Shane's up to today, but he made himself scarce yesterday and again this morning. The sky's overcast this morning, so I transfer Jas's clothes to the drier and put mine in the machine.

My phone buzzes with a text, and I pull it from my pocket.

CASS

So I just got off the phone with Mom ;)

ME

Yeah, me too

CASS

She's staying for another week ;)

ME

She told me. It's great that she connected with a high school friend

CASS

Did you notice it was a HE? :0

Oh yeah. Hmm, I *did* notice.

ME

Do you think she's "connecting" with him? Lol

CASS

God, I hope so. She deserves it

ME

She so does

CASS

Anyway, I was hoping you'd let Jas come for a
sleepover until Sunday

Poppy's missing her cousin

I'm onto my sister but I'm not about to say no.

ME

Jas misses Poppy too

CASS

Great!

I'm finishing work early today, so bring her over
after school

ME

Okay, see you then

And, thanks ...

I know exactly what you're doing, and I
appreciate it

CASS

You're welcome ;)

Hmmm, I need a plan for the weekend. Perhaps we can start
with a nice dinner, some sexy lingerie, candles, music ... maybe
dancing in the living room. I'll have to wait for the laundry to
finish but I have heaps to do.

SOFT MUSIC FILLS the house when I hear the front door open and close. Goosebumps race across my body like wildfire, and my nipples pucker in readiness.

It's time!

In all the time I've known Shane, this is the first time we've been truly alone and in a situation where we won't be interrupted. His footsteps echo down the hallway but pause for a moment at what I assume is the doorway to the living room. Then he's on the move again as he approaches the kitchen entry. A shiver works its way through my body knowing he's so close, and I turn to look at him over my shoulder, finding him leaning against the doorframe with his arms crossed. *He's such a beautiful man.* I scan his face, noting the five o'clock shadow on his strong jaw and the slight narrowing of his eyes.

"Oh, hey. You're home." *I hope that sounded normal.*

His dark eyebrows slash down over his gorgeous eyes. "Yeah. Are you going out or something?"

"Uh ... no, why?"

He traces my body with his gaze and shifts on his feet. "You're dressed up. Where's Jas?"

I turn to face Shane fully. "She's staying with Cass, Toby, and the girls until Sunday morning."

His eyebrows shoot up while he drops his hands to tuck them in the front pockets of his jeans. He knows the girls often have sleepovers, so this isn't unusual. "So it's just you and me?"

"Yeah." *Shit, that came out a little breathy.*

He takes a predatory step toward me, and my breath stalls in my lungs. There's a certain look in his eye that I've not seen before. It's dark and promises all sorts of things. Well, I hope it's promising all sorts of things. He takes another step and another until he has me backed against the counter. His hands drop to the surface on either side of my hips and this close, I can see the copper striations in his warm irises.

"Alone?" He leans closer and his warm breath ghosts across my lips. My tongue darts out to taste the air, and his eyes drop to watch. "All weekend?"

I nod, my voice suddenly missing. His lips tip up in a sinful smirk as he traces every inch of my face with his eyes. The man hasn't even touched me, and my heart's thumping triple time against my ribs and I'm finding it hard to breathe. His chest brushes my breasts, and I'm certain he can feel my diamond-hard peaks.

The buzzer on the oven sounds, breaking the crackling tension between us, and it takes him a few seconds to step away so I can deal with our dinner. Inhaling a deep breath, I turn off the oven and grab the oven mitts with shaky hands. Once I have the dish of tetrazzini safely in my grasp, I carry it to the table as Shane lights the candles I placed in the center. He holds up the bottle I opened earlier. "Wine?"

"Please." I hold my glass up, hoping he doesn't notice the slight tremor, and he pours a healthy amount into it, then fills his own. *I'm gonna need this to take the edge off.*

"This looks great. Smells good, too."

"Thanks. It's one of my favorite dishes and easy to cook, too."

He scoops a decent amount onto his fork, and I watch for his reaction. His eyes widen slightly and he nods his head a little, then goes straight back in for another scoop. I breathe a sigh of relief because it seems as though he likes it. "This is delicious. Thanks for making dinner."

"You're welcome and I'm glad you like it." I take a bite of my pasta dish, ensuring I have a little of everything on my fork, chew and swallow. "What did you do today?" *Way to make the conversation mundane, Vi.*

He swallows the food in his mouth. "I spent the day at *The*

Bunker." I narrow my eyes and try to think if I've heard him talk about the place before but I'm drawing a blank. "Where is it?"

"It's on the outskirts of the city center. It's a place for returned servicemen and women." He takes a sip of his wine, and I do the same. I like this Shane. The one who shares parts of himself with me. "When I'm not doing something with Toby, I spend a lot of time there. We restore discarded bikes and gift them to underprivileged kids and groups that work with children in low socio-economic areas." I'm not surprised that he does something that gives support to the community; he can't help but help others. He twists the stem of his wine glass, his eyes dropping to watch the action. "That place and the people there have saved me from myself on several occasions."

My heart splinters and without thinking I reach across the table to lay my hand on his for a quiet moment. "I'm glad you have a support system."

His eyes rise to meet mine and he lifts his shoulder. "It's only when I look back, I can see how far I've come from the man I was when I first came home, and it's all thanks to Toby and the support I've had from the people at *The Bunker.*" He twists his glass around in the other direction. "I do my best to give back now that I'm in a better place." Even in the two years I've known Shane, I've seen a difference in him. It must be difficult to go to war and see and do awful things and then have to return to normal society. It's admirable, really, and I wonder if he realizes how strong he is.

We spend the remainder of the meal talking about general stuff. I tell him that Mom's decided to stay away for another week and brag that I got some Daisy snuggles this afternoon to which he responds that he got his snuggles this morning. I sometimes forget how entrenched he already is in our family.

As we clean up from dinner, the tension between us ratchets up with every *accidental* brush against each other. I've always been physically attracted to Shane, but over this past week, as he's opened up a little to me, I've fallen harder for him. Not to mention watching him with Jasmine is enough to have me falling at his feet.

As I bend over to put the last dish away, Shane's hands land on my hips sending heat racing through my body. "Why don't you go into the living room and put your feet up? I'll bring what's left of the wine."

"That sounds like a plan I can get behind." I smile at him as I stand, then head into the living room to change the playlist and light the candles. Since I've already moved the coffee table to the side, we have room to dance. Ever since we danced together at Cass and Toby's wedding, I've wanted to be back in his arms where I feel safe and protected. I sway to the soft song playing as I watch the sun sink below the rooftops, painting the sky in dusky pinks and oranges.

A glass of wine comes into my vision over my shoulder, and I turn to take it from Shane. We watch each other as we both take a sip, the sweetness of the wine coating my tongue. Shane dips forward and licks the seam of my lips, and I could die with relief right now that he's made the first move, and I don't have to wonder if he wants this as much as I do. I hold myself still, allowing him to take the lead and he doesn't disappoint as he presses his mouth firmly against mine, coaxing me to reciprocate. The feel of his lips is like a bolt of lightning to my core that heats my blood on the way.

His free hand goes around my waist and he sways to the music with me as he teases my mouth with his until we open to each other. The sweet taste on his tongue as we move together sensually sends goosebumps racing across my skin. My panties are already soaked beyond anything the fabric can absorb and the wetness coats my thighs. My thumping heart matches the beat of the music, and I press against him, feeling his hardness against my stomach.

He disengages and takes the wine from my hand, placing both of our glasses on the table beneath the window. "I've been dying to taste your lips from the moment I knew we were alone, and there'd be no interruptions." As if to punctuate his sentence, he presses his lips gently to the space beneath my ear, nuzzling into my neck and placing soft, lazy kisses against my skin, making his way slowly along my jawline to my mouth. His hand lands on my hip and he grips me almost painfully. "You torture me in the best possible way, Blue," he murmurs against my mouth. His soft lips sweep over mine in a whisper of a touch, his breath warming the supple pillows, and a sigh slips past my lips. He presses more firmly and his tongue pushes inside my mouth. He's not requesting permission to enter, he's taking what he wants, and I couldn't be happier to give it to him.

I rest my palms on his pecs while his big hands cup my face, his fingers weaving through my hair as his tongue seeks out mine with sensual strokes. My body melts into his when he angles my face to deepen the kiss, tasting and licking, dancing and stroking. I press closer, soaking up everything he's giving me, and eagerly return his ministrations. A moan barrels out of me as lust bubbles in my veins. It's embarrassing how wet I already am and we've barely started. I've been wanting this moment for such a long time; I almost can't believe it's finally happening.

His hands move from my face to my neck and down to my shoulders. They smooth their way along the edges of my breasts, tracing the dip of my waist until they land on my hips. He squeezes the extra softness there, then glides his hands over my ass, not once pausing our kiss. His exploration of my dips and curves is sensory overload and has my synapses firing all over the place. He grips my backside hard, almost to the point of pain, pressing his cock into my stomach and it's impossible to miss how hard he is for *me*. *For me*.

With a panting breath, he pulls his lips away, traces his nose up the side of mine, and kisses my forehead. It's such a different kiss from the ones we just shared that I open my eyes to study the man before me. His lips are puffy from our kisses, swollen to the point they almost look feminine and his pupils are dilated, nearly swallowing the warm brown that I love so much. I feel his heart pounding a heavy beat that matches mine beneath my touch and his heavy breaths are uneven as they blow across my lips. "As much as I loved this dress on you the first time you wore it and as much as I love it today, I'm gonna need you to take it off." His words rumble across his lips, and he takes a small step back from me. I miss his heat immediately, and my instinct is to follow him and plaster myself to his body but I keep myself steady.

Heat rises through me, and my legs tremble beneath his heavy-lidded gaze. Slowly, without taking my eyes off his, I find my courage and bravely bend forward to grip the bottom of my sweater dress, pausing for a moment before I begin to slide it up my legs, past my knees, and higher still to the tops of my thighs. His gaze doesn't stray from the edge of my dress and I can tell the moment the fabric breaches my panties by his sudden sharp inhale and the slight widening of his eyes. His throat bobs as I expose the emerald silk covering my pussy, and he licks his lips when the knitted material reaches my waist.

"Keep going." His voice is barely a roughened whisper, but I feel it like a heated caress everywhere. My nipples pucker to the point of pain and an embarrassing amount of slickness from my pussy coats my thighs.

Can he see how wet I am for him?

I continue the slow torturous glide up my body, exposing the bottom of my matching silky bra, then slide it up and over my head, sending my hair cascading down my back. Catching the fabric in one hand, I toss it onto the single couch near the window and I stand before him in my underwear, acutely aware that all of my flaws are on display for the perfect man before me.

Shane's hands twitch but he remains rooted to the spot as his heated gaze traces every curve and dip, crease and bulge. I suck in a shaky breath under his perusal, my heavy breasts rising and falling as I do. When I flick my eyes across his body, I can't miss the huge bulge behind his zipper.

"Cup your breasts and push them together for me."

I continue with my show, sliding my hands slowly up from my thighs, across my stomach which still has the evidence of my pregnancy stretch marks, and up to my boobs. Doing as he asks, I cup each one and push them up and together, creating cleavage while my nipples do their best to press through the fabric. A deep groan vibrates through Shane's body and he roughly adjusts his cock in his jeans. I follow the action and unintentionally lick my lips. The memory of him in my mouth, his taste, how big he is … like the most decadent of treats I can't wait to sample again and again.

Without hesitation, Shane steps closer and his hands land at the dip of my waist. His touch sends fire shooting through my veins like flames racing uphill and I rub my thighs together seeking some form of relief. He bends at the knees and dips his head, burying his face in the space I've just created and kissing the exposed skin. His roughened cheeks are a beautiful contrast to his soft lips against my sensitive flesh making my heavy breasts ache in the confines of my silky bra. At once the pressure releases and Shane gently slides the straps from my shoulders with his calloused fingers and tosses the bra aside to join my dress. The air in my lungs escapes with a gasp when his warm mouth surrounds one nipple, and he bites the peak.

God, how I want to touch him. To grip the strands of his hair, if only to keep myself grounded. "Mmm, that feels so good." He rewards me with a moan and swaps to the other side, doling out the same attention. "Your mouth feels incredible."

He pulls back and one side of his lips tip up in a sinfully sexy grin. "I plan to keep it on you until you beg me to stop." *Well, I can't imagine that happening anytime soon.* Picking up his glass of wine, he dips his fingers into the sweet beverage and then rubs his wet fingers around my nipple causing it to bead further. "Let's see how they taste with a little Moscato." The tip of his warm tongue is striking against the coolness of the wine and I gasp, swaying my body into his. He repeats the process and not for the first time, I wish I could touch him somehow.

Pulling away, he studies his handiwork, pinching each peak between his fingers and twisting them. The small amount of pain shoots straight to my core, and I swear to God, if I weren't still wearing my panties, my arousal would be sliding down my thighs. Kissing and nipping, he makes his way back up to my mouth while his fingers skate over the softness of my stomach, straight to the soaked fabric covering my slit. We both moan at the same time and I eagerly widen my stance. I'm so freaking ready to get to the good stuff. I hope against hope that we'll actually get to the good stuff tonight.

He chuckles against my lips, our eyes locked tight. "Don't worry, Blue, I'll take care of you."

His words send a shiver through me and I have to tear my gaze away from his to hide what they do to me. The strength of his declaration. The certainty that he'll take care of me—not just in this moment but I sense he means in *every* moment—is like an aphrodisiac. I've been taking care of everything for so long, it feels foreign to give up that control to someone else but I have every confidence in Shane to do as he promises.

He dips his fingers between the silk and my mound and tugs, giving me no choice but to follow as he leads me toward the couch. The candles flicker and the music plays softly in the background but the man in front of me steals all of my focus. Sliding his fingers around to my hips, his knuckles drag across my flesh and leave a wave of goosebumps in their wake. Hooking his fingers in either side, he slips my panties down my legs, then taps each foot in turn, to remove them, and tucks them in his pocket.

He takes my lips in another heated kiss. This time, it's a little messy with lots of tongue and I move as close as I can to him, pressing my naked body against his fully clothed one, and whimper. Our tongues twist and delve, taste and stroke, tease and tempt.

We haven't kissed all that much but there's a familiarity ... a comfort I can't describe.

After a long moment, he slows the kiss, finishing with small pecks, and drops his forehead to mine.

We pause like that.

Our breaths heavy.

Our eyes connected.

Our hearts thumping in our chests in a heavy staccato.

"If I don't get my mouth on your pussy in the next thirty seconds, I don't think I'll survive." He exhales, his breath coating my lips. "Knees on the edge of the couch, lean your elbows on the back for me, Blue." Always a man of few words.

With my heart thumping so hard and my breaths as shallow as they are, my head spins a little as I turn to do as I'm told. I rest my knees on the edge of the cushion then drop forward to rest my elbows on the back of the couch, leaving my heavy, achy breasts hanging and exposing my pussy. The thump of Shane's knees hitting the carpet is the only warning I get before the first swipe of his tongue. The firm stroke makes me jolt, and I peek over my shoulder to watch him work his magic. Our eyes lock as if some magnetic force is at work as he devours me so completely that I battle to keep my eyes open and on him. The sight of his lustful gaze on me fills me with power and makes me feel sexy, something I haven't felt for a long while, if ever.

Our moans fill the living room and drown out the music as he plunges two fingers inside me, stretching me deliciously. Stealing his eyes from me when he dips down to tease his tongue around my clit, I shiver and close my eyes. Tension builds through my limbs and I know this orgasm is going to barrel down on me like a freight train. I drop my head to the couch and prepare myself to fall apart because there's no way to hold off with the way he's working me over, and as great as his mouth and fingers feel, I'm hoping I finally get his cock at some point tonight. The muscles in my legs tense, and I'm on the brink of breaking into a million pieces.

His mouth disappears and his fingers slide out of my pussy. I snap my head around. "Wha—"

With his eyes locked on my pussy, he hurriedly unbuckles and unzips his jeans, pushing them below his ass to free his magnificent penis. I'm not a penis expert, but his just seems so … *perfect*.

"Are you ready for me, Blue?"

I exhale a long breath. "So ready."

He reaches across to the side table and grabs a condom I left there earlier—a girl has to be prepared for any situation, right?— and slides it down his thick shaft. *Yum!*

Gripping my hip, he lines himself up with my opening and teases me with his thick head. I try to push back and take him inside, but Shane's strong grip keeps me in place. "Patience," he murmurs with his eyes locked on where we're about to be joined. There'll be no turning back for either of us once we share this. He slips the thick head in and I tilt my hips back, eager to take him all the way inside. My spine dips and Shane grips the back of my neck, then slides the palm of his hand along the curve of my vertebrae until he reaches my ass. "So damn beautiful," he says, roughly as he slides his cock in a little further. I'm so impatient, I just want him to slam into me … over and over and over again. I want him to take us to paradise and never stop. But he continues his slow intrusion, torturing us both. "You should see how beautiful your pussy looks as it stretches around my cock."

"Show me."

Creases form across his forehead when he raises his eyebrows. A sinful smirk touches his naughty lips and he digs into his back pocket, grabbing his phone. He snaps a photo and shows it to me, and I swear to God I can feel myself dripping down my thighs. The pinkness of my lips stretched tight around his thick shaft, the prominent vein decorating his length disappearing inside me is so damn hot. He flips the phone back around, points it to where we're joined, and slides in further. Pulling out slowly, he pushes in a little further this time, the camera still focused on us. He moans as he pushes in all the way to the root, finally burying himself inside me as deep as he can. *Finally!*

"You know this means you're mine now. There's no going back to how things were," he growls.

His words make my stomach quiver and a mewl works its way up my throat, escaping my lips and my back dips further. I've waited so long. "So long as you know you're mine, too." My thighs shake as I adjust my position to accept him fully. "You feel so good," I breathe. *So good.* Better than I could have anticipated.

"Not as good as you feel wrapped around me," he rumbles, still holding the phone as he pumps leisurely in and out of me, his head tilted down on an angle to watch the action. I was so close to the edge before, I'm going to burst any second now. Every muscle in my body tenses and my breath stalls. He fills me and stretches me so perfectly that my walls are tightening around him already. *No.* I don't want this to be over yet. It's too quick and I've waited too long. "Don't hold onto it. Let go so we can work toward another one," he coaxes.

Oh God!

With both hands gripping my hips, he pushes back in harder than before with a feral-sounding grunt. I glance over my shoulder to find he's discarded his phone somewhere and his gaze is focused solely on our coupling. "I-I can't come like this, my clit needs attention, too."

His gaze snaps up to mine, and his brows dip down in concentration but he leans down over me, cloaking me with his big body and sliding one hand around to where I need him. His clothes are rough against my bare skin, sending a shiver through me and heightening my arousal. He rubs tight circles around the sensitive bud and I moan, pushing my ass back into him. "Like that?"

"God, yes." I meet his every thrust making the buckle of his belt clank. "Harder." He doesn't slow but he does add more force each time he plunges inside making my boobs swing. My walls tighten, and I suck in a sharp breath when his grip on my hip intensifies. "Mmmhm." The pressure on my clit increases, electricity shoots through my muscles making them lock tight, and my walls spasm around his talented cock. "Oh, fuuuck, Shaaaane!" I shout as my orgasm barrels through me and steals all my air.

"Ah, shit! Your cum is all over my cock," he growls as he slows his thrusts, working me through my orgasm. "Damn, I wish you could see this, Blue." He pushes in and slides out slowly. "You feel even better than I thought you would, and I've thought about this moment a lot."

Me too.

His hand grips the back of my neck, and he turns my head to the side, folding his big body over mine again, and taking my lips in a ferocious kiss. Blood rushes through my ears and I fear my heart is going to force its way out of my body. I taste my arousal as well as his desperation and relish in it. Knowing he's as desperate for me as I am for him repairs some of those cracks I've been working toward healing. As our mouths fuse, his hand glides down the side of my body, tracing the curves and dips, until he reaches my ass, then slides back up again in a soothing stroke that doesn't match the way he's ravaging my mouth.

When he slips his cock out of me, he strokes his fingers through my pussy lips and brings them to his mouth, sliding them past his lips. Closing his eyes, like he's savoring a decadent treat, he moans around his digits and the rumble makes my empty pussy throb. Even though I just came like a lightning bolt, I want him back inside me. I want it like nothing I've ever wanted before.

He makes me crazy desperate.

He opens his eyes and a predatory gleam locks onto me. With a smirk, he pulls my panties out of his pocket and takes a seat on the couch beside me. "Climb on." He taps his thigh while his other hand holds his cock, covered in my cum, straight up for me.

Oh my!

I shuffle closer and then straddle him. With my eyes locked on his, I hold onto the back of the couch and lower myself on his thick shaft. Moans escape both of us as I slide down until he's seated deep inside me. I drop my head forward and enjoy the stretch, the feeling of fullness, the feeling of *completion*. And that curve of his cock ... it hits me in the best place possible.

Shane gently guides each of my hands behind my back, and I drop my gaze to look at him as the position forces me to sit upright. "I know you can't keep your hands to yourself, so this is a gentle reminder." He twists the damp silky fabric of my panties around my wrists and I allow him. He's right, I can't help myself. It's unnatural for me to not touch my lover and I'm too scared he'll stop if I resist.

I definitely don't want him to stop and to be honest, it's hot how he binds my wrists. His hands trace back around my body until they reach my hips.

Using my thigh and stomach muscles, my breasts bounce as I rise and then drop back down under Shane's firm guidance. He leans forward slightly and his lips drop to my nipple and he draws it into his warm mouth, sucking and teasing me as I rise and fall again and again over his cock. His thumb circles my clit in delicate strokes and the delicious friction is exquisite. I'm thankful I've already had an orgasm because I want to drag this out for as long as possible. I increase my speed and use my full weight to drop down heavily landing on Shane's jean-clad thighs over and over, both of us building toward a release that can't be stopped.

"That's it, Blue. Come all over my cock." Shane pants as a sheen of sweat coats his forehead.

Our lips connect and lock, our tongues twist and stroke, and he wraps his arms around me tightly as we both fall apart. The edge of my vision goes fuzzy and it's hard to find my breath as his dick pulses inside me and my pussy squeezes him so tight in return that I'm worried I'm going to black out. Shane's thick fingers weave through my sweaty hair and he tightens his grip, pushing the intensity of the kiss upward as we each ride out our release.

Oh my God, I think I just had an out-of-body experience. Tearing my mouth from his to catch my breath, I drop my forehead to his shoulder and suck in much-needed oxygen while he pets my hair and kisses the side of my face. "That was incredible and now I'm kicking my own ass that I resisted you for so damn long."

A chuckle bursts out of me and I roll my forehead back and forth on his shoulder. "You only have yourself to blame, I kept giving you all the signals."

His hand strokes my hair and he rests his cheek on top of my head. "I know, Blue. Believe me, I got them loud and clear." He pauses and his throat bobs as he swallows. My tongue darts out to swipe his Adam's apple, tasting his salty perspiration. "I wasn't sure I could be what you deserved."

I raise my head and capture his eyes. "I just need you to be you."

26

I LIE WITH MY HANDS BEHIND MY HEAD AS A DEEP satisfaction settles over me but there's also an ache that wasn't there before. My mind flashes back to the disappointment on Vi's face when I wouldn't climb into her bed with her. I didn't want to risk having a night terror and scaring her. Or even worse, harming her in some way. I would do anything to be able to sleep beside her, have her curled up in my arms and her hair in my face.

Before I can think twice about it, I climb out of bed, throw on a pair of sweats and a long-sleeved T-shirt, grab a condom, and head next door. I reach for the handle without overthinking what I'm about to do. I want her taste on my tongue again because she's my new favorite flavor and I'm tired of denying myself what I want.

Opening the door, I quietly step inside Vi's room. She raises her head and her eyes latch onto me. Her shoulders drop slightly and a soft smile touches her lips. Fuck, she's so damn gorgeous. She pulls back the covers on the empty side of the bed and pats it, welcoming me without question or recourse.

It's then I pause.

She waits patiently but I can tell she's straining to keep her smile in place. I didn't expect her to be awake. I thought I'd sneak in here and wake her with my tongue on her pussy.

"Do you want to come in?"

"Why are you awake?"

One smooth shoulder rises and falls. "Couldn't sleep. You?"

"Couldn't sleep, but that's nothing new for me." I take a few steps to her bed and climb in.

She twists her body so she's facing me and crosses her legs. "Why do you have so much trouble sleeping?"

Resting my hand on her smooth thigh, I consider my answer. If I'm truly going to have something real, something worthwhile and long-lasting, I need to be truthful. "My time away left me with some deep trauma. I have night terrors some nights and even when I don't, my body doesn't seem to be able to stay asleep. It's always on high alert. It's fucking exhausting." I rub my hand down my face, then chance a look at hers. She laces her fingers through mine but she's not looking at me like I'm broken. "I'm so tired, Violet."

Her eyes flick between mine. "So lay beside me and sleep. I'll watch over you. I promise I won't let anything happen." She leans forward and presses the gentlest of kisses against my lips and I snap my hand up to tangle in her hair to hold her mouth to mine.

Her words. So fucking simple. But so damn beautiful.

Her offer to protect me does something to the deepest parts of me. It stitches together a small part of my broken soul and I deepen the kiss. Before I realize it, I've laid her down and I'm climbing over her body, pinning her hands above her head. I kiss her in a way that I hope portrays what her words mean to me. Her promise to take care of me when it should always be the other way around. She wraps her legs around my ass, and I grind down on her mound, dry-humping her like a teenager. Sexy moans escape her lips and I greedily swallow them down, collecting them like they're precious gems.

Within moments, I have her panties cast aside and a condom sheathing my cock and I'm sliding home into her warm heat.

"Mine," I murmur as I piston my hips slowly, grinding down on her clit each time as she whimpers. It was so hot how she told me exactly what she needs to come, so I make sure to hit all the spots that need to be stimulated as I kiss her deeply, ravaging her mouth and her pussy at the same time. Tangling my fingers through hers to keep her from touching me, I tease her with my tongue, mimicking the action and speed of my hips. Long, slow, seductive strokes in and out of heaven as we both build toward our release.

Tension intensifies through my muscles and electricity shimmers through my veins. My back aches, but I ignore it in favor of enjoying the moment. Vi's legs tense around my hips and her velvet walls tighten around my cock. She feels incredible. I tear my mouth away from hers. "You were made for me. Feel how good we are together." My heart tightens as it expands with the emotions I have for her.

She nods, her eyes rolling back in her head and her mouth forming a beautiful O when I hit that special spot inside her. Keeping my eyes locked on her face, I swivel my hips each time I bottom out. Puffs of warm air coat my face every time I push inside and Vi's mouth opens wider with a silent scream as her walls strangle the life out of my dick. *Fuck!* I try to hold out, gentling my strokes as she falls apart spectacularly beneath me but my body has other plans. I lower my head and take her mouth in a violent kiss as I fill the condom with ribbon after ribbon of cum. It's almost sweet agony as I push in as deep as possible emptying every last drop into the latex.

I drop my forehead to hers and suck in much-needed air before I black out and collapse on top of her. When I open my eyes, her lips are spreading slowly and there's a sparkle in her eye. "You make me come so hard, I almost blacked out."

I huff out a chuckle. "Same." Keeping our connection, I roll to the side, bringing Violet with me. I release her hands and she drags them down between us, laying them on my pecs, and buries her face in my neck. Using the tips of my fingers, I gently stroke her hair away from her face and lay soft kisses on the top of her head and across her temple trying to express my gratitude for the gift she's given me. She tries to slide her leg off my hip but I grip it and hold it in place. I like being wrapped in her, having her athletic legs encircling me and holding me close.

She pulls away slightly, tilting her head back and what I see in her eyes causes a lump to form in my throat. "I'm feeling some big feelings and I'm a little scared that I'm feeling them on my own."

She's so fucking brave.

It's time I took some risks, too. "You're not on your own, Blue. I promise you."

Her lips spread slowly, and her eyes twinkle as she exhales and snuggles back into me. We lie together in the quiet of the night, her hand on my heart, our breaths in sync.

As much as it pains me, I pull out of her heat. "I need to deal with the condom. Back in a minute."

"You're coming back?" Hope tinges her words, and I hate that I gave her any doubts.

"Yeah, Blue. I'm coming back." I do what I need to do and climb back into bed, ensuring I'm on the side closest to the door.

I lie on my back and she curls into my side, her head resting over my heart. Peace settles over me, and I close my eyes for a moment.

"SHANE!" Jas leaps for me as soon as I step through the front door after spending the morning at *The Bunker*. We needed to load up the bikes to take to a group foster home run by *The Parkerville Project,* so it was a matter of giving them all a final polish and adding the decals so they were ready to go. I came home to have a quick shower before I have to head over to Mom and Dad's so she can wish me happy birthday for tomorrow.

I chuckle as I swing her up into my arms. "Hey, Angel. Did you have fun with Poppy and Daisy?"

"Yeah. Daisy's so funny. She follows me everywhere, even the bathroom but I missed you and Mommy."

My heart squeezes at her words. I don't know what I did for this little girl to give me her love and trust so easily but I'll never take it for granted. "Well, we missed you, too." When we weren't *busy*.

Vi steps out of the kitchen with a slight limp—I may have gotten a little carried away this morning but I can't say I'm sorry. I mean, I'm sorry she's having trouble walking but I'm not sorry for what we were doing. I meet her halfway and wrap my arm around her waist, pulling her into me, and dip down to taste her lips. "Hey, Blue."

"You kissed Mommy," Jasmine almost shouts.

Without taking my eyes off Violet, I nod. "I did."

"Kiss me, too!" She bounces in my arms and I chuckle at her excitement, then press a kiss to her forehead. She drops her head onto my shoulder with a shy grin. "I love you, Shane," she whispers, and something weird happens in my chest. My stomach flips and I don't recall when it happened, but I've loved this kid for a long time.

"I love you, too, Angel." When I glance up at Vi, her eyes are glassy and she's biting that pouty bottom lip of hers, one hand teasing out the bottom of her hair. I catch her eye to check in with her. "Are you okay?"

She nods slowly. "Yeah." She wipes her finger beneath her eye and spins on her heel. "I've made lunch. Come on."

I follow her into the kitchen and place Jas on her feet, then wash my hands and help set the table. We sit to eat the grilled cheese sandwiches and I ask the girls about their afternoon plans.

Jas smiles at me. "We're weeding the garden. Aren't we, Mommy?"

"Sure are. We probably need to do some pruning and make sure the tomato plants are fixed to their trellis properly as well."

Jas smiles the whole time Violet explains what they're going to do, then turns to me. "Shane, you'll help, won't you?"

I'll have to message Mom and tell her I'll be a little late. "I can help for a while but I have to visit my mom this afternoon."

Her eyes widen. "Can I come?"

"Jas, you can't invite yourself along. That's rude," Violet chastises her gently.

Jas's face drops. "Sorry."

I don't like making her feel bad, and I don't want to see her sad but am I ready for them to come with me today? Mom will be making a fuss about my birthday, which I generally don't celebrate, and Dad will probably be his usual asshole self. Do I really want to subject them to him?

The thing is, I want a future with them. They're important to me. I know Mom would love Jas to pieces and she'll be thrilled to know I'm seeing someone as perfect as Violet is for me.

"If you would like to come, you're more than welcome. I'd love to introduce you to my mom. But I need to leave here around two if that's okay."

"Yay! Can we go, Mommy?"

Vi's eyes widen slightly as she looks from her daughter to me. "Are you sure?"

"Yep."

"Oh."

I grin. I think it's the first time Vi's been at a loss for words. Over the last week, I've opened up to Violet more than I have to anyone else, and she's been nothing but compassionate and understanding. This is just another way to open up to her and let her in. It's time. "Yeah, *oh*." I raise an eyebrow.

"Okay." She nods and smiles at Jas, tucking her hair behind her ear. "We can go."

Jas bounces in her seat. "Yay!"

27
VIOLET

Okay, shit!

I'm meeting his mom.

Don't freak out.

I don't know how I'm going to look his mother in the eye after everything we got up to this weekend but this is a huge step with Shane and there's no way I would turn down this opportunity. I've known him just over two years, but in the last week, I've learned more about him than in all the time before that.

"Jas, can you play quietly while I get changed to visit with Shane's mommy?" I ask her as I tie a ribbon in her hair.

"Is it okay if I watch some TV?"

"Sure. I won't be long."

I run the brush through her hair one last time and she heads downstairs to watch TV so I can close myself in my bedroom and go into panic mode. What the hell should I wear?

Now I know how Cass felt when we shared our first Thanksgiving with Toby's family, not that today's a celebration or anything, but it's still an important moment. I have no clue how much time Shane spends with his family but I want to make a good first impression.

Opening my closet, I look through my clothes but nothing

feels appropriate for a meet the mom of the guy I've fallen in love with moment.

Quinn will know.

Grabbing my phone, I press her name.

"Hey, girl. Please tell me you've banged that hot hunk of man you have living with you."

A chuckle escapes me. Trust Quinn. "A girl doesn't kiss and tell."

"Oh my God, you have! Now I don't need specifics, but was he worth the wait?"

I exhale a long breath. She knows I'd never give details but I can answer this. "So worth it, Quinny."

She squeals and I have to drag the phone away from my ear. "I hope you're happy over there living your best life while I live vicariously through my books," she says light-heartedly.

"I'm actually panicking a little because he's taking us to meet his mom this afternoon, and I have no idea what to wear."

"Oooo, meeting the folks. That's serious stuff."

I blow out a long breath. "I know and I want to make the best impression."

"You know I'd never lie to you, right?" Her tone has lost all humor.

"Yeah." That's what makes her the best friend a girl could ever have.

"It doesn't matter what you wear because once they meet you, they're going to know you're the best person for their son." My heart grows with her kind words. "But let's swap to video so I can see what you have."

Relief pours through me. "Thanks, Quinny. You're the best."

"I know. Now switch."

We swap to a video chat and I show her my options.

"Wear your black jeans and that tan sweater that crosses over, then you can wear your boots."

I do always feel good in my black jeans and I need to feel confident today. "You don't think the V sits too low?"

"Nope. It'll look great and it won't look like you're trying too hard."

I smile at my friend. "Thanks, Quinn. You saved my ass."

"Not all heroes wear capes, you know." She laughs and I join her.

"You're the best. I've gotta go."

"Bye. And, Vi … they're gonna love you. Relax and have fun."

I choke up. "Thanks … bye." I end the call before she makes me cry and quickly change. A knock sounds at my door as I'm pulling my hair back into a high ponytail. "Come in," I call.

I see the door open in the reflection of the mirror and inhale sharply when I see Shane wearing his dark jeans and a long-sleeve Henley. I still haven't seen the man naked, which seems crazy after all the sex we had this weekend. As I turn to face him fully, he makes his way around the bed to me.

"You look gorgeous, Blue," he tells me as he grips my hips and pulls me flush into his body.

"You don't look so bad yourself." I press up on my toes and touch my lips to his in what is meant to be a chaste kiss but Shane's tongue darts out for a taste and before I know it, his hand is on my ass, and he's grinding into me as he mauls my mouth. I moan and press against him, enjoying the feel of his hard body against mine.

He slows the kiss with light pecks to my lips and drops his forehead to mine. "Now that I've had you, I don't think I can keep myself in check when I'm around you. It was murder watching you bend over in the garden and not pull your pants down and fuck you."

I giggle like a schoolgirl and heat rises up my neck to my cheeks. Damn. "Hold those thoughts. After Jas is in bed, we can get busy. Right now we need to go visit your mom."

He kisses the end of my nose, then steps away, and I could kick myself in the ass for dropping a bucket of cold water over us but I don't want to make him late for his visit. "You're right." He nods as if to convince himself. "Are you ready?"

"Yeah, just let me put some fresh gloss on my lips." I wave my hand down my body. "Is this outfit okay?"

He frowns. "You look gorgeous. But then again, you always do. It doesn't matter to me what you wear."

I tease out the bottom of my hair and look down at the floor between us. "I just want to make a good impression. This feels ... important. And I won't get the opportunity to make a good first impression again."

He steps in close and his hands land on my shoulders, his fingers cupping the back of my head and he uses his thumbs to lift my chin. "I'm glad you think this is important because it is. I've never taken a woman home to meet my parents."

I inhale sharply and I'm certain my eyes are as wide as saucers. "Never?"

He shakes his head and presses his lips into a tight line. "Never. I want you and Jas in my life which means opening up more. Letting you in. It's foreign to me but I'm trying my best." He presses his lips to my mouth, then pulls back, his eyes searching mine. "I hope you know how important you are to me." My heart expands to double its size and it fills with hope. "I'm trying to be as brave as you are but I'm not used to sharing ... to being open." *He* thinks *I'm* brave. "You'll need to be patient with me as I find my courage."

I gently lay my hand over his heart, feeling it thump heavily. I've always sensed that he doesn't share a lot of personal stuff with others but he's just confirmed it. "I'm glad you think I'm brave, but I'm really not. I stayed with a cheating ex much longer than I should have because I was too scared to leave. You're braver than you realize and you have courage for days." I press a tender kiss to his lips. "But I want you to know that I'm here whenever you're ready to share pieces of yourself, and that when you do share, your pieces are safe with me."

He drops his forehead to mine. "Thank you," he murmurs, then presses the softest of kisses to my lips.

I wish we could stay in our bubble, but I don't want us to be late. "Shall we go?"

He swallows harshly. "Yeah."

I quickly apply a coat of gloss to my lips, then tuck my hand in Shane's and we make our way downstairs to grab Jas and head out.

SHANE PULLS into the driveway of a quaint house with a sweet garden and my stomach twists. I'm so freaking nervous.

"Is this your house?" Jas asks from the back seat.

"This is my parents' house. They moved here after I left for the army."

"It has a pretty garden."

"My mom likes to keep busy." He glances across at me. "Are you okay?"

I nod. "Yeah," I squeak like I haven't used my voice in a while. I clear my throat and try again, this time adding a smile. "Yeah."

He narrows his eyes at me but climbs out of his SUV, as do I. Shane opens Jas's door, unbuckles her, and lifts her out of her seat. The man dotes on her and she's happy to let him but she's more than capable of climbing out of the car herself.

The front door opens and a woman steps out with dark chin-length hair streaked in silver. Her eyes grow wide and she brings her hand up to her chest when she notices Shane isn't alone. A smile spreads as she comes toward us. "Well, who do we have here?" She looks between the three of us and her gaze pauses on me. "I'm Fiona, Shane's mom." She holds out her hand to me, and when I take it, she presses her other hand over mine. "You seem familiar."

I take a moment to look at her carefully. There's something

familiar but I can't place her. I chuckle. "You're familiar, too, but I can't work it out."

Shane steps closer to his mom, holding Jas's hand. He wraps his free arm around his mom's shoulders and kisses the top of her head, which barely comes up to the middle of his chest. "Hi, Mom. This is my girlfriend, Violet, and her daughter, Jasmine. I hope you don't mind that I brought them over."

I snap my eyes up to Shane as he winks at me. He called me his girlfriend ... *girlfriend*! I almost feel like a giddy schoolgirl who's been asked to go steady by the popular boy in school. By inviting us here today, and by the way he's been opening up to me, he's made it plain that he wants to build something meaningful, so I'm not sure why his label has me in such a spin.

She tsks and pats his firm stomach, her eyes sparkling with clear affection for her son. "Of course not. It's not even *my* birthday and you've brought me the best surprise." She grins down at Jasmine and then crouches down to her level. "Hello, Jasmine. Such a pretty name for a pretty little girl."

Jasmine's lips tip up at the compliment. "Hello." She drops her chin to her chest and twists her body side to side. She looks up at Shane, and he squeezes her little hand. "You're Shane's mommy?"

Her eyes go soft, flicking back up to her son. "I am," Fiona says proudly.

"But he's so big, and you're so little."

Shane's Mom guffaws and I flame with embarrassment. "Jas!"

"Well, he wasn't always this big. He was small like you once," she explains.

Jas's head snaps up to Shane and her eyes widen. "Really?" He nods. "Do you think I'll grow up to be as big as you?"

He chuckles and bends down to scoop her into his arms. "I don't think so, Angel."

Her bottom lip falls. "But I want to be big and strong like you."

His eyes soften, and my heart does this squishy thing it always seems to do when he's being so sweet to my little girl, which means it happens a lot. "You don't need to be big to be strong. Just look at your mommy."

Ah, geez. This man. He gives me all the big feelings and he doesn't even have to try.

Jas grins at him and looks at me. "My mommy's the best. I want to be just like her."

He bounces her in his hold. "How about you just be the best Jasmine?"

"Yeah. I'll do that." She throws her little fist up into the air.

Shane's mom tears her eyes away from her son and my daughter and grins at me. "Violet. That's not a very common name. I think I know why you're so familiar. You helped me the day I was struck by cyclists in the par—"

Recognition hits me like a bolt of lightning before she can finish. "Oh my goodness. I'm so glad to see you're okay. You've often crossed my mind. Was your hip okay?"

Shane's eyes flick between me and his mom like he's trying desperately to keep up with our conversation.

She waves her hand in the air as if to dismiss my concern. "Yes, just badly bruised and a pinched nerve in my spine from the heavy landing."

"When was this?" Shane interrupts.

"Uhm … let's see." Her eyes widen. "Just over two years ago, now. You remember. I was still sore when you came over for your birthday."

Shane nods. "I remember now." He turns to me. "You were the park ranger who helped her?"

"Yeah. Gosh, it's such a small world."

Fiona wraps her arm around me. "Oh, I'm just so happy to see you again. I was so impressed with how calmly you helped me, and you were so caring and lovely." She looks up at Shane. "She was so wonderful and kind to me." She steps away from me and holds her arm out toward the front door. "Come inside, William will be so happy to see you."

I doubt it. William didn't seem like the happy-to-see-anyone type. He was an asshole if my memory is correct, but maybe it was because of what happened—everyone has a bad day. We step inside Fiona's tidy home and I spot William sitting in a recliner watching some sort of war movie with the volume at an obnoxious level. On the table beside his chair, there are several empty beer bottles and Fiona rushes forward, collecting them, then disappears around the corner. I hear the clanking of glass, and then she returns to the living room.

"William. Look who's here," Fiona says brightly. William glances up at us, then drops his eyes back to the screen in front of him. "Shane brought his lady friend and her daughter." He grunts but doesn't tear his eyes away from the TV. "You might remember her, she's the young woman who helped me that day in the park. Remember, when I was hit by the cyclists?" His head snaps up, and he studies me more closely with narrowed eyes.

Obviously, he's still an asshole. I give him an awkward smile. "Hi, William. This is my daughter, Jasmine." I lay my hand on Jas's back. "Jas, say, hi."

She steps forward and gives him her best smile. "Hello, Shane's daddy."

He drops his eyes to her and grunts, then turns back to his TV show. When I look up at Shane, the tic in his jaw is in full swing, and his eyes are as hard as flint as he looks down at his father. He places his hand on Jas's shoulder and turns her away from his dad. "Come on, let's head into the kitchen." Shane doesn't acknowledge his father in any way as he directs us away from the man and the negative dynamic between them makes my heart break for him.

Fiona smiles awkwardly at me. "He sometimes forgets his manners when he's in the middle of watching one of his favorite movies."

I nod and return her awkward smile as we step into the

kitchen. When I look up, balloons are tied to the backs of the chairs, there's a birthday cake on the counter with two candles—two and nine—a happy birthday banner across the window, and other birthday treats already on the table which is set for three people. I'm pretty sure she said it wasn't her birthday, or maybe she said it *was* her birthday. I was so nervous, I probably got mixed up. But the two and the nine …

She spins and holds her hands up with a huge grin. "Happy birthday, Shane!"

What?

It's his birthday and he never said a single word.

Jas jumps up and down excitedly. "I love birthdays. Happy birthday, Shane." Then she freezes and her face drops. "I didn't get you a present."

He crouches in front of her. "I don't need a present, Angel. I have you and your mom, and that's perfectly enough for me."

My daughter wraps her little arms around his neck and hugs him tight, landing a kiss on his cheek. "I'll give you this big hug as your present."

He wraps his arms around her, accepting her hug, his eyes closed as a smile touches his lips. "Thank you. It's the only thing I need because you give the best hugs."

She pulls away and smiles at him. "You're welcome."

I'm frozen and I don't know whether to be pissed that he didn't share this information with us or happy that he brought us here to celebrate his birthday. I peer around the room, at the decorations and the food, and I decide to be happy. This is Shane opening up to me little by little. He's let Jas and me into his world and shared a piece of himself with us. I take the few steps I need to close the distance and place my hands on his pecs, the only part of him he allows me to touch. "Happy birthday."

He leans down and kisses my forehead. "It's tomorrow but thank you."

Hmm. Tomorrow. That means I have time to organize something.

Fiona busies herself, adding two more settings to the table, grinning like a Cheshire Cat. "I wasn't expecting anyone else. This is just wonderful."

"Can I help with anything?" I offer but she waves me off.

"Now what can I get you both to drink?" She looks between me and Jas.

"We can just have water."

"Nonsense. It's a party. Coffee, juice, maybe?"

"Violet drinks tea, Mom."

"Of course. I have tea." She looks at Jasmine. "What about you, young lady?"

Jas chuckles. "Can I please have juice?"

"Absolutely." Fiona bustles back to the kitchen and fixes our drinks.

Shane pulls out a chair next to his and gestures for me to sit, then pulls out the chair beside mine for Jas. "Thank you."

Once the drinks are ready, she calls out to William. "Are you going to join us today?"

There's no response and I study Shane. There's no outward sign he's disappointed that his father isn't joining us but he's clenching his teeth, something he's been doing since we arrived. Fiona hands out plates like nothing's amiss and tells us to help ourselves. Shane helps Jas choose some food and places it on her plate and she happily digs in, oblivious to the tension in the room.

Once Fiona's happy that we each have enough food, she sits. "So, Violet, how long have you been working at the park?"

I chew quickly and swallow my food. "Ever since I finished my bachelor's degree in environmental science, so about eight years now. I love working there. I couldn't imagine working in an office, and they've been flexible with maternity leave as well as allowing me to work part-time."

We chat about the environment and some of the issues we're

facing as we eat our party food. She tells me that she tries to take nature walks every few weeks but she doesn't like to go alone since the incident.

"And how old are you, Jasmine?"

Jas grins. "I'm five! I go to school and everything."

Fiona widens her eyes and lays her hand on her chest as if surprised. "No! Are you the teacher?"

Jas laughs loudly. "Of course not. I'm onl—"

"Can you all shut the fuck up? I'm trying to watch my movie."

My blood freezes in my veins at the all-too-familiar phrase and Jasmine jolts in her seat, her bottom lip trembling. Her eyes grow glassy, and I collect her from her seat and bring her to my lap to keep her safe. Not that I think Shane would allow anything to happen to her or me. But those words bring back one of the worst days of my life and I have to concentrate on holding steady; I don't want to feed into Jas's already frightened state.

Fiona covers her mouth with her hand and Shane shoots to his feet, pushing his chair back with a loud scrape, the tic in his jaw working overtime.

"Mom, how about you show Jas and Vi your garden out back? They like to grow vegetables, too."

Fiona gives him a tremulous smile and stands. "Sure," she says brightly. "I can't wait to show you my squash. Maybe you could help me pick some?" she says directly to Jasmine with a forced bright tone.

I climb to my feet with Jas in my arms and we follow Fiona outside. I glance back at Shane over my shoulder and he lifts his chin and sends a wink my way but I can't stop my worry for him.

As soon as the back door closes behind me, Jas wriggles her way down my body until her feet touch the ground. "Mommy, look at the tomatoes. They're bigger than ours."

Fiona stops me with her hand on my wrist. "I'm so sorry. William sometimes forgets his manners."

I smile at her. She shouldn't have to apologize for her husband's behavior. "You don't need to apologize to me, Fiona."

She nods. "I hope you won't take what he said to heart. I don't want my husband's bad manners to reflect poorly on Shane. I would be devastated if you distanced yourself from my boy because of his father."

I rest my hand over hers. "There's nothing, and I mean nothing, that will make me distance myself from Shane. He's the best man I've ever known, and I consider myself extremely lucky that he's opening his heart and his life to me and my daughter. I promise you have nothing to worry about."

A tear slips over the edge of her lash and she nods at me, a shaky smile touching her lips. "Thank you."

I smile back. "No ... thank *you* for raising an amazing son."

28

I SEE FUCKING RED. I DIDN'T THINK MY RESPECT FOR MY father could sink any lower, but I see that it can. Once the girls are outside and the back door closes behind them, my first instinct is to storm into the living room and have an all-out brawl with the old man but I drag in a long breath, then tuck my chair into the table in a controlled manner in a bid to calm down.

Striding to the opening that leads to the living room, I stand and watch my father as he drinks his beer without taking his eyes off the television screen. "Don't ever speak to my girls like that again," I grit.

MY girls.

That's exactly who they are. They're important to me and I won't tolerate anyone treating them poorly. Especially the man who made me feel unimportant and unwanted for most of my life.

He ignores me and takes another pull of his beer. My barely-tamped fury returns, and I step in front of the TV so he has no choice but to acknowledge me. Something he hasn't done in longer than I care to remember. My body vibrates with anger, and I'm doing my best not to explode at him—a courtesy he didn't offer my girls.

"What the fuck?" His eyes finally make their way to my face.

"Get out of the way." He points at the screen behind me. "I'm watching that."

I reach down to the table next to him, snatch the TV remote, and switch it off. "Do I look like I care?"

"Watch who you're talking to. This is my goddamn house and you'll show me the respect I deserve."

I scoff, shoving my hands on my hips. "Respect. You have no idea what respect is and I have zero ... actually make that less than zero respect for you."

His face turns red and he pushes the footrest of his chair down to stand. "Finally decided to grow a backbone?" He sneers.

"It's been years and years of suppressing what I really feel to keep the peace for Mom. She's prepared to put up with your ignorant, disrespectful bullshit and that's her business. But I"—I strike my chest with my closed fist—"will not tolerate you showing any form of disrespect to my girls. I don't fucking care what you've been through. You have no right to treat the people around you like they don't matter."

"You have no fucking clue what I've been through, you ungrateful piece of shit!" he shouts at me, spittle flying from his mouth. Finally, he's saying how he really feels about me. "You think you can come into *my* home and speak to me like this? I'm your father."

I scoff. "You're my sperm donor. You checked out of your role as a father and husband a long time ago." He was never there to guide me or offer his wisdom as a father should. I watched Toby with his dad and wished that mine was half the dad Mr. Summer was ... still is.

He steps forward. "I've always provided for my family. You had a roof over your head"—he flings his arms around, wildly gesturing to the walls and ceiling—"and food on the table. And you have the gall to tell me I checked out. What more did you want, you ingrate?"

"You!" I bellow. *How can he be so blind?* "You showing some level of interest in your wife and son. Even a minor level of interest would have been better than what you gave us. You may have physically been here and you may have provided food and shelter, but you never gave us *you*." I point at him like I'm trying to stab him with my words. To wound him the way he's wounded me.

"Me! There was nothing of me left when I came home and you and your mother just kept going along like my life hadn't completely changed—you'd turned into a Mommy's boy." He sneers. "You were doing well enough without me, you didn't care about me or what I'd been through. You spent more time out of this house than in it. *You* made it very clear that I didn't matter to you." He paces behind his chair and rests his hands on the back, his knuckles turning white, his chest rising and falling rapidly like he's come back from a run. "I was just returning the favor and staying out of the way."

"I was a fucking kid!" I seethe. "You talk about what you'd been through. Did you ever stop to think about what we'd been through here without you? We may not have been at war but we missed you. Mom was sick with worry about you more often than she wasn't. She was so distracted with her concern for your safety; whether or not you would make it home that she'd forget to look after herself and me some days. I became her caregiver when she fell into a depression and couldn't make it out of bed because you hadn't written to her." His eyes widen. "Yeah, you didn't know about that. She did her best but some days she struggled. I was happy to help but I was a damn kid. You don't think that created a strong bond between us. You call me a Mommy's boy like it's the worst thing possible, but we only had each other. We didn't have it as easy as you imagine," I snap, my chest rising and falling with angry breaths.

He grips the back of his chair tightly, his lips thinning. "It's not like I had a choice. I didn't want to leave you and your mother, but every man in my family was expected to enlist and defend our freedoms. I couldn't be the first one to break family expectations, to turn my back on the family tradition. I had to do my part to ensure you and *your* children could enjoy freedom." His voice softens and his shoulders slump and when I study him, he looks tired and defeated—much like I used to look.

I huff out a sarcastic laugh and run my hand through my hair. "And yet you forced the same expectation onto me." He deflates a little more. "And just so you know, you're not the only one who saw and did awful shit. I did too, but I'm doing my best to battle my demons and not wallow in them like you have."

He scoffs. "You were on a peacekeeping mission. How fucking awful could it have been?"

With a heart full of anger and frustration, I spin around and raise my shirt over my head. When I hear his sharp gasp, I turn back around to face him, pulling the shirt back down as I do. "I fucking got blown up and when I woke I found out my best friend had died in the blast. Then I spent weeks in a German hospital getting patched back together. I was so fucking broken. Is that awful enough for you? You think you're the only one who had terrible things happen, but you're not. Wake the fuck up, old man, before you lose out on everything." I storm out of the living room before he can respond.

I need to check on my girls and apologize to them. I need to make sure they're all right. I knew bringing them here was a risk but I figured he'd just ignore them the same way he always ignores me. I never once expected to come to verbal blows with him today. If I had, I would have come alone. I pause at the back door and calm my breathing. I don't want to scare them.

The back door bangs closed and the girls turn toward me. Jas smiles and calls out, "Shane, look at how big your mommy's tomatoes are!" The tension that had bunched in my shoulders releases knowing she's okay after the way my father spoke. I make my way over to one of the sweetest kids I've ever met and crouch down where she is. Her little arm automatically wraps around my neck and I can breathe again. This little girl and her mom are everything right in my world. They make me want to be a better man. Better than my father. And for the first time ever, I think I actually will be better than my old man.

"Show me which one is the biggest."

She tugs me around to the opposite side of the planter and points. "This one. It's almost the size of Mommy's hand."

"It's pretty big. That would be great in one of your salads."

Jas nods with her eyes wide. "Uh-huh."

Mom steps closer to where we are. "Why don't you take that one home?"

"Oh, we grow our own tomatoes and have plenty," Vi points out, but Mom plucks the tomato from the vine and hands it to Jasmine.

Jasmine's eyes drop to the heavy tomato resting in her hands. "Thank you. I'll add it to our dinner tonight. Do you want to come over?"

Mom chuckles. "Oh, thank you for the invitation but I need to make dinner for William."

Jasmine's face drops and creases form between her brows, then she looks back up at Mom as she twists her body side to side. "He could come, too, if you like." After the way he just yelled at her, she still invites him into her sanctuary. I swear this kid is too good for this world.

Mom's eyes grow glassy and she brings her hand up to cover her chest. She looks up at me and her lip trembles slightly, then drops her eyes back to Jas. "Oh, you're too sweet. Maybe another time." She bends down and presses a soft kiss to the top of her head. "How about we go inside and sing 'Happy Birthday' so we can have some birthday cake?"

"Yeah!" Jasmine's mouth spreads wide. "I love birthday cake."

While Mom guides Jas inside, I fall in beside Violet. "I'm sorry about my father."

She smiles tightly at me. "Your mom already apologized. And

honestly, neither of you should apologize for him. His behavior is all his own."

"Yeah, well. It was rude and unnecessary. He's been like that most of my life." I run my hand across the top of my hair. "It's why I spent most of my time with Toby's family."

She links our hands together and brings them up to her mouth, brushing a soft kiss across my knuckles as we walk through the back door and my stomach flips with her quiet support. Mom's frozen in the doorway to the kitchen and when I come up behind her I see the reason why.

Dad looks up from lighting the candles on my cake; his eyes red-rimmed. "Happy birthday, Son," he says in a ragged voice. His gaze skates from Vi to Jas. "I'm sorry I was so rude earlier. Please accept my apology."

I turn to look at Vi and she gives my dad a soft smile. "Apology accepted. We all have bad days." That's a freaking understatement. She steps fully into the kitchen once Mom steps forward, tugging me along with her and I feel like I've just walked into the *Upside Down* from *Stranger Things*.

Dad nods stiffly, then grins at Jas. "Shall we sing 'Happy Birthday?'"

Jas smiles back. "'Happy Birthday' is one of my favorite songs!" she says, then skips over to Dad to stand beside him, and I watch his entire demeanor soften. I think I'll call it the Jas effect because she does the same for me.

For the first time since I was a young boy, my father sings 'Happy Birthday' to me along with Mom, Vi, and Jas. It's a surreal moment and hope blooms bright that maybe my chat with Dad will have a positive impact on our family. Mom cuts the cake after I make my wish and we all enjoy the birthday cake she baked for me. Dad doesn't join in with the conversation but he's sitting at the table with us so I'll take it.

BLUE

Jas wanted to play at the park after school
today

Meet us there?

ME

Sure

See you in five

A SMILE CREEPS across my lips remembering the birthday present Vi gave me this morning. I don't think I'll ever tire of having her mouth on me but this morning was something else. Waking up to her tasting my lips was awesome, but when she dropped to her knees and handed me a silk sash then held out her wrists, I thought I'd died and gone to heaven. I don't think I've ever acted as quickly as I did this morning. Tying that silk around her slender wrists almost had me coming in my sweats but I really had to hold back when I finally slid down her gorgeous throat. The heat and warmth ... her swallowing around my length ... the moans that vibrated around my cock ... fuck! The woman is a goddess.

I adjust myself as I flick the indicator for the parking lot and find a place to park. I'm familiar with this park after spending several afternoons here with Poppy and Jasmine when I was driving Poppy to and from school. I climb out of my car and narrow my eyes when I spot Toby's car in the parking lot alongside Hope's car.

Scanning the park, I find my friends chatting among themselves next to a table with party decorations, waiting for *me*. I've avoided birthdays like the plague since I returned ... out of guilt mostly but also because I didn't feel my life was worth celebrating. There have been so many times over the years that I've wished I was the one who didn't survive the blast. But now, looking at everyone here ...

A large hand lands on my shoulder, and I tense, ready to twist and punch. "Never thought I'd see the day."

When I turn my head toward Nix's familiar voice, a wide grin greets me and the tension evaporates from my muscles. "You didn't say a word about this when I left you at *The Bunker* twenty minutes ago."

He laughs. "That would have ruined the surprise." He pats my back. "Happy birthday."

"Thanks." Something happens inside my chest that these people are here for *me*. I guess they've always been here for me, but now I'm finally prepared to let them in.

Together, we walk toward the most important people in my life, and as I get closer, I notice Mr. and Mrs. S among the group as well as Kate and Oliver—my surrogate family. The girls break away from the group and run toward me, Poppy in the lead, closely followed by Jasmine with Daisy trailing behind, giggling her head off. Poppy plows into me, wrapping her arms around my torso then Jas comes at me from the side. "Happy birthday, Shane!"

I lift her with both arms, kiss her forehead, and swing her up onto my shoulders. "Thank you, Angel."

Daisy finally makes it to me and wraps her arms around my leg, looking up at me with her six teeth proudly on display. "Birf-day!"

I chuckle and scoop her up, careful of Jas on my shoulders. "Thank you, Daisy."

Poppy releases me, steps back, and brushes her flat hand over her heart a couple of times, then touches her middle finger to her chin and down to her chest.

"Thank you," I say as I sign.

Wearing his soccer uniform, Evan steps away from the group and walks toward me with his hands buried in his pockets. "Happy birthday, Shane."

"Thanks, Ev. I'm surprised to see you and your mom here."

He shrugs. "We're just stopping by quickly before we go to soccer. I don't want to be late and get in trouble with Coach Mathers. I've been in enough trouble lately." He looks up at me sheepishly.

"Well, thanks for coming. I appreciate it."

"Shane, let me down, please. I need to hug Evan." Jasmine twists her body on my shoulders.

"Hang on a sec." I tighten my hold on Daisy and then help Jas slide down my body until her feet touch the ground.

The minute she's steady, she takes the few steps to Evan and throws her arms around him without any warning. "I hope my hug makes you feel better, Evan. Hugs always make me feel better."

He stands stiffly for a moment and looks up at me with confusion. I tip my head to him and widen my eyes. He relaxes and then wraps his arms around Jas, returning her embrace. She smiles against his chest and I watch Evan's body relax—the Jas effect. Jas tightens her hold briefly, then lets him go.

He stares at her with a look of wonder. "Thank you. I ... uh ... feel much better now."

Jas's smile is as wide as I've ever seen as she twists her body from side to side. "I'm glad. If you need another hug, just say so." He grins at her and they walk side by side toward our little group.

Collecting Poppy's hand in mine, the kids and I make our way to everyone else. "Happy birthday!" they all shout at once, bringing a smile to my lips and gratitude to my heart.

I chuckle and make my way around the group. When I stop at Toby, he wraps his hand around the back of my neck and pulls me in tight. "I'm so incredibly happy to be able to wish my best friend a happy birthday face-to-face. It's been too long, man." The emotion in his voice and etched on his face is like a punch to the gut. I never considered that I was hurting him when I ignored my birthday. In some ways, I'm no better than my father, and that realization makes me sick to my stomach.

"I'm sorry. I've been so caught up in my head that I didn't stop to see what I've been doing to the people who care about me. I promise to do better." Emotion clogs my throat, and I swallow it down so I can pull myself together.

"We're always here whenever you're ready." He winks at me and pats me on the back, then tips his head toward Vi and Jas. "They've been the best thing to ever happen to you. I'm happy for you, man."

I watch Nix fuss over Jas and the way she has her chin tucked into her shoulder as Violet chuckles at something he says and the love I have for them grows. I'm content and thankful that she persisted and I finally relented to what had been building between us since the first moment I laid eyes on her. "Thank you." I turn to look at him with a smile. "For everything."

He simply nods and I continue making my way around the group, thanking each person for being here to celebrate my birthday.

Hope wraps her arms around my middle and squeezes me tight. When she pulls away, her eyes are shiny but her lips are tipped up. "Happy birthday, Shane. I'm so happy and relieved to see you building the life you deserve. Wyatt would be proud of you."

I swallow and blink away the sting in my eyes. "You know he'd want that for you, too."

She looks past me but nods subtly. "When I'm ready."

"That's all anyone can ask." I squeeze her hand. "Thanks for coming."

"Of course. We wouldn't miss this for the world but we can't stay for long."

Last but not least, I make it to Vi and grip her hips, pulling her roughly into me. "You did this?"

Her hands land on my chest and she looks up at me sheepishly, a worried smile touching her lips. "Yeah. I hope you don't mind."

I shake my head at her and grin. "I haven't wanted to acknowledge my birthday since I got back"—her smile drops, and she opens her mouth to speak but I place a finger over her lips—"but

I'm glad you did this because it's time to live my life. Thanks, Blue."

"You're welcome." She presses up onto her toes, and I bend down to meet her in the middle to share a safe-for-public-consumption kiss. She pulls away slowly and when her eyes meet mine, they're full of heat that I can't wait to build into an inferno later. "We'd better sing and cut the cake because Hope and Evan need to get to soccer."

I tuck her loose hair behind her ear. "Thank you for including them."

"They're important to you. There's no way I would have left them out. It took a little effort to work out how to get in touch with them but we got there in the end." She smiles and it lights up her face as she calls everyone together. And here, in the middle of the park on a Monday afternoon, my friends sing 'Happy Birthday' to me and share a slice of cake to celebrate my life.

29

SHANE

Through the living room window, I watch the storm roll in. Thick, dark clouds have been building all day and intermittent claps of thunder sound in the distance as the darkened sky flashes with light. Violet had just finished her shower, and I was sharing a story with Jas when the electricity went out. I had to finish reading the story using the flashlight on my phone.

Vi hands me a cup of chamomile tea, and I look at her questioningly. "Gas hot water heater, so it's not going to be as hot as it should be."

I nod and take a sip. "Thank you." This has been our routine since my birthday, and I like it.

I like it a lot.

It's a quiet moment at the end of each day, once Jas is in bed, where the two of us connect simply over a cup of Vi's favorite tea. I brush her wet hair over her shoulder and wrap my arm around her, then pull her into me and take another sip of the hot tea while we both stare out of the window in silence. I don't know whether it's a psychosomatic response to the tea or if it's the sex we've been having every night but I've been sleeping better lately—which I'm certain is the initial reason Vi started making the tea for me each night. Maybe it's because I'm feeling more settled and stable than I have for a long time. Perhaps it's because I'm not as stuck in the past and I'm beginning to think about the future. Whatever it is, it's made a huge difference for me. "It's gonna be a rough night."

From the time we both arrived home, we worked together to secure everything outside to keep any damage to a minimum during the storm. Even Jas helped where she could, checking the bindings on the tomato plants were secure. We worked great as a team and it has me thinking that maybe it's time to find a house instead of going back to my apartment. While I don't mind the simplicity of apartment living, I know that for Jas and Vi to be truly happy, they'll need a backyard with enough room to grow their beloved fruits and vegetables.

Violet hums her agreement, and the innocent sound vibrates through me like a cannon, waking up my cock and I tug her closer until there's no space between us. To be fair, I don't think my cock is ever not semi-hard when I'm near her. "I'm glad we moved the outdoor furniture and packed away our gardening tools."

"Better to be safe than sorry. I checked with Toby and Cass and they've secured everything in their backyard too."

"That's good. I checked on Quinn and she's done the same." She looks up at me in the candlelight. "Mom called to check if we were ready for the storm. She also needed to tell me that she's staying until the weekend." She raises her brows. "I have a feeling she's reconnected with the guy from high school in more ways than one."

My lips tip up at the lightness and approval in Vi's voice. "Good for her."

"Yeah," Vi breathes. "She deserves to be happy. She's given so much of herself to me and Cass and our girls, it's time she put herself and her happiness first."

I lean down and kiss the top of her head, soaking up the fresh scent of her shampoo as a particularly strong wind batters the window. "You do the same with Jas. You put her first and give her everything you have, that's why she's such a great kid."

She smiles up at me and it's so damn breathtaking. "You really think so?"

"Absolutely." I take the cup from her hand and place both of them on the table beneath the rattling window, then turn back to the woman who's grown to become one of the most important people in my life. Sliding my hands up her arms until I reach her neck, I cup her face gently and tilt her head back until I can gaze into her vivid blue eyes. A flash of lightning illuminates her face for a mere second and my breath catches in my lungs at the desire I see. Lowering my head, she meets me partway, and our lips touch softly as thunder crashes in the night. A gentle press followed by another and another.

As I nip along the bottom pillow a soft moan escapes Vi and her hands come up to rest on my pecs. I could kiss this woman every day of my life and never tire of tasting her, hearing her moans, swallowing her sighs and whimpers. Feeling her beneath my touch, sharing tea with her before bed, reading bedtime stories to Jas, and everything else that comes with sharing their space. I tilt her head back and use my tongue to encourage her to open to me which she does beautifully. Slipping my tongue inside, I stroke and taste her and make love to her mouth. Weaving my fingers through her wet hair, I cup her head and tilt her to suit my needs as our tongues tangle and dance like we've been kissing for years, not weeks. My cock grows even harder, and I grind into her soft stomach as thunder rumbles overhead, rattling the glasses in the cabinet.

I only wish I had a body that was worthy of her touch because I crave her hands on me beyond anything I've ever wanted before. I tear my lips away from hers as a dose of cold water washes over me. How will I have a long-term committed relationship with this woman if I can't expose myself to her fully? Touching my forehead to hers, disappointment douses my arousal, and I murmur, "I wish I could give you everything, Blue."

Her eyes flick between mine, a furrow forming between them.

"You do. I have never felt as safe, as accepted, or as valued as I do when I'm with you. What else is there?"

Her words give me pause. "Why are you prepared to accept less than you deserve?"

"You're everything I deserve and more, Shane." I open my mouth to interrupt but she presses her thumb over my lips and shakes her head a little. "You're so kind and patient with Jas, more than her father ever was. You give her so much of your time and attention and she's blossomed because of it. She clearly feels safe with you and adores you to the moon and back. Do you know how important those things are to me after the relationship I had with her father?" I understand what she's saying but all of those things she mentioned are about Jas. "And I can see your mind ticking over. You're the most giving and kind human being. Your morals and the standards to which you hold yourself surpass anyone I've ever met before. You make me feel cherished and important. Desirable and sexy." She presses her palms against my chest firmly. "You see my worth and value me as well as my choices and the things that are important to me. I didn't have that before and until I saw Toby with Cass and Poppy, I never believed it could happen in real life. I was so happy for Cass that she'd found a good man and then there was you. I knew you were a good man. A solid man. A man with a strong character. A man who would do anything for the people in his life as well as those on the periphery." She raises her brows. "Like me and Jas. How could I not fall for you? That would be asking the impossible. And sure, you come in a beautiful package"—I flinch internally as she strokes my cheek—"but it's your kind heart and your beautiful soul that has me coming back time and again and wanting more with you." She presses up on her toes and touches her lips to mine, then pulls away slightly to catch my eyes. "You're a good man, Shane. One of the best."

As much as I love that she thinks I'm a good man, I'm not. I've let people down in the worst ways possible. "There are so many things you don't know about me. Things I'm not sure how to share." I swallow thickly.

Her eyes soften and she cups my cheek. "I know enough and I can wait until you're ready for the rest."

I dip my head and touch my lips to hers with gratitude. I don't know why I ever fought my attraction to her. I've wasted so much time. Our breaths combine and I close my eyes, absorbing the softness of her touch. The love and care she's showing me. We lose ourselves in a kiss that feels like it's repairing some of my broken pieces, smoothing out the roughened edges, and healing my wounds. Her kiss is like the balm I've needed to put myself back together.

The storm builds outside, matching the building emotions Vi's words have unleashed in me. I want to be the best man for her and Jas, it's what they deserve. Our tongues tangle and taste and the need to make love to her builds rapidly.

But I need to think.

About the future.

About showing her all of me.

About being brave.

I slow the kiss and finish with soft, sexy pecks to her lips. Dropping my forehead to hers, I exhale a long breath. "I need to take a shower." I kiss the tip of her nose. "Be ready for me when I come out. I want you naked and spread out on your bed for me." I tap her ass. "Don't touch your pussy. It belongs to me. Understood?"

Her lips tip up on one side. "Understood."

As I PULL my boxer briefs up my legs, the room lights up momentarily and an ear-splitting bang shakes the house, making the walls vibrate. A scream pierces the air, and I sprint toward Jasmine's bedroom, my heart hammering against my ribs. Lightning flashes again—followed by another bang, not quite as loud as the last one—allowing me to see Jasmine sitting up in her bed. I scoop her into my arms and hold her tight to my body. In an instant, her little arms wrap around my neck and her legs around my torso. I stroke my hand down her tangled hair in a soothing motion as her heart beats rapidly against my chest. "It's okay, Angel, it's just the clouds bumping together. You're safe." Her body shivers, and I hear Vi's footsteps as she steps into the room. The room is suddenly bathed in light, and I realize I forgot to turn Jasmine's bedroom light off.

Vi gasps behind me and I tense, my stomach rolling and sinking like an anchor to the floor beneath my feet.

I close my eyes and inhale a long breath as I continue to make Jas feel safe again, trying to relax my muscles. Her body calms, the longer I stroke her back and I feel Vi move closer. I stiffen again— my secret on display. This will be it. The end of the line for us. She'll finally realize what I've been telling her, that I'm broken beyond repair.

Her heat warms my back as she stands close and raises her arm to brush her daughter's hair out of her face. Jas burrows further into my neck with a hiccuping sob. "You're okay, JJ. It's just the storm. Shane and I are here with you."

"It scared me," she whimpers.

"It was a loud bang. You're allowed to be scared but I promise you're safe," I reassure her.

Her arm stretches out to wrap around her mom and she pulls her in. Vi's front presses to my back and her heat scalds me as her perfection touches my ugliness. We stand quietly in Jas's bedroom, the three of us huddled together as the little girl in my arms slowly calms after her fright. Her breathing slows, and her body relaxes against mine. Her head drops to my shoulder and her body grows lax.

"She's asleep," Vi whispers, her breath hot against my shoulder.

I don't want to break this moment but I reluctantly lay Jasmine back in her bed and pull the covers over her tiny body. Violet tucks them in, smooths her hair away from her face, and kisses her forehead. Once I'm happy she's settled, I head back into the bathroom and close the door, taking my time to finish dressing, then close myself in my bedroom. Leaning against the door, I bang my head against the timber.

I wasn't fucking ready for her to see the monster I hide.

30

SHANE

After a long while, a soft knock sounds through the door. "Shane?" *She's so damn brave.* Here I am hiding and she's confronting the issue head-on. Blowing out a long breath, I step away from the door and open it, then move closer to the bed. Her worried gaze flits over me, and then she steps inside, closing the door quietly. When she turns around her eyes are filled with mischief. "I was waiting for you as requested." She takes a step closer and unties the silk ribbon holding her robe together exposing the space between her breasts and a smooth area of her soft stomach. She can't possibly still want me after seeing the damage that covers the entirety of the back of my body. "I grew tired of waiting, so I thought I'd come to you." She takes another step forward and I take one back. Her eyes narrow and she closes the distance. As I retreat, my legs collide with the bed and I drop to my ass. She wastes no time, climbing over my lap, her legs straddling me. The heat of her pussy scorching my thighs through my sweats.

Like this, our lips are level and it would be so easy to kiss her, to ignore the discussion we need to have. "About what you saw—"

She places her finger over my lips just like she did earlier and shakes her head. "You're supposed to be defiling my body right about now, we don't have to talk about it until you're ready."

"That's the thing, I'm not sure I'll ever be ready but you've seen it now and ... to be honest, I don't know how to talk about it but I feel we probably should."

She nods as compassion fills her eyes. "I'm guessing that's the reason you don't like me touching you."

"Well, yeah. It's not that I don't *want* you to touch me, I've been desperate to have your hands on me. I'd love nothing more than to have your hands exploring my body, but who wants to touch a monster?" I tear my eyes away from hers because I can't bear to see her look at me any differently than before—like I'm less of a man. "The scars you saw barely scratch the surface of the scars I hide inside, Violet. I'll never be the man you deserve. I'll never be whole. My only saving grace is that *I* don't have to look at the scars marring my skin."

She moves so she captures my eyes in her stunning gaze, only this time, what I see is fire, honesty, and respect. "*You* don't have to like what you see, but I need you to know that *I* love everything about you." Her voice is full of steel. "Those scars on your body don't repulse me or make you any less of a man in my eyes. In fact, they make my feelings for you stronger because these scars show a strength that muscles don't have. They show you're a survivor. That you've been through something utterly horrendous and you've fought to come out the other side. That's incredibly attractive, Shane." She leans forward and presses a tender kiss to my lips. "I'm not sure why you felt the need to keep them hidden but you don't have to hide anything from me. I love you for exactly the man you are today. And so does Jasmine."

See, *fucking brave.*

My heart grows to triple its size knowing this remarkable woman loves me, and she didn't hesitate to tell me. I wrap my arms around her and drag her into my body. "I love you, Blue. And

Jasmine, too. I'd closed myself off to the possibility of love because I don't think I deserve it, but I'm too weak to fight what we have between us."

She moves in and as she kisses me, her fingers slide beneath my T-shirt … and it's incredible to finally have her hands on my flesh. A groan resonates through my body at the feel of her hands on my skin as a shiver makes its way through my body like a wave. Teasing her tongue inside my mouth, she slides her hands up my body, over the ridges of my abs, tracing each indentation on the way and lifting the fabric as she moves higher. Pulling away slightly, her eyes scan my face, then stop on my eyes. "Can I take this off?"

I draw in a breath for fortitude and nod sharply, then smooth my hands down the front of the silky robe and over her perfect breasts. "Only if you take this off."

She grins. "No problem." She slides my T-shirt over my head, and my first instinct is to pull it back down to cover the ugliness of my back but I draw on Vi's bravery and raise my arms so she can remove it completely. Goosebumps rise over my flesh and my nipples bead as she tosses the material to the side. She doesn't say anything as her eyes drink in every inch of my torso. My heart grows to the point I fear it's going to escape my chest with her eyes on me. From the front I appear untouched—my skin is smooth, my muscles defined and I don't mind her perusal … but my back … that's another story.

She raises her hand toward the tattoo over my heart, her gaze laser-focused on it but pulls back at the last second before touching my skin. I wrap my fingers around her wrist and place her palm over the tattoo. Closing my eyes temporarily, I absorb her warmth, drawing on her strength. "You can touch me," I whisper harshly around the lump in my throat as I fight the feeling of being exposed and vulnerable.

I didn't want to feel this way.

I wasn't ready.

It's the very thing I've been trying to avoid all these years. My breaths are heavy and uneven as I fight my instincts, but I remind myself that I'm safe with and accepted unconditionally by this woman.

She nods and swallows, removing her palm and using the tips of her fingers to trace the lines of my Army Ranger tattoo. Concentrating as she follows each line meticulously, her eyes flick up to mine. She licks her lips, and I can read the reluctance in her eyes, so I nod slightly. "What does this represent?"

I look down at the tattoo and remember the day Wyatt and I decided to get them. Even though I was reluctant, his eagerness made me want to do my part. "I was in the Third Battalion of the Army Rangers. This is the symbol."

She points to each letter R L T W in turn. "What do these letters stand for?"

"*Rangers lead the way.* We're always the ones who go into situations first."

Her eyes snap up to mine. "That sounds dangerous."

"It can be." I cup her magnificent bare breasts, weighing them in my hands—they really are a work of art. "I don't want to talk about it anymore tonight." I don't want to slip into a dark place while I have this beautiful woman sitting in my lap.

I lean forward and suck one peak into my mouth, but Vi pulls away. "Don't distract me, Shane. I'm on a mission." She pushes me back slightly, then stands and slides the robe from her shoulders, allowing it to slide down her arms and then dropping it to the floor, leaving her in matching panties.

"Jesus, fuck, Violet. You're so damn perfect," I groan as my cock hardens further in my sweats.

Her smile is vibrant. "Thank you, but I'm far from perfect."

I slip my hands up the back of her thighs, sliding them up the smooth muscle until I cup her silky-covered ass. Her hands drop to my shoulders, her fingers spreading across the muscle, and I cringe when she finds the divots there. She leans down and kisses the top of one shoulder, her breath brushing against my heated skin, and then she moves across and repeats the process on my other shoulder. Her kisses fill me with tenderness, love, and care. "It feels so good to have your hands on me," I breathe.

"If you'll let me, I'll keep my hands on you forever." Her hands slide down my arms, over the five-inch scar where I have missing muscle thanks to shrapnel from the IED that stole Wyatt's life. I suck in a sharp breath. "Are you okay?"

I nod sharply as the wind picks up outside and rain taps angrily against the window. "Yeah."

She moves and climbs onto the bed behind me. I hear her suck in a sharp breath, then she whispers, "Oh, Shane." Her fingers feather over my skin, tracing from one scar to the next, her lips following the path, pressing healing kisses to each reminder permanently marked on my flesh. Her shaky finger traces the two-inch scar about halfway down my spine. "Can you tell me about this?"

I swallow past the lump that's growing in my throat as my mind flashes back to the blast.

The force of pressure.

The pain.

The heat.

Being thrown forward.

Hitting the ground ... then nothing.

"It was a result of an IED. I was walking away, so I had my back to the blast. As a result, my T10 vertebra suffered a compression fracture, so the doctors had to operate. They injected cement to restore the bone to its correct height, then stitched me back together."

Her hair brushes my spine and then her lips brush my skin. "Does it still hurt?" she murmurs.

"It aches when it's cold." Goosebumps radiate from where her fingers ghost across my scars like she's tracing the constellations in the night sky.

"And what about all of these scars?" Her fingers glide across my pockmarked skin.

I shrug. "Shrapnel."

"Do they hurt?"

I swallow and nod slowly. "Yeah." But it's my reminder. I'll take the pain because I got off lightly compared to Wyatt.

The bed creaks, and then Vi's soft lips press against my skin. She does it again and again until she's kissed every mark she can reach on my back and arms for a second time. My stomach twists, and it's difficult to swallow past the lump that's blocking my throat. My nose tingles and the backs of my eyes sting so I blink quickly. Her hands wrap around my middle and she rests her damp cheek against my shoulder blade—she's been crying. Crying for *me*. "I'm so glad you're still here," she whispers.

I exhale a long breath and press my thumb and forefinger to my eyes as I cover her hand with mine and tangle our fingers together. The feel of her soft cheek against my back, her silky hair on my skin, her breath warming me is messing with my mind. I'm so close to crying like a damn baby, and it's all because I can't remember the last time someone touched my bare skin with affection. After the blast, the touches were purposeful and impersonal. Their perfunctory application of bandages and ointments was only to heal the wounds on a superficial level. But Vi's touch is *truly* healing. It's doing something to me on a more fundamental level than that of my epidermis.

I bring her hand up to my lips and press a kiss to her knuckles. "I'm glad I'm still here, too." I've thought it before in passing, but this is the first time I've truly meant it. Through my darkest days, I was angry I'd survived. I felt undeserving and that feeling only deepened into self-hate. But I see now that I had to go through that to understand this beautiful moment with the woman at my back.

She lifts her head away and glides her hand down my spine, over the scar from my spinal surgery and I use our tangled hands to pull her around to my front so she can straddle my lap. Cupping her face, I wipe away her tears with my thumbs. "Don't cry for me." Before she can argue, I guide her mouth to mine and kiss her deeply. I kiss her in a way I hope expresses how much I appreciate her comfort and acceptance. She gave no indication of being turned off by my scarred back, in fact, the way she kissed each scar, with so much reverence and compassion made me fall deeper in love with her. I slide my tongue against hers in a dance that's quickly become familiar to us.

Weaving one hand into her hair, I hold her in place as her hands smooth over my chest and loop around my shoulders to play with the short strands of my hair. I will be forever grateful to have her hands on me after such a long hiatus from human touch. I really don't know how I ever survived. She grinds down on my dick, and the heat of her pussy is sensational. Falling backward, I take her with me, then roll over, so I'm balancing over her on my forearms. When I gentle our kiss and pull back, Vi's eyes flutter open slowly, the blue almost completely swallowed by the black of her pupils. I dip down and kiss the tip of her nose then whisper gruffly in her ear, "Move up to the middle of the bed for me, Blue." I watch her throat bob as she swallows, but she does as I ask. "Such a good girl."

Once she's exactly where I want her, I peel her panties down her sexy legs, then push her knees up, placing her feet flat on the bed. Thunder cracks in the distance followed by a lightning flash. My hand trembles slightly as I make contact with her smooth skin but steadies instantly when I feel her warmth. Sliding my palm along her shin, to her knee, I follow my path with light kisses. Vi trembles beneath my touch and when I look up at her, she's watching me with a heavy-lidded gaze while she presses her teeth into her bottom lip. "You're so damn beautiful, Violet."

Her lips tip up. "Not as beautiful as you."

I huff out a laugh. "I'm far from beautiful. You've seen the mess."

"As I said, beautiful. The scars you wear don't detract from that." Her fingers slide into my hair, sending tingles down my spine.

I nip the inside of her knee as my stomach flips at her compliment. I guess I should be offended that she called me beautiful instead of handsome or even hot but I'm not. She likes what she sees and accepts all of the ugly parts as well as the parts of me that came out unscathed. Moving up the inside of her thigh, the scent of her arousal fills my nose and I suck in a long breath to take the sweet aroma deep into my lungs. When I get to the apex of her thighs, I bury my nose in her pussy, then swipe my tongue through her lips making her shiver and her fingers tighten in my hair. "You always smell so damn good," I say, smiling against her sensitive flesh, then swipe my tongue up and around her clit in a light, teasing stroke. Wrapping my hands around her thighs, I open her wider and feast. Like a man who hasn't had sustenance for weeks.

Her moans and sighs fill my temporary bedroom and as she pushes her hips into my face, I revel in her taste, her scent, her obvious enjoyment of what I'm doing to her. I pulse my tongue against her clit and her hips fly from the bed.

"Shaaaane! God, that feels so good. I'm not gonna last much longer."

Pressing my tongue into her opening, I circle her clit with firm pressure and tease her nipple. Her thighs tremble and her fingers tug on the strands of my hair, ratcheting up my need for her. I don't know how I ever thought I could keep having sex without her hands on me. Her clit pulses beneath my fingers, and I pinch it firmly but not too hard. I watch her closely as her body stiffens, her chest freezes as she holds her breath, her stomach quivers, and she falls apart beautifully beneath my touch, calling out my name like a prayer. I swap out my tongue for a single finger and feel the tightening of her walls through the aftershocks of her orgasm. I grind my dick into the mattress to hold off my release and she loosens her grip on my hair, then lightly scratches my scalp with her short nails. Dragging my finger out of her opening, I replace it with two, then three, and begin to pump. "I want you to come again," I grumble against her clit.

She lifts her head from the pillow and looks at me with a grin and I know that whatever's about to come out of her mouth is going to be sassy. "I'm not going to say no to another orgasm. Do your worst."

I chuckle against her pussy and accept her challenge, using my tongue and fingers to build her to a second release. Her hips push against my mouth and I reluctantly tear my hand from her breast to hold her in place. Flicking my tongue against her clit, I increase the intensity of my fingers and she rewards me with a long, sexy moan. I love learning what she likes and what she responds to best, it makes me feel like a king. Her legs stiffen on my shoulders and the fluttering of her internal muscles warn me that she's close. Keeping up my momentum, I suck her clit between my lips and feel her body tighten beneath my touch. Her orgasm takes her like a slow-rolling wave and her inner muscles pulse around my fingers. Contentment fills every molecule of my body while I lead her through her release. She melts into the mattress, her legs and arms going limp. Her breasts tremble with each panting breath and I soak in the spectacular sight. Fuck, I'm a lucky man.

My dick begs me for release, so I gently remove my fingers once her muscles relax, rub gentle circles across her swollen pussy slowly, and place a tender kiss on her clit. Then I work my way up her trembling body, kissing a path across her stomach, to each breast in turn, where I lick each nipple as I line up my aching cock. Her hands find my hair again and she guides my head higher up her body. I feel as though my balls are going to explode at any moment and I need to concentrate hard so I don't come as soon as I slide into her tight, slick heat. Kissing my way up her neck, I suck on her hammering pulse point as I notch the head of my cock at her opening. Her heat scorches me immediately and I fight to hold myself steady and slide in slowly as my heart hammers.

Heaven.

This has to be what heaven feels like.

We both groan at the sensation of me filling her. "I'll never get tired of feeling you around my cock. The way your body welcomes mine." I'm glad we had the birth control talk so we can enjoy this without worrying about condoms.

"Same." She sighs against my ear.

I kiss my way across to her mouth and take her lips in a passionate kiss. As our tongues dance a sensual tango, I shift my hips in a slow, steady retreat followed by an equally slow and steady advance. I fill her repeatedly, building us progressively closer to our peak, murmuring praise between kisses. "You feel so hot and tight around my dick." For the first time, I'm making love to Violet, not just having sex.

My heart is completely open as it pounds in my chest, and a feeling of warmth envelopes me. When I gaze into Vi's eyes, I see nothing but deep acceptance and love. So much so, that it fills me up and makes me feel things I never thought I deserved but am grateful to have. I deepen our kiss, expressing the love and gratitude I feel for her. The only one patient enough to break through my defenses. The only one I feel safe enough with to share the darkest parts of myself and know with certainty that she won't judge me or that her feelings for me will diminish. I hold myself still inside her as I confess. "I love you," I murmur against her lips —the words tumbling out on a wave of emotion and connection.

She grins up at me as her arms tighten around my shoulders, pressing her breasts against my chest and removing any space between us. "You have no idea how much it means to me when you say those words." She leans up and presses her swollen lips to mine. "I love you so much, and I want you to know that I'm here for you. Whatever you need."

My cock swells with her words. They're not sexy but she's expressing a level of loyalty that shows how pure her heart is. And after what happened with her ex, being that open with someone else has to be scary for her. But as usual, Violet is nothing but brave. "I've said it before, but it bears saying again. You're so fucking brave. You know that?"

Her eyes snap to mine and creases form between her brows as confusion fills her face. "The only brave one in this room is you."

I shake my head. "There are different types of bravery, Vi. You have the bravest heart I know. You lead with your heart, never afraid to be honest about how you're feeling or to express your thoughts and emotions." I dip down and taste her lips again because I can't stop. "So damn courageous."

Her body melts beneath mine and a slow, sexy smile slides across her lips. "I'm glad you see me that way. You're the first man to do so." Her legs tighten around my waist and the heels of her feet dig into my ass. She drags her hands along my flanks and around to my back, running over the multitude of scars. She lifts her head and captures my mouth with hers and we waste no time in opening to each other and tangling our tongues in a dance as old as time. Our kiss is long and passionate, heating the blood in my veins and I begin to move again. Slow and sensual movements of our hips, matching our rhythm, syncing our breaths, and uniting our souls. The staccato of her heart increases as does mine as we build toward our peak. She holds onto me like I'm her lifeline as her pussy tightens around my cock and she falls apart beneath me. "Oh, God. Shaaane," she cries as she tightens her legs around my waist, and I push in deeper, relishing the rhythmic pulsing of her muscles around my dick and ignoring the ache in my back.

An electric charge moves through my body, from the extremities of my fingers and toes, like lightning heading straight to my balls and I don't even try to stop my impending orgasm. I hold myself deep inside her as jets of cum flood from me. Pulse after hot pulse and in that moment, my mind drifts toward a thought I briefly considered once before.

What would it be like to see Violet round with *my* baby?

I groan at the image playing in my mind of her swollen with

my child. Of our baby cradled between us and Jasmine looking on at her baby sister or brother. When I open my eyes, they immediately catch on Vi's as hers flutter open, and a slow, sexy grin tips up her lips.

I drop my head to press soft kisses all over her face, making her chuckle.

31

VIOLET

I wake with my hand over Shane's steady heart, my head on his muscular chest, and a grin on my lips. Without moving, I glance up at his handsome face. I've never seen him asleep because he's always awake before me, and this moment almost feels like an out-of-body experience. He looks completely different when he's relaxed, and I quietly sigh to myself. We've been growing closer and our affection for each other has certainly deepened, but last night, I felt the shift.

I felt him finally surrender to me.

To us.

To what's been growing since we first met.

I drop my eyes down his torso, focusing on the smooth texture of his skin, the definition of his abs, that sexy V that points straight to his perfect dick, and the tattoo permanently marked over his heart. My lips tip down as I remember the multitude of scars etched on his skin and how my heart shattered into a million pieces when I saw it last night as the storm battered the house. The pain he must have felt—both physically, mentally, and emotionally. The strength it's taken for him to get to where he is today is mind-boggling. He says I'm brave, but he doesn't see his own bravery. It's staggering to think about everything he must have experienced.

The surgeries, the healing, the pain, the anguish, the trauma, the heartache. Never being the same man as you once were. How does a man come to terms with such tragedy and come out the other side as strong as he is?

Pressing a kiss to his chest, I sigh as I watch the faintest hint of pink begin to color the sky through the window. The storm is long gone, and there's nothing but peace. It's even too early for the birds, but I don't want to go back to sleep. I move my leg and take stock of the delicious aches in my body which have become commonplace since we started sleeping together.

Well ... sleeping isn't exactly the correct term.

He's a generous lover with stamina that I would have never believed possible. He's stretched muscles that I hadn't realized existed.

He stirs beneath my hand, and I tip my head back to look at his face. A sleepy smile greets me as his warm brown eyes take me in. He lifts his hand and uses his thick fingers to slip my loose hair behind my ear, then traces the curve of my face down to my jaw with his knuckles. "Hey," he murmurs softly, his morning voice a little rough. *So sexy.*

"Hey," I say, grinning up at him.

I push myself up and press a kiss to his lips. He weaves his fingers into my tangled hair and holds me in place as he deepens our connection. I melt into him, my body liquifying when his other hand digs into my hip and pulls me across his body until I'm sprawled over him. His hard length presses against my thigh, and I shift so I can feel it against my clit and rub myself against him. Both of us moan, and I adjust myself so the head of his cock is notched against my opening, then push myself upright so I can slide down his hard length. That curve of his dick that I admired the first time I saw it is as perfect as I thought it would be. As he bottoms out deep inside me, I drop my head back on my shoulders, soaking up the fullness. "I love having you inside me," I whisper as I drop my gaze back to Shane's.

His fingers dig into my hips, and he pushes up. "I want to live inside you, Violet. Never let you go." His hands trail up to my waist and higher still until his large palms span my rib cage beneath my breasts. "You feel so damn hot and tight around my cock," he grumbles as his thumbs swipe over the droop of my breasts and he cups each boob. He pushes them together, then sits up to bury his face between the soft mounds. "I love your tits. They're perfect." *They're not really but I'm glad he thinks so.* He squeezes my nipples, then dips down to suck each one into his hot mouth in turn, lavishing them with attention. Tracing his hands down my body and around my waist, he grabs the globes of my ass and squeezes. "And your sexy ass. Feel how perfect it fits in my hands. Made for me." He grips each cheek, pulls them apart, and pushes roughly into me. *Oh my God!* A moan slips past my lips. Sliding his hands down my taut thighs, he groans. "And your fucking legs. These legs of yours make me so hard. So damn strong and sexy." Groaning, he nips my nipple and slides one hand around to my clit.

I rock over him slowly, swiveling my hips as I slide my fingers through his hair, gripping the short strands to help ground me. A pink hue paints the wall behind Shane as we move together, creating a beautiful rhythm that builds us both toward our release. Our lips meet in a sensual kiss as a sheen of sweat coats our bodies. The slickness blends where our flesh meets while our breaths combine and his thumb circles my clit tightly, taking me ever closer to the edge. Never before have I felt so close, so in tune with another human being as I do with Shane. Being with him feels different now.

Deeper.

Like we're more connected.

He's bound me to him with his soft heart, strong moral compass, and stoic determination.

He makes me feel safe and cared for.

Appreciated and admired.

Respected and desired.

He lifts me from him with ease and flips me onto my back, then climbs over my body and presses himself inside while he licks and sucks on my neck, paying extra attention to that spot just below my ear. His mouth always feels amazing on me but this morning there's the additional sensation of his morning scruff as it scrapes along my sensitive flesh. I'm engulfed beneath his huge body and it feels as though nothing else exists except for him and me. A long moan escapes me as he hammers into me over and over, shunting me toward the end of the bed until my head hangs over the edge and my hair drags on the carpet. I wrap my arms and legs around him, digging my short nails into his shoulders and he grunts. Tingles erupt along my limbs, sending waves of sparks through my body, building in strength until they crash at the apex of my thighs. My body tightens and my breath stalls in my lungs. Sparks fill my vision and I shatter, falling ... forever falling into oblivion.

His cock grows thicker, and I feel it pulse inside of me, sending tiny shockwaves through my core. A deep groan escapes his lips and he wraps his arms around me, holding me tight. It almost feels like he's trying to merge us into one as he fills me with his release. I gasp in a breath, filling my lungs with Shane's sexy scent. He drops his forehead to mine and we both spend a few moments breathing heavily as our hearts pound against each other. Once our bodies have calmed a little, he pushes up on his elbows and cups my face, taking his weight with him and I miss him immediately. When I try to pull him back down, he holds strong meaning I have no hope of getting him to do what I want. Sliding his nose along mine, he murmurs, "I don't want to crush you."

Without breaking our connection, he rolls so I'm on top of him and slides us down the bed. "What about me crushing you?" I giggle.

"Not possible." He scoffs. I drop my head to his chest, nuzzling into his neck as he strokes his fingers slowly through my hair. I'm surprised his fingers aren't getting caught in a million tangles after the night we shared. "I want to watch the sunrise with you," he whispers roughly and when I look up at him, I see a hint of nervousness in his eyes and I sense this is important to him.

I nod. "Okay."

He gently slides out of me and I roll to my back. Climbing out of bed, Shane grabs a wad of tissues and comes back to clean me up, then helps me to stand on shaky legs. He collects my robe from the floor and slips it over my shoulders. "You might need something warmer," he whispers as he kisses my shoulder.

"Probably."

"I'll meet you downstairs."

He gives me one last heated kiss, and I head to my bedroom to put on warmer clothes. I change quickly, not wanting to miss a moment of watching the sunrise with Shane. When I make it to the kitchen, he's already boiled the kettle and has my tea steeping in my favorite cup, making me smile. While he finishes making his drink, I grab a blanket from the back of the couch and head to the back porch. The pink hue across the sky has been joined by a soft orange slash that adds a touch of warmth to the early morning horizon and I inhale a deep breath of the fresh morning air, absorbing the negative ions created by the storm.

I hear the back door open and close and feel Shane at my back as he passes my tea to me over my shoulder. One solid arm wraps around my shoulders from behind and he tugs me into his body. We stand in silence as the colors of the sky change, casting the garden in different hues.

"I've avoided watching the sunrise since I returned." I hold still even though I have a million questions running through my mind. *Why would he avoid it? Why does he want to see it this morning? What's changed for him?* "It reminds me it's a new day. A day that Wyatt doesn't get to spend with his family. Another day that I'm still here while he isn't. But my feelings surrounding the dawn are slowly changing." He kisses the top of my head. "And it's because of you and Jasmine." I melt into his body when his hold around my shoulders tightens. "I met Wyatt at Basic when we were screened for the Rangers together. We were inseparable. Our backgrounds were so similar, it was uncanny. The only difference was he was already married with a baby and he wanted to serve his country to make the world safer for his wife and son." My heart pounds in my ears and the need to turn and comfort him is overwhelming but I keep as still as possible so he keeps sharing. "The attack that caused all of my wounds, stole Wyatt from us. He was closer to the blast. Didn't stand a chance. I was unconscious while my friend died and I could do nothing to help him." His voice sounds distant, lost.

I place my tea on the railing and spin in Shane's hold, no longer able to hear the pain in his voice without comforting him. Wrapping my arms around his middle, I bury my face in his chest, feeling his heart thumping steadily against my cheek. I soak in his warmth and vitality—grateful that he's still here but sick to my stomach that he lost a good friend. That Hope and Evan lost someone incredibly important in their lives. I absorb the pain dripping from him, trying to soak it up and take it from him. He's been carrying this burden, this sadness for such a long time and it's time he had someone help him share the load. I don't want to give him false platitudes because *sorry* feels grossly inadequate for what he's experienced. So I say nothing. I only hold him—hoping he takes what little strength I can offer him.

Just when I think he's not going to say anything more, he sighs. "I've tried my best to be available to Hope and Evan, but I can't replace what they lost. I've done my best to step in wherever I could but now that Hope's asked me to stay away I feel lost and inadequate." He kisses the top of my head and I tighten my hold on him, then look up at his face. The tortured expression catches me off-guard. "I don't know how to help them from a distance. I feel as though I've broken my promise to Wyatt."

"I don't think she sees it that way. Hope seems like a strong, independent woman. I can't imagine it would be easy for her to ask for help. And maybe she worries that they're stopping you from having your own life and moving forward."

Shane rubs his hand down my back and cups my ass. "She is. So fucking strong, but she doesn't see it in herself." He squeezes my ass again and tugs the bottom half of me against him so we're touching at every available inch. He dips down, and I press up on my toes to meet him partway. Our lips meet in a tender kiss of support and understanding.

The back door bangs open. "Mommy? Shane?" Jasmine's sweet morning voice breaks our moment and she walks toward us. Wrapping her arms around both of us, she squeezes us together in a group hug. Without letting go of me, Shane bends down to collect my daughter and bring her into our embrace. Her arms wrap around our necks, and she presses a kiss to each of our cheeks. "I love you, Mommy." Kiss. "I love you, Shane." Kiss.

"We love you, too, Angel," Shane responds.

Jasmine's eyes widen and a wide grin splits her face. "You *really* love me?"

Shane's eyebrows dip over his chocolate irises. "Of course. I've told you before." He rubs his nose across hers. "I love you *and* your mom." His words make my heart melt into a puddle at my feet. He's shown me time and again that he loves Jasmine and he's told her that he loves her, but I think it's finally sinking in that this man ... this stoic man actually *does* love us.

"Does that mean you're my daddy now?" I'm not surprised by her question and hold my breath waiting to hear his response.

He glances at me briefly before turning his attention to my daughter perched between us. "I'd be honored to be your daddy if you think I'm good enough." I feel his body tense beneath my touch as he waits for Jasmine's response.

Pfft. As if he wouldn't be good enough. He's already treated my daughter better than her biological father ever did. I can't believe he has doubts.

My daughter looks at him like he's a crazy person then leans in and kisses his cheek before squeezing both of them between her tiny hands to make him look at her. "You're the best daddy. You read me stories and color with me. You play with me at the park and take me for ice cream. You help me in the garden and come to my school. You give me the best hugs, and my heart feels big when you're around," she declares with a smile.

His body relaxes, and his smile slowly grows wider with each point that Jas makes to show him that he's already a great dad. He looks even more devastatingly gorgeous with that smile on his lips and a lightness dancing in his eyes. He chuckles and squeezes us both tighter, kissing each of us on the top of our heads. "My girls," he murmurs against my hair, and contentment washes through me. Settling me and making me feel as though everything's going to be all right. *Finally.*

"Mommy? Can we clean up the garden now?"

I chuckle at how quickly Jasmine's thoughts jump from one idea to the next, completely oblivious to the importance of the moment we just shared. "Not right now. We need to get you ready for school, and Shane and I need to get ready for work."

"After school?" she asks hopefully.

"Sure thing. We'll have it cleaned up in no time this afternoon. We can even use some of the fallen vegetables in our dinner tonight."

"Okay. I better get ready." She shuffles down our bodies until her feet touch the wooden porch and then skips inside.

When I turn to follow her inside, Shane reaches out and grips my wrist, pulling me back into his embrace. He brushes my hair away from my face and studies me intently. "Thank you."

I look at him, confused. "What for?"

"Everything." He kisses my forehead and then pulls away to lock his gaze with mine. "For last night. Your acceptance of me into your life ... both of your lives. For being patient with me."

"You don't need to thank me, Shane. I would have honestly

waited for you forever, but I'm glad I didn't have to wait that long. We love you." I press up onto my toes and plant a kiss on his bristly cheek, and while I'd love to get lost in another kiss, I need to make sure Jasmine hasn't become distracted and is getting dressed for school.

32

VIOLET

 for an available parking space. Jasmine insisted on making a sign to welcome Mom home, so instead of pulling into the pickup line, we need to find a place to park.

I point to the right. "Oh, there's a couple walking toward their car. Let's follow them."

Shane nods and flicks the indicator, slowing down to follow the couple. Once they pull out, we park and climb out, careful not to bend the sign for Mom. She's going to be so surprised. We make our way through the busy terminal and find the arrival gate for her flight.

"When's Gramma coming?" Jasmine asks as she holds her colorful sign in front of her.

"Soon. Keep watching for her." People mill about the large open space, moving from one area to another.

"I can't see with all the people in the way."

"We can't have that now. We don't want your gramma to miss out on seeing the sign you worked so hard to make."

Jas smiles up at Shane and he bends down, scoops her up, and sits her on his shoulders so she can see above the crowd. "Thank you, Daddy."

My heart does a flip every time my daughter calls Shane *Daddy,* and I've noticed how his face softens and his shoulders relax whenever it happens. She has no concept of how special it is to have him take that role in her life ... in *our* lives but I do, and it's a gift I'll always treasure. A man who takes on the role of father for a child who isn't his own is truly a special man.

Jasmine bounces on Shane's shoulders, waving her sign around, and he tightens his grip on her. "There she is! Gramma! Gramma!"

I press up on my toes, but I'm too short to see over the crowd so I turn toward the direction Mom will come from now I know she's through the gate. I finally lay eyes on her, and I realize I've missed her. This is the longest we've ever been apart. She surges forward with a bright smile and sparkling eyes, looking well-rested and energized from her vacation.

Shane places Jas on her feet, and she drops her sign, then bolts toward Mom with Shane's eyes locked on her like a heat-seeking missile. "Gramma! I missed you."

Mom laughs and bends down to scoop up her granddaughter. "Oh, my beautiful girl. I missed you so much." She squishes her tight, rocking back and forth, and my smile widens as I watch them reunite.

Shane tangles our fingers, his grin matching mine as we watch Mom and Jas. Suddenly, his smile disappears, his muscles grow taut, and he takes a step forward, dragging me with him. I follow his flinty stare with confusion. What has him on alert?

A man, who looks remarkably like Hugh Jackman, steps close behind Mom and places his hand on her lower back. My eyebrows must be almost at my hairline and I tug on Shane's hand until he looks down at me. I drag him in close and whisper, "Not once did she mention she was bringing her *friend* home."

He relaxes as he chuckles, and his warm breath ghosts across my cheek. "I think he might be more than a *friend.*"

"Me too." I wriggle my eyebrows up and down.

"Violet," Mom says with her arm outstretched to hug me while still holding Jas in her other arm.

I wrap both arms around her and my daughter. "Mom. It's great to have you home. We missed you."

"I missed you, too." We kiss each other on the cheek, then she pulls away and smiles up at Shane. "Hello, Shane. It's wonderful to see you. Thank you for taking care of my girls."

He looks down at me, sin filling his gaze. "It was my pleasure." *Wow! Is it hot in here?*

"He's my daddy now!" Jas almost shouts.

Mom's eyes widen along with her grin. "Oh my, I see a lot's happened while I've been away."

I lift my chin and gesture over her shoulder. "It seems that way."

Her cheeks flush and she turns, holding out her hand. Her *man* friend takes it with a smile and nods at me and Shane as he steps into our circle. "I'd like you to meet Lloyd. Lloyd, this is my eldest daughter, Violet and her little girl, Jasmine. And this is Shane."

Lloyd holds his hand out with a warm smile but I push right past it and engulf him in a hug. "It's great to meet you."

He chuckles as his free arm wraps around me. "Nice to meet you, too. Your mom's told me so much about all of you; I feel as though I already know you."

Well, he's one step ahead of us, but I don't say that. I don't want to make the man uncomfortable. "How long are you staying?"

He looks down at Mom with affection. "Indefinitely. I couldn't bear to part from your mom, so I'm going to finish up my current projects from here and then start working with her."

"Oh, wow! That's a huge step." My eyes must be as large as saucers.

"When you know, you know." He winks at Mom. "No point wasting any more time."

"Ain't that the truth," Mom pipes in, taking his hand in hers. "Shall we collect our luggage and go home?"

"It should be at baggage claim three," Shane points in the direction we need to head, then grabs Mom's pull-along carry-on luggage.

Jas slides her hand into Mom's free hand, Lloyd grabs his carry-on, and we make our way to the baggage claim area. Luggage is already making its way around the carousel, and he tells Mom to wait with us while he and Shane collect their bags.

I don't waste a second. "Soooo. This is an interesting turn of events."

She beams at me. Literally beams and I'm thrilled for her. "I know. I couldn't believe it when he showed me his ticket this morning and told me he was coming with me. We had spoken about him moving here when he's finished his current projects but he said he would miss me too much." She's almost giddy, and I adore seeing her happiness.

"I'm so freaking happy for you, Mom." I lean in and embrace her. She's sacrificed so much over the years, raising two daughters on her own and stepping in to help Cass and me raise our girls. "You deserve every bit of happiness."

She squeezes me tight. "Thank you. I was worried you'd think it was too soon."

"Are you crazy? You've waited almost thirty years, how is that too soon?"

"I mean that we're moving in together so quickly after meeting."

I wave off her concern. "*Pfft.* I'm pretty sure you're old enough and wise enough to make decisions that are the best for you. If he makes you happy and he's a good man, then we're all gonna be happy for you both."

Shane heads toward us through the thinning crowd with two large bags and a duffle bag slung over his shoulder while Lloyd pulls their carry-ons behind him, and we head to the parking lot.

Luckily, we brought his SUV because we would never have fit everything in my car.

We pull into our driveway behind a brand-spanking new SUV and it takes me a moment to put two and two together. Toby said he was buying Cass a *family* car the last time we spoke, and I guess this is it.

The screen door flies open, and Poppy and Daisy burst out of the house, heading straight for Mom with Cassia and Toby pausing on the front porch to watch the girls fuss over her. I can tell the moment my sister realizes we have an additional passenger when her eyes go comically wide and she blinks several times, then looks up at Toby. He shrugs and pulls her down the front steps and across to Shane's car, immediately going to the back to help him unload the luggage.

While Mom catches up with Cassia and her girls, Lloyd stands beside me. "Wow, there's a lot of love here."

I turn to him. "We've never been away from Mom for so long. She's the glue in our family and we missed her." He tucks his hands in his pockets and rocks back on his heels as he watches her fuss over Daisy and Poppy. "But we're thrilled she took some much-needed time out for herself and that she connected with you. She's sounded happy ... really happy every time we've spoken while she's been away and I think I know why."

He gives me a boyish smile. "I actually crushed on your mother in high school but I was too shy to do anything about it."

"Ha! I know what that's like," Toby interrupts with a chuckle from behind us. He holds out his hand to Lloyd. "Hi, I'm Toby. I'm Cassia's husband."

He shakes Toby's hand. "Lloyd. Great to meet you, Toby. Rose has talked about you all non-stop."

I nudge Toby's arm. "Nice car."

He huffs a laugh and runs his hand through his hair. "Yeah, I finally got around to upsizing."

We all make our way inside, and the scent of garlic and tomato sauce wafts through the house in greeting. I grab Cass's arm and pull her to a stop. "I said I'd make dinner."

She shrugs. "Toby insisted. You know how much he loves Cristo's, and he had a hankering for his favorite *moussaka*. We have enough to feed all of us for three days." She rolls her eyes and chuckles.

"Where do you want Lloyd's luggage?" Shane asks Mom, and Cass and I wait with bated breath for her answer.

Without skipping a beat, she tells Shane to take it to her room, and Cass and I grin at each other like a couple of kids at a birthday party. Maybe Shane should just move into my bedroom, too. There's really no point in him keeping Cassia's old bedroom since we spend every night together now. Shane nods and he and Toby carry the bags upstairs.

"Mom, why don't you show Lloyd around and we'll set up for dinner," Cass suggests.

Jas rushes to Mom's side. "Can we show him our garden first, Gramma?"

Lloyd crouches so he's at Jasmine's height. "I've heard a lot of good things about your garden and how you help your gramma grow the fruit and vegetables. I'd love to start there."

Jas twists her body from side to side in that shy way she does when she first meets new people but her happiness at Lloyd's praise is plain to see. She slides her hand into his and leads him out the back door, telling him all about the storm and how we had to clean up afterward. Mom collects Daisy and Poppy and follows them out back.

"He seems nice."

I watch them through the same window I watched Jasmine lead Shane around the backyard when he first moved in; it's almost like déjà vu. "He does. And look how happy Mom is." I turn toward Cass. "I feel like our family has finally fallen into place."

Cass nods and comes closer to me, wrapping her arm around my shoulder and spinning me back toward the window. I wrap my arm around her waist and lean my head on her shoulder. "We all deserve this, Vi. Good men who love us and our kids unconditionally."

"Yeah," I whisper, feeling emotional that we've all found happiness.

"Everything okay in here?" Toby's voice breaks through our moment.

When I spin, both of our guys are standing in the kitchen doorway and my heart skips a beat, just as it does whenever I think of Shane as mine. "Yeah, we were just watching Mom and Lloyd with the girls."

"He seems like a decent guy," Toby says absentmindedly as he carries dishes to the table. He and Cass work together to place the dishes along with spoons ready for serving. Shane and I grab the plates and silverware, and before long, we're ready to eat whenever Mom comes back inside.

THE GIRLS CHAT and eat happily at the table we set up for them next to Mom's dining table, and the adults settle in with full plates and glasses of iced tea. As I'm scooping up my first forkful of food, Toby stands and taps his fork against his glass.

"I hope you don't mind the interruption, but Cass and I have something we'd like to share with you."

I flick my eyes to my sister who's looking up at her husband with a grin. Her eyes are bright and clear and she almost looks as though she's glowing. Giddiness grows as I study her closely, and I think I know what Toby's about to tell us.

He looks down at my sister with so much love, then turns back toward the table. "Cass and I are excited to announce that Cass is pregnant with our third child."

Mom and I both bolt out of our seats to embrace Cass and Toby with our congratulations as cheers fill the dining area. The guys do that back-slap-come-hug thing they do and I ask Cass when she's due.

"We're due the second week in May, around Poppy's birthday."

I can't stop my smile. "I can't wait to be an aunty again. This is so exciting. How have you been feeling?" I grab Poppy and hug her, using sign language to congratulate her, too.

"Yeah, good. I've been feeling fine so far. Just a little morning sickness but it's gone by ten." She takes her seat again.

"Well, that explains the need for a bigger car." I raise my eyebrows at my sister.

She grins at me, then fills her mouth with food. I was wary of Toby when we first met him but I'm so glad he's part of our family. He's been amazing for my sister and niece, as well as for our family. Not to mention he's the reason I met Shane. I owe him a huge amount of gratitude.

"Daddy,"—everyone turns toward Jasmine and Shane climbs to his feet—"can I please have some more juice?"

"Sure," he says as he grins at our daughter and grabs the juice out of the fridge. After he fills Jas's cup, he tops off Poppy and Daisy's drinks, too.

Cass looks at me with raised brows, her mouth dropped open. "When did that happen?"

"Wednesday morning." It's a day I'll remember forever. It's the day I felt Shane's final wall tumble.

"I knew I sensed a deeper level of contentment in you, I just wasn't sure why." She squeezes my hand. "I'm so happy for you guys." She looks up at my man. "Welcome to the family, Shane." She winks at him. "Finally!"

He grins at her as he puts the juice back in the fridge, then winks. "Thanks, *Sis*."

Toby stands and wraps his arms around Shane. His eyes look a little glassy, and I swallow past the lump in my throat as I watch two best friends embrace in Mom's kitchen. It's such a powerful moment for both men. Cassia told me that Toby worries about Shane and the way he closes himself off from people, keeping himself on the periphery. To see Toby so emotional about Shane's growing relationship with Jasmine and me makes me grateful that Toby's quietly been in Shane's corner all these years.

The guys return to the table and we finish our meal. Mom and Lloyd tell us all about the conference and innovations they want to include in their future projects and I love how they're talking about doing things together as if it's as natural as breathing. This is exactly what Mom needed.

LEANING against Shane's hard body while we enjoy our chamomile tea on the couch, I sigh.

He wraps his arm around me and I sink further into him. "That was a loud sigh. What's up?"

"I'm just so happy for Mom and Cass." I look up at him. "It feels like our family is finally complete."

He nods. "Your Mom seems so different from the woman I dropped off at the airport. She seems ... younger almost."

"I know. Like she has a new lease on life." I tease out my hair. "I'm a little worried because she's still technically married to Dad."

His eyebrows shoot up. "Shit."

"Yeah," I breathe. We're quiet for a few minutes, each of us sipping on our tea. "Hey, I was thinking that you should move your stuff into my room. We've been together every night so I don't see the point in having two rooms."

He's quiet for a long moment, and if I felt less secure in our relationship, I might worry, but this is Shane taking a moment to consider everything carefully. He pulls back a little and slides his fingers along the side of my face, following the action with his eyes. "You don't think it's disrespectful to your mom if we share your room?"

My heart does that squishy thing again. He's always thinking about everyone else. I grasp his hand and bring it to my mouth, kissing his knuckles. "I don't think Mom will mind at all but if you would prefer, I can ask her." I entwine my fingers with his, admiring how big his hand is compared to mine and how safe he makes me feel.

"I know we're not kids anymore but this is her home, and I would feel more comfortable if we had her blessing." I stretch up and kiss his lips tenderly.

"You're such a good man, Shane," I murmur against him, the bristles around his mouth scratching my face.

He smiles against my mouth. "If I'm such a good man why do I always want to do such bad things to you?"

I chuckle. "I wouldn't say anything you do to me is bad. In fact, I'd say it's all pretty great."

He closes the distance and presses his mouth to mine tenderly. His fingers slide into my hair, and he tilts my head as he swipes his soft lips across mine. I lick across the seam of his mouth and he opens for me. Wasting no time, I dart my tongue inside and moan at the taste of him. Our kiss heats up quickly as our tongues swipe against each other and Shane guides me to straddle him without missing a beat. I grind down on him, aching to have him buried deep inside me.

"Ahem." I register the sound of Mom clearing her throat from the doorway and tear my mouth from Shane's, then peer up at her. She smiles at me in that motherly way of hers. "I just came down to tell you that Lloyd and I are turning in for the night. We'll see you in the morning."

"Okay." I climb from Shane's lap and stand in front of Mom. "I ... uh ... wanted to ask if it was okay with you if Shane moves into my room."

Her eyes widen and she glances between Shane and me. "Do you mean to tell me that you've been sleeping in separate beds while I've been away?"

I turn and look at Shane, silently asking him if he's okay for me to share and he stands. "Well, no. I'm sorry if I was disrespectful to you and your home, Mrs. Phillips." He buries his hands deep in his pockets.

Her eyes skip to Shane. "Rose. And it's not disrespectful at all. It's what I was hoping for." She grins. "I'm thrilled the two of you are finally where you belong ... *together*."

I lean in and kiss her cheek. "Thanks, Mom."

"You're welcome. Good night, you two."

"Good night, Rose. And thank you again."

"Good night, Mom."

"See you kids in the morning."

Lloyd steps behind her and wraps his arm around her waist. "I just came down for a glass of water and to say goodnight. Thanks for being so welcoming, especially since you weren't expecting me." He looks down at Mom, and I love how he's looking at her like she's the air he breathes. "When it came down to it, I didn't want to miss a single minute with this amazing woman now I have my chance."

Oh my gosh, he's so sweet. Mom melts into him, and I don't think she's stopped grinning the entire time she's been home. I point to Mom's face. "Anyone who puts that smile on Mom's face will always be welcome."

He tips his head. "Thank you. I'm going to head up to bed." He kisses Mom's cheek. "See you soon."

Mom takes his hand. "I was on my way up. Good night, kids. See you in the morning."

"Night."

"Good night," Shane says. Once Mom and Lloyd are out of sight, he links his fingers with mine, pressing a kiss to my forehead. "I'm just going to check all the locks, and we can head up.

Pressing up on my toes, I kiss his cheek. "Okay. I'll be waiting."

I spin toward the stairs and Shane smacks my ass. "Be naked."

Great. Now my panties are soaked. It seems that's the permanent state of my underwear these days. I take the stairs two at a time and strip off the minute I close myself in our bedroom—*our* bedroom—and squeal quietly with happiness.

Shane's footsteps sound on the stairs and I scramble onto the bed to get into position. My heartbeats increase in speed when I see the doorknob turn and the door open. The man of my dreams steps through the opening and closes the door softly behind him. He gracefully moves forward dragging his T-shirt up his body and over his head in one swift action. My heart sings with happiness that he's so comfortable getting naked with me now. I drink in the perfection of Shane's physique, his defined abs, and that incredible V that makes my mouth water. "You're so beautiful," I murmur. I know I should probably use handsome, but he really is a beautiful male specimen.

He tosses his shirt to the side with a smirk, then his hands drop to his pants. I crawl to the edge of the bed and sit, then gesture for him to come closer. He obliges and I take over removing his pants, pushing them down his legs and he steps out, kicking the fabric to the side to join his T-shirt. I immediately stroke his dick and dip down to lick around the head, paying special attention to the slit, and tasting his salty precum. His fingers weave into my hair and he grips the strands tightly, eliciting a moan from me. He uses his hold to pull my head away from his cock and holds his finger over his mouth. "You're gonna need to keep the noise down, Blue. Can you do that?" I nod the best I can as he holds my hair. "That's my girl." He smirks at me and pushes my head back down on his cock, his other hand holding it upright for my mouth.

I go to work, sucking, licking, and stroking his beautiful dick —the experience is so much better now that I can touch him with my hands. I collect his balls in one hand and gently massage them as I take his cock as far as I can down my throat. "Oh fuck," he grunts quietly.

Pressing my flat tongue along the underside of him to add pressure, I moan softly around his shaft. He pushes his hips forward and my eyes water as his cock thickens in my mouth. Suddenly, he pulls out, and if it weren't for his grip on my hair, I would fall flat on my face. Looking up at him in confusion, I ask, "Why'd you stop?"

He cups my cheek. "Because I don't want to come down your throat. I want your pussy." He kisses my lips as his hands slide beneath my ass and he lifts me from the bed. "Wrap your gorgeous legs around me." I do as he says and he carries me over to the wall. "I need you hard and fast and the bed squeaks too much." He takes my mouth in a messy kiss as my back meets the cold wall and he impales me on his cock. I moan into his mouth as he withdraws and pushes back inside repeatedly, pressing against my clit each time just the way I need it. He hammers inside with precision, and I have no idea how he does it while he's holding me up.

I press my feet into his ass and grip him tightly as my body winds tighter and tighter like a rubber band ready to snap. Our kiss mimics the actions of our hips and everything that he's doing to my body sends me into overload. My vision goes fuzzy around the edges and my breaths seize in my lungs as I grind against him relentlessly. My pussy tightens to the point where Shane's movements are restricted, and I feel him thicken inside me while his groan rumbles through his hard body as we reach our peak.

We break apart to catch our breath and Shane drops his forehead to mine, our eyes connecting and locking. Breathlessly, I chuckle. "Oh my God, I'm pretty sure I was close to suffocating."

He chuckles silently with me, kisses the tip of my nose, and then carries me across to our bed. "I won't let anything happen to you, Vi."

I liquify in his arms. "I know," I whisper. And I do. He would protect me and Jasmine with his life, of that I'm one hundred percent certain.

His face looks pained as he withdraws from me, and I miss him immediately. Grabbing a wad of tissues from the bedside table, he gently presses me back onto the bed and then sets about cleaning me up. His gaze rises from my pussy to my face and he gives me a boyish grin. "I can't wait until it's our turn to announce that we're the ones having a baby."

Surprise rises thick and fast. "You want to have a baby with me?" I whisper, part of me afraid that he'll rescind his words. After all, Jasmine was the reason Allen no longer wanted me. He wished we'd never had her. "A baby is a huge commitment, and it changes a relationship. They need a lot of care and attention which means less attention for you, especially when they're newborns. I'll probably be tired and won't feel like having sex as much, especially in the first few months." I tease the bottom of my hair with my fingers. "Some men don't like being second best."

He balls up the tissues and tosses them in the trash. "Hell yeah. I want to have a baby with you. You're an incredible mom and I'm not a child. I don't need to have all of your attention all of the time." His dark eyebrows slash low. "And I'm here to help. You won't have to do everything on your own like you did with Jas." He crawls over me and tenderly presses his lips to mine. "Would you consider going off your birth control?"

I wrap myself around him and kiss him all over his face, making him chuckle. "I won't take it anymore but it may take a while to clear my system."

He blows out a breath and his shoulders relax. I hadn't even noticed he was tense. "Thank you. You have no idea how much that means to me." *I think I do.* Dropping his lips to mine, he pushes me back onto the bed, presses his body against mine, and slides back inside. "We'd better start practicing."

Slowly, steadily, silently, he makes love to me until we both come undone again.

33

SHANE

Toby, Peta, and I sit in a quiet booth tucked in the back of *Declan's Diner*. Toby had a hankering for a kebab today, and while I'll never understand why he can't just get the food delivered to his house, I understand his craving. The kebabs here are the best around. We were going to bring Daisy with us but when Rose found out about Toby's meeting with his manager today, she and Lloyd decided to tag along with me to Toby's place so they could fuss over her for a couple of hours.

Peta peers down at her phone and I swear she'd be lost without that thing. She has her entire personal and business life on it. "So when are we thinking for your next tour?" She looks up at Toby when he doesn't respond, which he can't while his mouth is stuffed with kebab.

He chews and swallows. "Uh ... so ... Cassia's preg—"

"Again?" Peta slaps her hand on the table.

"Yeah," Toby answers, looking at Peta like she shouldn't be surprised.

I rub my hand over my mouth to hide my grin but she catches me and her head snaps across to me. "You knew?" she asks with raised eyebrows.

I simply nod. I have nothing to contribute to these meetings.

I'm just the hired muscle but I do find Peta entertaining on occasion. Most times I just find her abrasive but she's damn good at her job and more often than not she has Toby's best interest at heart.

"When is she due?"

"Second week in May."

"Fuck. It's October. How am I supposed to set tour dates? I know you're not gonna travel with a damn newborn."

He takes another bite of his kebab like he doesn't have a care in the world. He chews and swallows. "You'd be right about that. I was thinking I could do ten days up the West Coast ... San Diego, Los Angeles, San Jose, San Francisco, Sacramento, Portland, and Seattle. Allow a day to drive between LA and San Jose and again from Sacramento to Portland, one show in each city. It's not like I have a complicated stage setup because I'm going to do a solo acoustic tour this time." He grabs a fry and pops it in his mouth while Peta madly types the details on her phone. "Let's look at doing it in February."

Peta's head snaps up, her eyes ablaze. "February? Are you serious?"

"Yeah, why?"

She inhales a deep breath and I watch her shoulders drop. "I know you think I'm amazing at my job, and I appreciate your faith in me but I'm not a miracle worker. I'm not sure I can find venues available within such a short time frame."

"You know I'm just as happy to play at small venues, even pubs. I want this tour to be intimate. If you can't find a suitable venue in one of the cities, then we skip it this time. Don't stress. It'll all fall into place."

She huffs. "One of these days, I'll manage my response better when you drop a bombshell on me."

Toby chuckles and flicks his wrist in the air. "Nah, this is far more entertaining."

Peta half-stands from her seat opposite Toby and slaps him

playfully with the back of her hand while wearing a grin. "You want to know what's going to be entertaining?"

He tries to dodge her attack but fails miserably. She waits for him to respond with her eyebrows raised. "Even if I didn't, I'm sure you'll tell me." He playfully rubs the spot she struck.

"Watching you deal with not one but two and possibly three teenage girls." She breaks out into hysterical laughter.

Toby's eyes grow wide like he hasn't thought that far ahead. He glances at me and then back at Peta. "That's not even a little bit funny."

My smile grows and I snicker. "It actually is, man."

His head snaps toward me. "You'll have a teenage daughter, too. Don't get too cocky."

That statement sobers me and my grin slides from my lips. "Damn."

He raises a single brow, nodding at me. "Yeah."

"So, I'm assuming since you'll be ready to tour in February, you're writing is coming along?"

He nods. "Yeah, it is. I tested my new material last month at *Brady's*. The response was really positive wasn't it, Shane?"

"The crowd there always loves you, but you're right, they were going crazy for your new songs." My phone vibrates in my pocket, and I tilt my hips to grab it, finding my landlord's name on the screen. I look up at Toby and Peta. "I need to take this." I stand from the booth, press the green button, and turn my back to Toby and Peta so I'm still blocking him from public view. "Hi, Roger."

"Shane. I have some disappointing news."

I tense. "What is it?"

"The contractors are running behind schedule, and your apartment won't be ready for another two weeks."

"What the hell? This is ridiculous. First, you gave me barely any notice. You increased the rent. You're still charging me rent, and I'm not even living there, and now you're telling me it'll be another two weeks?" I snap, dragging my hand over the top of my head.

"Settle down, big guy." My eyebrows shoot upward. "I can't help that the contractors are running behind schedule, and even though you're not living in the apartment at the moment, I still have mortgage repayments to make, so for you to expect a handout is deplorable." What in the actual fuck?

I grit my teeth. "I'm the deplorable one? Feel free to rent the apartment to someone else, I'm not coming back."

"Are you telling me you're going to break your lease agreement?"

"As far as I can tell, you've already broken the agreement," I snarl.

"But ..." I press the red button and jam the phone back in my pocket. I was already thinking about finding somewhere else to live, but now the decision is made.

"You okay?" Toby's concerned voice breaks through the red haze and I turn, sliding back into the booth.

"Yeah. I'm gonna need to find a new place to live. I think I just broke my lease." I exhale a long breath, releasing the sudden tension. "I was going to look for a place with a backyard for Violet and Jasmine anyway. This just forced my hand."

Crinkles form around Peta's eyes. "You finally made a move."

I glare at her. "Not that it's any of your business, but yeah. I made a move."

"Good for you."

"Thanks," I grunt.

"I doubt Rose will mind if you stay longer while you look for a place."

"I don't think she will, but Vi and I need our privacy. We keep forgetting where we are and end up getting caught by Rose or Lloyd."

Toby loses it, slapping his hand on the table as he rocks back in the booth. "I'd love to be a fly on the wall."

"Yeah, well ... I feel like a damn teenager." Not that I was ever caught making out with a girl by my parents but I can guess what it feels like now.

Once Toby calms down enough, he turns thoughtful. "There's that new development over on the east side. It would be closer for Violet to get to work."

"I checked them out the other day. The yards are too small, and Jas would have to move to a different school. She likes it where she is and has a solid group of friends."

He nods thoughtfully. "Well, if you need any help, let me know."

"Thanks."

I CLOSE the laptop with a heavy sigh and drop my head into my hands.

"Everything okay?" I look in the direction of Rose's voice as she breezes into the kitchen.

Rose has been nothing but gracious to me, opening her home at short notice, providing storage space in the garage, and she's been nothing but understanding every time she catches me making out with her daughter. I should probably do her the courtesy of keeping her up-to-date with my plans. I point to the laptop. "I've been looking for a new place," I explain about my landlord and the increase in rent as well as the contractors running behind schedule.

She pulls out a chair opposite me and places her glass on the table. "You know you're welcome to stay here indefinitely, Shane." She looks down at the glass and traces her fingers along the rim. "I assumed that since you and Violet were *together* together you'd just move in here permanently."

My heart misses a beat, as it does whenever Jasmine wraps her arm around my neck, and I drop my gaze from Rose's for fear she'll see that I'm barely holding in my gratitude. I swallow thickly and clear my throat. "Thank you, I appreciate that but I don't want to impose any more than I already have." I grit my teeth and run my hand over the top of my head. I remember the day Toby took Rose to lunch and asked her permission to propose to Cassia. He was quietly shitting himself and at the time I thought it was amusing. Toby's fantastic with words and he struggled when it came time to talk to her and while I'm a man of few words, I should probably discuss my plans with Rose. "Do you have a minute?"

"Of course." Creases form between her brows but she gets more comfortable in her chair. "Do we need a drink? You sound serious."

I stand and head to the kitchen to make a coffee for each of us and return to the table, Rose watching my every move. I sit and stare into my coffee, the steam rising into the air and try to formulate my words. I lift my eyes to find Rose watching me with a glimmer in her eye. "I love Violet and Jasmine with all of my heart." She nods and her lips widen slightly. "They shattered the armor I'd created to protect my heart and have wrapped themselves around it. I can't imagine my life without them in it. I'm not as good with words as Toby, but my plan is to make them mine one day. I'm not sure when since I don't have a home at the moment." I shift in my seat and wrap my hands around my cup. "They mean more to me than my own life and I want to give them the very best of everything because they only deserve the best. They make me want to be a better man, and I'm determined to be the best husband and father I can possibly be. I promise I'll always treat them with the utmost respect and kindness. I'll always consider their needs before my own, and I'll love them with everything that I have." When I look back up at Rose, she wipes at her cheek, her lips quivering.

She reaches across the table. "I don't know how you can say that you're not good with words because everything you just said was perfect. I really couldn't ask for a better man for my girls,

Shane. I've never seen them happier or more settled than they've been since you've been in their lives. I'm thrilled that you're going to be joining our family, and I'll be incredibly proud to call you son."

The backs of my eyes sting, and my nose tingles. I drop my eyes from hers and work hard to hold in my emotions. "Thanks, Rose, but I know I'm not good enough for Violet. I still have a lot of stuff to work through, but she makes me *want* to work through it so I'm the best person I can be. I promise I won't ever let them down." I hope she understands how seriously I take that vow.

"I know you won't, Shane. *I* believe in you. Violet and Jasmine do, too. Now you just need to believe in yourself," she says with a soft motherly smile.

The front door bangs open, and little footsteps sound on the timber floor. I quickly look at Rose. "Please keep this between us for now."

She nods as Jasmine barrels through the doorway. "Daddy! Look what I made for you today." She makes a beeline for me, waving a piece of paper above her head, as if she hasn't even noticed that Rose is sitting at the table.

I chuckle as she climbs onto my lap and holds the paper an inch from my face. "Let me see." I take it from her, and as soon as I can see the image clearly, my heart explodes with joy.

"It's a picture of you hugging me and Mommy on the back porch. See." She points at the figures and grins at me. "It's our family." I swallow past the thickness in my throat, and with a trembling hand, I pull her back into me, tightening my hold on her to keep me grounded to stop myself from floating away. The smile drops from her face and it fills with concern. "Do you like it?"

I shake my head slightly. "I don't like it, Angel," I say as her chin trembles. "I love it. I love that you've drawn a picture of *our* family. This is the most special gift you could have made for me." Her smile returns, and she twists her body, flinging her arms around my neck. I return her embrace, and when I glance up, Rose and Vi are both watching us closely, their hands clenched tightly over their hearts.

Holding out my hand to Vi, she makes her way around the table and I wrap my arm around her hips and draw her in tight, pressing a kiss to her stomach. "How was your day?"

"It wasn't as good as this moment right here." She leans down and kisses my lips but pulls away too soon.

"I'm hungry, Mommy."

"Don't I even get a hello?" Rose pretends to be affronted but the smile she's trying to hide gives her away.

Jasmine scrambles off my lap and races around the table. "I'm sorry, Gramma. I didn't mean to forget you."

Rose opens her arms wide and welcomes her granddaughter with a chuckle. Vi and I step into the kitchen to make an afternoon snack, and then we sit around the table while Jas fills us in on her day.

34

SHANE

As I wash the last dish from breakfast, Vi snakes her arms around my waist from behind and presses a kiss between my shoulder blades. I'll never tire of having her hands and mouth on me. "How would you feel about a picnic in the park today?"

I turn my head to the side to look at her over my shoulder. "It's a nice day out. I think it's a great idea and Jas will enjoy it."

She grins at me. "I thought that, too." Her lips make contact with my shoulder and the rhythm of my heart spikes at the simple gesture. "Let's surprise her."

"Okay." I lean down and press a kiss to her lips and then we set about packing everything we'll need and loading it into the car while Jasmine's out back checking on the veggies with Lloyd in tow.

When they come back inside, Vi collects the vegetables they've gathered from Lloyd and takes them to the sink. "We need to stop by my work real quick. Do you want to come with us or stay here with Gramma and Lloyd?"

Without taking a moment to think about her answer, Jasmine responds, "I want to come with you. Can we go for a walk too? Please, Mommy."

Vi makes a big production about thinking about it. "I guess we could. Go put some long pants and boots on and grab your hat."

With a cheer, Jas sprints up the stairs to her bedroom and returns less than a minute later, wearing her favorite hat. In the mudroom, she drops to her butt and pulls on her boots. "I'm ready!"

"All right, go and say goodbye to Gramma and Lloyd and meet us at the car."

"Okay, Mommy."

Once Jas is out of earshot, Violet laughs. "She has no clue about our plans. I love doing little things to surprise her."

I chuckle, pull Vi into me, and lead her outside. "That's what makes you such a great mom."

The screen door slams and Jas calls out as she runs across the grass. "I'm here!"

I bend down, scoop her up, put her in her booster seat, secure her seatbelt, and close the door, then check that Violet has her seatbelt on too. On the drive, we play classic rock and when I look in the rearview mirror I smile at the sight that greets me as Jas rocks out to an Eagles classic.

We pull into the parking lot nearest to the place Vi wants to have our surprise picnic, and Jas kicks her feet against the seat. "I love this place, Mommy!" I release Jas from her booster seat and she scrambles out of the car, gripping my hand tightly and pulling me along. "Come and see the stream, Daddy. It's so pretty."

I chuckle when she freezes as her eyes land on the picnic basket in Vi's hand. "Surprise!"

Jas's eyes light up and she jumps up and down on the spot. "I love picnics." She grabs my hand again. "Come on, Daddy. Let's go."

I smile at Violet and let Jasmine lead me toward the track. The little girl that's stolen my heart is clearly familiar with the way. As we walk, the sound of trickling water grows louder and we eventually stop at a grassy area beside a stream. Butterflies flutter all around and birds chirp above us. The day is mild and perfect for spending the afternoon in the girls' happy place.

Tugging the little angel to a stop beside me, I crouch down and she grins at me. "Do you like it, Daddy?"

I gaze around, taking in the beauty of the spot. "I love it. I can't wait for you to show me all of your favorite places."

Vi lays out a blanket and places the picnic basket next to it. "Come on, let's eat first and then we can explore."

The three of us sit and I help Vi remove all of the containers from the basket, spreading them in the middle of the blanket so we can all reach the food. Vi and Jas talk excitedly about the butterflies and birds they can see and then talk turns a little somber when they discuss the low water levels of the stream but they explain it's always low like this at this time of the year.

Once we've all eaten our fill, Vi drags out her camera and starts taking photos of me with Jas as she leads me down to the stream. The water is barely flowing, but we still manage to have some leaf races. Jas throws her arms up. "I win … again!" she shouts with glee. I had no idea how competitive my angel could be and I'm enjoying seeing this side of her.

I point at her playfully. "You cheated." I look at Vi. "She cheated. Did you see how she dropped her leaf onto the water before I did?"

Vi laughs and snaps another photo of me appearing to be upset by Jas's cheating ways. It really is the perfect afternoon with my girls and it makes me want to spend more afternoons like this with them. While Vi practices taking photos of the stream with an open shutter, Jas and I explore the area around the picnic site and a little beyond.

"Daddy, come and look at this flower," Jas calls as she crouches down.

I hear a distinctive rattle sound coming from beneath the bush behind her and instinctively step between her and the bush snatching her up by one arm in an instant. My heart pounds and sweat coats the back of my neck when I realize what could have happened to the angel in my arms. I hold her tight to me, needing to keep her safe.

Feeling a brief sting on the back of my calf, I lean down to swipe the area, noticing the juvenile snake coiled tightly. When I bring my hand away from the spot, there are specks of blood on my fingers and I wipe them on the back of my shorts, careful not to touch Jas. I quickly step away and look back down at the dark-colored snake that's moved further back under the bush and realize the damn thing tried to bite me. I must have frightened it when I moved quickly to grab Jas and it retaliated to protect itself.

Slight pain radiates from the site and I carry Jas back to Violet, who's packing up the picnic. "Uh, we should probably head home," I suggest.

"There was a rattlesnake, Mommy."

Vi's eyes widen. "You didn't get close, did you?"

"No, Mommy. Daddy picked me up before it could bite me." She tightens her hold around my neck and squeezes me.

Vi's worried gaze moves to me and her features relax. "Thank you. A rattlesnake bite is no joke." Her eyes go back to Jas. "You always need to look where you're walking, okay?"

"I will."

"All right, well, let's get this stuff loaded in the car. It's my turn to cook dinner tonight."

I shift Jas so she's sitting on my shoulders, grab the picnic basket from Violet, and grip her hand in my free one. The pain in my leg begins to intensify but it's not so bad that I can't handle it —I've had worse. By the time we make it back to the car, my leg is aching like a bitch and once I have Jas secured in her booster seat, I take a look at the area. Shit, the area's swelling quickly and blisters are forming.

Violet closes the back of the car and comes around to her door, noticing me looking at my leg. "Shit!" Her head snaps up to mine.

"You were bitten, and you didn't say a word." She bends down and takes a closer look.

"I thought it had just broken the skin. It didn't hurt at first. Now it's hurting like a bitch," I grit, holding onto the side of the car for balance.

"Do you have a first aid kit in your car?"

"Yeah, in the trunk."

She rushes back to the trunk and comes back holding a bandage. She helps me sit in the passenger seat and carefully wraps the bandage over the bite and up my calf toward my knee. I feel like a failure that she's having to take care of me when it should always be the other way around.

"We need to get you to the hospital, Shane. This could be bad."

I nod because at the rate the pain is spreading and the amount of swelling, I'm inclined to believe her. She works in this environment and is familiar with the wildlife so I trust her judgment. If she thinks I need to go to the hospital, I'm not going to argue with her.

Vi quickly climbs into the driver's seat and holds out her hand. "Keys, please."

Lifting my ass, I suck in a sharp breath at the pain in my leg, then pull the keys out of my pocket to hand them to her and she tears out of the parking lot and onto the road before I can put my seatbelt on. I lean my head back against the seat and try to relax my body but the pain is becoming overwhelming. Gritting my teeth, I buckle in quickly.

Vi looks across at me with eyes full of worry. "If it had bitten Jas, she wouldn't make it. She's too small and the venom works too quickly." Tears trickle down her cheeks, and she swipes them away, turning her eyes back to the road. "You saved her life today, Shane," she murmurs. "I'll be forever grateful."

Thank God it was me and not her, I couldn't bear it if I had let another person down—a person who means the world to me and so many other people. I reach across and take her hand in mine as sweat coats my body. My tongue feels too big in my mouth but I do my best to reassure her. "You girls are all that are important to me." I swallow past the excess saliva forming. "You girls are everything right in my world." Nausea begins taking hold, and I wind the window down to get some fresh air blowing on my face.

Fire lances my leg, and I close my eyes for a moment while listening to Violet talk to someone through the Bluetooth speakers, and I think ... maybe I shouldn't have worn shorts today.

35

VIOLET

Oh my God, he's passed out. My hands shake on the steering wheel, and I grip it tighter, turning my knuckles white. He has to be okay. The universe wouldn't be so cruel as to steal him away from us now. I glance up at the sky and ask, "You wouldn't do that to me and Jas, would you? You're not that sadistic?" Looking forward again, I spot the hospital entrance just ahead. *Thank fuck*!

"Mommy, why are we at the hospital?"

With my heart pounding, I glance over my shoulder. "The snake bit Daddy. He needs help." I daren't tell her how bad it is, I don't need a full-on meltdown at this point because I may just join her. The blood in my veins races too fast and my skin is too tight as I pull up to the emergency doors. I'm not sure how I'm managing to drive in a straight line with the amount my body's shaking. Two nurses come running out immediately with a gurney and I don't know how they're going to manage to get Shane out of the car and onto the bed—he's twice their size.

"Is he going to be okay?" I glance at my daughter. Her tear-streaked face and worry-filled eyes break my heart.

"He'll be fine. The doctors will give him some medicine, and he'll be all better." *I hope.* I don't know what I'll do if something happens to him. He has my heart and soul. He and Jas are my entire world. He's our rock. Our safe place.

I shut down the negative thoughts and focus on one step at a time.

Step one: Get him the help he needs.

I climb out of the car and greet the nurses, leaving my sobbing daughter inside but Shane has to be the priority right now. I explain where we were and the type of snake that bit him. I point to the location of the bite on his calf and try to calculate the amount of time that passed since he was struck. "It's probably close to two hours since he was bitten. We walked a trail back to the car for almost an hour, then I wrapped his calf and drove here, which was another forty minutes."

"We'll take it from here." They glance at each other before maneuvering him expertly out of the car and onto the gurney, communicating their movements with each other efficiently. No time is wasted. "You can park your car and come inside!" one of them calls to me as they wheel the man who owns my heart away.

Tears trail down my cheeks as I watch him disappear through the doors, feeling completely and utterly helpless. He has to be okay. There's no way he can survive a bomb blast to be taken out by a reptile, right? I shake out my hands and quickly climb back into the car to find a parking spot.

"Mommy. Where's Daddy?" Jas's tiny voice breaks through the fog of worry that's quickly taking over and suffocating my rational thought process.

"He's with the nurses. They're going to take care of him for us." I find a spot and park, then twist in my seat to face my daughter. "He'll be okay." I hope I haven't just lied to my daughter. I promised myself I would always be upfront and honest with her after I lied to her about her father.

I carry Jas into the emergency area and head straight to the desk trying to tamp down my panic so I don't set Jas off. "Hi, uhm, Shane Sutton was just brought in with a rattlesnake bite. Where can we go to be with him?"

"Are you family?"

"He's my daddy," Jasmine cries.

The woman behind the desk looks at Jasmine with sympathy. "Well, we'd better get you to your daddy then." She points to a set of doors to the right. "Go through those doors and follow the red arrows on the floor. They'll take you to another desk and a waiting room." She smiles softly at us.

"Thank you."

I turn to the right and push through the doors with Jasmine wrapped around me, crying her little eyes out. When I arrive at the next desk, I explain again and we're told we need to wait in the waiting room until a nurse comes to get us. We could be here for hours before we know what's going on and as well-behaved as Jasmine is I don't think it's a good idea for her to be here.

I dial Mom and she answers on the third ring. "Are you enjoying your afternoon in the sunshine?" I can hear the smile in her voice and it causes a flood of tears to escape. "Violet? What's wrong?"

Shudders rack my body. "Sh-Sh-Shane's been bitten by a rattlesnake. I'm at the emergency department."

She gasps. "Oh my gosh. Which hospital? Lloyd and I will come right away."

I sob into the phone. "Mercy Vale."

"Hold tight. We'll be there shortly." She disconnects the call, and I stand with Jas still in my arms.

We're as bad as each other, both crying, and I absently think to myself that I should be holding it together better for my daughter. I pace laps around the waiting area, soothing Jasmine with long strokes from the top of her head down her back and repeating the process over and over. The activity helps to calm her as well as me.

I draw my phone out of my pocket and quickly text Quinn with one hand.

ME

Shane's been bitten by a rattlesnake

Tell me he's going to be okay

QUINN

WTF?????

Of course he'll be okay

Where are you?

ME

Mercy Vale Emergency

QUINN

OMW

My relief is palpable. If anyone knows snake bites, it's her, and if she says he's going to be okay, then I need to try to believe that. Jas lifts her head from where she's been snuggled in my neck. "Why is it taking so long, Mommy? I want to see Daddy." Her tears stain her cheeks and my heart breaks.

"Well, they're busy looking after him." I *hope* they're busy looking after him and nothing's happened. "We want all of their focus to be on him, and if they have to stop to come and talk to us, then they're not looking after Daddy when he needs them. So we'll just wait until they're finished, and then we'll be able to see him. Okay?"

She nods against my shoulder and snuggles back in. I exhale a long breath, trying to release my worry so Jas doesn't feed off of my distress, but it's tough. My mind runs through all of the possible *what-ifs*. Some of them are too frightening to consider, and I shut the thoughts down before they can set seed.

"Vi! Jas!" Mom calls from the entrance of the waiting room. I turn and she rushes forward with Lloyd close behind, worry creasing both of their faces. "Any news?"

I shake my head. "Nothing yet."

"Well, that's good. It means they're working on him. That's a positive sign." I love how she automatically goes to the most positive scenario; it's exactly what I need. She rubs Jas's back. "Hey, JJ, why don't you give Gramma a hug?" Mom tries to lift her from my arms, but she tightens her hold.

I smile softly at Mom. "She's okay with me."

"I'm going to pop over to the café I noticed across the road and grab us all a drink." Lloyd points in the direction he'll be heading. "Any requests?" He's a lot like Shane in the way he always wants to help the people around him.

I smile shakily at him. "Jas would probably like an apple juice and a cookie, thank you." She'll probably need some sugar to counteract the shock. "I'm happy with whatever." Not that I can think about food right now, but I'll need to keep up my energy if I want to be here for Shane.

"Thanks, Lloyd." Mom squeezes his forearm and he tips his head before leaving us.

"Why don't you come and sit down?"

"I can't. I need to keep moving."

Mom nods in understanding and paces slowly with me around the room. On our third lap, Toby rushes through the door, tightly holding Poppy's hand with Cass—who has Daisy in her arms—by his side.

He comes straight for me and wraps his arms around me and Jas, engulfing us. The tears I've been holding back escape and slide down my cheeks. I'd been sort of holding it together until now. When he pulls away, I'm left feeling bereft until Cass wraps her arms around me, squashing Jas and Daisy between us. I burrow my face into her shoulder and bawl my eyes out. "He's strong, Vi. And he's healthy. Those two things will work in his favor. He'll be okay."

"He has to be. He's our everything," I say shakily.

"I know," she murmurs as she strokes my back.

Quinn walks into the emergency room like she owns the place and wraps her arms around all of us. "There's no way that behemoth of a man will be taken down by a snake, Vi. You have to know that. He'll be fine. You wait and see." Maybe if everyone tells me the same thing enough times, it'll make it true.

Lloyd returns with our food and drinks—as well as extra supplies—along with Mr. and Mrs. Summer, Kate, and Oliver. Our group takes up most of the waiting room as we wait for news about Shane. The promise of a cookie the size of Jas's head has her crawling down my body to go to Lloyd. He sits with the girls and pretends to have a tea party to distract them from our situation.

I tug on Toby's shirt. "Hey, do you think we should call Shane's parents to let them know he's in the hospital?"

He runs his hand through his hair, messing it up. "Shit, yeah. I'll call them. Nix, too."

"Can you ask him to let Hope know? They're important to him." He nods as he digs out his phone. "Thank you."

THE KIDS ARE restless after waiting for three hours with no updates. "How about we take the girls home? It's getting late."

I smile gratefully at Mom. "Thanks, Mom."

"Let us know when you have news."

I nod and reach forward to embrace her, then kiss Jas and the girls goodbye. Flopping down into a chair, I blow out a relieved breath that Jas went willingly ... it's been a long afternoon and she's exhausted; poor kid. Even I feel like I could curl up into a ball beneath the blankets and sleep for a week. Mom used the need to harvest the cauliflower so we can make it into rice to coax her home, otherwise, I don't think she would have left.

She loves Shane so much.

We both do.

I cover my mouth when a sob breaks free at the thought of possibly losing him. Our lives would be irrevocably changed, and I'm not sure how we could possibly recover from the devastation losing him would cause. Quinn, Hope, Kate, Cass, Mrs. S, and Shane's mom gather around me, sharing their support and strength with me, reminding me how strong he is and telling me that he'll be doing everything he can to pull through this for me and Jas.

"The family of Shane Sutton."

I stand faster than I should on shaky legs, and my head spins a little. Cass supports me as I make my way toward the nurse. "That's us."

Her eyes scan our group, taking in the number of people here for Shane. *Does he realize how many people love him?* "I can only take two people." My heart sinks. That means I won't be able to see him.

"Can you give the rest of us an update at least? Is he ... is he okay?" I manage to ask.

"He was in pretty bad shape. The amount of walking he did before he received assistance meant the venom made its way through his system. However, he was brought in within two hours of the bite, and we immediately started antivenom treatment. While he didn't have an allergic reaction to the treatment, his condition worsened, and we had to give him another dose and move him to the ICU where he'll be monitored closely and continue to receive further treatments every six hours."

My legs give out, and strong arms catch me from behind before I hit the floor. I can't believe this is happening. "Will he be okay?"

She presses her lips together. "He's improving, which is a positive sign. I can't tell you any more than that. You'll need to speak with his doctor. But I'm happy to take two people through to see him."

My heart sinks, and I turn to Fiona. "Please tell him how much I love him and that I'll be waiting out here for him."

William moves next to his wife. "You and Fiona should go through. You can tell him how much you love him yourself."

My relief and gratitude are instantaneous, and I exhale a long breath. "Thank you so much." I lean forward and wrap my arms around Shane's dad. He stands stiffly, but I squeeze him tighter, and he softens in my hold.

His arms come around me, and he returns my embrace. "You tell that boy of mine that I love him, and I'll be waiting out here."

When I pull away, I look up at his face. His eyes look a little glassy but he's putting on a good front. "I will."

Nix and Toby quickly embrace me and tell me to stay positive, then Fiona and I leave our group behind and follow the nurse through to the ICU. She slides her hand into mine as the nurse stops at a door. "He's in here. You can go in."

"Thank you."

I open the door and gasp, my stomach twists, and my wobbly legs barely support me so I reach out to grip the door frame. The giant of a man I've fallen in love with lies helpless in a hospital bed, hooked up to noisy machines. Fiona rushes forward but it takes me longer to find the strength to take the few steps to his bed. It's completely foreign seeing him still like this, and my mind fills in the gaps of how he would have been lying all alone in an ICU in Germany. My heart shatters for everything this man has already endured. The amount of healing he's already done and the amount of healing he has in front of him.

This time he won't be on his own. I'll be supporting him every step of the way.

His eyes open slowly, and his unfocused gaze skims the room until it lands on me. One side of his mouth tips up and my breath bursts out of me in a rush of relief. I quickly wrap my hands around his and bend down to place a kiss on his knuckles. When I lift my head, his eyes are closed and his face is relaxed as though he's still asleep.

I glance at Fiona, and she gives me a watery smile. "I think he sensed you in the room."

My heart does a flip that she thinks our connection is so strong.

Seven and a half hours later, Shane finally opens his eyes with a groan and then promptly falls back to sleep. Fiona went home with William late last night, leaving me alone with Shane as nurses came and went throughout the night, checking his vitals and administering the precious medicine his body needs to heal.

When Toby walks through the door carrying a cup of coffee for himself and tea for me as well as breakfast wraps for each of us, telling the staff that Shane is his brother, relief overwhelms me. I don't think the nurses believe him but they let him in just the same. He hands breakfast to me with a kiss on the top of my head, and I mumble my thanks. Taking a seat on the opposite side of the bed, he asks, "Any change?"

"He sort of woke up earlier. He's moving around more, so the nurse thinks he'll fully wake soon, though he'll still be groggy for a while."

"Did you get any sleep?"

I shake my head. "Nope. Every little move or sound and I was on my feet, studying him like a science experiment. How about you?"

"Not a wink." He drops his gaze to his long-time friend. "I was so scared," he murmurs, peering around the room. "It was hard coming back here, and I had hoped I wouldn't be back here anytime soon."

I nod. "Yeah. Me too." The memories of Cass have been fighting for attention but I've managed to push them aside and focus on Shane and what he needs while trying not to think about the worst-case scenario.

We sit in companionable silence for a while both of our gazes trained on the giant of a man lying unnaturally still in the bed between us. Shane twists his head from side to side with a groan, and I jump to my feet, sliding my palm across his forehead and down the side of his face in calming strokes. His eyes flutter open, revealing unfocused brown eyes that I'm elated to see. A tear splashes his cheek and I quickly wipe it away, then wipe my cheek to swipe at the wetness while giving him a shaky smile. I lean down and press my lips to his forehead, leaving them against his skin for a moment before pulling away. "Hey," I whisper.

"Hey." His lips tip up slightly as his roughened voice forms the simple word, mending some of the cracks in my heart.

Quickly, I grab the cup of water from the table and press the straw to his dry lips. "Drink."

His eyes clear, and I see the mirth at my bossiness but he takes a sip. "Thanks." He takes another drink, then asks, "Is Jasmine okay?"

My bottom lip quivers, and the tears return to my eyes but I swallow past the painful thoughts of how this situation may have turned out if not for Shane's quick thinking. "She's perfect, thanks to you." He smiles tiredly and closes his eyes. "I don't know how I'll ever thank you for what you did." I lean down and press my lips to his in what is meant to be a kiss of gratitude but his hand weaves into my messy hair and holds me in place as he teases my lips.

He pulls away slowly and presses my forehead to his. With his eyes on mine, he murmurs, "No thanks necessary, Blue." There's something new in his gaze replacing the usual regret I see there. I can't quite place it but he seems more at peace.

Toby shifts in his seat and Shane turns toward the sound. Something passes between the two men and I step back as Toby rises from his chair. He bends over Shane, grasping the back of his neck and pressing their foreheads together. "You scared the shit outta me. Don't do that again."

Shane huffs out a laugh and pats Toby on the back. "I don't intend to, brother."

I watch Toby's body deflate, the tension falling away from him as he taps Shane's cheek with a slight grin. "You're one tough motherfucker."

They both break into quiet laughter, and the mood in the room lightens considerably.

The door opens and the doctor I met this morning walks in wearing green checkered pants, a purple paisley shirt, an orange bow tie with white spots, a yellow jacket, and bright red glasses. His outfit hurts my eyes but his demeanor is unlike other doctors I've met in the past. He grins when he sees Shane is awake. "Well, good morning!" If he notices the famous rock star in our midst he doesn't show it, keeping his focus on his patient. "Great to see you awake." He squeezes Shane's foot. "How are you feeling, young man?"

Shane takes a moment, and I can almost see him working through every part of his body. "I've been worse."

The doctor nods, his humor falling away. "Yes, I noticed that." Toby's brows scrunch together over his oceanic eyes, forming creases. "We've been dosing you up with antivenom and pain meds, and we're happy with the improvements we're seeing. We'll keep you in another night and you should be fine to go home tomorrow. It'll be a couple of months until you'll have full use of that leg, so we'll need to sort out physiotherapy and crutches for you."

Shane nods. "Thanks, Doc."

"Now, I'm just going to check a few things, and I'll be out of your hair." He busies himself as he checks Shane over thoroughly as well as the machine monitors showing various details that I have no idea about.

Once he leaves, Toby leans forward, studying Shane intensely. "What did the doctor notice?"

My eyes jump to Shane's, and I can see the resolve there. I know he's never told anyone but me and his dad what happened to him. It was even tough for him to open up to Mom when she noticed the scars on his legs when he came downstairs wearing shorts yesterday morning. God, was that only yesterday? He looks at me and I nod slightly, telling him without words that he should share his truth with his best friend. I watch him swallow and make the decision that I know is hard for him.

With a grunt, he slowly sits up and turns his back toward his friend. Toby gasps when the exposed portion of Shane's back comes into view. He reaches around to release the ties, but I push his hands away so I can help him. I want him to know that I'm here to support him in any way I can. As the fabric falls away, revealing the broad expanse of Shane's back as well as his arms, I glance up to watch Toby carefully. His eyes are glassy and his chest rises and falls quickly as he flicks his eyes up to me and back again.

"Fuck!" Toby curses under his breath. Shane just grunts and looks up at me, telling me he's ready to cover himself again. I redo the ties and he turns back to lean against his pillows. "What the hell happened to you?"

I pass Shane his cup of water and he takes a greedy drink then launches into his story. Toby covers his mouth with his hand, tears running down his face as he explains the cause of the scars that mar his body from top to bottom. I've grown somewhat accustomed to them now but it doesn't hurt any less knowing how much he's endured.

Toby stands abruptly, pushing his chair back with a loud scrape. His hands dive into his hair and his expression is livid. He points angrily at Shane and snaps, "I'm so fucking angry with you. You had no right keeping that from us. Not allowing us to be there for you. I would have fucking flown to Germany to be by your side, you stupid dick." He turns his back to us and I study Shane closely after Toby's outburst. He doesn't seem to be angry, more like he's resigned to accept Toby's ire. "You didn't need to deal with that by yourself." Without looking at us, he makes his way to the door and Shane calls his name to stop him. He freezes but doesn't turn around, holding up his hand. "I can't right now. I thought we were friends, man." He steps through the doorway and disappears.

Shit!

"Fuck!" Shane grunts. "That was fucking awful." He looks up at me. "I've made so many mistakes. Let so many people down. Hurt so many people." His eyes skate away from mine and he exhales a long breath, running his hand over the top of his head. His jaw clenches and that tic of his comes to life.

I carefully lodge my ass on the edge of his bed and cup his cheek, turning his face toward mine. Flicking my eyes between his, I absorb his anguish as I lean down to press my forehead to his. "Why did you shut everyone out?" I have to know. "Make me understand."

He tries to break our connection but I hold him in place and watch him swallow. "I didn't want them to see the mess I was. How weak. I was so fucking broken I wasn't sure I'd ever be whole again and I didn't want anyone to see that version of me. If I'd died, I wanted them to remember me how I was, not the broken man I'd become."

"Oh, Shane," I whisper against his lips.

He shakes his head. "I didn't ... don't ... want pity. I didn't ... still don't ... deserve it."

"It's not pity I feel for you. My heart breaks for the man you were. The man you *thought* you were. You couldn't have been more wrong." I draw on my reserves because he needs to hear what

I'm about to say to him. "I wasn't there, but that IED … it wasn't your fault. *None* of it was your fault. Wyatt's death wasn't your fau—" When he opens his mouth to argue with me, I press my thumb to his lips and shake my head. "It wasn't. None of it. If I know you, and I feel that I mostly do, you would have done everything you could if you hadn't been rendered unconscious. But, honestly, looking at you and your scars, I don't see how the outcome for him could have been any different when he was right next to the boy with the device."

Tears fill his eyes and escape the corners, trailing down the side of his face into his hair and I wipe them clear with my thumbs. He closes his eyes at the contact. "I know," he whispers, his breath licking my lips.

"It was so tragic, Shane, and I'm sorry right down to my bones that you've had to experience it. Nobody should have to go through what you've been through. But I want to make sure that you understand you have friends and family around you who want to support you. Who love and cherish you. Please don't shut us out." He nods as best he can in my hold. "I know you're tormented right now because you've hurt Toby but I know you guys will sort this out and get back to how things were."

His hand threads into my hair, and he pulls me toward his lips, taking my mouth in a passionate kiss full of gratitude and promise.

37
SHANE

I fall back against my pillows in frustration. I desperately want to go home but the doctor insisted I stay another night. I miss Jasmine, even though Rose brought her up to visit yesterday afternoon. Violet's been with me the whole time, only leaving my side to grab coffee and snacks which is where she is right now. As thankful as I am to have her by my side, guilt consumes me that I'm keeping her away from her daughter and job.

"It's here, Mom." Evan steps through the door with Hope close behind. He's wearing his soccer uniform and cleats. Damn, it was my turn to coach this week. "Shane!" he calls as he closes the distance to my bed.

I smile. "Hey, big guy."

His eyes start at my feet and trace their way up my body with concentrated focus until he reaches my face. I smile, hoping to calm his obvious worry. "Hey."

I tip my chin toward Hope. "Hey, how are you doing?"

"Better than you."

I shrug. "Yeah, well ... better me than Jas."

"While we were waiting to hear if you were going to be okay when you were first brought in, Jasmine told us all about how you saved her from a rattlesnake." She leans down and kisses my bristly cheek. "You did good."

I shrug. "Better me than her."

Hope nods. "I haven't stopped thinking about it all." She bites her bottom lip. "And I was thinking ... maybe ..."—she glances at Evan, then returns her gaze to me—"maybe you were meant to survive the blast so you were here to save Jasmine's life," she says with a shaky voice.

Oof.

I feel like she slammed my solar plexus with a sledgehammer. I force air into my lungs and swallow past the boulder-sized lump in my throat. She knows my struggle. That I was furious that I'd survived when Wyatt didn't and I can't believe she can stand at my bedside and point out the serendipity of the situation. Once I regain my composure I acknowledge her thoughts with a simple nod and turn my attention to Evan. "Sorry I can't make it to training this afternoon."

He looks down at the floor, then back up at me. "That's okay. Ben said he'd come down and help even though he doesn't know anything about soccer. He said I could tell him what you usually do and I could be his assistant coach." His eyes are alight with excitement and it's great to see a glimpse of the old Evan.

"Who's Ben?" I glance between Hope and Evan, as she shifts on her feet.

"He's the police officer that ... you know," Evan says, dropping his eyes from mine as pink stains his cheeks.

I look between the two for a few moments, and then I realize that Ben, the police officer, must be spending time with Hope and Evan for him to step in as coach on my behalf. Maybe Hope's ready to open her heart. Smiling, I muss up Evan's hair. "That's great. Please thank him for me, and if he gets stuck, he can give me a call."

Evan's head snaps up. "You're not mad?" His eyes widen.

I chuckle. "Why would I be mad? I'm grateful he can step in to help."

He blows out a long breath, and I watch the tension release from his and Hope's shoulders. Evan smiles and looks up at his mom. "He said he can help out as long as you need, provided he's not working." He moves in closer and lowers his voice. "I was worried it would hurt your feelings. I'm glad you're not mad because Ben's really cool."

Ben's really cool. I think he's smitten. I glance at Hope, noticing she looks a little lighter, the gray cloud overhead seems to be dissipating.

She titters. "Ben and Evan have become fast friends, but I think Evan loves Ben's police dog, Rex, more than he does Ben."

"Well ... Rex *is* pretty cool."

Violet steps into my room with a tray of drinks and snacks, and my smile is instant. When Toby steps through the door behind her, it drops along with my stomach. I'm surprised he came back at all, let alone the day after I shared my secret with him and trampled our friendship into the ground.

Everyone says hello, chats for a while, and then Hope tells Evan it's time to leave for soccer practice, leaving me and Violet in awkward silence with Toby. He makes no move to strike up a conversation, but after knowing him for as long as I have, I can read the hurt in his body language.

Violet glances between us, implores me with her eyes to open up to my friend, then jabs her thumb over her shoulder. "I'm gonna call Jas to see how her day was."

As soon as she leaves and we're alone, Toby lowers his ass into the chair next to my bed. He drops his head into his hands and grips his hair. After a long while of silence, he raises his head and his tortured gaze locks onto me. Fuck, I'm an asshole.

"I need to know why you didn't have faith in me. In our friendship."

I huff and shake my head, frowning. "It wasn't that I didn't have faith in you. I didn't have faith in *me*."—I thump my chest—"I was broken beyond repair." I swallow thickly and turn away from him, I can't look at him as I make my confession. "I didn't want to survive. I was so broken mentally and physically, that I wanted to die. I was so pissed that I'd survived the blast and a good man with a wife and son died. I had no one waiting for me at ho—"

Toby stands suddenly, pushing his chair back. "*I*"—he points at his chest—"was waiting for you. I loved you then, and I love you now. You're like my brother, and it fucking guts me that you clearly don't think of me the same way."

I push up—thank fuck I actually have clothes on today—to stand, balancing on one leg. "I *do* think of you as my brother, but I was ashamed that I'd sunk so low. You were so damn proud of me when I enlisted and left for Basic. Your entire family was." I huff. "I failed in the worst way possible over there. I didn't know how to come back here and see the disappointment on everyone's faces. It was bad enough coming home and having to face Hope and Evan, knowing their husband and father didn't make it when I did. It should have been me, Toby." I drop my voice to a murmur. "It should have *fucking* been me."

Toby drops his hand to my shoulder. "I don't believe that for a second. Look, obviously, I wasn't there but I know you well enough to know that if you could have prevented your friend's death, you fucking would have. The circumstances were out of your control, therefore, it wasn't your fault. I *know* you would have done anything in your power to ensure he came home in one piece to his family."

"How can you say that? Look at what happened to Cass and Sam because of my poor decision-making. They could have been killed because I refused to listen to you." I slam my fist against my sternum, then run my hand over my hair, gripping the short strands. "*I* fucking knew better," I say sarcastically. "I don't know how you can even look at me." My chest rises and falls rapidly, my breaths shallow.

Toby looks at me as though I'm a stranger. "What the hell are you talking about? As if either of us had a clue about Jake's state of mind. Last time I checked you can't see the future, man. Have you really been blaming yourself all this time?" He's completely puzzled.

I narrow my eyes at my long-time friend. "Of course I'm to blame. I don't know how you all look at me with anything less than contempt."

He digs his hands into his hips and shakes his head. "How?" He studies me closely and as I open my mouth, he holds up his hand to stop me. "I've heard some bullshit in my time, but that takes the cake, Shane. The blame for Jake's behavior lies solely at Jake's feet, and I'm guessing the same could be said for what happened as a result of the IED. I know for a fact that your friend's death wouldn't have been your fault either." He slides his hand through his long blond hair. "Look, I'm truly sorry your friend didn't make it. I really am. Losing any life is devastating but losing a friend ... I can't imagine the pain in your heart. But I'm fucking grateful that you came home to us, broken or not. I don't even want to think about the possibility of you never coming back." His eyes are shiny when he looks up at me. "I think of you as a brother, man."

The tension I always hold in my body slides away, leaving me feeling off-balance. I grip the back of his neck and pull him into me for a brotherly hug. "Me too, man. Me too." I squeeze his neck. "And for the record, after a shit load of therapy, I'm glad I made it home, brother."

He grins at me, the sparkle returning to his eyes. "Promise me that you'll let the blame go."

I nod. "I mostly have ... sort of."

"And no more secrets?" he asks with wide eyes and raised brows.

I shake my head and chuckle. "No more secrets." I pause and look him square in the eyes. "Maybe one more." I wink.

"No. From now on you tell me everything. I won't settle for anything less." He slashes his hand through the air.

I sigh dramatically for effect. "Okay. Well ... I'm going to ask Vi to marry me."

He bursts into loud laughter and slaps me on the shoulder. "Ah, man, that's no secret. I knew it was coming, it was just a matter of when."

"Shit! Do you think she knows?"

"She's probably hoping more than anything. I've never seen you so gone over a woman in all the years I've known you, so I guessed it was coming. Have you spoken to Rose?"

I nod and shove my hands into my pockets, rocking back on my heels. "Yeah, I spoke to her last week. I don't think I've ever been so nervous."

"Why the hell were you nervous? Rose loves you. You have to know that."

I drop my ass to the bed. Fuck, I feel tired. "It's one thing to have your daughter dating a guy like me, it's a completely different story to know you'll be stuck with someone like me as a family member."

"What the fuck do you mean, *a guy like you*? I've told you before, you're the best man possible for Violet and Jas. Nobody will ever love and care for them the way you do." He paces the room, messing up his hair further. The agitation coming from him fills the room.

"It's not like I had a great role model showing me how to be a good father and husband. And ... well, my time away left more than physical scars."

His posture softens and he steps in front of me. "I've watched you with my girls as well as with Jas and the few times I've seen you with Evan. You're doing a great job. You give those kids everything they need. As far as being a husband, keep doing what you're already doing with Vi. You're killing it there too."

"You really think so?"

"Absolutely and I bet Rose was fucking over the moon."

My lips tip up at the memory of how her face lit up like a damn Christmas tree when I asked her if it would be okay to ask Vi to marry me and make both the girls mine. I nod. "Yeah, she was happy."

"Of course she was. She loves you for her girls. When are you going to propose?"

I shrug. "I don't know. I don't have a fancy plan like you did. I'll just do it when it feels right."

He nods, humming his approval.

SIGHING when my ass finally hits the couch, I drop my head on the backrest. I know I sleep for shit, but with the nurses coming in every couple of hours to check on me, I got zero rest, and I'm exhausted. It probably doesn't help that my body's been fighting against the effects of the venom. I feel the cushion next to me move, and I roll my head in the direction. Violet hands me a cup of coffee and then takes a sip of her tea. I drop my free hand to her thigh with a grateful smile. "Thanks, Blue."

"You're welcome. I'm so glad to have you home." Her voice still holds a tinge of fear, and I take a moment to study her. Black smudges beneath her eyes give away her exhaustion from spending every minute at the hospital with me.

I squeeze her thigh gently. "Why don't you have a nap before Jas gets home from school?"

She grins. "Only if you join me."

I chuckle. "Sure. I actually think I could sleep."

We finish our drinks, and I follow Vi upstairs on my crutches.

"We could move into the downstairs bedroom that Cass used when she was in her wheelchair if it'll make it easier for you." I grunt in response. I don't want to feel any more incapable than I already do. She grins at me over her shoulder. "Back to the grunting, I see."

"I'll show you grunting in a minute."

Vi chuckles and jogs the last few steps, leaping playfully across the landing and disappearing into our bedroom. By the time I make it there, she has the bed covers pulled back and is stripping down. "I'm ready."

I stop and study her. Her chest is rising and falling quickly, and the pulse at the base of her throat is fluttering like crazy. Her pupils are dilated and she looks so damn gorgeous. "You're so beautiful. I can't believe I'm lucky enough to call you mine." I move forward awkwardly and run the back of my hand down the side of her face, then tuck her soft hair behind her ear and cup her smooth cheek. "Thank you for staying with me."

She nuzzles into my palm with a gentle smile. "I would never leave you in the hospital alone." I read the meaning behind her words and my heart doubles in size. I clumsily toss my crutches to the side and balance carefully, then grip the back of my T-shirt to drag it over my head. Her hands land on my pecs and glide down over my abs to the buckle of my belt. With swift fingers, she has it unbuckled and the button and zipper undone. Her hand dives into my jocks without preamble, and I groan as she squeezes my shaft.

I press my hips forward and push my underwear and jeans down my legs. "Fuck, do that again." She does, setting me on fire. Gently, she guides me backward until I'm sitting on the edge of our bed, and she drops to her knees. Almost reverently, she removes my shoes, socks, jeans, and boxers until I'm naked. I can't bear to keep my hands to myself any longer and slide my fingers into her soft hair, tangling them in the strands and tugging on them until she's looking up at me. Leaning forward with a wince, I press my mouth to hers and tease my tongue along her lips. She opens eagerly and I slip inside, swiping my tongue along hers, tasting the tea. I swallow her moans and tug her higher, feeling her silken hips brush against my knees as she rises. Pulling back the smallest amount until our lips are barely touching, I tell her, "Straddle me, Blue."

Her lips spread against mine and I return her smile, then dive back in for more of her kisses. Her taste ignites my blood, sending sparks arcing through my veins and I need more. I'll always need more. She grinds down on my cock, her already wet folds sliding against my hard length. Gripping her hips, I hold her to me and grind against her, pushing through the ache in my leg. Damn, I can't do that and I hate feeling incapable ... less than.

"I-I need you." Her hot breaths coat my lips along with her desperate words. Gripping her hips, I lift her and she wraps her hand around my dick, notching it at her entrance. The heat of her pussy scorches my needy head. Between one breath and the next, she slides down, sheathing me deep inside her warm body. Her silky walls tightening around me is pure bliss, and I hold her hips to keep her in place—I could sit here filling her forever. Her arms wrap around my neck, and her slender fingers slide into my short hair. Her breasts press against my chest, and we're touching everywhere possible.

I pull back slightly so I can see her eyes. They're beautifully dilated and unfocused, filled with lust and sinful intent. "Marry me and let me adopt Jas as my own," I murmur. This isn't exactly how I thought I'd ask her to marry me. Not that I'm great with words or sophisticated with fancy plans or anything, but this is probably a shitty way to ask her to spend her life with me. But I've said it now. "Be my wife. Let's be a real family," I say with more conviction as my heart tries to escape my chest cavity.

She chuckles, pressing her lips to mine. "Sure. We'll go see the county clerk tomorrow. We could be married by the end of the week and then we can work on the adoption." She finishes with a wink and a grin.

Moving my hands around to her ass, I grip it and squeeze it roughly. "I'm serious, Vi. I'm asking you to marry me. To spend your life with me, walking beside me." Her smile drops as she recognizes that I'm being serious. "I know it's not the most romantic of proposals and I don't have fancy flowery words for you or a ring but I want you to be my wife. I want to be part of your life. I want to spend every day and night with you. I want you to be the first person I see every morning and the last person every night." She tightens her arms around my neck and goosebumps cover her silky flesh. "Let me adopt Jas because I want to parent alongside you and watch Jasmine grow into the fine young woman I know she'll become." I press my hips up. "I want to have babies with you and learn how to be the best father and husband I can be. Say yes." I beg her with my eyes.

Her gaze softens on mine, those electric-blue eyes I love so much peering into my soul. My heart pounds heavily against my sternum and with the way her breasts are pressed against me, she has to feel it. She has to feel my anxiety as I wait for her to respond. She touches her lips against mine. "Yes," she whispers. "But I need to make one thing clear. You're already the best father. I honestly couldn't ask for a better man."

I slam my mouth onto hers and ravage her as my body sags in relief. There's no teasing, just savage appreciation of her acceptance of my proposal. Our tongues unite, sliding and tasting, twisting and stroking. Using my grip on her sweet ass, I guide her up and down my cock, celebrating our future with deep penetrating thrusts. My leg aches like a bitch but I won't let it slow me down or stop me.

Our bodies, slick with sweat, slide against each other as we connect on the most elemental level a man and a woman can. It's primal and urgent. It's me laying my claim to her body and her heart. I kiss my way from her lips across to her ear and whisper, "Thank you." Then, I continue my way down her throat and across her collarbone as I lick, nip, and suck her heated skin, tasting the saltiness of her sweat. I kiss my way farther down and suck her nipple into my mouth and am rewarded with her walls tightening around my cock. This woman has me body, heart, and soul.

Her moans fill the bedroom, sending my pulse skyrocketing. "Oh my God, you feel so good filling me up." Flames lick my skin and my focus narrows to making her come, to feel her strangling my cock and falling apart in my arms. I kiss my way back up to her mouth and I take her mouth messily … hungrily … without finesse. Short, rough breaths burst out of me with each thrust, my heart thumps in a crazy rhythm, and the blood in my veins heats to the extreme. Each slide, each contraction of her muscles pushes me closer to the edge. Using one hand, I keep her moving on my cock, then find her clit to rub tight circles with my free thumb.

Our bodies slap and grind against each other, her beautiful ass landing on my thighs each time I bottom out. My balls draw up tight, and I grit my teeth to hold off my orgasm while puffs of hot air burst from me, blowing strands of Violet's hair across her face. I increase my ministrations against her clit and it pulses against my digit. "Get there, Blue," I grunt.

She adjusts the angle of her hips, and it feels fucking sensational when she swivels slightly as she drops. With each slam of her hips, sounds of ecstasy leave her lips, casting her warm breath across my cheek. Her walls tighten and pulse and she drops her head back on her shoulders with a long moan, exposing her neck to my tongue. "Aaaah, Shane!" she shouts as her arms tighten around my neck and her thighs grip mine like a vice as she detonates in my arms.

Electrical pulses race through my body with a singular destination in mind. Every synapse fires from my toes, up my legs, from my head, and down to the base of my spine, all accumulating in my balls. My body locks as pulse after pulse of electricity sends me over the edge and I shout Violet's name. Wave after wave of my release shoots out of me as my body vibrates against Violet's. I wrap my arms around her tightly, probably crushing her but I need her as close as possible. I need to meld her flesh with mine. I need every part of me to be connected to every part of her—mind, body, heart, and soul.

She shivers in my hold, and I grab the bedcovers to drag them around her body. "Thank you," she murmurs against the base of my neck, her breath skittering across my heated skin sending out a wave of goosebumps. She licks the skin and then sucks on it like the minx she is and I smack her ass in retaliation, making her giggle which feels amazing around my cock.

"I love you, Violet. With everything that I am and for the man I want to be when I'm with you and Jasmine ... I love you." I squeeze her impossibly tighter and press my lips to the base of her throat.

Her body shudders, and she pulls back slightly. Her arms slide from around me and she cups my cheeks, her gorgeous eyes flicking between mine. A slow smile curves her swollen lips and I feel my chest puff up with pride that I get to see her like this. Touch her like this. Experience her like this. "I love you, too. So much. You are an incredible man, and I couldn't be more thankful that you're in our lives and want to become a permanent part." She leans forward, melding our lips and pushing me until I fall back on the bed. She drops down and rests her head on my pounding heart, which must be deafening against her ear, but she doesn't complain.

38

VIOLET

I startle awake at the sound of a slamming door and little footsteps running up the stairs. Oh my God, Mom's home with Jas and we're sprawled out on the bed stark naked. Thank goodness I have the bed covers half tossed over me but I do not want my daughter to see this. I quickly jump to my feet, my heart pounding, and rush to the door, flicking the lock just before the doorknob rattles.

"Mommy!"

Shane shoots up in bed, wincing. Shit! We probably shouldn't have gotten so carried away before but I'd missed him so much and I'm so relieved he's going to be okay.

Jas bangs her little fists against the wood. "Mommy, are you in there?"

"Yeah, JJ. I'll be out in a minute. Meet me in the kitchen for a snack?" I quickly scoop up my clothes and shove my feet into my panties, then pull up my jeans. God, I feel like a teenager who's been caught making out in the backseat of a car by her boyfriend's mom.

"I want to see Daddy," she calls through the door, and I can hear the pout in her voice. Shane rolls over, until he's sitting on the edge of the bed and I pass him his boxers.

"He'll be out in a minute. He was napping because he's tired."

It's quiet for a long while as I put my bra and T-shirt on. "I'm sorry I woke you."

"That's okay, Angel. We'll be down real quick because we missed you," Shane calls as he zips his jeans. I kiss his lips as I push my arms into my sweater.

"Okay." I hear her feet on the stairs and exhale a long breath.

Shane pulls me against his still-bare chest. "I'm sorry I didn't keep track of the time." He pecks my lips. "I should have set an alarm or something."

I chuckle. "We were"—I trace my hand down his pecs, over his abs, and to his cock—"busy." Winking, I push away from him. "I'll see you downstairs."

Closing the bedroom door behind me, I sag back against the wood with a grin that must be the size of the Mississippi. I can't believe he asked me to marry him and he wants to adopt Jas. I squeal internally and push away from the door to float downstairs and into the kitchen. The worry in his soulful brown eyes while he waited for my answer was almost comical. As if I would have ever said no.

Jas spots me the instant I step through the opening like she was watching and waiting to pounce. "Mommy!" She leaps into my arms and wraps her little legs around my waist and her arms around my neck, kissing me and making me laugh. I wrap my arms tightly around my daughter and soak up her joy. She's going to be so happy when I tell her that Shane and I are getting married and that we'll be a family. She'll finally have the family she deserves ... as will I.

I bounce her in my arms. "How was your day?"

"Long and boring. I just wanted to come home and see you and Daddy." Her little hands cup each of my cheeks. "I missed you."

I kiss the tip of her nose. "We missed you, too."

Mom steps into the kitchen and embraces me. "You look happy to be home."

"I feel as though I'm floating," I tell her as I return her hug.

Her eyes widen as do her lips. "Any particular reason?"

I pull Jas into our embrace as I tell them both the news because I'm too excited to wait for him to come downstairs. "Shane asked me to marry him, and I said *yes*!" I'll keep the adoption part quiet for now. That's something Shane should ask Jas first.

"Oh my gosh, congratulations, I'm so happy for you all." Mom's eyes sparkle with joy, and I know she's genuinely happy for me. She loves Shane so much.

Jas squeals in delight and the three of us jump around the kitchen like we've won the lottery, but this is so much better. "What's going on in here?" Shane asks as he walks into the kitchen on his crutches. "Can I join in?"

"Daddy!" Jas reaches across for Shane and he moves closer, balancing on his crutches, he holds out his hands to take her. She wraps her arms and legs around him. "You're gonna marry Mommy! This is the best day ever."

Shane chuckles and kisses her cheek. "You don't mind? It means I'll always live with you guys."

Jas shakes her head adamantly. "That's the best part ever. I never want you to leave us, and I never want to leave you!" She presses her cheek to Shane's and as happy as I am about marrying the man I love, it hurts that Jasmine has that memory of leaving her father. She never asks about him anymore because Shane's filled that need for her but it still makes me sad that she doesn't have that relationship with her biological father.

"Well, that works out perfectly because I never want to leave you or your mom." He rubs his nose against hers with a grin as big as I've ever seen.

Lloyd wanders into the fray, chuckling at us as he kisses Mom on the cheek. "Quite the love fest happening here this afternoon."

He turns to Shane and me. "Great to have you guys home where you belong."

"Shane proposed to Violet and she said *yes*," Mom explains and they share a look which I can't quite decipher.

His attention turns to me and he embraces me. "Congratulations."

"Thank you."

He turns to *my* fiancé. *MY fiancé!* "I'm thrilled for you, Shane."

Shane grins. "Thank you."

"Take a seat, everyone. I'll get us some snacks." Mom looks across at Lloyd, and they share a secret smile. I narrow my eyes. Something's going on there. Shane, Lloyd, and Jas sit around the table, and I help Mom make cups of coffee and tea, while she prepares some sweet treats. I raise my eyebrows at her because we never have treats like this on a school day. "What? It's a special occasion." She shrugs like she doesn't have a care in the world but I sense that's not completely accurate.

We take everything to the table and dig in. Mom and Lloyd share another secret look and I can't take it anymore. "What's going on?" Mom feigns innocence but she's not fooling me. I raise my eyebrows and wait her out.

She glances at Lloyd and he nods slightly. "Well ... not to take anything away from your special day, but Lloyd and I also have an announcement and a proposal."

"Oh my gosh, could this day get any better?" I jump out of my chair and wrap my arms around Mom. "Congratulations."

Mom laughs and pats my hand. "Not that sort of proposal. But I'll take your congratulations."

I deflate and drop back into my chair, confused by what she means. *Shit!* I forgot for a second that she's still legally married to Dad, so she can't marry Lloyd. I wonder if she'll look for him so she can finally divorce his ass. "What are we congratulating?"

Lloyd slides his hand over Mom's resting on the table between them and links his fingers with hers. "I asked your mom to move in with me and she agreed." He leans over and kisses her temple and Mom's eyes flutter closed. My heart flips for her. Finally, she has a love that she deserves.

Okay, cue the confusion. "Aren't you already living together?"

"Yes. Of course, but Lloyd bought a property with more land." She glances at him with a soft smile. "He's accustomed to having more space."

"Wow! That sounds awesome. When are you moving?" Does that mean she's going to sell this place? That means we'll have to find somewhere else to live too. I glance at Shane, but I don't think he's realized what this will mean for us.

"Closing on the house will be next month and we need to do some work on it before we can move in. Now … about that proposal." She claps her hands and grins like a Cheshire Cat. "Would you and Shane like to buy this house?" My eyes widen and I cover my mouth. "We wouldn't worry about market value or anything like that. We'll work out a fair price. We want to help you guys, after all."

I snap my head toward Shane, lost for words. It's a generous offer but I'm not sure if he had any plans and I don't want to overstep. I need to get used to making decisions as a couple now. "That's really generous, Mom. Would you mind if Shane and I talk about it and get back to you?"

She flicks her wrist as if to dismiss my question. "Of course. There's no rush."

Shane smiles at me as his hand lands on my thigh beneath the table. He squeezes the thickness and shoots me a wink. "Whatever you want to do is okay with me. My home is wherever you and Jas are."

I lean over and press my lips to his and whisper, "I love you."

He grins, his lips spreading against mine. "Love you, too, Blue."

EPILOGUE

IO MONTHS LATER ...

39
VIOLET

A LARGE ARM WRAPS AROUND MY MIDDLE, STARTLING me, and my brush slips, sending a smear of sage green paint onto our bedroom window trim—thank goodness we haven't painted them yet. I lean back into my husband's warm body and plant a kiss on his chin as I chuckle, then tap his nose with my paintbrush. His eyebrows shoot up as he spins me around so I'm facing him, my hands trapped between us bringing my paintbrush dangerously close to his chest.

"Oh, now it's on, Mrs. Sutton." He smirks down at me with a wicked gleam in his eye, and I don't think I'll ever tire of him calling me *Mrs. Sutton*. He leans in and takes my mouth in an almost violent kiss without giving me a chance to prepare for his invasion. His tongue lashes against mine, and our teeth clash as his large hand slides into my hair, tightening around the strands and angling my face to suit his needs. I moan into his mouth when his other hand squeezes my ass roughly and presses me into his hard body. This man has the ability to set me ablaze in less than ten seconds. He pulls away as quickly as he began kissing me, leaving me dizzy but he doesn't let me go completely until I have my balance.

I narrow my eyes. "That was cruel."

He grins down at me. "You painted my nose." He points to the tip where the green paint is smeared, which means some of it is probably on my face now. "I was just returning the favor." And that's when I feel the wetness on my chin. Damn him. He kissed me so far out of my mind that I painted myself with my damn paintbrush. I rub the area and sure enough, my hand comes away covered in light green paint. I swipe at him but he darts out of the way with speed he really shouldn't have for a man his size. "It's almost time to pick up Jas from school."

"Damn, I lost track of the time. I wanted to get these walls finished."

Shane picks up a roller. "There's not much left. If we both work on it, we'll get it done."

While I finish painting around the window trim, he rolls the paint on the wall which means we'll be able to give it a second coat tomorrow. When we're finished, we both step back and inspect our work. Since buying the house from Mom, we've been gradually working through each room to renovate. Our bedroom is the last room to be done, and I'll be so glad to have it finished. It's been a huge task to renovate the place but I'm so happy with the result. Mom and Cass can't believe how different our family home looks and feels.

He wraps his arm around my shoulder and tugs me into his side. "It's looking really good, Blue. We should be finished by the end of the weekend, then we can bring in the new furniture from the garage, and you can work your magic with the finishing touches."

I grin up at him. "I'm really happy with how everything's coming together." I press up on my toes and kiss his cheek. "We'd better get cleaned up so we can get Jas."

"I can clean up if you want to head out," he offers.

"I was hoping we'd all stop for ice cream. It's been a while, and I think we deserve a treat."

"Jas will love that." He smacks my ass. "Alright, let's get moving."

We work together, cleaning up the brushes and rollers, sealing the paint tin, and washing the paint from our faces—thankfully we're using water-based paint. I quickly tidy my hair and change into a fresh pair of shorts and top, then meet Shane downstairs who's also wearing fresh clothes. I wrap my arms around my husband and look up at his handsome face, still amazed that he's mine. "Thank you."

His eyebrows dip over his dark eyes. "What are you thanking me for?"

I shrug. "Just wanted to say thank you. I don't ever want you to think I take you for granted. And we've been so busy with the house and Jasmine and work that I worry I forget about you among everything else."

He leans down and gently swipes his lips across mine. "I know that, Vi. You don't need to worry that you're neglecting me because you never do, and I'm not a child that needs your undivided attention twenty-four seven. I *know* you appreciate me in the way you show me with the little things you do for me every day. The way you put our family first and the way you love and care for our daughter as well as the work you've put in to make our home as warm and beautiful as you have." He nuzzles into my neck. "I should be thanking you. Every." Kiss. "Single." Kiss. "Day." Kiss. "That you were brave enough to kiss me beneath the moonlight. And strong enough to battle my demons." Kiss. "Honestly, Vi, I don't know what I ever did to deserve you and Jas, but I'm always thankful for both of you."

My heart does that squishy thing it does whenever he says such beautiful things to me. "You say you're not great with words, but *that* was beautiful, Mr. Sutton."

He gives me a boyish grin. "I do my best, Mrs. Sutton. Now, shall we get Jas and surprise her with ice cream?"

"Absolutely." We climb into the car and make the drive to Jas's school. Sometimes we also pick up Poppy but she's away at camp until Sunday afternoon, so it'll only be the three of us today. Now that Jas is six, she likes to exert her independence, so we've been forbidden from picking her up at her classroom. We have to wait at the front of the school with the other parents. Shane suddenly stiffens beside me and I push up onto my toes in an attempt to see whatever's grabbed his attention. "What's happening?" He doesn't answer because he's too focused. Sometimes I hate not being tall. I return my gaze in the same direction as his and I don't have to wait long to see what has him on alert. My lips tip up when I spot Jas walking next to Jason. I rub my hand up and down Shane's back. "Calm down, big guy. Remember, he's only six."

He momentarily drops his gaze to me and then returns it to the kids. "He's the kid who told our girl she was ugly."

When Jas spots us, she runs the rest of the way, leaping at Shane who catches her easily and lands a smacking kiss on her cheek. "How was your day, Angel?"

She wraps one arm around his neck and perches her little butt on his forearm. "It was so good. Jason was upset today, and I hugged him and made him feel all better, and now he's my friend." She turns to me. "Isn't that great, Mommy?"

I chuckle as Shane gives Jason the evil eye, and I'm surprised the boy hasn't combusted on the spot. "Good for you. You can never have too many friends."

"I know!" She wriggles in Shane's hold and he places her on her feet, taking her backpack and tossing it into the back of our car. She grabs Jason's hand and drags him closer to us. Shane stands to his full height and folds his arms across his broad chest but Jason doesn't seem bothered by his posturing which makes me giggle. "Mommy and Daddy, this is my friend, Jason."

"Hi, Jason. It's nice to meet you."

"Uh, you too, Mrs. Sutton." Well, at least the boy has manners. I glance at Shane and smile at his narrowed eyes. He doesn't make a move to say hello, so I nudge him.

His eyes cut to mine and then he softens his posture a little and tips his chin. "Jason."

The boy returns the gesture. "Mr. Sutton."

Shane's eyebrows almost hit his hairline with the attitude coming from the boy, and I can't hold in my snicker, so I turn my back and pretend to cough into my hand. Shane's onto me, though, and glares at me. Once I have myself under control, I turn back around. "Well, it was nice to meet you, Jason. We really must be going. We have a surprise planned for Jasmine."

Jas's eyes widen and her lips tip up. "A surprise. Is it ice cream? Please tell me it's ice cream. Can Jason come too?"

"No." I think it's the first time Shane's ever said *no* to Jas, and her head snaps up toward him in shock.

"Do you mean *no* it's not ice cream? Or do you mean *no*, Jason can't come?" she asks him sweetly.

He throws another glare Jason's way, then softens when he looks at our daughter. "We can't tell you what the surprise is, Angel, or we'll ruin it. And Jason needs to get home."

Jas claps her hands together. "I love surprises." She turns to Jason. "See ya next week." Without another glance at the boy, she climbs into the car and Shane smirks at the six-year-old who's been quickly forgotten in favor of a surprise. Shane reaches inside and ensures she's safely buckled in and I say goodbye to Jason, then we climb in the car and head to *Brain Freeze*.

Jas sings along to the music and I pinch Shane's hard thigh once I'm certain she's distracted enough. "What was that all about? He's six."

"I don't care how old the kid is. He hurt our girl's heart or did you forget?"

"Of course I didn't forget, but she's moved on and so should we."

He grunts and turns his attention back to the road. As crazy as it is, my heart flips at how protective he is of our daughter. And I know he'll always keep her safe but I dread to think how he'll be when boys start coming around when she's older.

Shane pulls into the parking lot down the street from the ice cream shop and Jas cheers. "I knew it was ice cream. Thank you!"

"How do you know we're having ice cream?" he teases.

"We always park here when we go to *Brain Freeze*. You can't trick me."

We climb out of the car. "She's too smart for us." Shane nods solemnly as he helps Jas out of the car and positions her on his shoulders. He takes my hand in his and we wander down the busy street toward our favorite ice cream shop. I love coming here because it holds great memories for us. I squeeze his hand in mine. "Life's pretty great, you know."

"It really is." With his soft gaze on me, he carefully leans down and kisses my temple, and I swoon, just as I always do.

I almost feel like I need to pinch myself. I'm so deeply happy; I almost feel as though I'm glowing. This life I've created with Shane is like a fairytale, and it's made me realize that I needed to go through all of the shit I went through to get to this point. I could almost kiss Allen for being such an asshole the day I walked away from my marriage. If he hadn't exploded so epically—as unbelievable as it is to think—I would have probably still been stuck in a miserable marriage with a cheating husband and disinterested father. I would have missed out on *this*. I grin up at Shane and Jas.

"Violet?"

I freeze and glance forward to find the owner of the familiar voice. Like I conjured him with my thoughts, my ex-husband stands before me. He's clutching the hand of a beautiful woman standing next to him and I wonder if she's the woman he moved into our home. Shane tenses and squeezes my hand as my gaze takes in the couple before me, pausing on the woman's very pregnant belly covered in a delicate sun dress. I snap my eyes up to Allen's face to find him openly staring at Shane, and when I raise my eyes to my husband, he's glowering down at my ex like he could kill him with laser beams. The glaring difference between the two men is almost comical. Allen isn't much taller than me which means he looks positively pitiful next to the man I now call mine.

"Allen." Shane tugs me in closer, wraps his arm around my shoulder, and presses a reassuring kiss to the top of my head. He's letting me know that he'll let me deal with my ex but he's ready to step in at any moment to defend my honor and I love him even more for his faith and steady support. I know I can do anything with him by my side. "I was just thinking about you."

He stands taller, a smirk touching his lips. "Yeah?"

"Daddy?" Jas's voice is small and uncertain.

I glance up at her as Shane squeezes her leg and says, "Yeah, Angel?"

At the same time, Allen's head snaps up to her and he says, "Yeah, kid?"

She grips each side of Shane's face and tips his head backward as she bends down to ensure they have eye contact. "Daddy, can we get our ice cream now?" The look on Allen's face is priceless, and I don't know how he could expect anything different. *This* is what he wanted, and I wouldn't change a single thing.

Shane grins at her. "Sure. Mommy just needs to talk to these people for a minute. Okay?"

She nods down at him. "Okay."

"I won't be long, JJ. Promise." I turn my attention back to my ex. "As I said, I was just thinking about you." I release Shane's hand and step forward, then briefly press my lips to Allen's cheek. Growling, Shane takes a step forward and grips my hip, pulling me back against him, and I soak in the warmth of his big body behind me. "Thank you. If it weren't for you being such a huge ..." I lean as close as I can to his ear and whisper, "asshole." I pull away and smile sweetly at him. "I wouldn't have the beautiful life I have now. I wouldn't have a loving husband who dotes on Jas and me like we're the only people in his world. I would never have known what it was like to have a husband who supports and encourages me in every single thing I do. Jasmine would never have had a father who is one hundred percent devoted to her and ensuring she feels happy and loved every moment of the day." I spare a glance at the woman obviously carrying Allen's baby. "I owe you a world of gratitude." I lean in close again. "Oh, and I would never have experienced the mind-blowing sex I have every single day with my amazing husband." I move back into my husband, taking his hand in mine. "So … thank you." I glance between Allen and the pregnant woman by his side. "I only wish you the life you deserve."

For the first time in all the years I've known Al, he appears to be lost for words. A red tinge makes its way up his neck, and I smile because I know exactly what that means. He's pissed. And I'm glad. Without giving him another moment of my time, I step around him, pulling Shane along with me. I feel so fucking powerful and mighty as we walk into *Brain Freeze* and order our ice creams.

As Jas tells the girl behind the counter her order, Shane tugs me into his body, wrapping his arm around my neck and kissing my forehead. "You're so fucking brave, and I'm so damn proud of you, Blue." He kisses me again as I bask in his praise. "But don't you ever put your mouth on another man again. Do you hear me?"

I look up at my husband with a grin. "Never."

He raises an eyebrow. "Promise?"

"Promise."

His eyes flick between mine, studying me, and I know he's checking to see if I'm okay. "You know our love is everlasting, right?"

I nod and press up on my toes to kiss his cheek. "Everlasting. Always and forever."

40

SHANE

the brown pants and black boots as I adjust the elastic straps digging into my armpits.

"Because you love our daughter and would do anything for her." Vi lands a kiss on my cheek, and I wrap my arm around her, tugging her into me. I never seem to get enough of her. "And because the school decided it was a good idea to include daddies in book week this year." She snickers and raises her eyebrows at me.

"This is true, but I think this is going too far." I turn to the left, studying the giant green wings rising from my back. "Where's the shirt that goes with this?" I'm sure there was a shirt in the photo.

Vi's eyes skate away from mine, and she bites her bottom lip. Teasing out the bottom of her hair, she looks back at me. "Uhm … it didn't come with a shirt." She brings her hand up to smooth over the silver adornment that rests over my shoulders and drapes over the top portion of my chest, barely covering my nipples. "You look amazing without it, though." She licks her lips, and I flick my eyes between hers, paying attention to the slim line of China blue that's shrinking by the second. "All the other daddies are going to feel so inadequate next to you," she breathes then her eyebrows slash down, causing creases between her eyes.

"What's wrong?" I drop my hand to her ass and pull her body against mine, squashing her breasts against me. We both groan at the sensation. If only we were both naked.

"Daddy!" Jas twirls into our freshly renovated bedroom. "Look at me!" She freezes in place when her eyes land on me. "Wow! You're the best fairy king I've ever seen."

My chest puffs up with pride that she thinks I'm the best fairy king she's ever seen ... and well ... maybe the costume isn't so bad after all. I grin at Jas. "Thanks, Angel." I hold up my hand and gesture for her to turn around, which she does with her lips spread wide. Her rainbow tutu flares out as she turns, her chestnut locks that Vi decorated with a halo of colorful ribbons flow down her back, and I grin at how colorful her princess fairy costume is. When she completes the turn and faces me again I tell her, "You look beautiful."

She tilts her head to the side and tucks her chin into her shoulder. "Thank you, Daddy."

"Okay, well, we'd better get going. We don't want to be late. Parking will be a nightmare today." Vi scoots us out of the bedroom and downstairs where Jasmine collects her school bag. As soon as Jas tries to climb into the car, we realize our mistake.

"I don't fit, Mommy!" Jas's bottom lip trembles and Violet crouches down to her level.

"We'll take the wings off for now. Okay?"

Jas nods and Violet carefully removes the wings. I'm going to have the same issue, so I remove my wings too, which are probably four times the size of Jasmine's. Now I wish I had a shirt to wear because I feel ridiculous. We lay the wings carefully in the back and reverse out of the driveway, listening to Jas's favorite song, which she sings loudly from the back seat.

I smile to myself.

Did I ever think I'd dress up as a fairy for book week at school?

Nope. Not even in my dreams did I think this was a possibility.

Am I happy about it?

You bet your ass, I'm happy about it.

Ecstatic.

I turn into the parking lot at school and find an empty spot which is a miracle on a day like this. I look around at the other fathers and not one of them is exposing as much flesh as I am. "Are you sure it's appropriate for me to go shirtless?"

Vi glances around the car, then turns to me with a shrug. "It's the costume. It's not like you're showing anything."

I'm still not convinced as we climb out of the car and grab the wings from the back. Vi helps Jas put hers on, and as I struggle to get my arms through the elastic straps, someone wolf whistles across the parking lot. I snap my head up and narrow my eyes to find Toby walking toward me with Poppy's hand securely tucked in his. He looks like he's about to step on stage with his guitar slung across his body. Poppy's hair is teased up and she has a blue and red lightning bolt painted across her face. Cass walks behind, holding Daisy's hand with their three-month-old daughter strapped to her chest.

When they reach me, Toby slaps me on the back. "Nice wings, man." He snickers, raising a single eyebrow.

"Where's your costume?" I grunt.

"I'm a rock star. This *is* my costume." He smirks and I roll my eyes. "Poppy's David Bowie, and I'm her lead guitarist."

"What book is that from?"

He shoves his hands into his pockets and rocks back on his heels. "*Starman: David Bowie*, the definitive biography."

"And how does that meet the theme of book week?"

"Music transports us to magical places." Can't fault him there. He scans my costume, helping me to straighten the elastic holding my wings on. "And what are you?"

I raise my brows and stand tall. "Jas and I are garden fairies. I'm the king garden fairy, and she's the princess garden fairy because fairies love nature and use their magic to care for all of the plants and animals," I say with pride.

Toby nods thoughtfully. "Makes sense."

"Rosemary," Jasmine sings and Cass bends down so she can kiss her baby cousin.

We all spend a few moments greeting each other, then Vi claps her hands. "Okay, we need to get to class."

Jas's hand is securely tucked into mine as we separate off to our classroom, and I don't miss the looks coming my way from the other fathers and the moms. Even though I'm used to the looks from the moms since I'm a regular helper in Jas's classroom, they still make me feel uncomfortable, especially as I'm more exposed than usual today.

When we arrive at Jasmine's classroom, her teacher is directing the kids. "Put your school bags on your hook. We'll unpack when we get back from the gym after the parade." Her eyes land on me and Jas and she brings her hand to her chest. "Oh, my. You two look fantastic!"

Jas beams. "Thank you, Mrs. McKinley. We're fairies!"

"I can see that." Her eyes stray to my bare abs, then dart back up to my face. "I think these costumes will be very popular with the audience."

My daughter bounces on her toes with glee as she looks up at me. "I told you we would be the best."

I chuckle. "That you did." But I'm not sure that's exactly what Mrs. McKinley meant.

Once everyone has arrived, we make our way to the school gym. After the principal welcomes everyone to the school and explains the theme of book week: *Reading is Magic*, she invites each class to parade across the makeshift stage. I walk proudly with Jas at my side, her hand tucked in mine, and I'm honored that I get to experience this with her.

I scan the audience until my eyes land on Vi's smiling face, and not for the first time, I thank my lucky stars that she saw the man beneath my emotional and physical scars.

Finally, I'm completely at peace with my survival, my life ... and it's all thanks to the little girl at my side, my wife, and my friends.

Would you like to check in with Shane, Violet, and Jasmine one year into the future?
Sign up for my newsletter to find out what they've been up to here:

https://tinyurl.com/everlastinglove-bonus

Are you ready to meet Toby Summer in **Second Chance Summer?**
A rock star/single mom second chance romance
A steamy, stand-alone contemporary romance about a magnetic,
protective rock star and a sexy single mom doing her best to
protect her deaf daughter.

https://books2read.com/dsj-2ndchancesummer

I put together a Pinterest board for Shane and Violet's story. If you're interested, you can check it out here:

https://tinyurl.com/everlastinglove-pinterest

The Summer Twins

Loving Summer | *Kate Summer & Oliver Stone*

Second Chance Summer | *Toby Summer & Cassia Phillips*

The Summer Twins | Complete Series

Kisses

Stolen Kisses | *Emma Miller & Theo Drivas*

Moonlit Kisses | *Max Stanfield & Molly Lewis*

Unexpected Kisses | *Sarah Stanfield & AJ*

Kisses | Complete Series

Monday Knights | *novellas*

Enemy Kisses | *Finn Brady & Harriet Dubois*

Everlasting

Everlasting Love | *Shane Sutton & Violet Jamison*

Debra has a list of her books available on her website.

You can find them here:

CONNECT WITH DEBRA

stalk me

You can stalk me pretty much everywhere!
https://debrastjamesbooks.com/connect/

How about joining my Facebook group?
https://www.facebook.com/groups/DebsBibliomaniacs

newsletter

Join Debra's newsletter to receive important updates before anyone else. Newsletters will be sent twice per month unless something really exciting is happening.

https://debrastjamesbooks.com/newsletter/

THANK YOU

Thank you so much for reading Shane and Violet's story. I know it's been a long time coming for my dedicated readers and I'd like to thank you for your patience. This was a tough story to write as I battled imposter syndrome. Several readers had asked for Shane's story and I was crippled with fear that I wouldn't meet reader expectations. You see ... he was only ever meant to be a side character. I only hope I did him justice.

I struggled with long COVID after catching it at RARE Melbourne at the end of April. It was tough to get my brain on board with producing sentences to write a story. I was so relieved when I finally came out the other side and could function like I should.

As I was closing in on completing my first draft of **Everlasting Love**, my sister was diagnosed with Stage IV Melanoma. I put everything on hold to support her through her treatments. She had such a positive attitude toward everything even though her diagnosis was dire. Her motto was: *"One Step at a Time"*. I was devastated when I lost her one month to the day after her diagnosis. My world is forever changed without her and this book will always hold a special place in my heart.

As always, I would like to thank Mr. St James and our two sons for their support and patience with me. My writing takes a lot of my time away from my family and their understanding and support is always appreciated.

Rachel. My gorgeous alpha reader. What can I say ... you are one patient lady as I wrote, rewrote, and tossed out chapters because I just couldn't get them to work. Without you, I really don't think this book would have seen the light of day this year or the next. I wanted to give up so many times but you kept nudging me forward. I owe you a world of gratitude. Thank YOU.

To my beta readers, Rachel and Kelly :) Thank you so much for your candid and thoughtful feedback while you read ***Everlasting Love***. You ladies provided me with plenty of laughs as well as points to consider.

I also need to thank Otsana for suggesting the perfect name for Violet's friend. Quinn was the perfect name for a female reptile rescue warrior! Especially when I think about what's in store for her.

Thank you to Matthew and Norma for your expertise and advice regarding Shane's military background. I appreciate your feedback which helped to make his character as authentic as possible.

Finally, thank you to Dr. Rory for your expertise regarding a suitable spinal injury and treatment for Shane as a result of the IED explosion. And, no, you can't read my book ... ;) I won't be able to look you in the eye if you do, *lol*.

To my online support network, you were there for me on the days when I doubted myself. Ladies, you are so very important to me. I'm grateful we connected and I can call you my friends.

To you, the reader. Thank you for taking a chance on me; for reading my book. I truly do appreciate your time. If you've enjoyed reading about Shane, Violet, and Jasmine, I'd love to hear from you.

ABOUT THE AUTHOR

Debra St James is an author of spicy, slow-burn contemporary romance that features cinnamon roll heroes who listen to their women's hearts and their words. She takes her time to weave a detailed tapestry of genuine characters, real-life struggles, love, and romance to create engaging stories that will have you so immersed in the story that you'll never want to leave. Her stories are always guaranteed to take you on an emotional journey that ultimately ends with a HEA!

Debra loves to read romance. Her family often finds her with her nose stuck in her iPad, swooning over her latest book boyfriend. She writes part-time from her Perth home, which she shares with Mr St James and their two sons, whose antics often make her roll her eyes and laugh in equal measure.

Writing a novel had never been on her radar. One morning, she was enjoying a coffee by the river and a story sprouted, seemingly from nowhere. At 51, she pulled up the Pages app on her phone and began to type, giving life to her debut, *Loving Summer*.

The rest, as they say, is history!

Debra xo

amazon.com/author/debrastjames

facebook.com/debra.stjames.books

instagram.com/debrastjames_books

bookbub.com/authors/debra-st-james

goodreads.com/debrastjames

pinterest.com/debrastjamesbooks

tiktok.com/@debrastjamesbooks